VROOOM

REVERSE WORLD

I want to go to the Reverse World!
I wonder if there's a bus line that
goes there.

– *Makoto Hijioka*

Makoto Hijioka is also the artist for
the series *Taiyoh Shonen no Django*,
which ran in *CoroCoro* magazine.

VIZ Kids Edition

Story & Art by Makoto Hijioka

Translation/Kaori Inoue
Touch-up Art & Lettering/John Clark
Graphics & Cover Design/Hitomi Yokoyama Ross
Editor/Leyla Aker

Editor in Chief, Books/Alvin Lu
Editor in Chief, Magazines/Marc Weidenbaum
VP, Publishing Licensing/Rika Inouye
VP, Sales & Product Marketing/Gonzalo Ferreyra
VP, Creative/Linda Espinosa
Publisher/Hyoe Narita

Printed in the U.S.A.

Published by VIZ Media, LLC
P.O. Box 77064
San Francisco, CA 94107

VIZ Kids Edition
10 9 8 7 6 5 4 3 2 1
First printing, May 2009

store.viz.com

Pokémon®

GIRATINA & THE SKY WARRIOR!

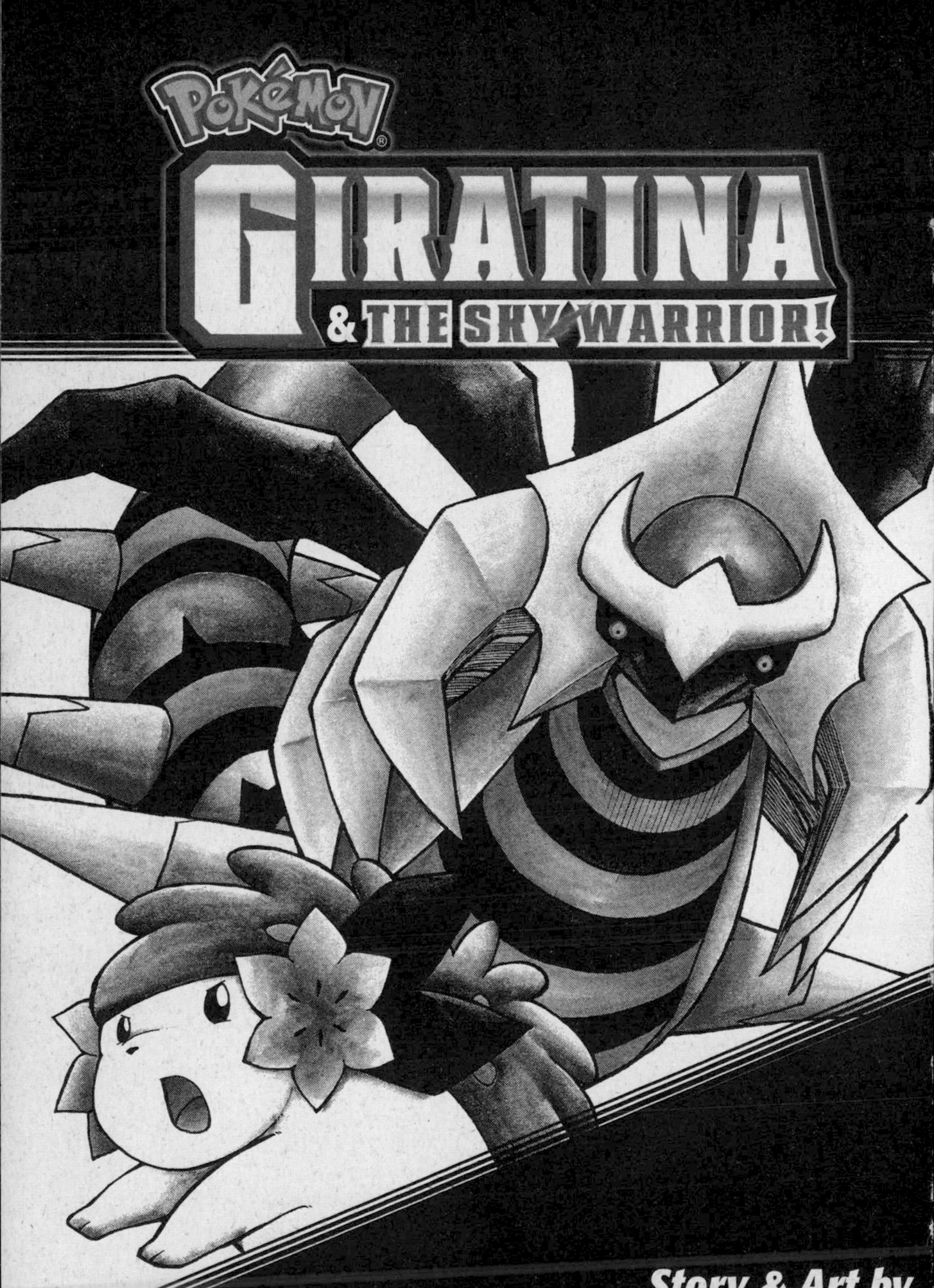

Story & Art by
Makoto Hijioka

MAIN CHARACTERS

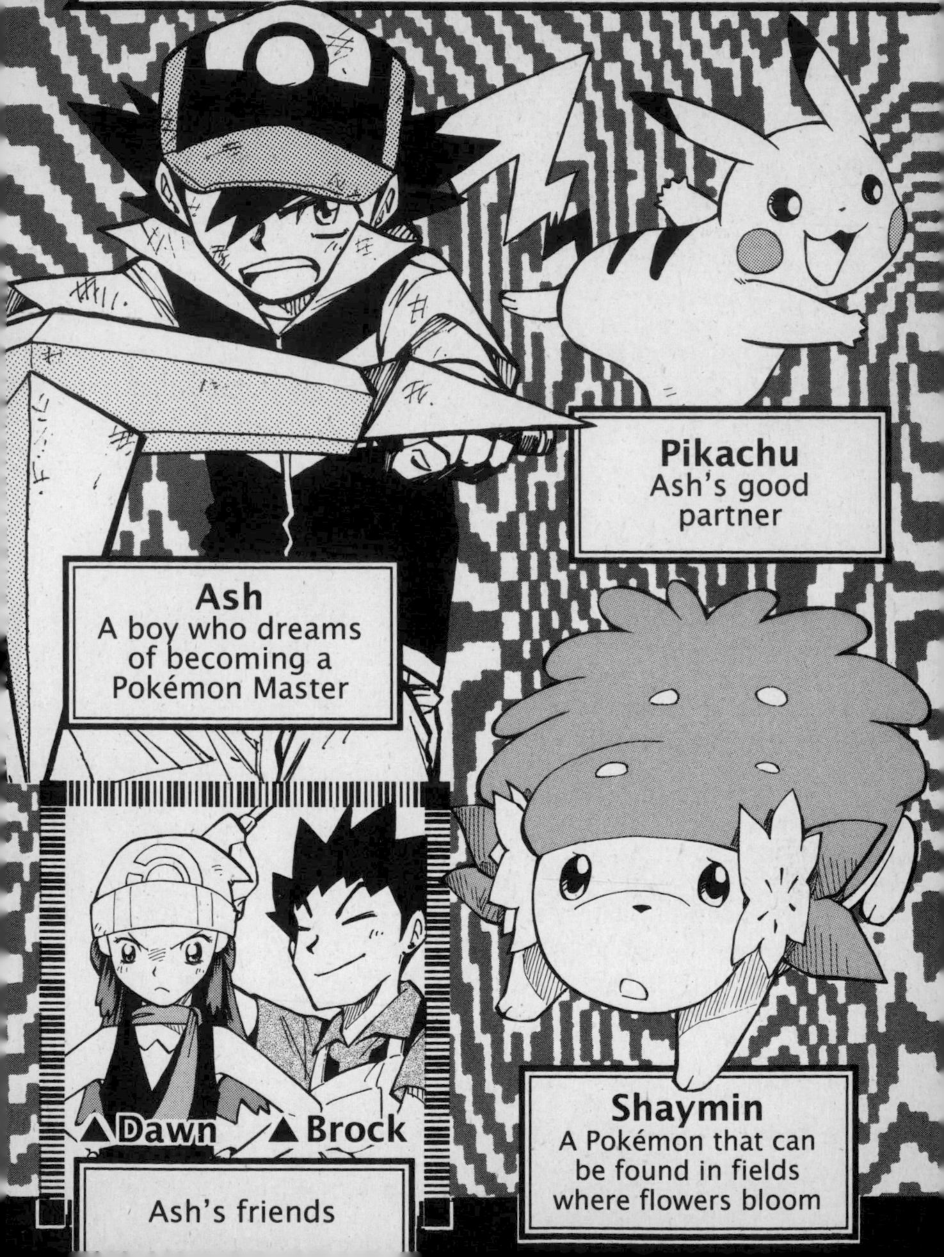
Pikachu
Ash's good partner
Ash
A boy who dreams of becoming a Pokémon Master
Shaymin
A Pokémon that can be found in fields where flowers bloom
▲Brock
▲Dawn
Ash's friends

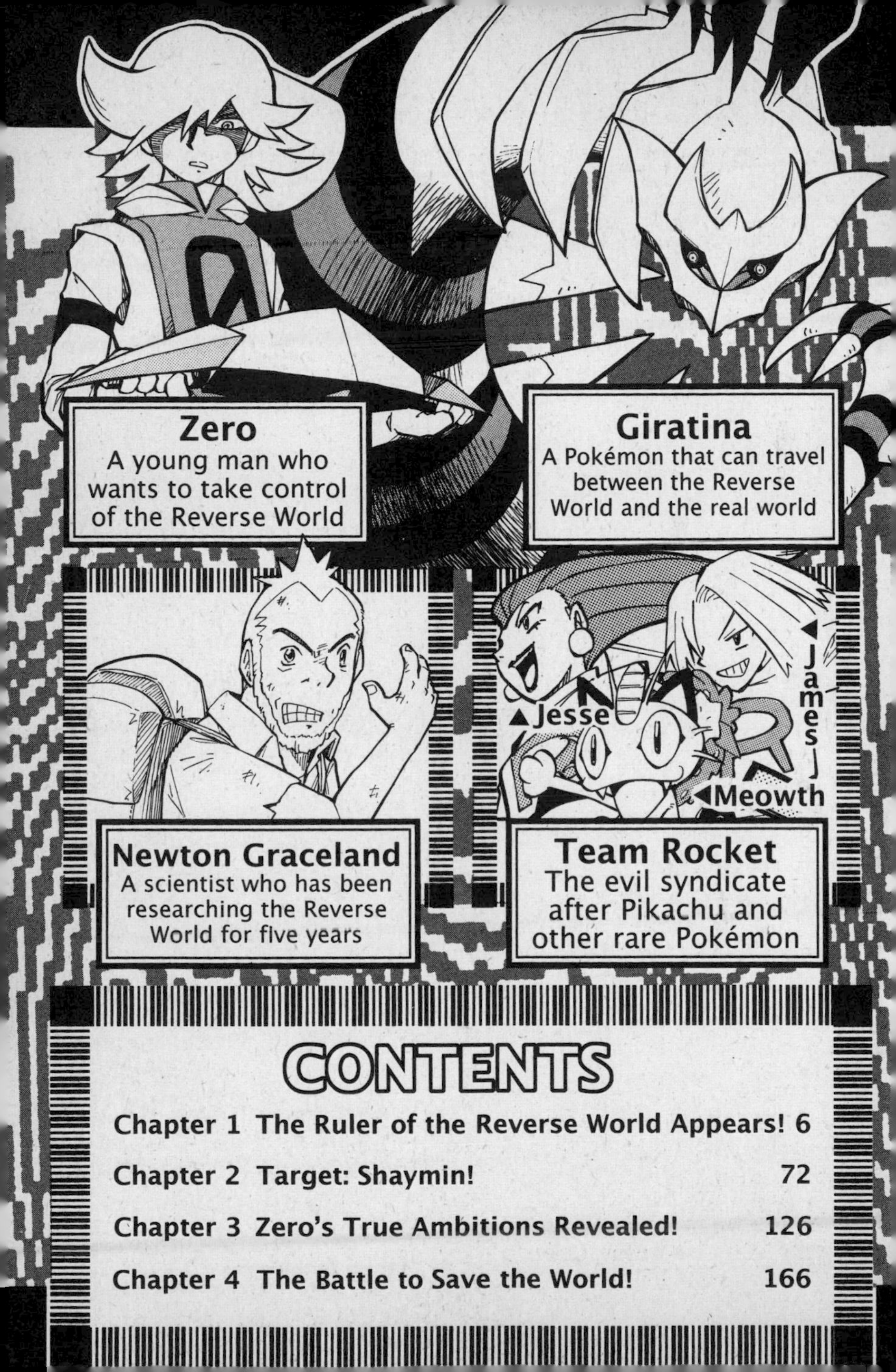

Zero
A young man who wants to take control of the Reverse World
Giratina
A Pokémon that can travel between the Reverse World and the real world
Newton Graceland
A scientist who has been researching the Reverse World for five years
Jesse
James
Meowth
Team Rocket
The evil syndicate after Pikachu and other rare Pokémon

CONTENTS

Chapter 1
The Ruler of the Reverse World Appears!

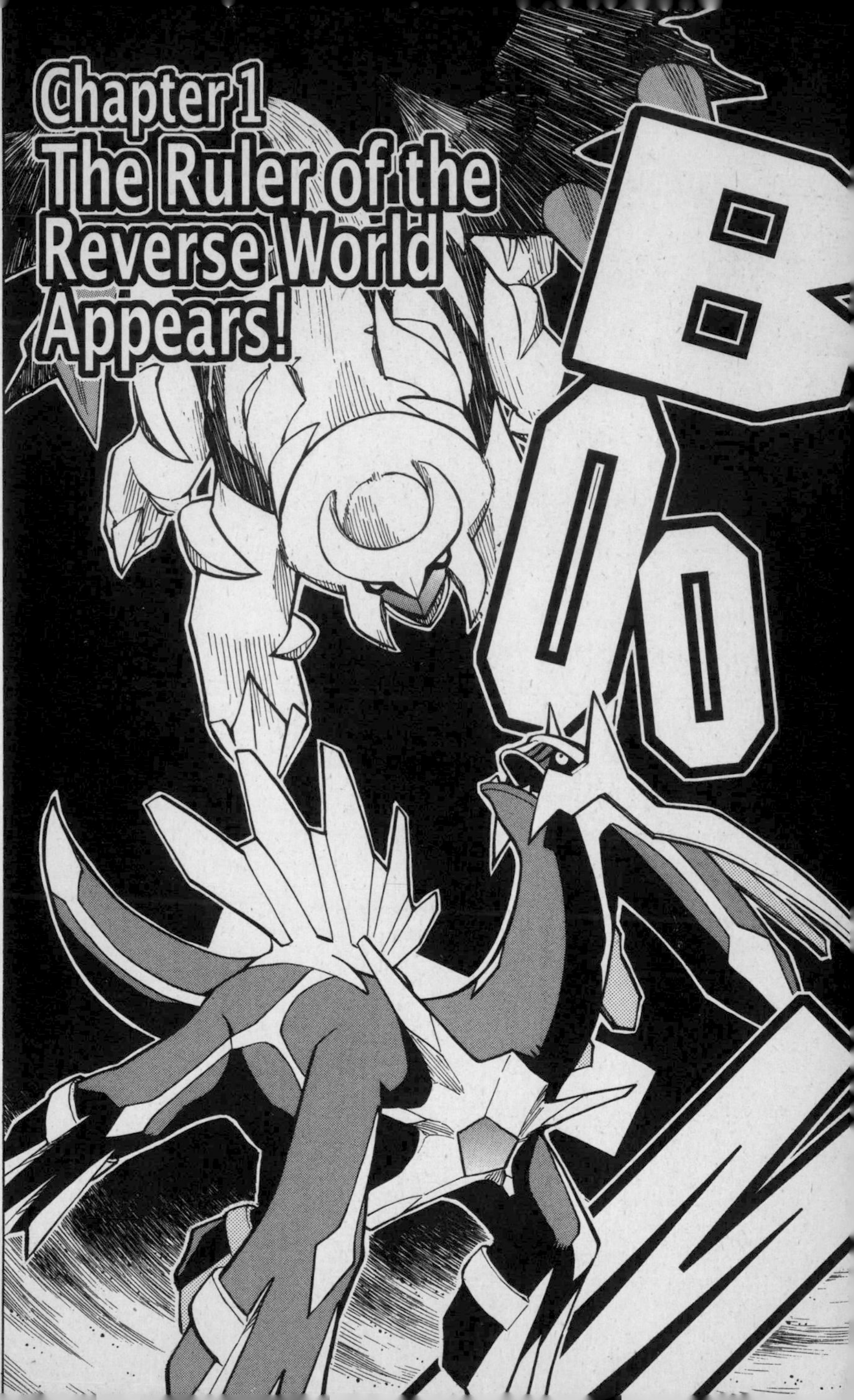

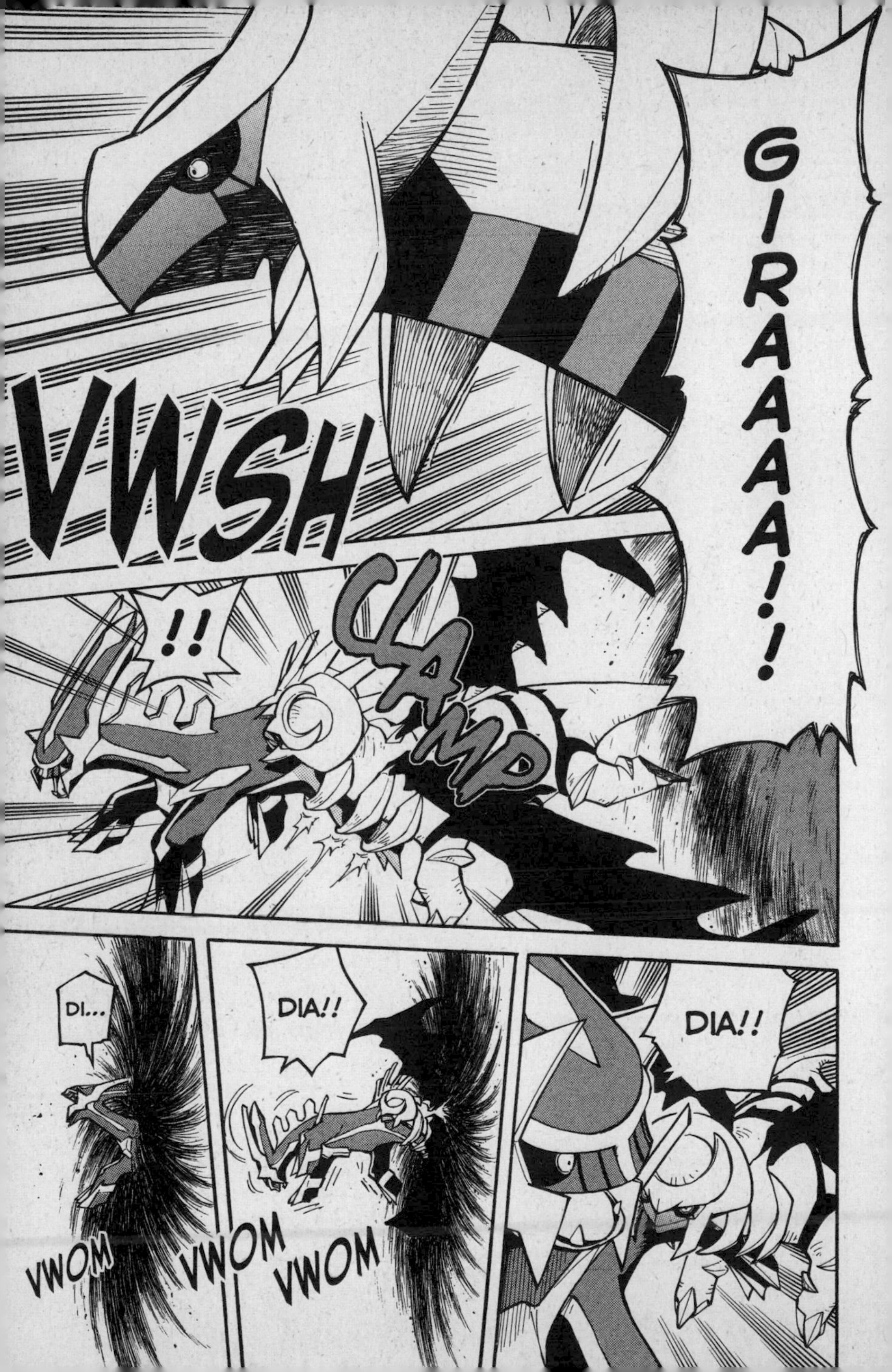
GIRAAAAA!!!
VWSH
CLAMP
!!
DIA!!
DIA!!
VWOM
VWOM
DI...
VWOM

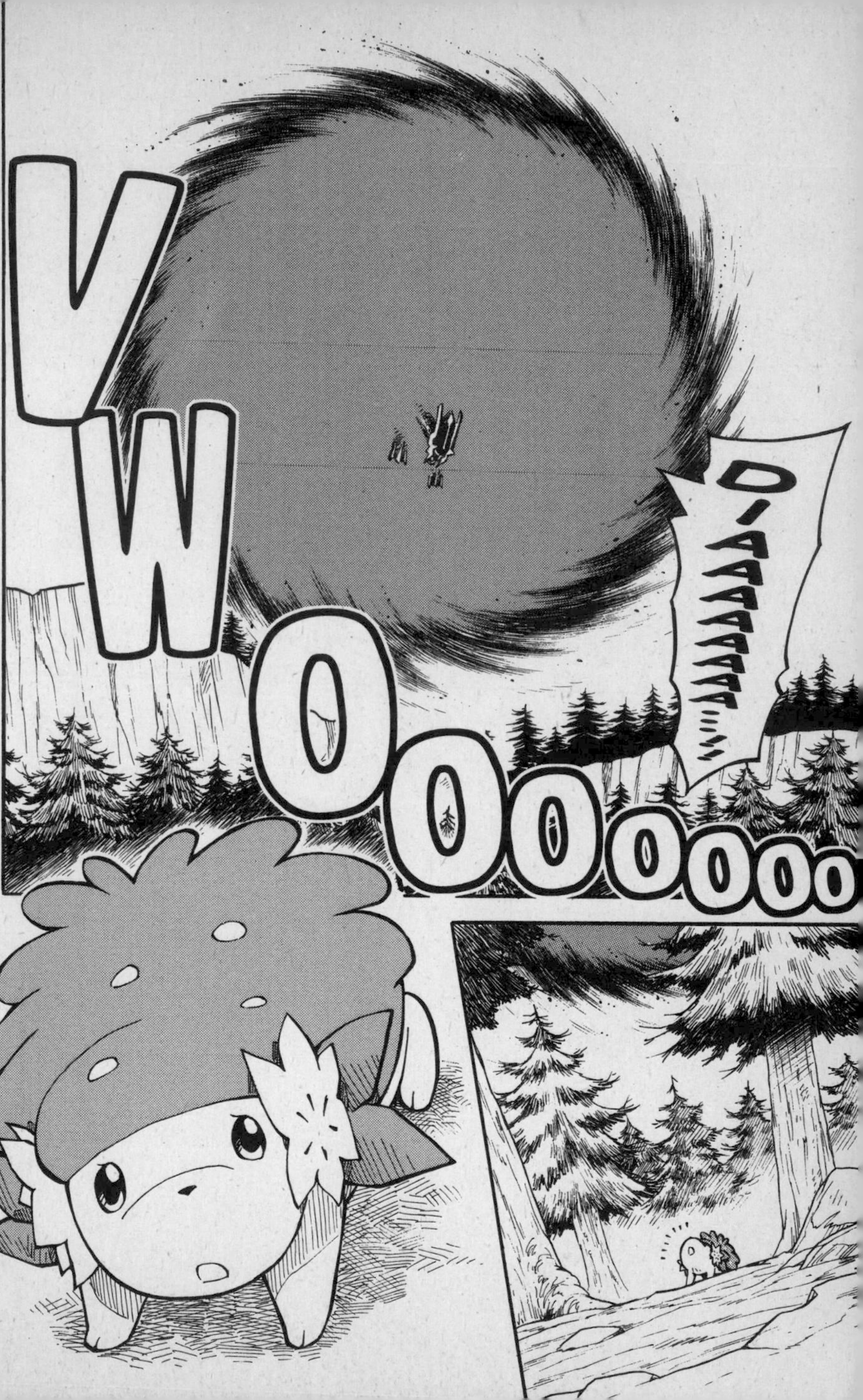
DIAAAAAAA...!!
VWOOOOOOO

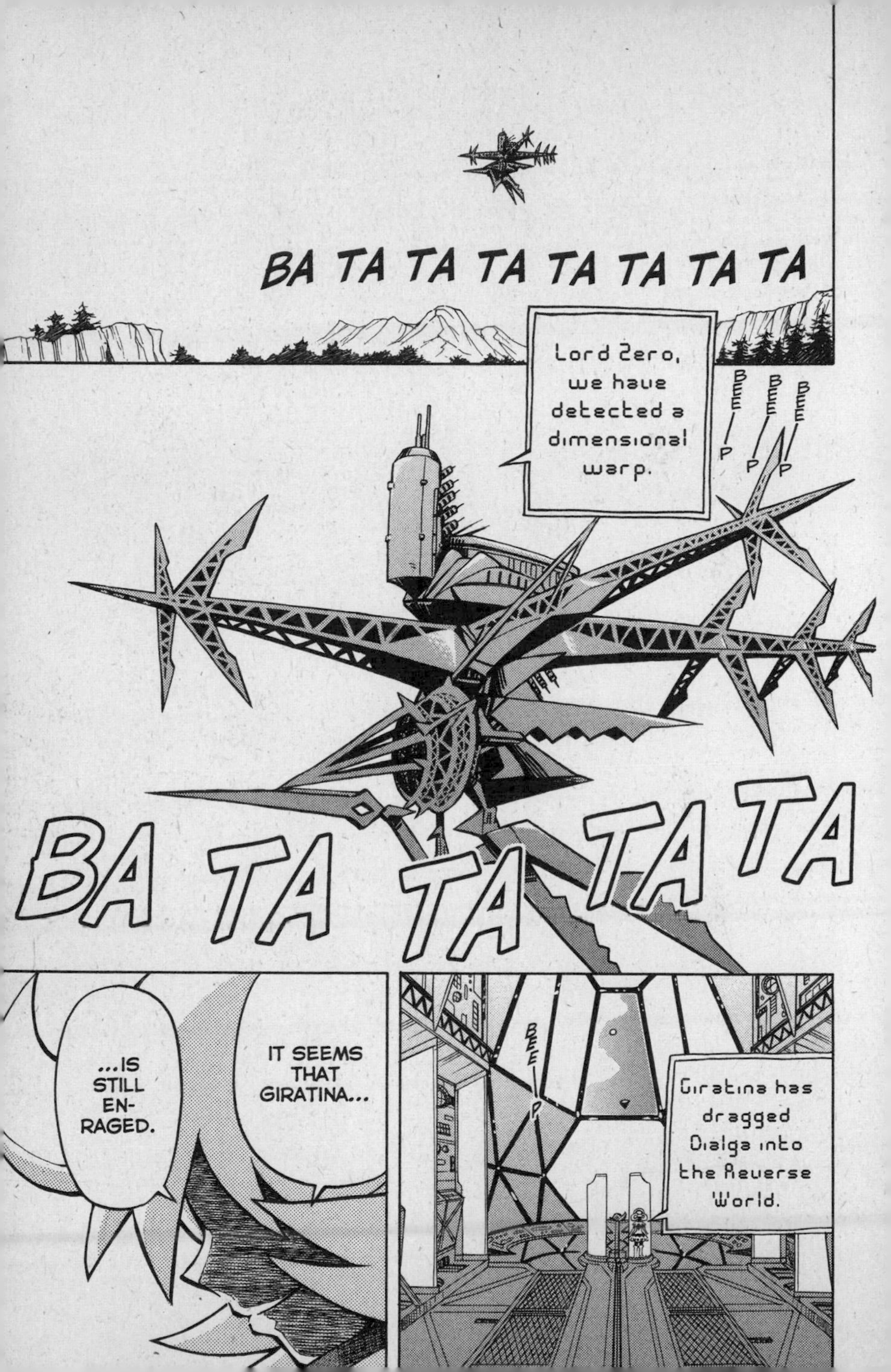
BA TA TA TA TA TA TA TA
Lord Zero, we have detected a dimensional warp.
BEEP BEEP BEEP
BA TA TA TA
Giratina has dragged Dialga into the Reverse World.
BEEP
IT SEEMS THAT GIRATINA...
...IS STILL EN-RAGED.

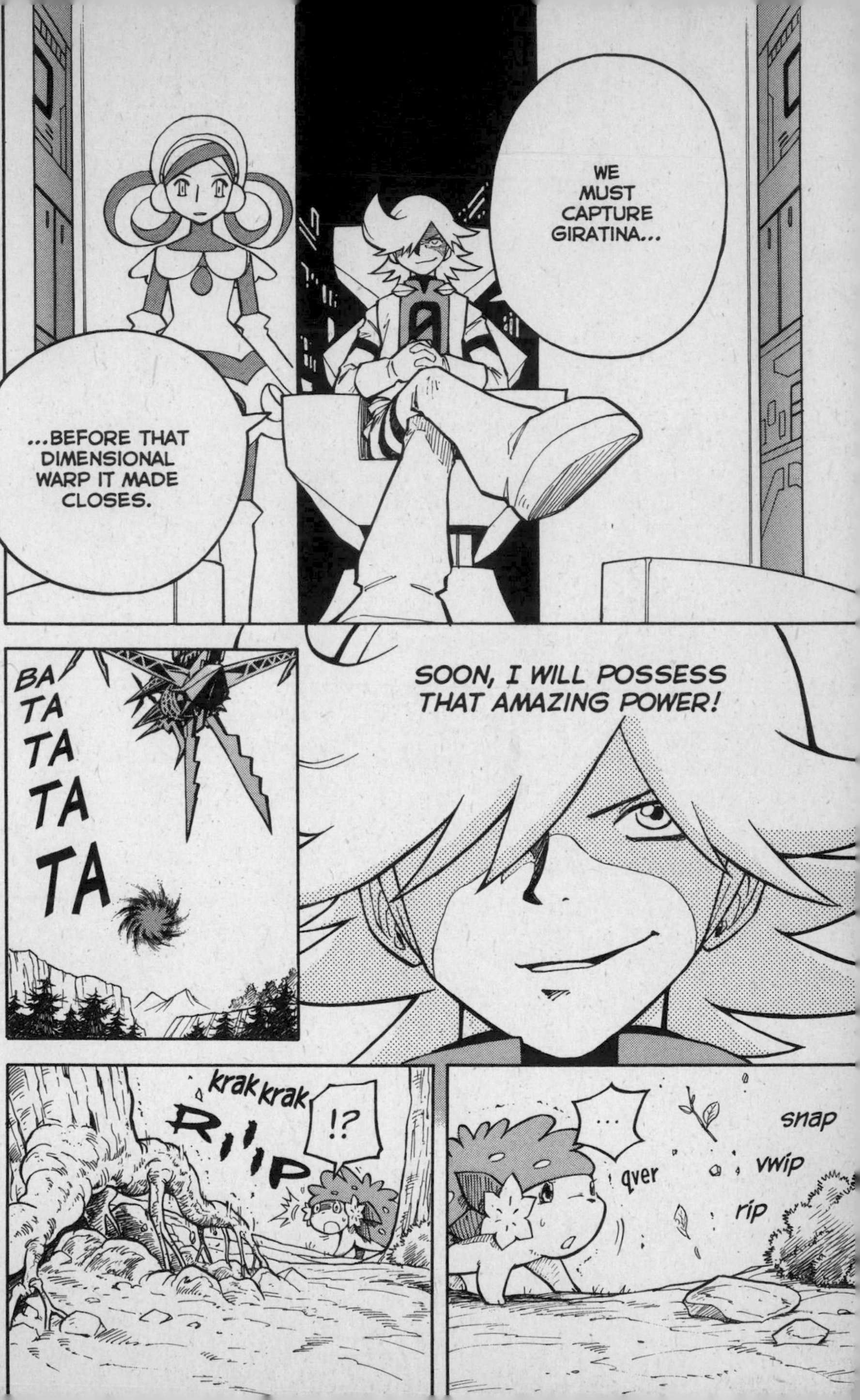
WE MUST CAPTURE GIRATINA...
...BEFORE THAT DIMENSIONAL WARP IT MADE CLOSES.
SOON, I WILL POSSESS THAT AMAZING POWER!
BA TA TA TA TA TA
...
snap
vwip
qver
rip
krak krak
RIIIP
!?

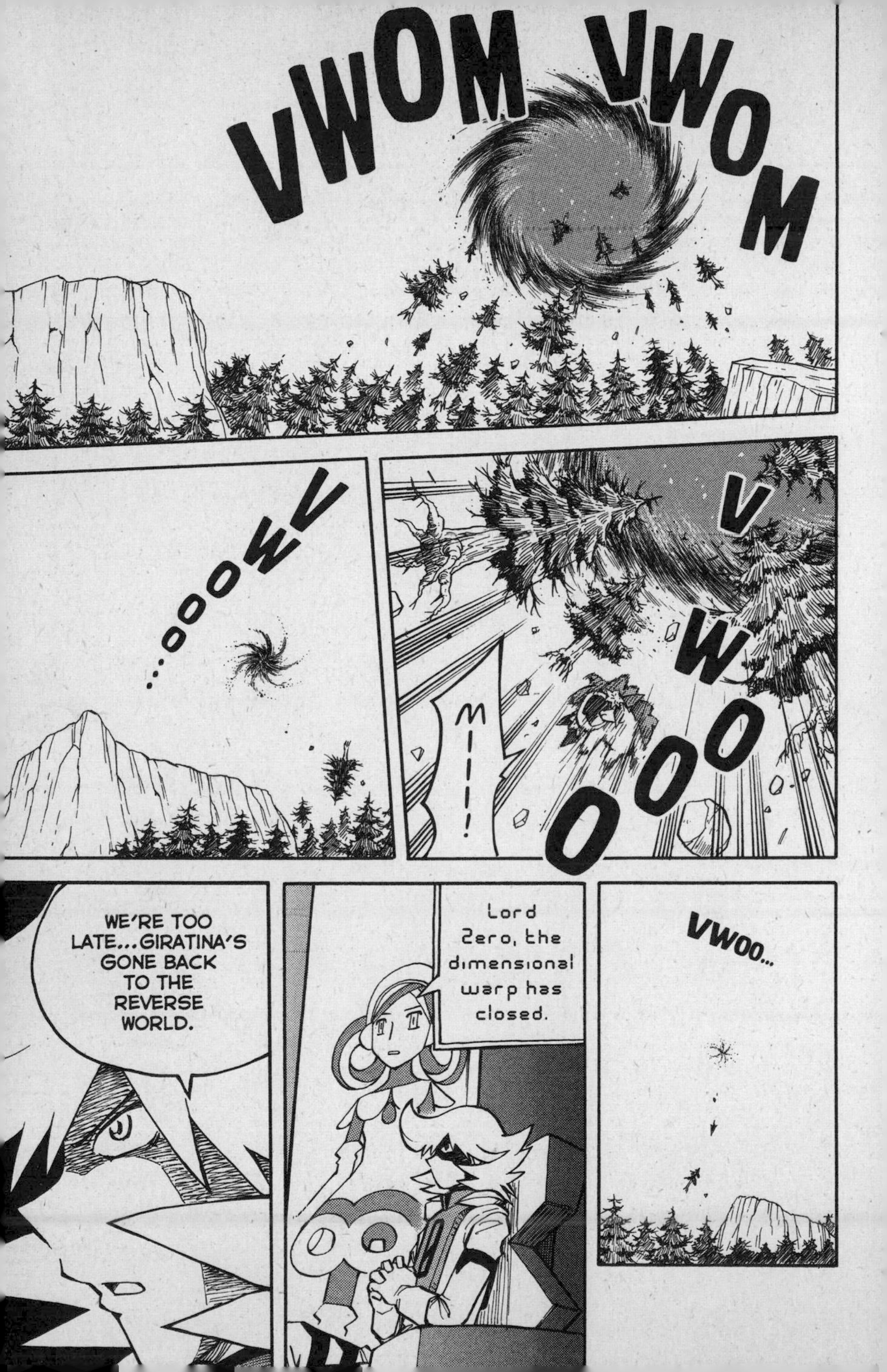
VWOM VWOM
VWOOOO
M!!!
...OOOWV
VWOO...
Lord Zero, the dimensional warp has closed.
WE'RE TOO LATE...GIRATINA'S GONE BACK TO THE REVERSE WORLD.

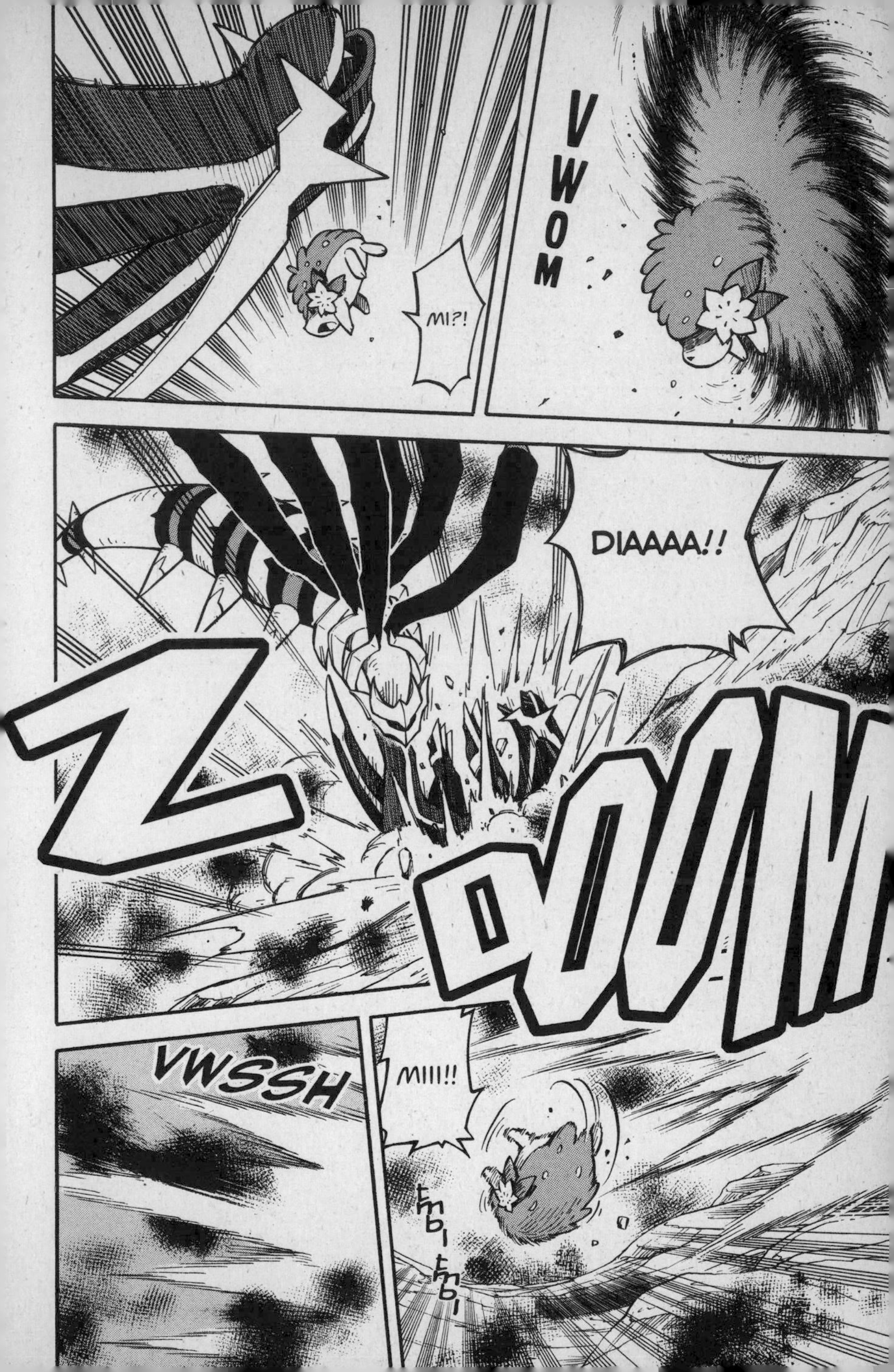
VWOM
MI?!
DIAAAA!!
ZDOOM
MIII!!
tmbl tmbl
VWSSH

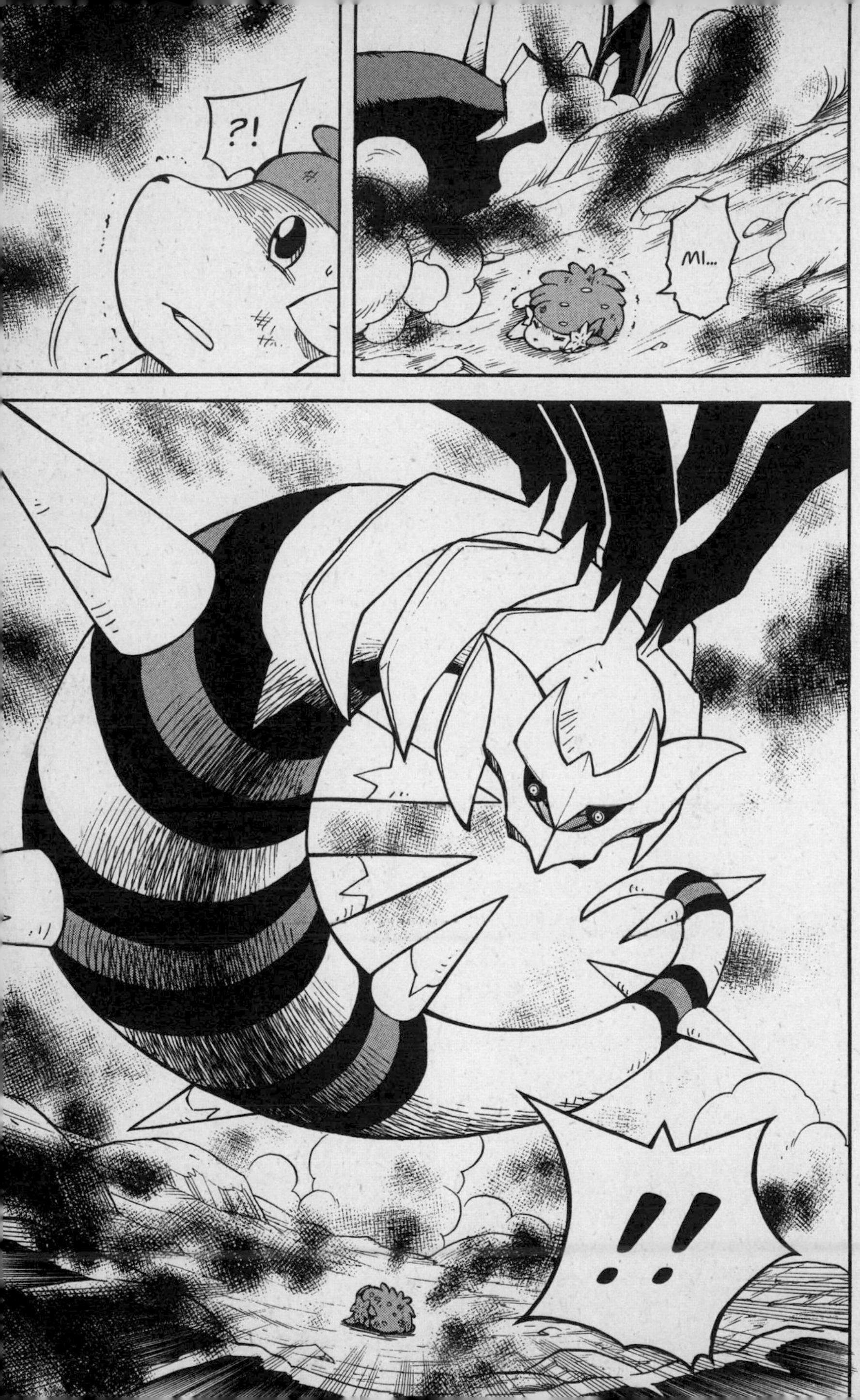
MI...
?!
!!

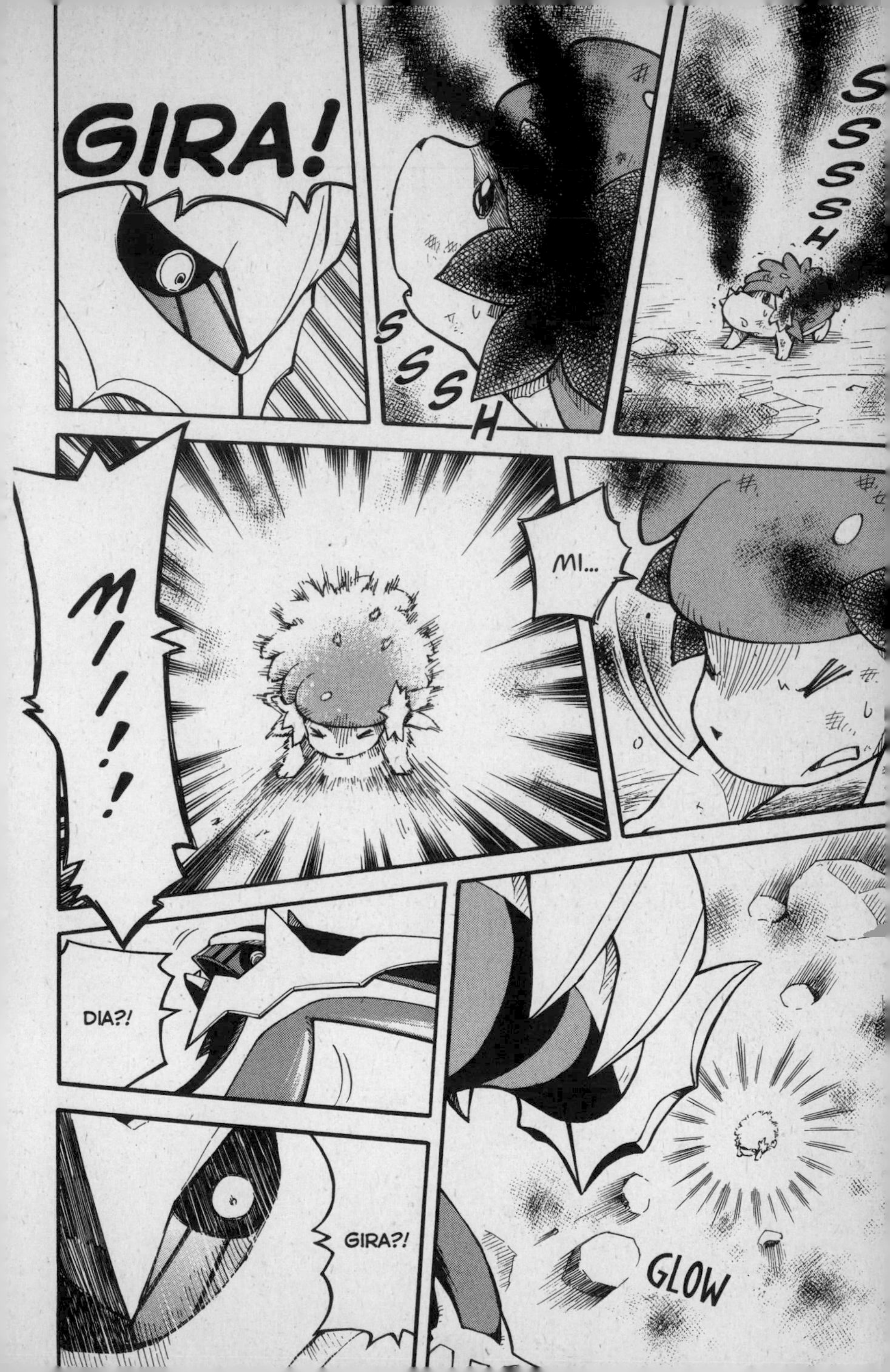
SSSSH
SSSH
GIRA!
MI...
MI!!!
GLOW
DIA?!
GIRA?!

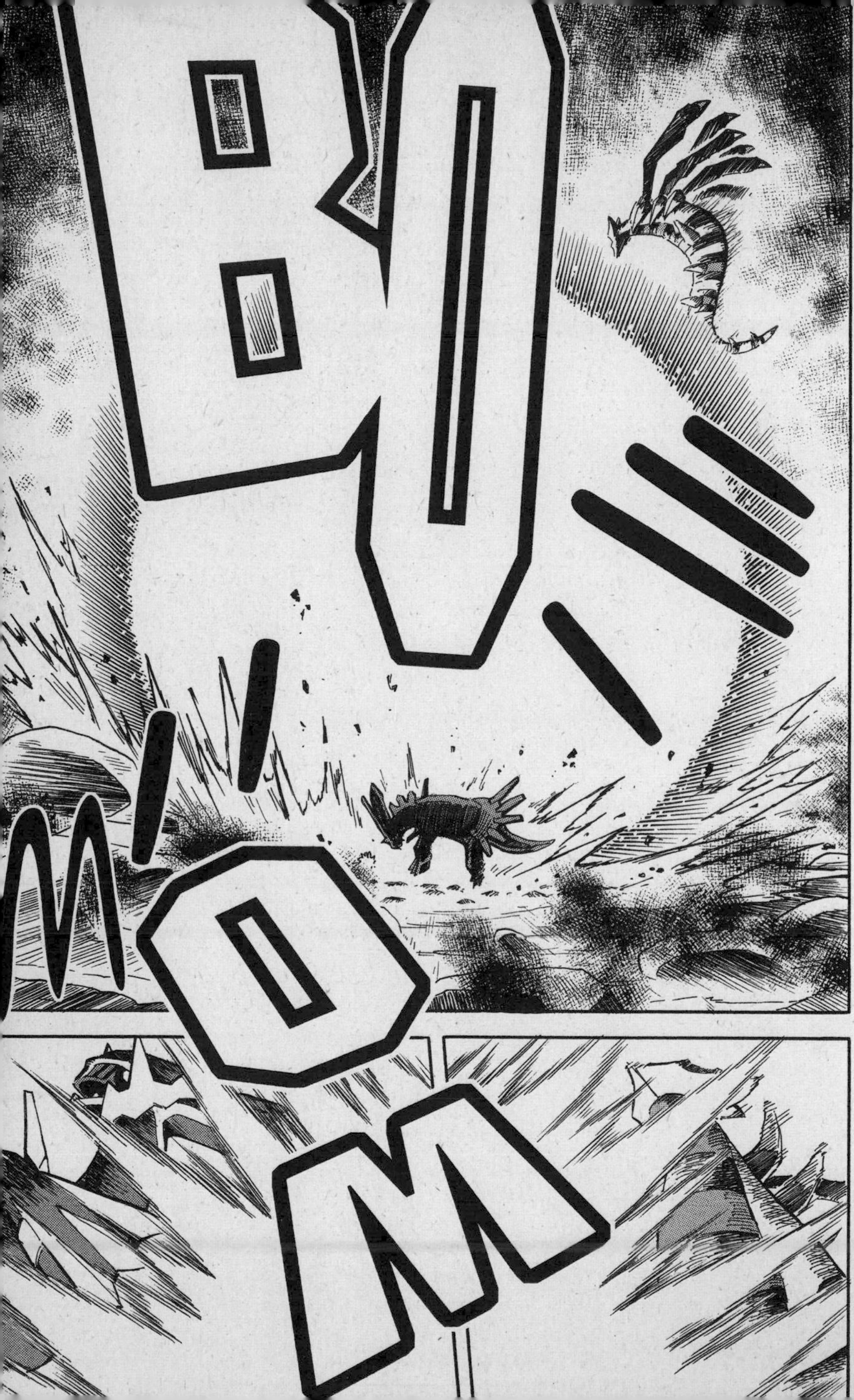

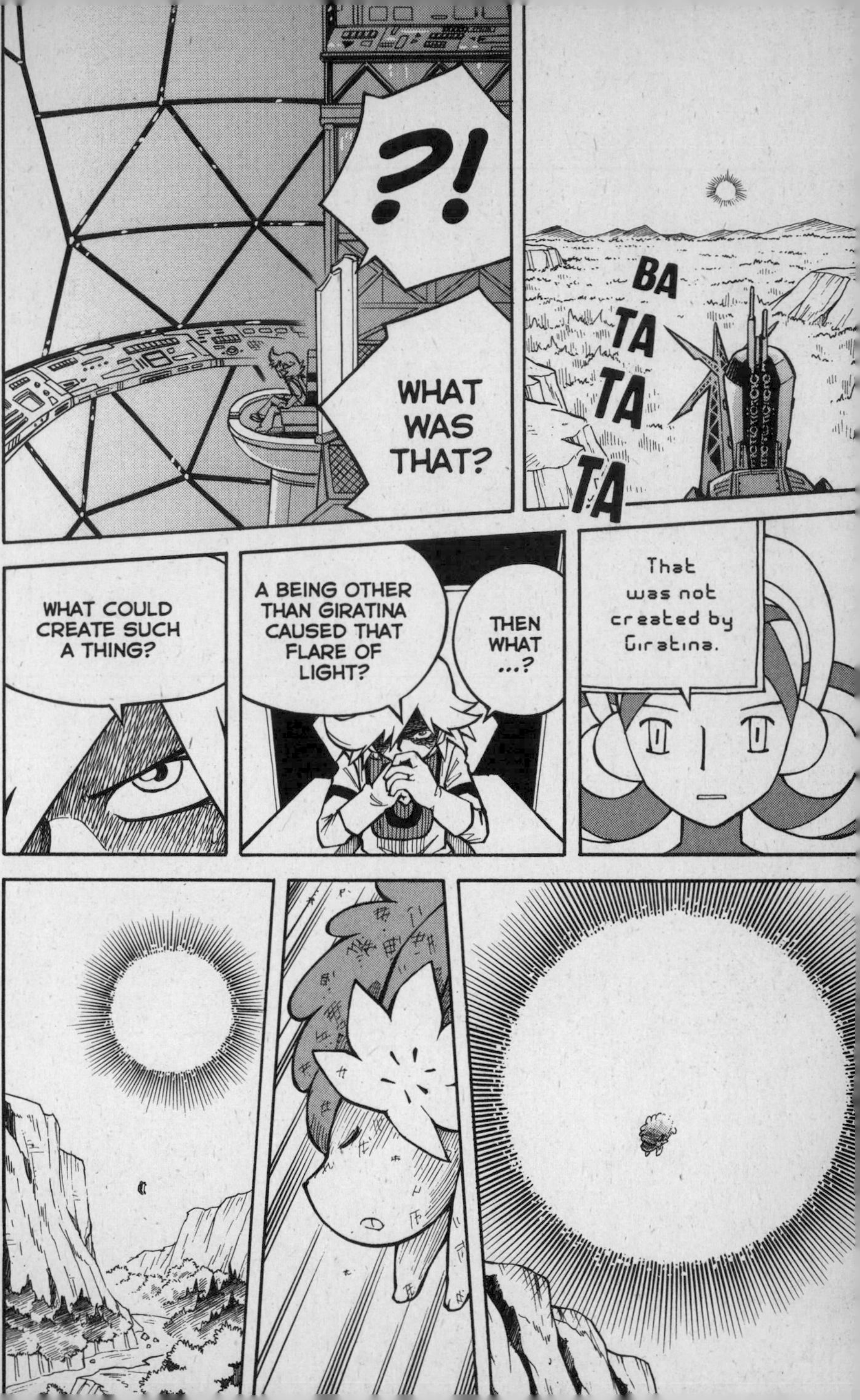
BA TA TA TA
?!
WHAT WAS THAT?
That was not created by Giratina.
THEN WHAT ...?
A BEING OTHER THAN GIRATINA CAUSED THAT FLARE OF LIGHT?
WHAT COULD CREATE SUCH A THING?

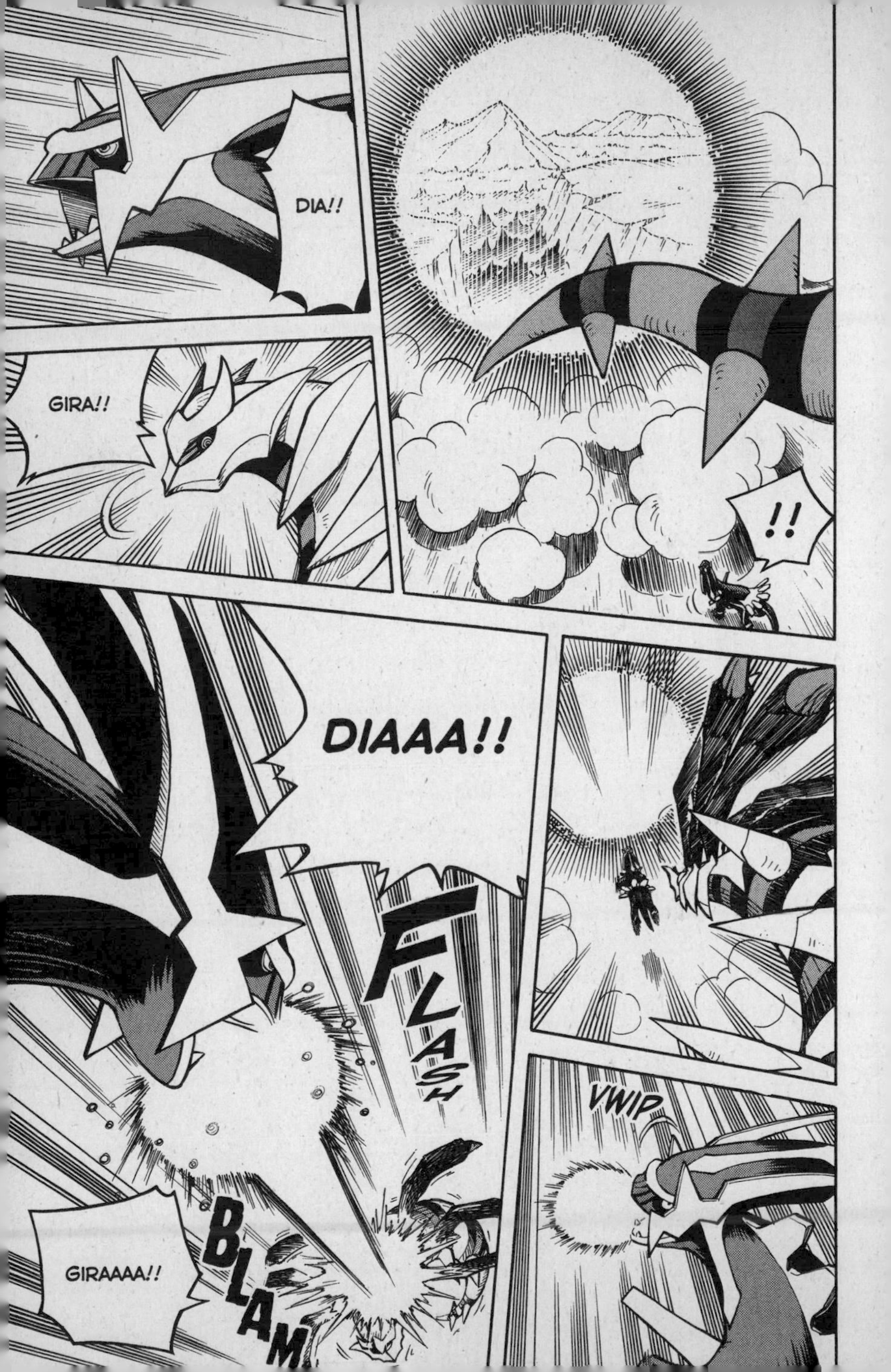

!!
DIA!!
GIRA!!
VWIP
DIAAA!!
FLASH
BLAM
GIRAAAA!!

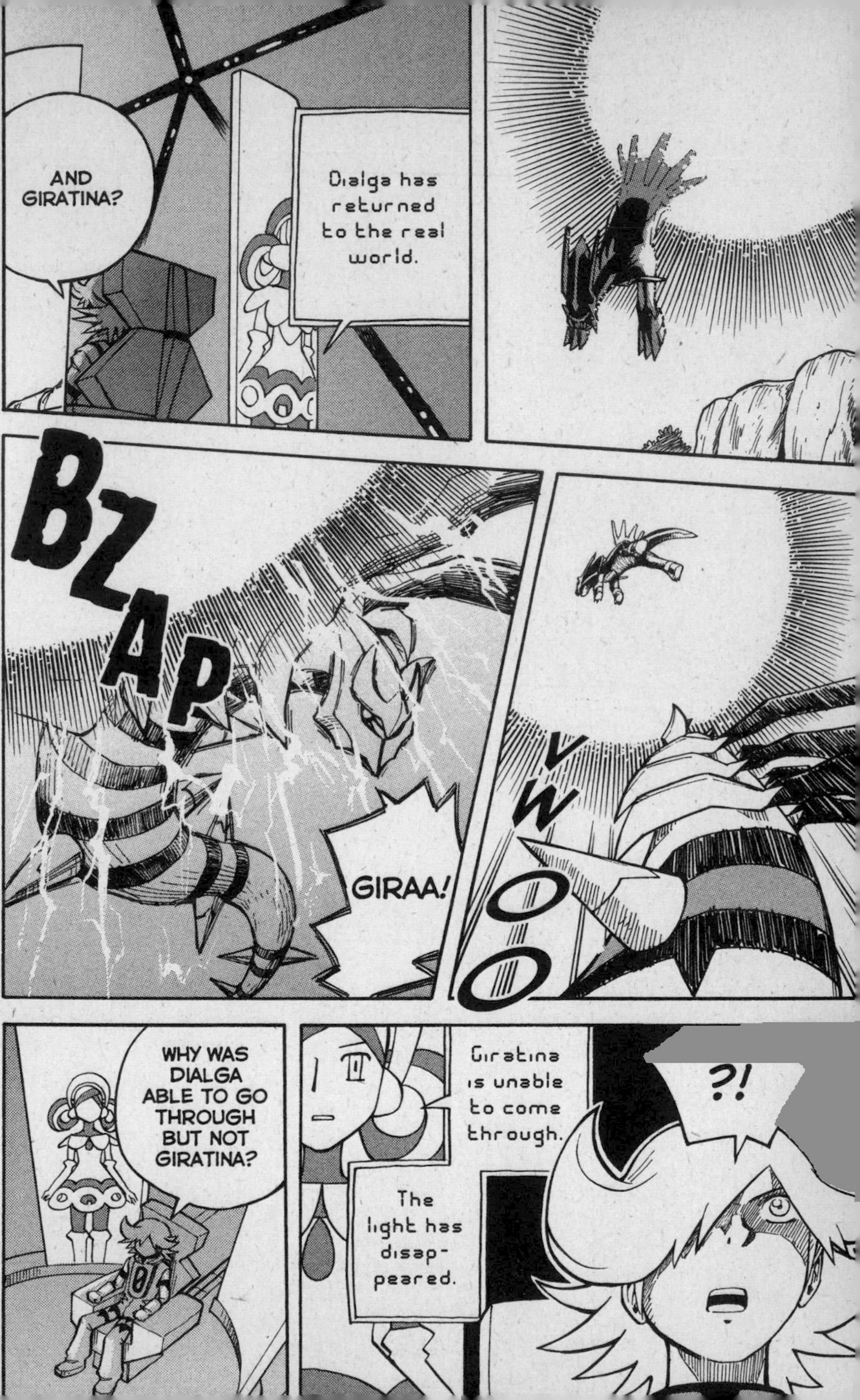

Dialga has returned to the real world.
AND GIRATINA?
VWOOO
BZZAP
GIRAA!
?!
Giratina is unable to come through.
The light has disappeared.
WHY WAS DIALGA ABLE TO GO THROUGH BUT NOT GIRATINA?

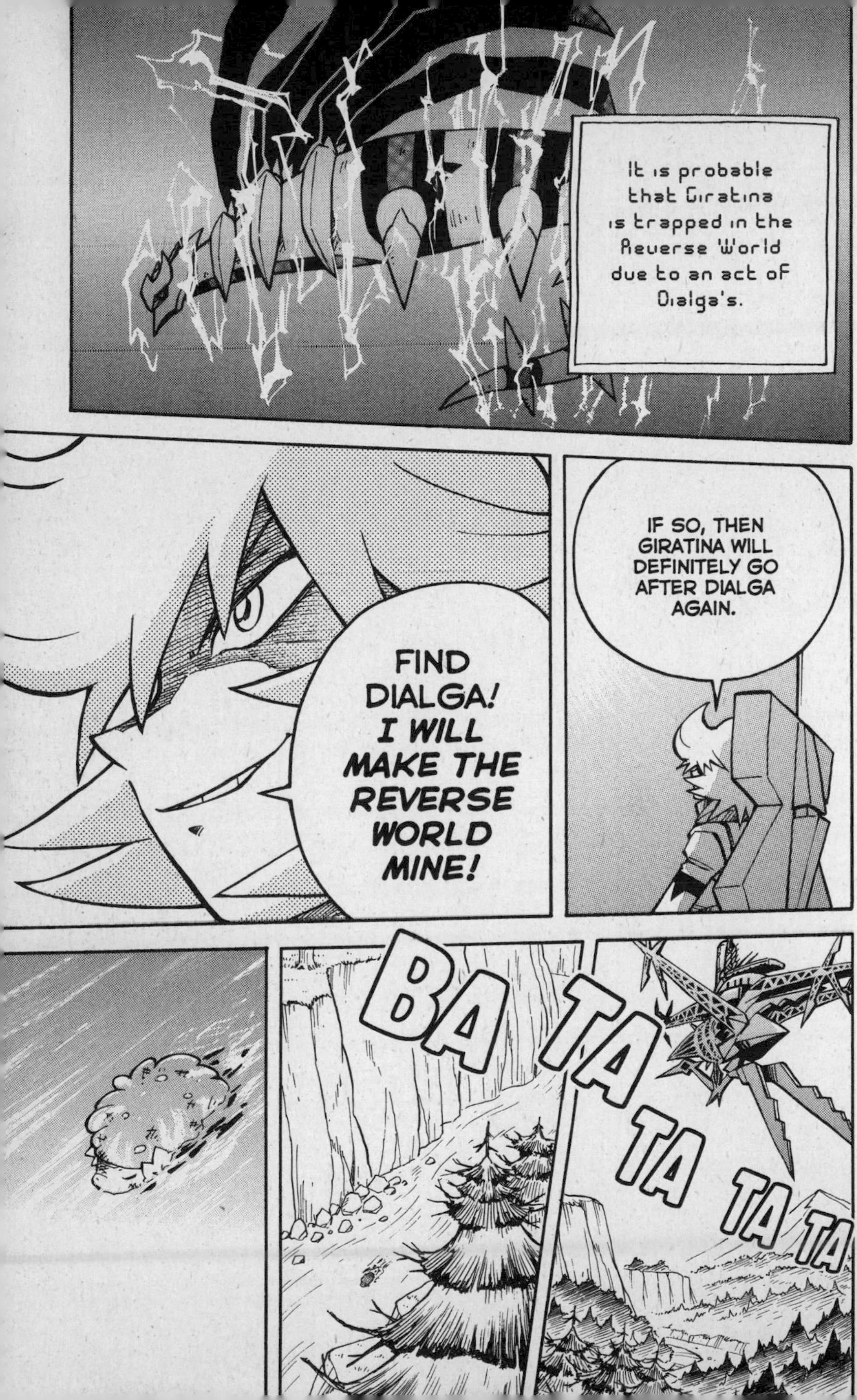
It is probable that Giratina is trapped in the Reverse World due to an act of Dialga's.
IF SO, THEN GIRATINA WILL DEFINITELY GO AFTER DIALGA AGAIN.
FIND DIALGA! I WILL MAKE THE REVERSE WORLD MINE!
BA TA TA TA TA

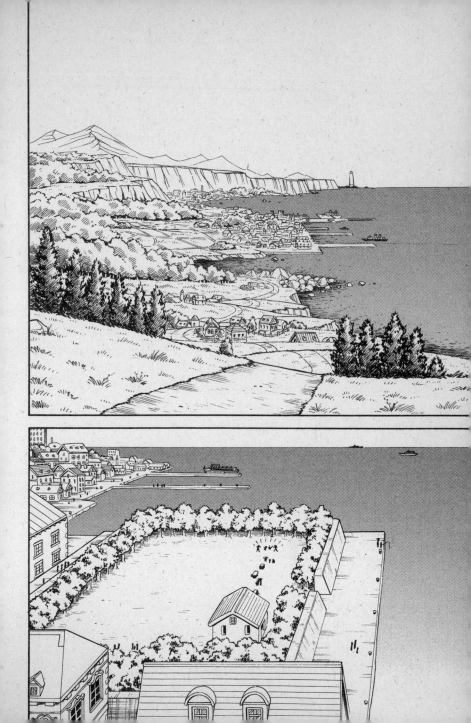

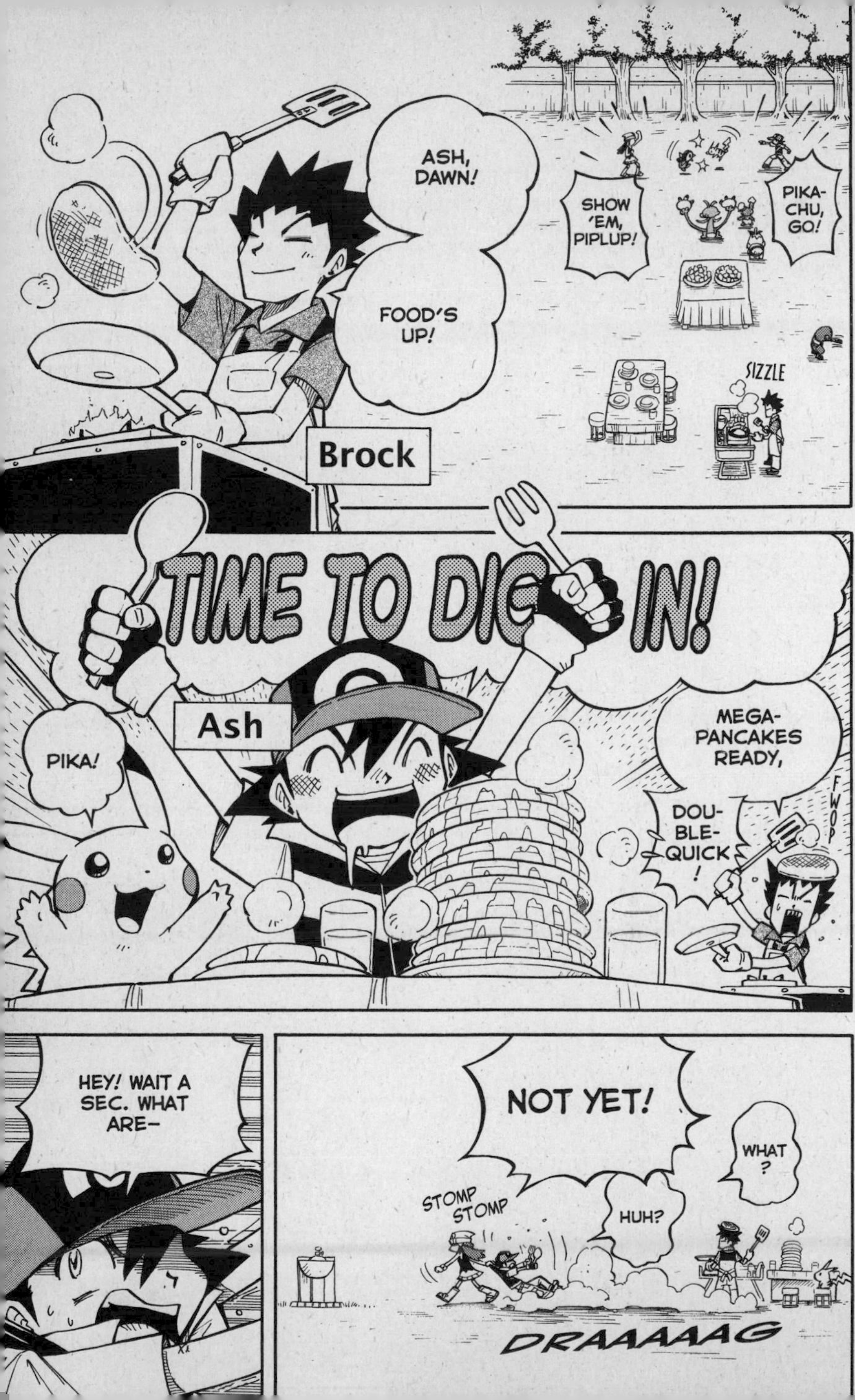
PIKA-CHU, GO!
SHOW 'EM, PIPLUP!
SIZZLE
ASH, DAWN!
FOOD'S UP!
Brock
TIME TO DIG IN!
MEGA-PANCAKES READY,
DOU-BLE-QUICK!
FWOP
Ash
PIKA!
NOT YET!
WHAT?
HUH?
STOMP STOMP
DRAAAAAG
HEY! WAIT A SEC. WHAT ARE–

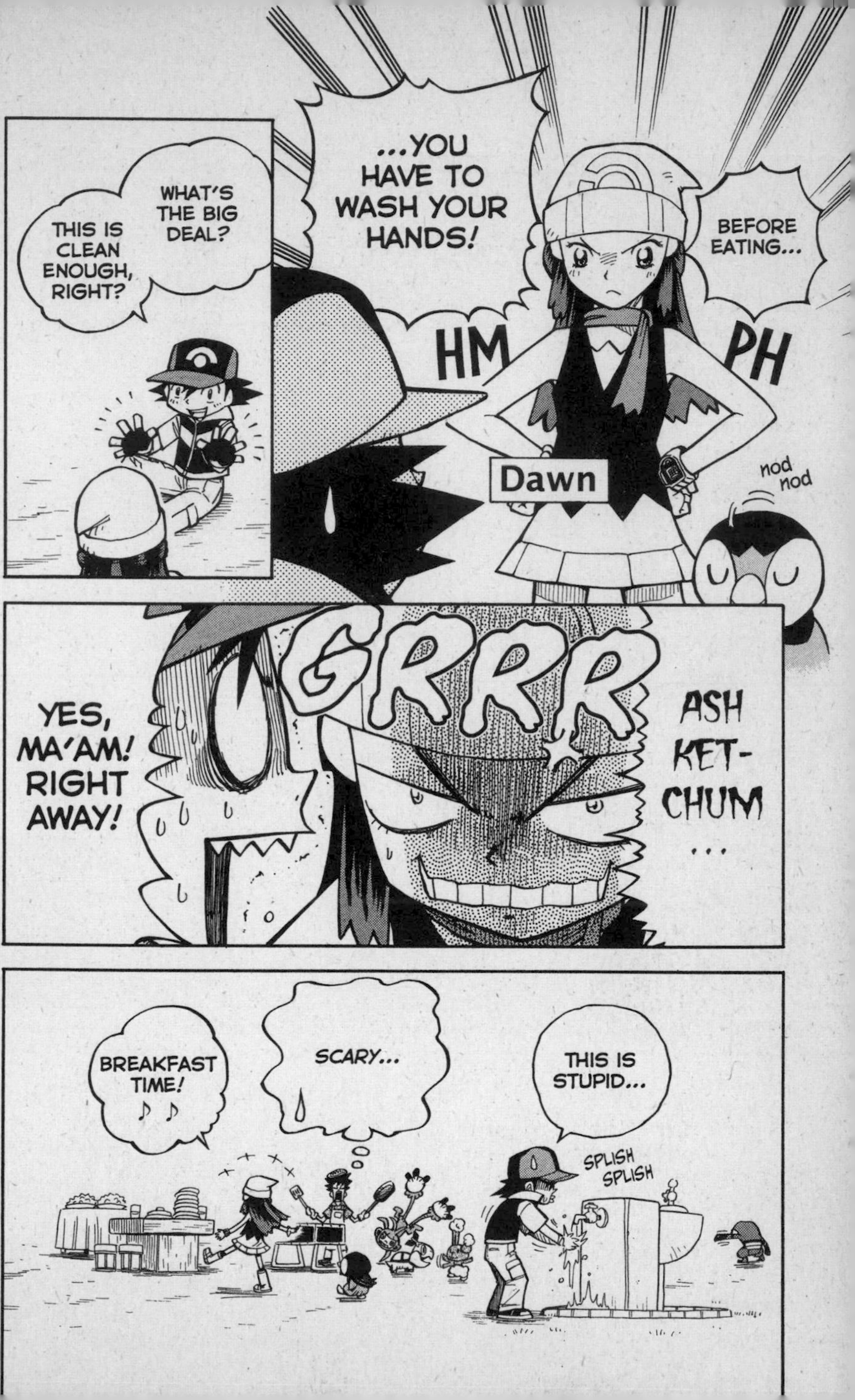
BEFORE EATING...
...YOU HAVE TO WASH YOUR HANDS!
HMPH
Dawn
nod nod
WHAT'S THE BIG DEAL?
THIS IS CLEAN ENOUGH, RIGHT?
ASH KET-CHUM...
GRRR
YES, MA'AM! RIGHT AWAY!
THIS IS STUPID...
SPLISH SPLISH
SCARY...
BREAKFAST TIME! ♪ ♪

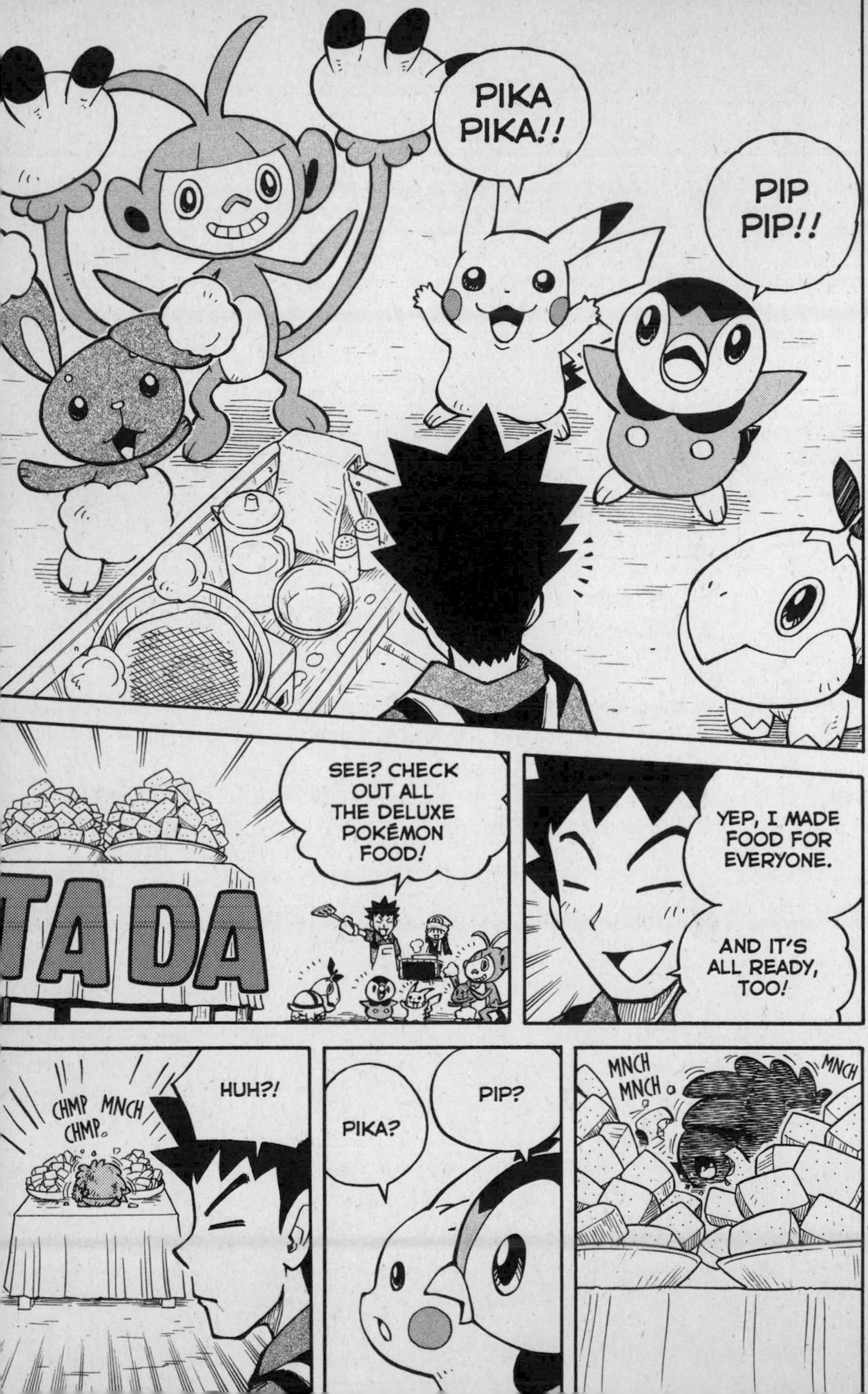
PIP PIP!!
PIKA PIKA!!
YEP, I MADE FOOD FOR EVERYONE.
AND IT'S ALL READY, TOO!
SEE? CHECK OUT ALL THE DELUXE POKÉMON FOOD!
TADA
MNCH
MNCH MNCH
PIP?
PIKA?
HUH?!
CHMP MNCH CHMP

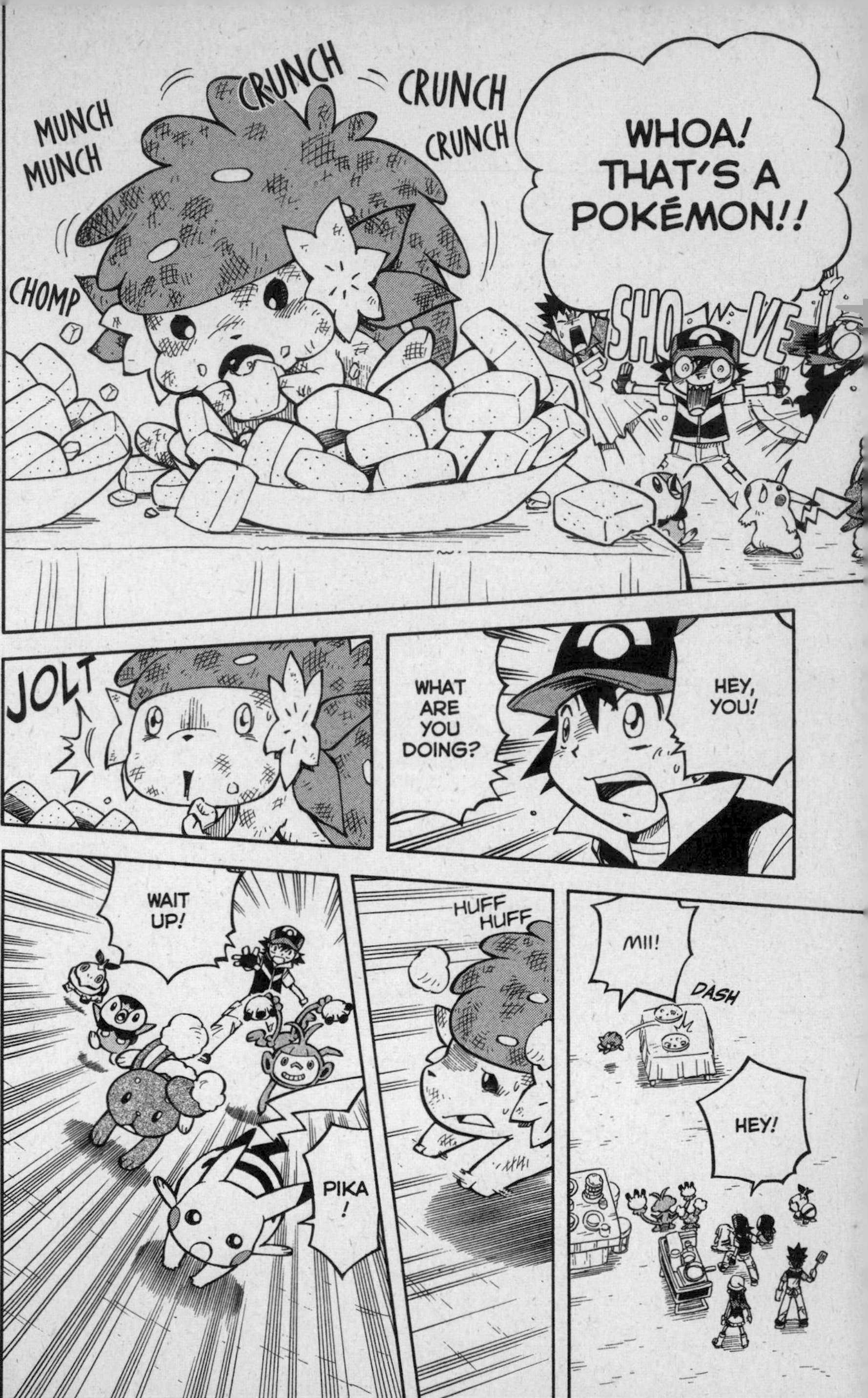
WHOA! THAT'S A POKÉMON!!
SHOVE
CRUNCH CRUNCH
CRUNCH
MUNCH MUNCH
CHOMP
HEY, YOU!
WHAT ARE YOU DOING?
JOLT
MII!
DASH
HEY!
HUFF HUFF
WAIT UP!
PIKA!

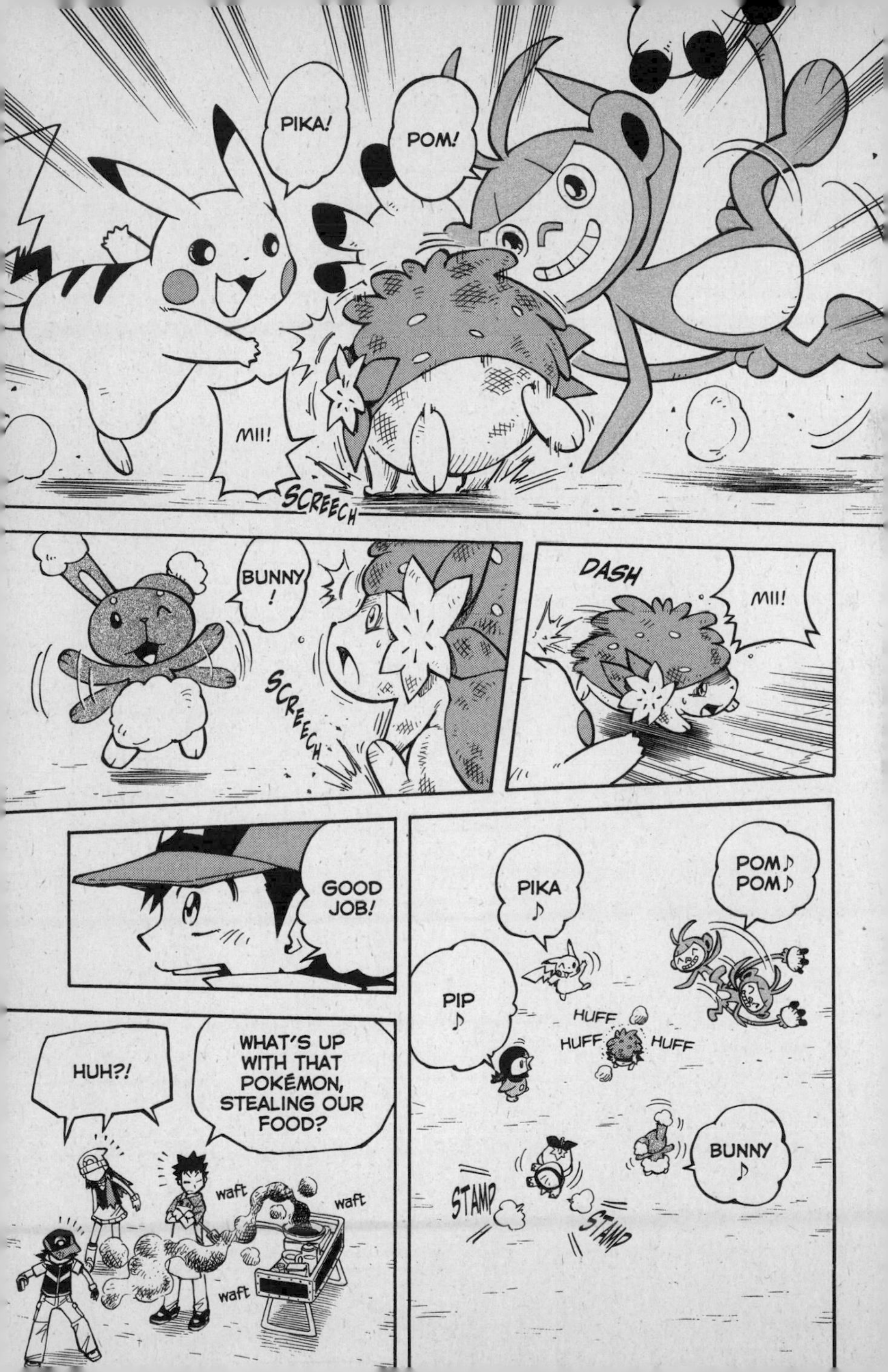
POM!
PIKA!
MII!
SCREECH
DASH
MII!
SCREECH
BUNNY!
POM♪ POM♪
PIKA ♪
PIP ♪
HUFF HUFF HUFF
BUNNY ♪
STAMP
STAMP
GOOD JOB!
WHAT'S UP WITH THAT POKÉMON, STEALING OUR FOOD?
HUH?!
waft
waft
waft

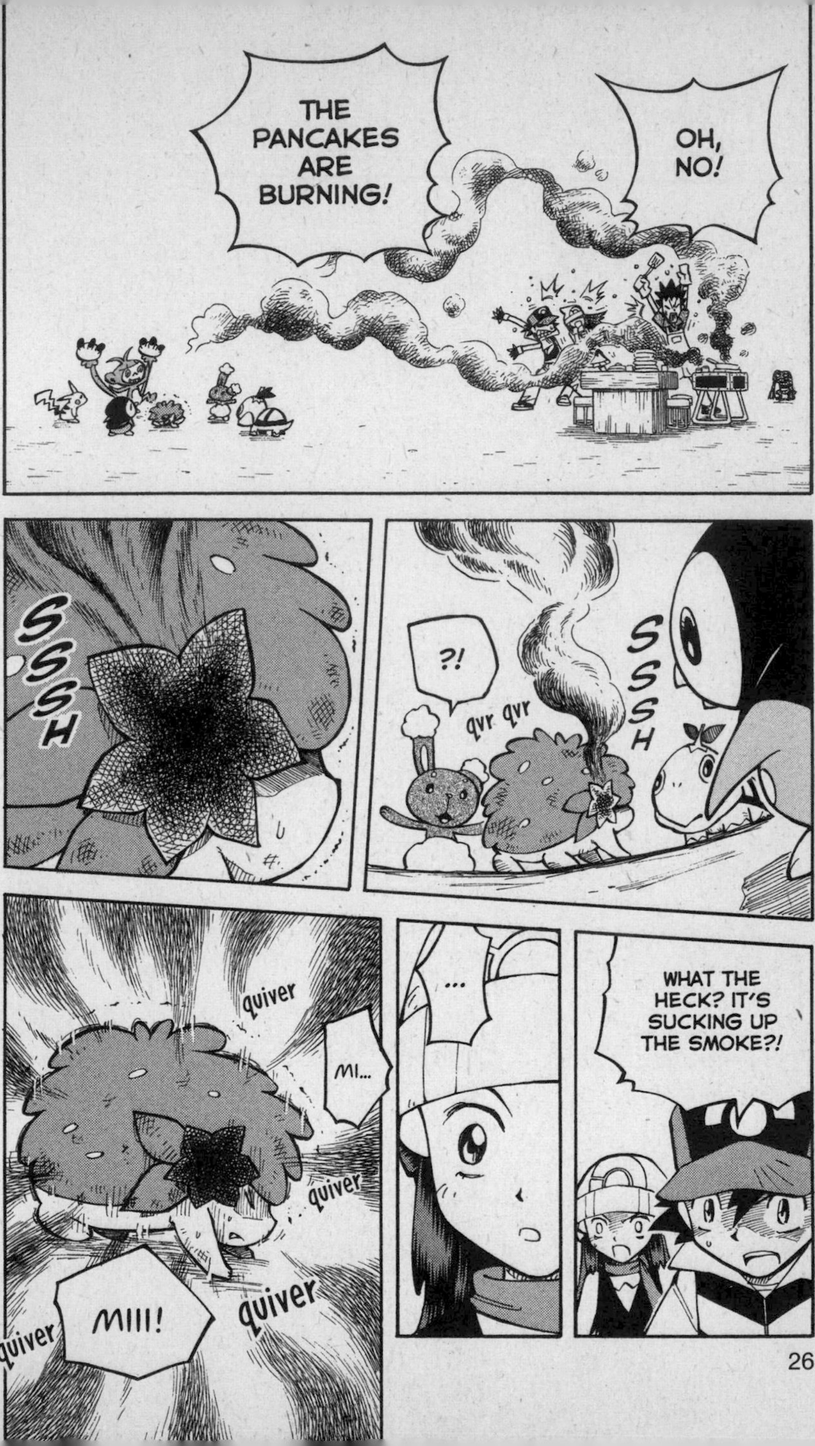
THE PANCAKES ARE BURNING!
OH, NO!
SSSH
?!
qvr qvr
SSSH
WHAT THE HECK? IT'S SUCKING UP THE SMOKE?!
...
quiver
MI...
quiver
MIII!
quiver
quiver

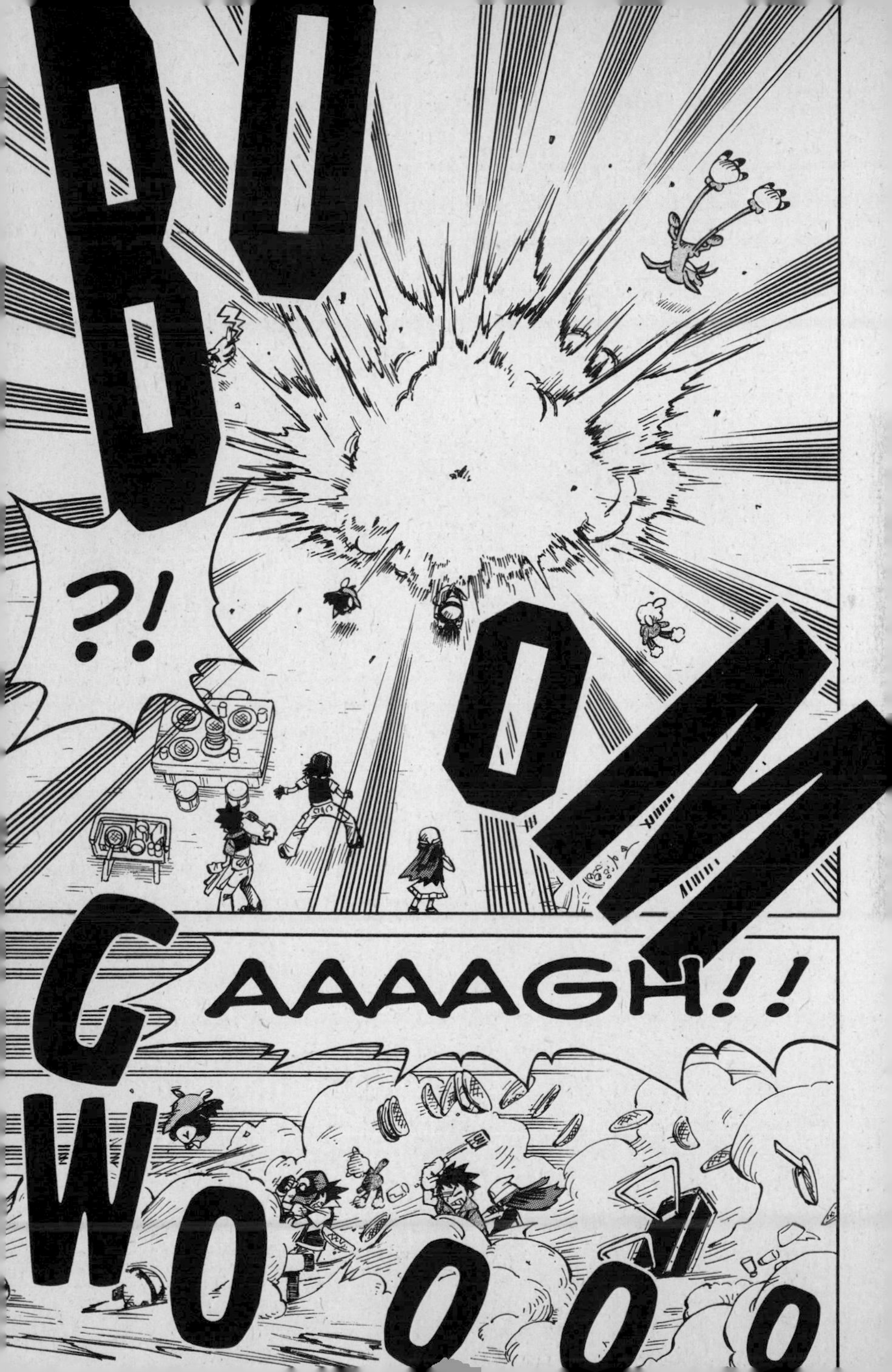
BOOM
?!
AAAAGH!!
CWOOOO

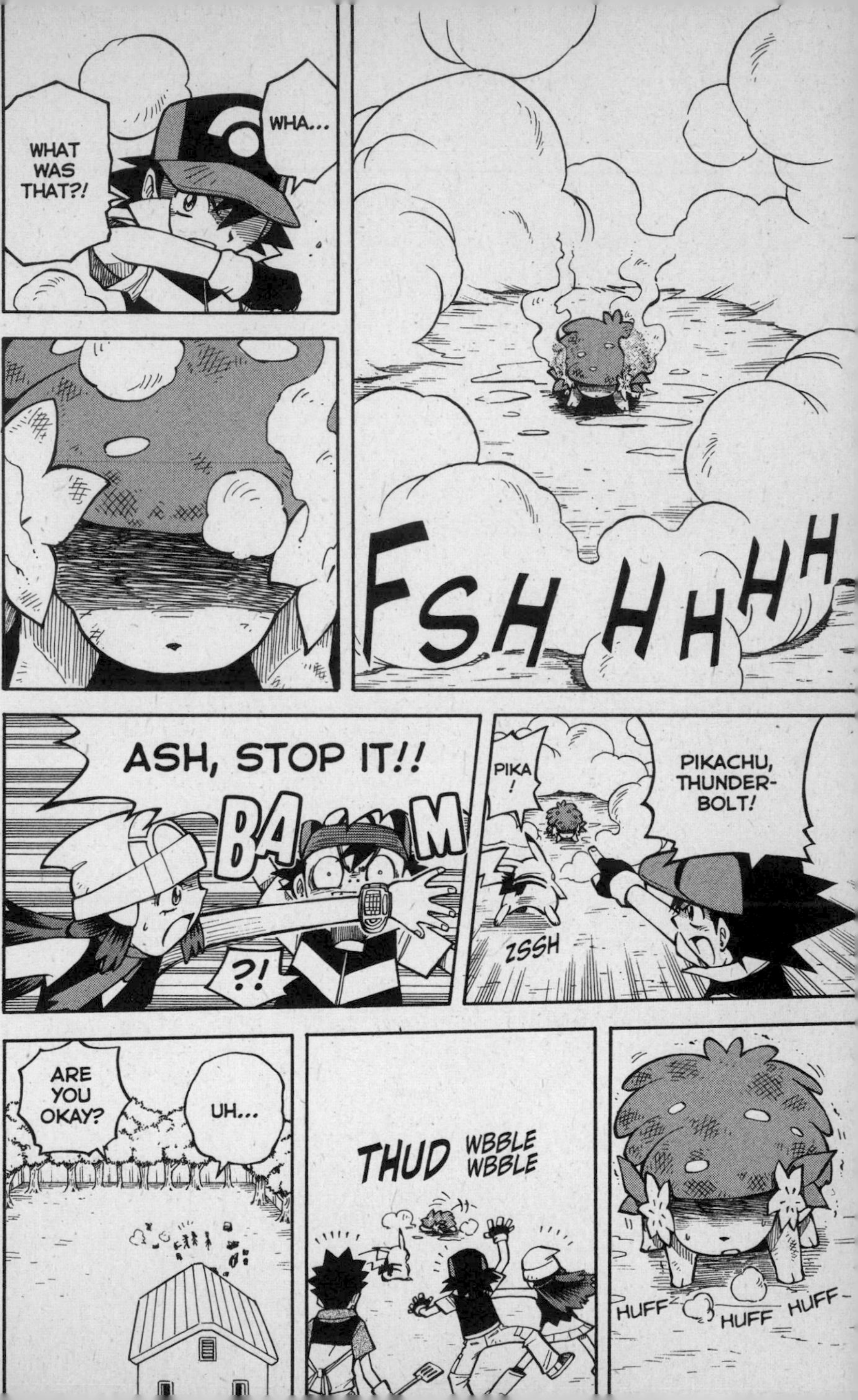
FSHHHHHH
WHA...
WHAT WAS THAT?!
PIKACHU, THUNDER-BOLT!
PIKA!
ZSSH
ASH, STOP IT!!
BAM
?!
HUFF HUFF HUFF
THUD
WBBLE WBBLE
ARE YOU OKAY?
UH...

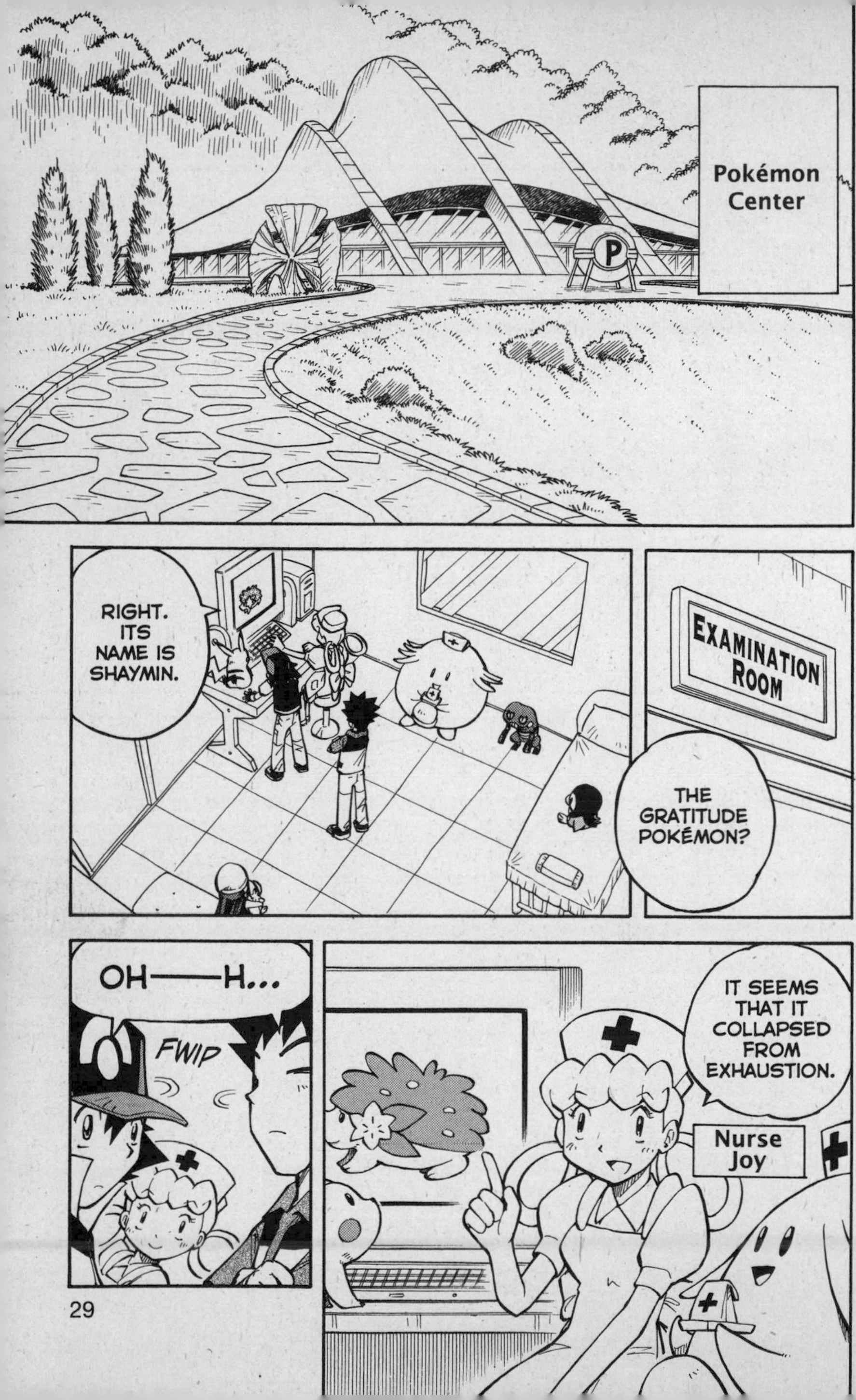
Pokémon Center
EXAMINATION ROOM
THE GRATITUDE POKÉMON?
RIGHT. ITS NAME IS SHAYMIN.
IT SEEMS THAT IT COLLAPSED FROM EXHAUSTION.
Nurse Joy
OH——H...
FWIP

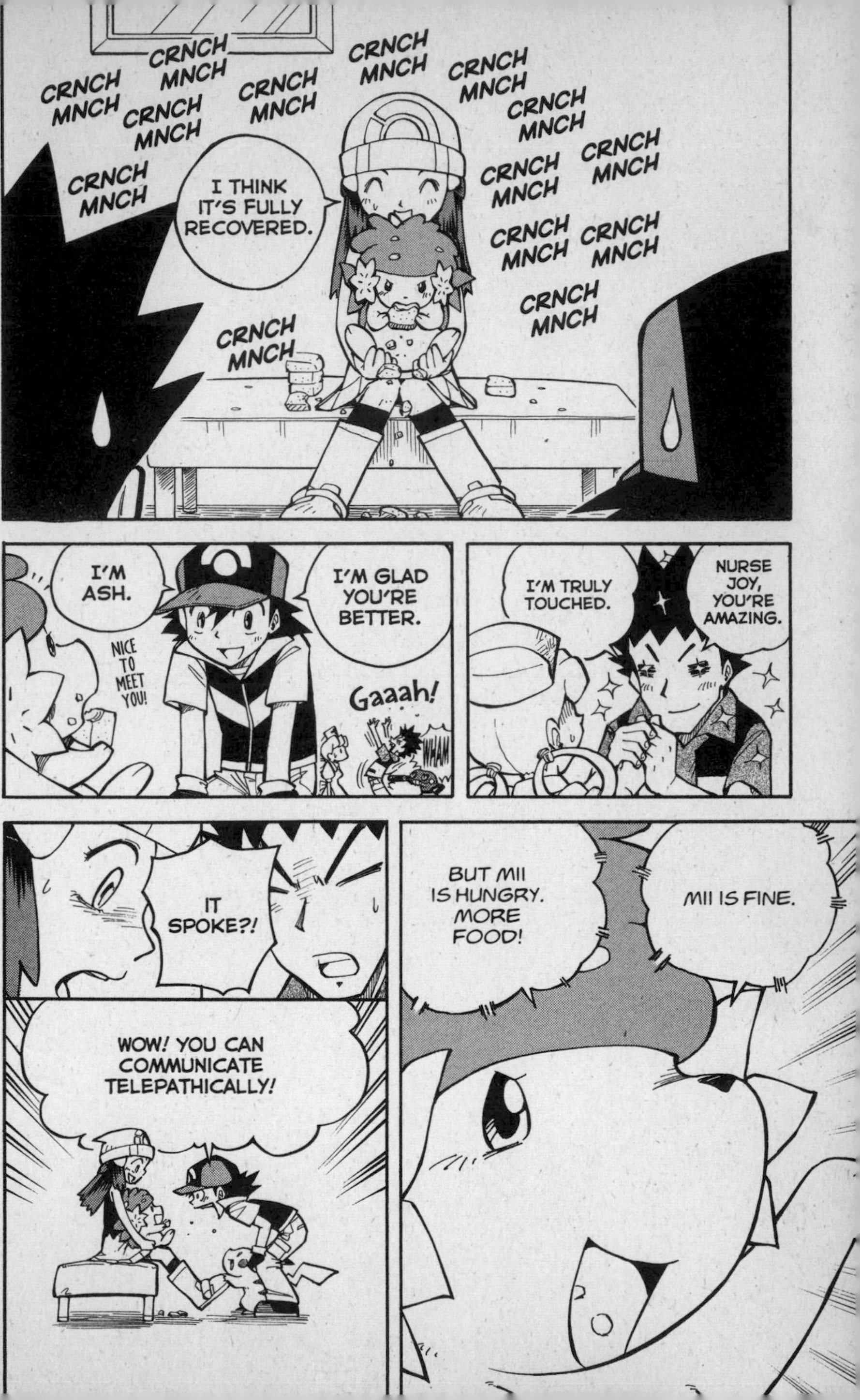
CRNCH MNCH
CRNCH MNCH
CRNCH MNCH
CRNCH MNCH
CRNCH MNCH
CRNCH MNCH
CRNCH MNCH
CRNCH MNCH
CRNCH MNCH
CRNCH MNCH
CRNCH MNCH
I THINK IT'S FULLY RECOVERED.
CRNCH MNCH
CRNCH MNCH
CRNCH MNCH
NURSE JOY, YOU'RE AMAZING.
I'M TRULY TOUCHED.
I'M GLAD YOU'RE BETTER.
Gaaah!
WHAM
I'M ASH.
NICE TO MEET YOU!
MII IS FINE.
BUT MII IS HUNGRY. MORE FOOD!
IT SPOKE?!
WOW! YOU CAN COMMUNICATE TELEPATHICALLY!

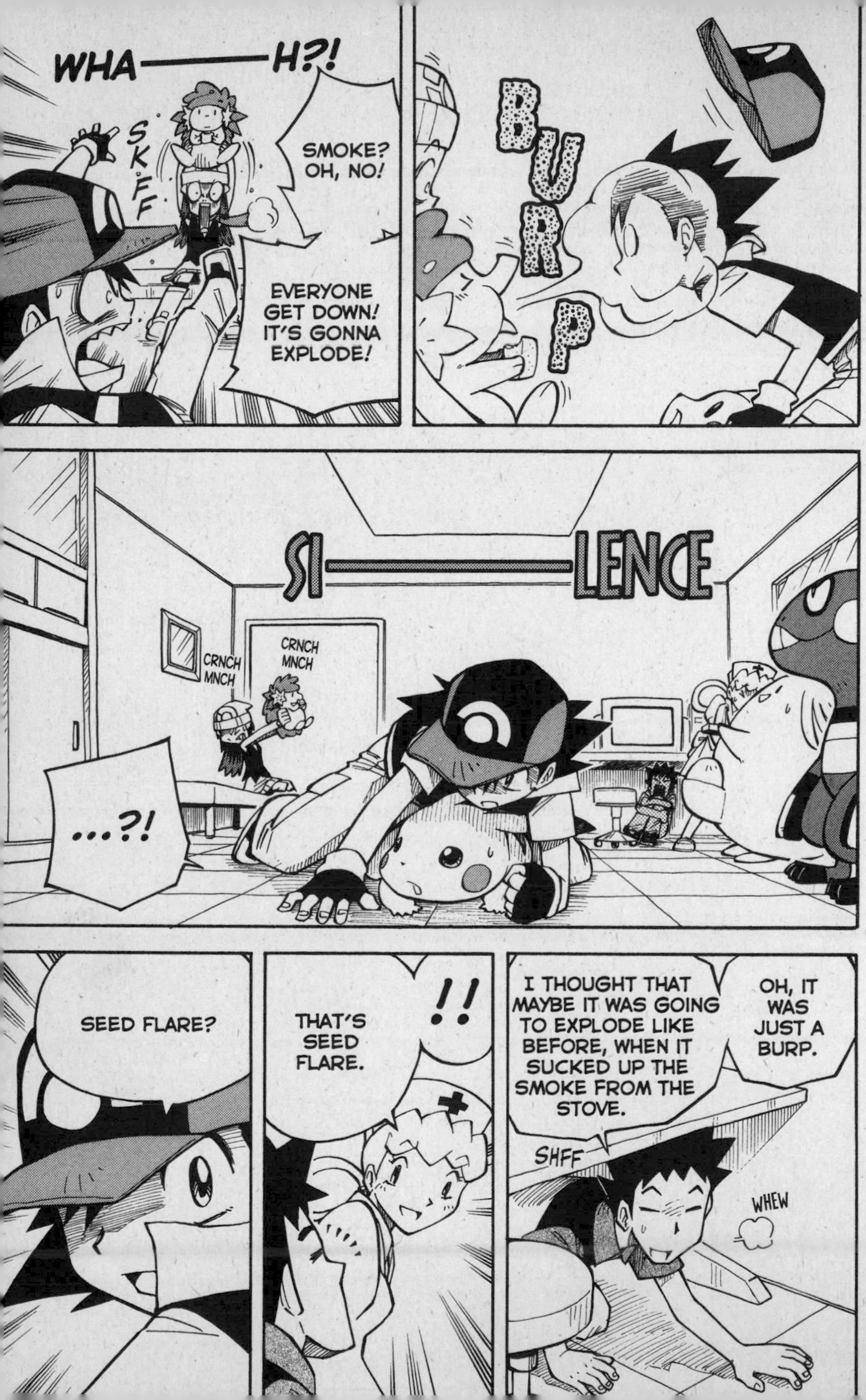
BURP
WHA——H?!
SKFF
SMOKE? OH, NO!
EVERYONE GET DOWN! IT'S GONNA EXPLODE!
SI——LENCE
CRNCH MNCH
CRNCH MNCH
...?!
OH, IT WAS JUST A BURP.
I THOUGHT THAT MAYBE IT WAS GOING TO EXPLODE LIKE BEFORE, WHEN IT SUCKED UP THE SMOKE FROM THE STOVE.
SHFF
WHEW
!!
THAT'S SEED FLARE.
SEED FLARE?

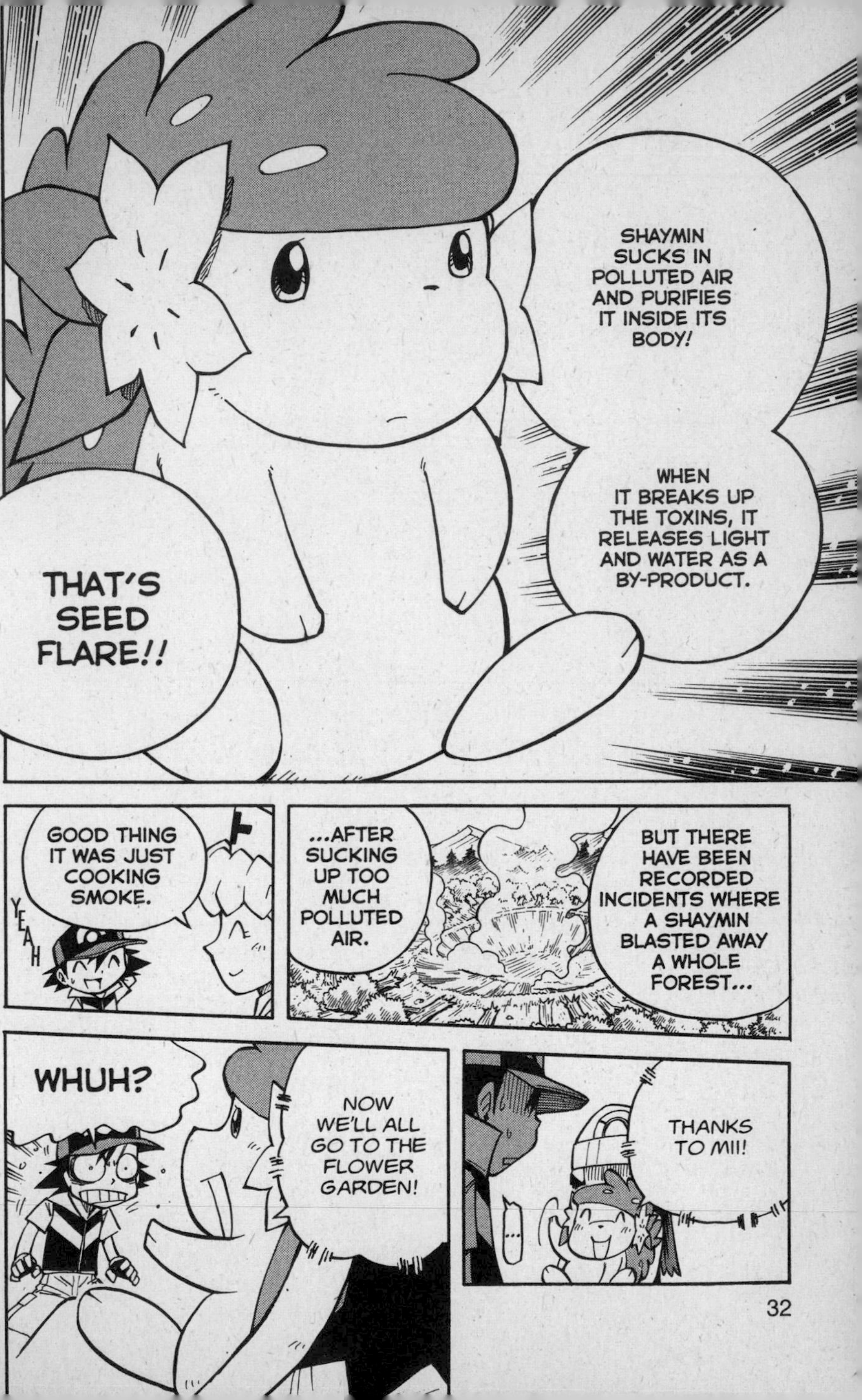
SHAYMIN SUCKS IN POLLUTED AIR AND PURIFIES IT INSIDE ITS BODY!
WHEN IT BREAKS UP THE TOXINS, IT RELEASES LIGHT AND WATER AS A BY-PRODUCT.
THAT'S SEED FLARE!!
BUT THERE HAVE BEEN RECORDED INCIDENTS WHERE A SHAYMIN BLASTED AWAY A WHOLE FOREST...
...AFTER SUCKING UP TOO MUCH POLLUTED AIR.
GOOD THING IT WAS JUST COOKING SMOKE.
YEAH
THANKS TO MII!
...
NOW WE'LL ALL GO TO THE FLOWER GARDEN!
WHUH?

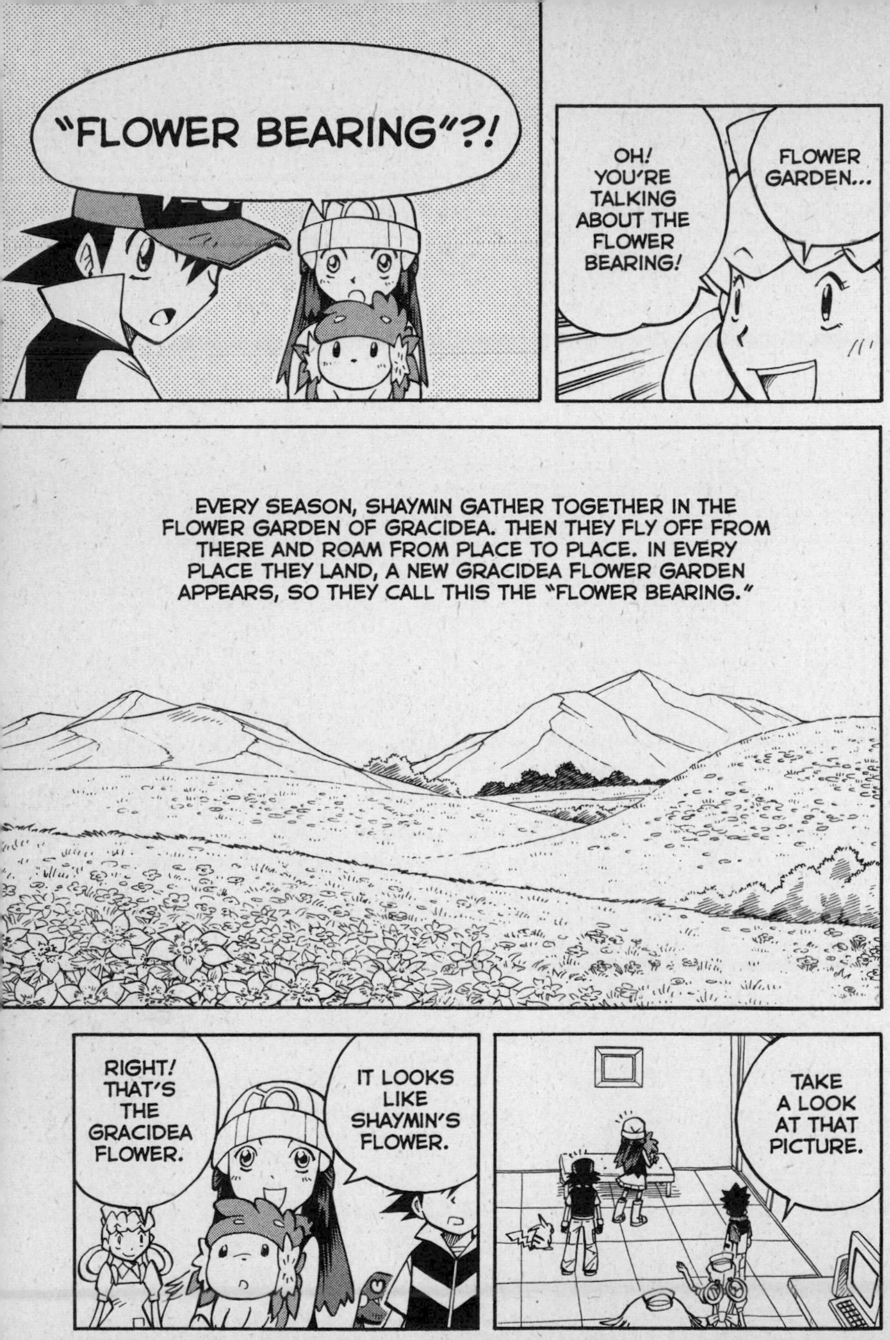
FLOWER GARDEN...
OH! YOU'RE TALKING ABOUT THE FLOWER BEARING!
"FLOWER BEARING"?!
EVERY SEASON, SHAYMIN GATHER TOGETHER IN THE FLOWER GARDEN OF GRACIDEA. THEN THEY FLY OFF FROM THERE AND ROAM FROM PLACE TO PLACE. IN EVERY PLACE THEY LAND, A NEW GRACIDEA FLOWER GARDEN APPEARS, SO THEY CALL THIS THE "FLOWER BEARING."
TAKE A LOOK AT THAT PICTURE.
IT LOOKS LIKE SHAYMIN'S FLOWER.
RIGHT! THAT'S THE GRACIDEA FLOWER.

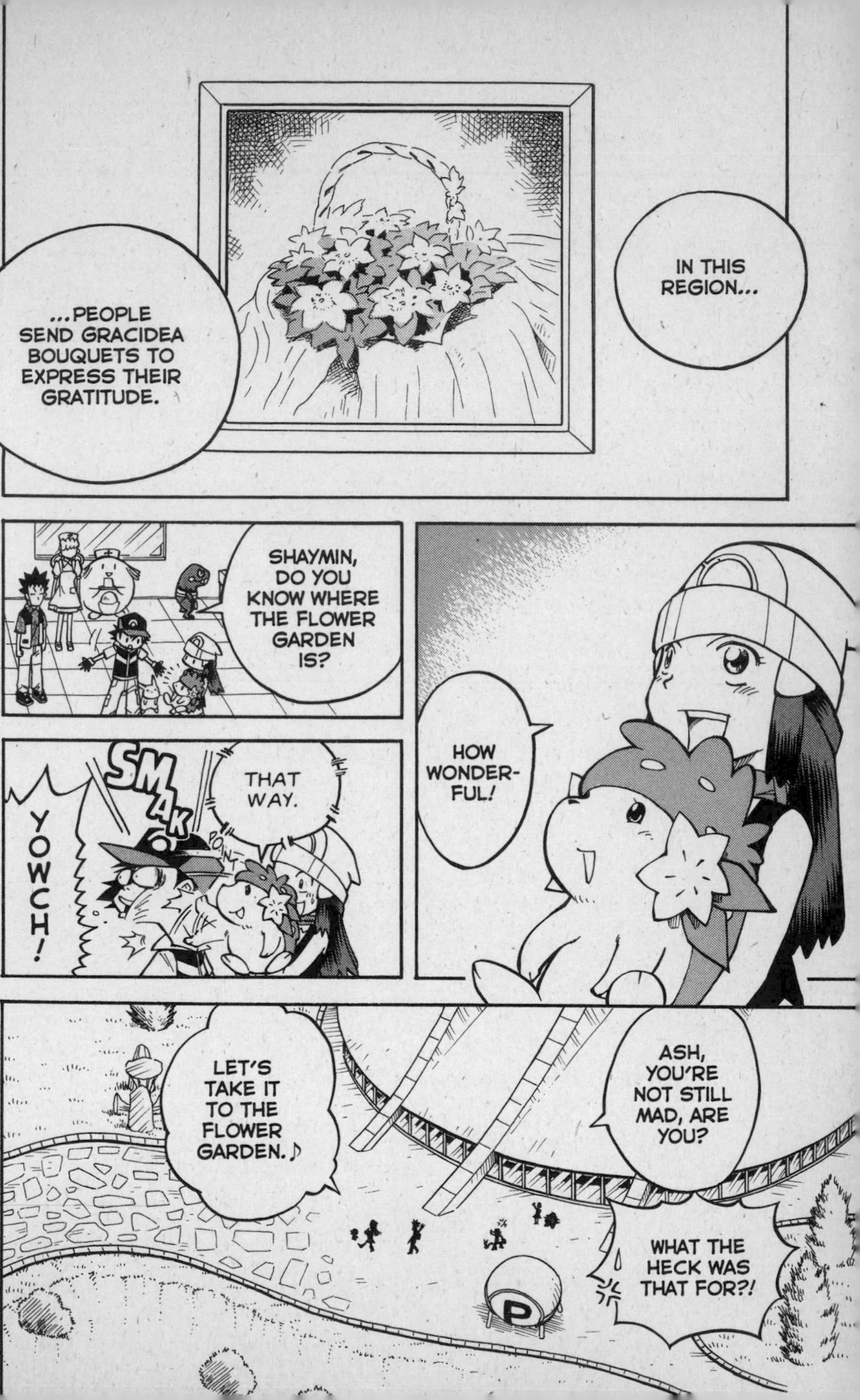
IN THIS REGION...
...PEOPLE SEND GRACIDEA BOUQUETS TO EXPRESS THEIR GRATITUDE.
HOW WONDER-FUL!
SHAYMIN, DO YOU KNOW WHERE THE FLOWER GARDEN IS?
THAT WAY.
SMAK
POINT
YOWCH!
ASH, YOU'RE NOT STILL MAD, ARE YOU?
WHAT THE HECK WAS THAT FOR?!
LET'S TAKE IT TO THE FLOWER GARDEN.♪

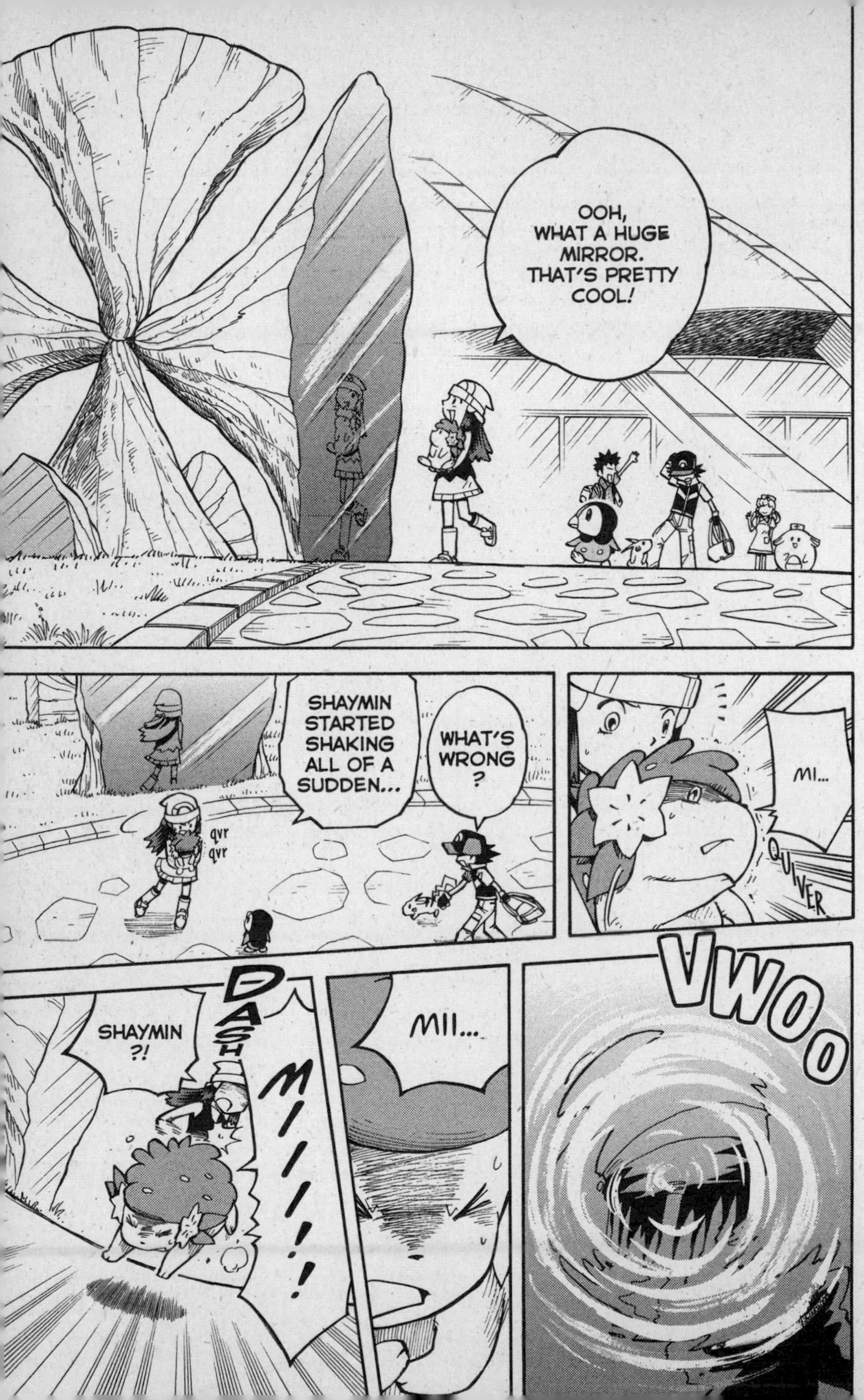
OOH, WHAT A HUGE MIRROR. THAT'S PRETTY COOL!
MI...
QUIVER
WHAT'S WRONG?
SHAYMIN STARTED SHAKING ALL OF A SUDDEN...
qvr qvr
VWOO
MII...
DASH
MI!!!!
SHAYMIN?!

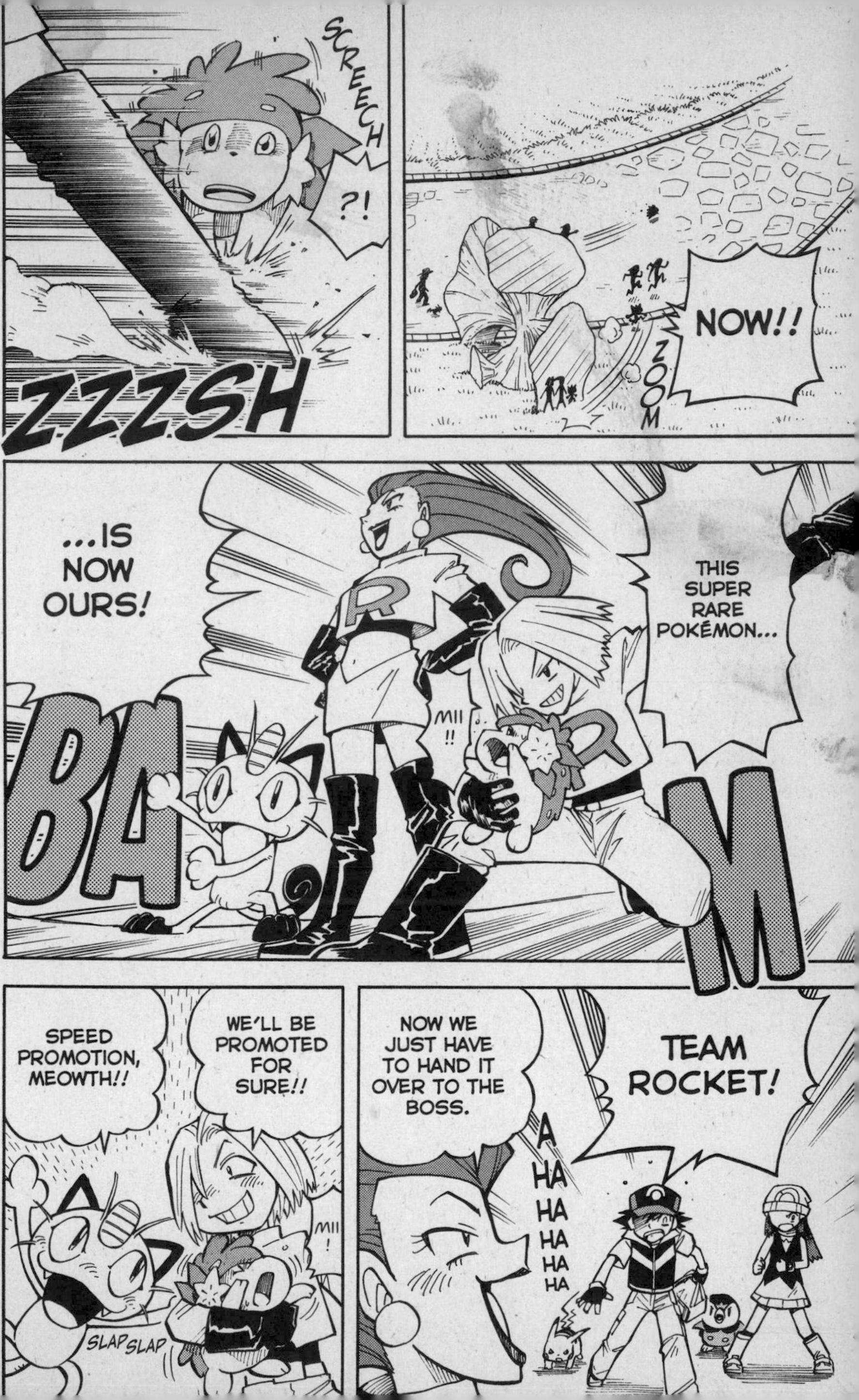
NOW!!
ZOOM
SCREECH
?!
ZZZSH
THIS SUPER RARE POKÉMON...
...IS NOW OURS!
MII !!
BAM
TEAM ROCKET!
NOW WE JUST HAVE TO HAND IT OVER TO THE BOSS.
A HA HA HA HA HA HA
WE'LL BE PROMOTED FOR SURE!!
SPEED PROMOTION, MEOWTH!!
MII !
SLAP SLAP

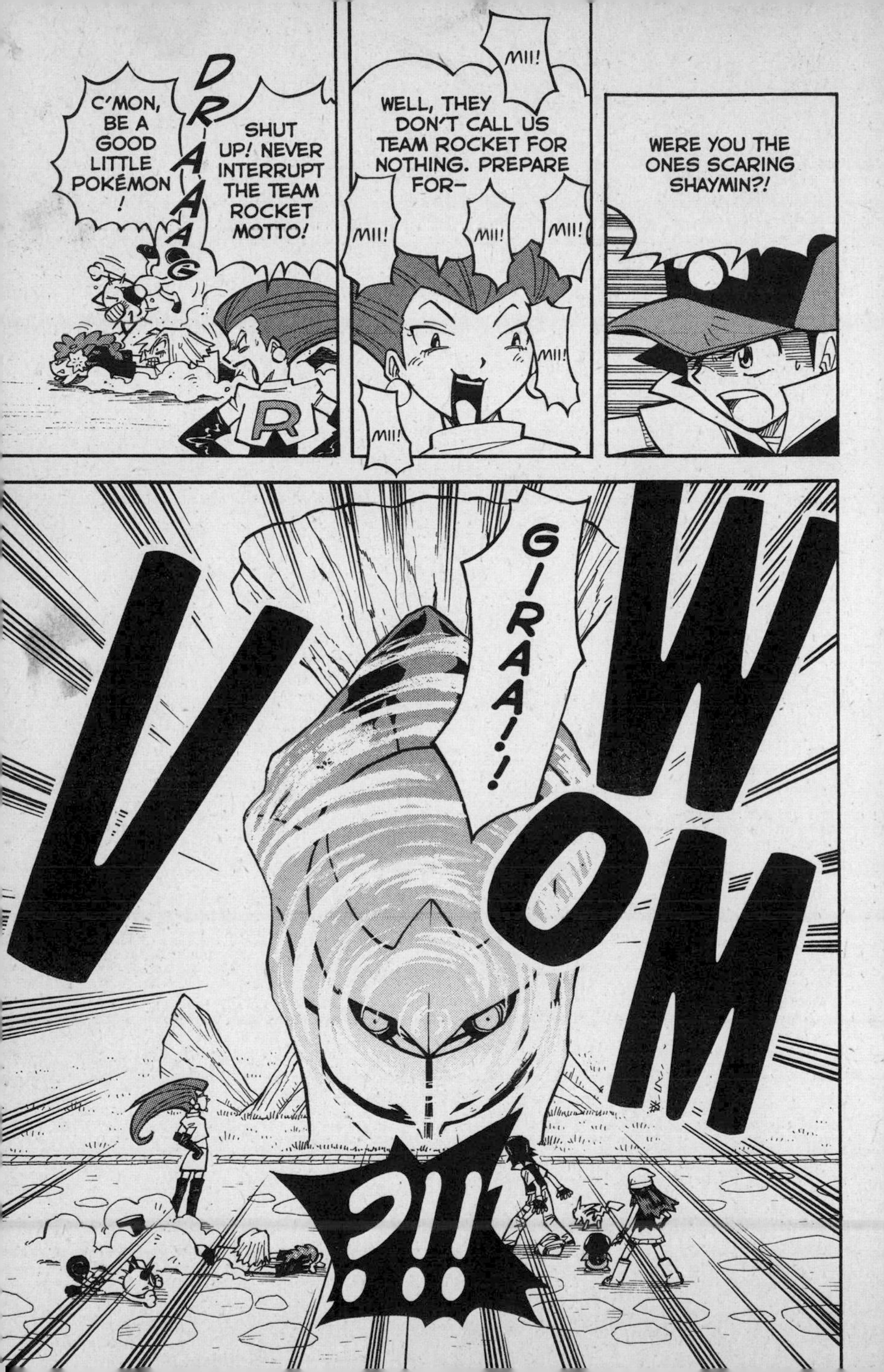
WERE YOU THE ONES SCARING SHAYMIN?!
MII!
WELL, THEY DON'T CALL US TEAM ROCKET FOR NOTHING. PREPARE FOR–
MII!
MII!
MII!
MII!
MII!
SHUT UP! NEVER INTERRUPT THE TEAM ROCKET MOTTO!
DRAAAAAG
C'MON, BE A GOOD LITTLE POKÉMON!
VWOOM
GIRAAA!!!
?!!!

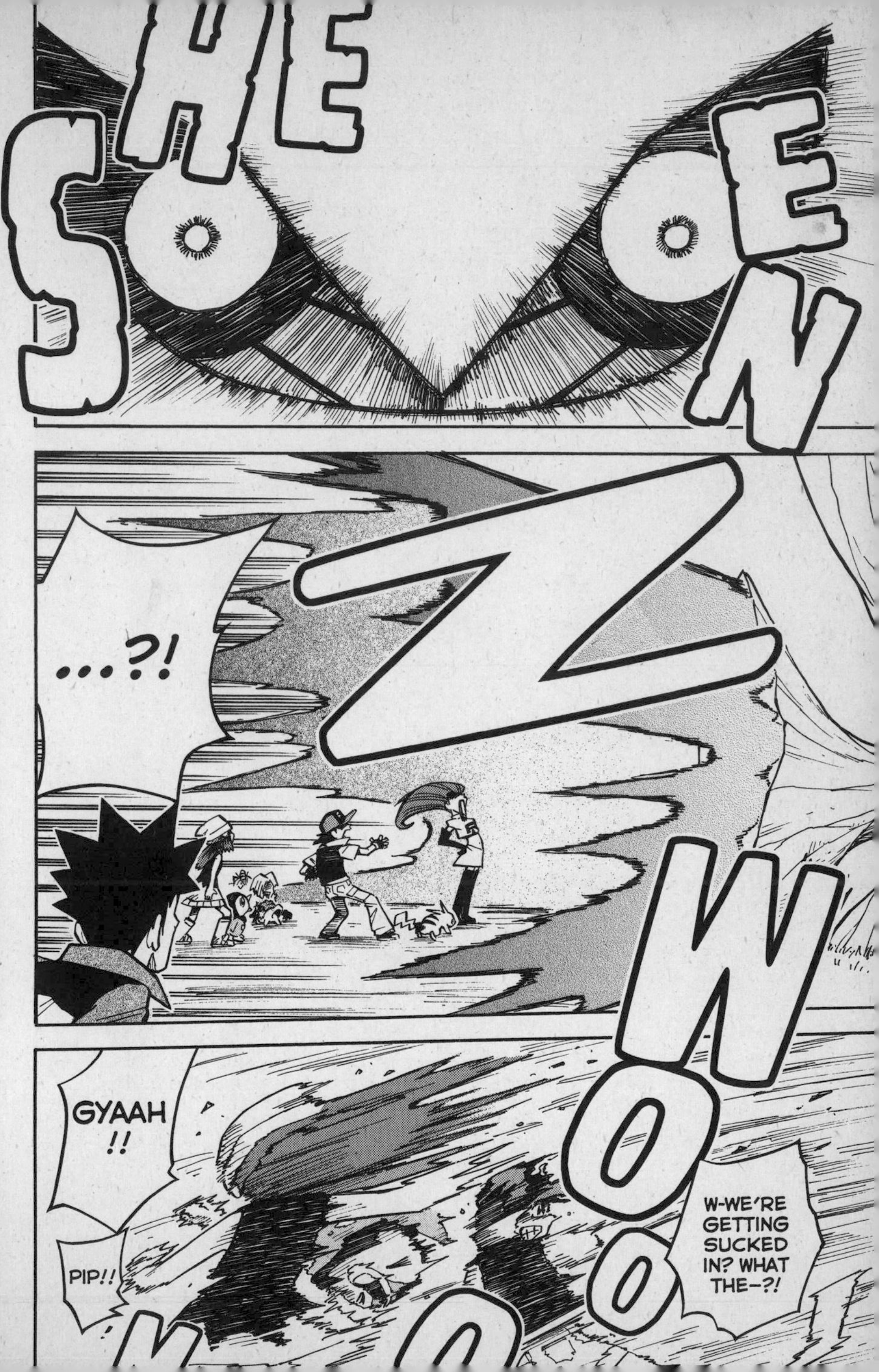
...?!
W-WE'RE GETTING SUCKED IN? WHAT THE–?!
GYAAH !!
PIP!!

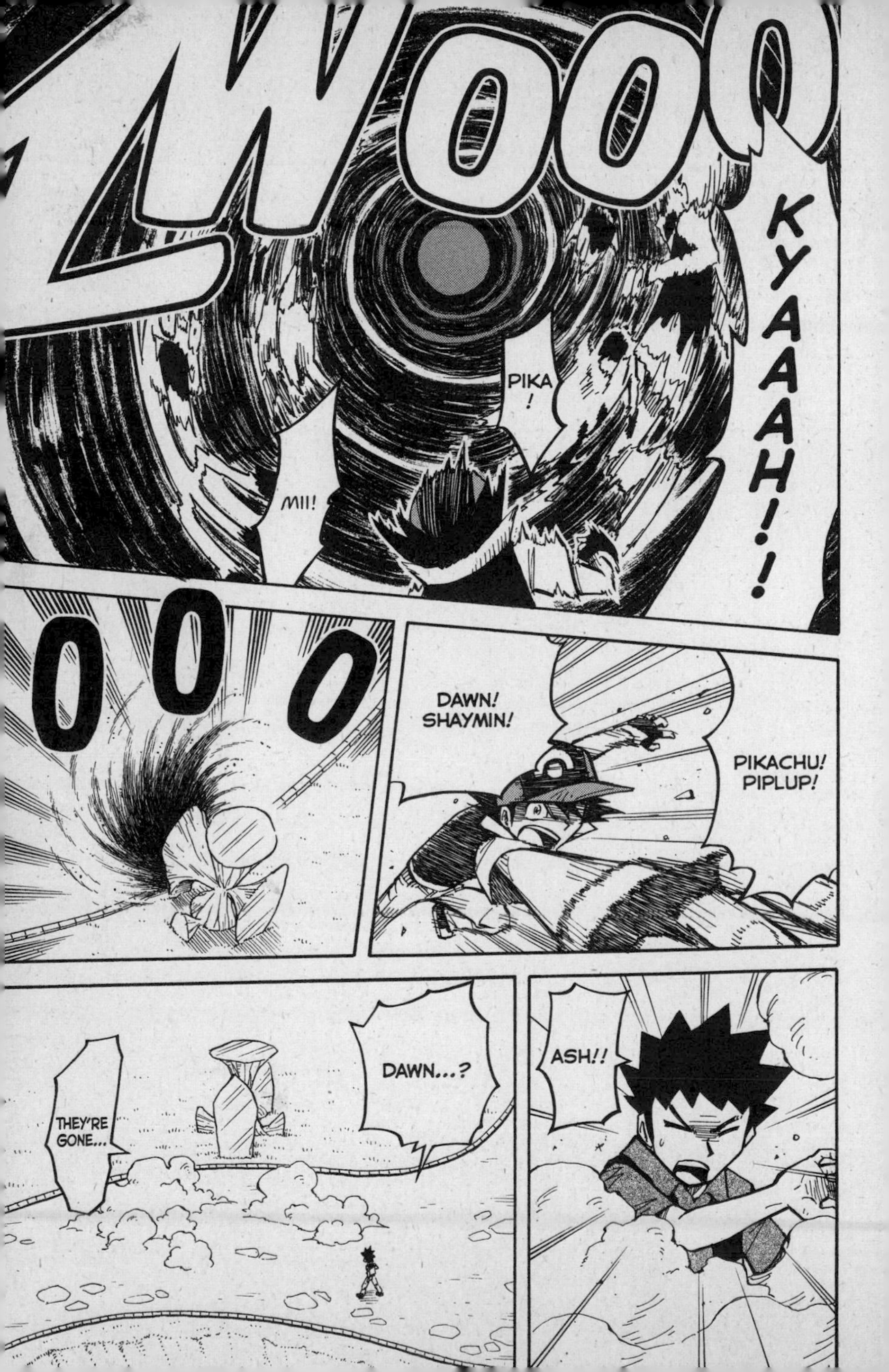
KYAAAH!!!
PIKA!
MII!
PIKACHU! PIPLUP!
DAWN! SHAYMIN!
OOO
ASH!!
DAWN...?
THEY'RE GONE...

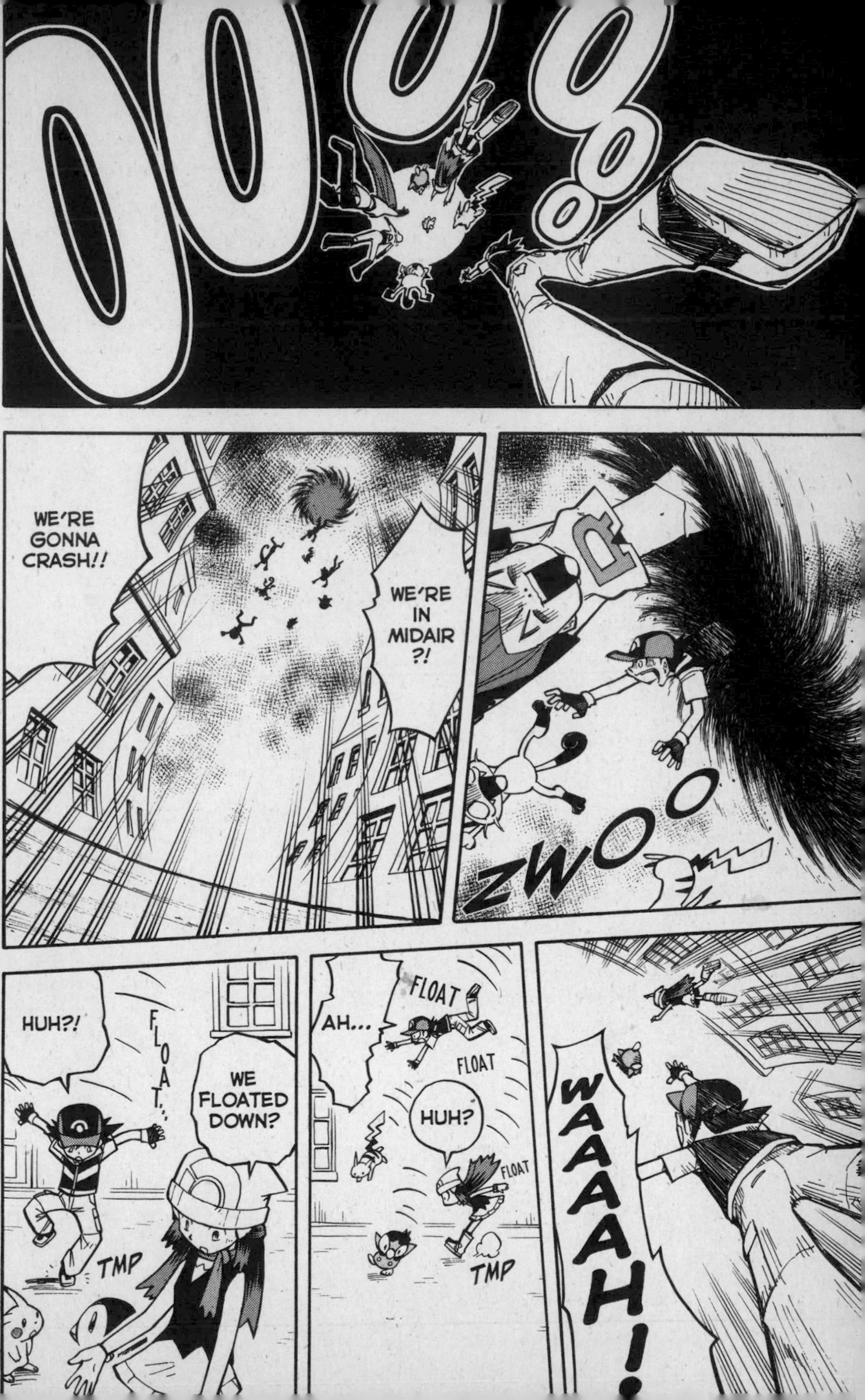

OOOOooo
ZWOOO
WE'RE IN MIDAIR?!
WE'RE GONNA CRASH!!
WAAAAH!
FLOAT
AH...
FLOAT
HUH?
FLOAT
TMP
HUH?!
FLOAT...
WE FLOATED DOWN?
TMP

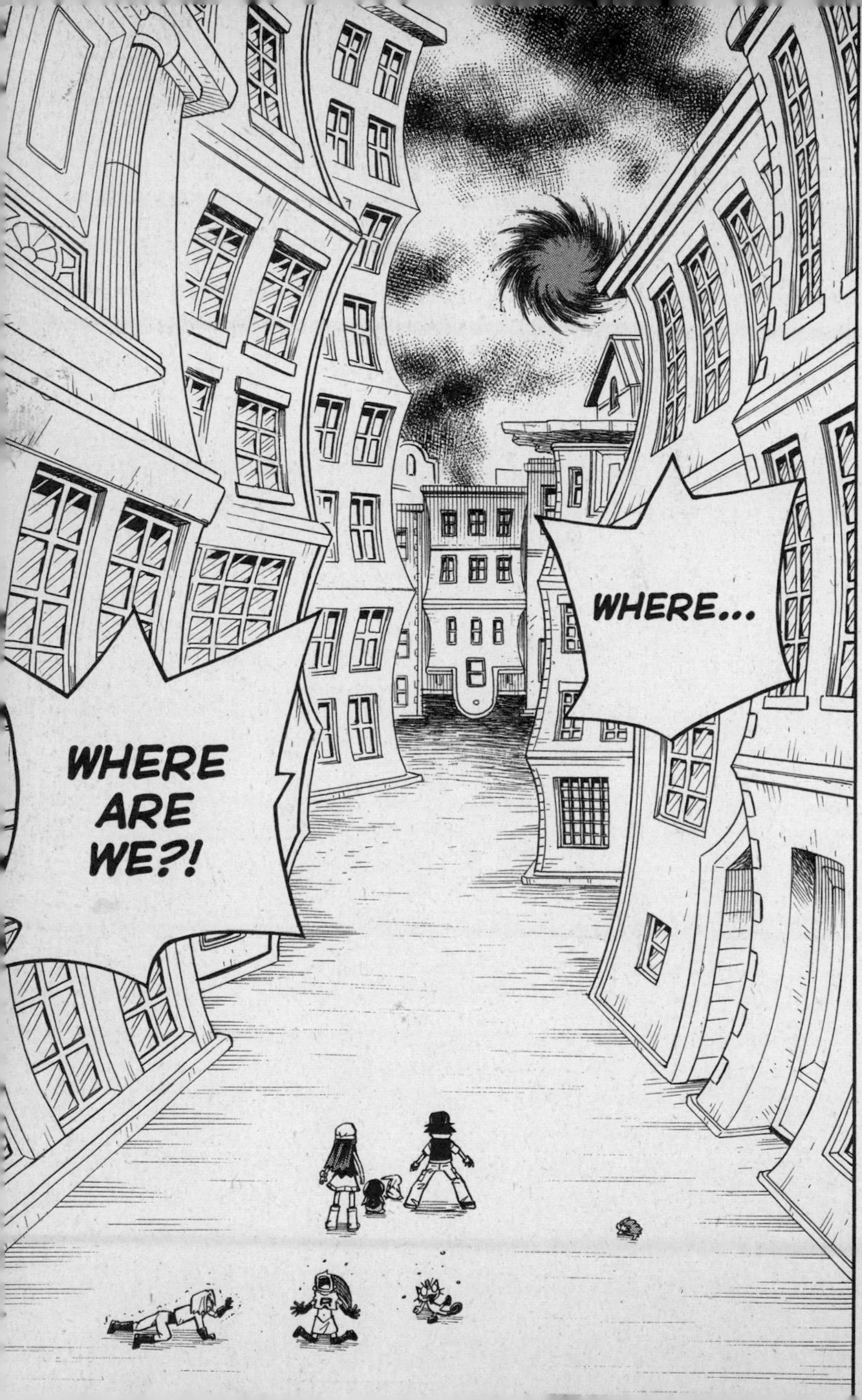
WHERE...
WHERE ARE WE?!

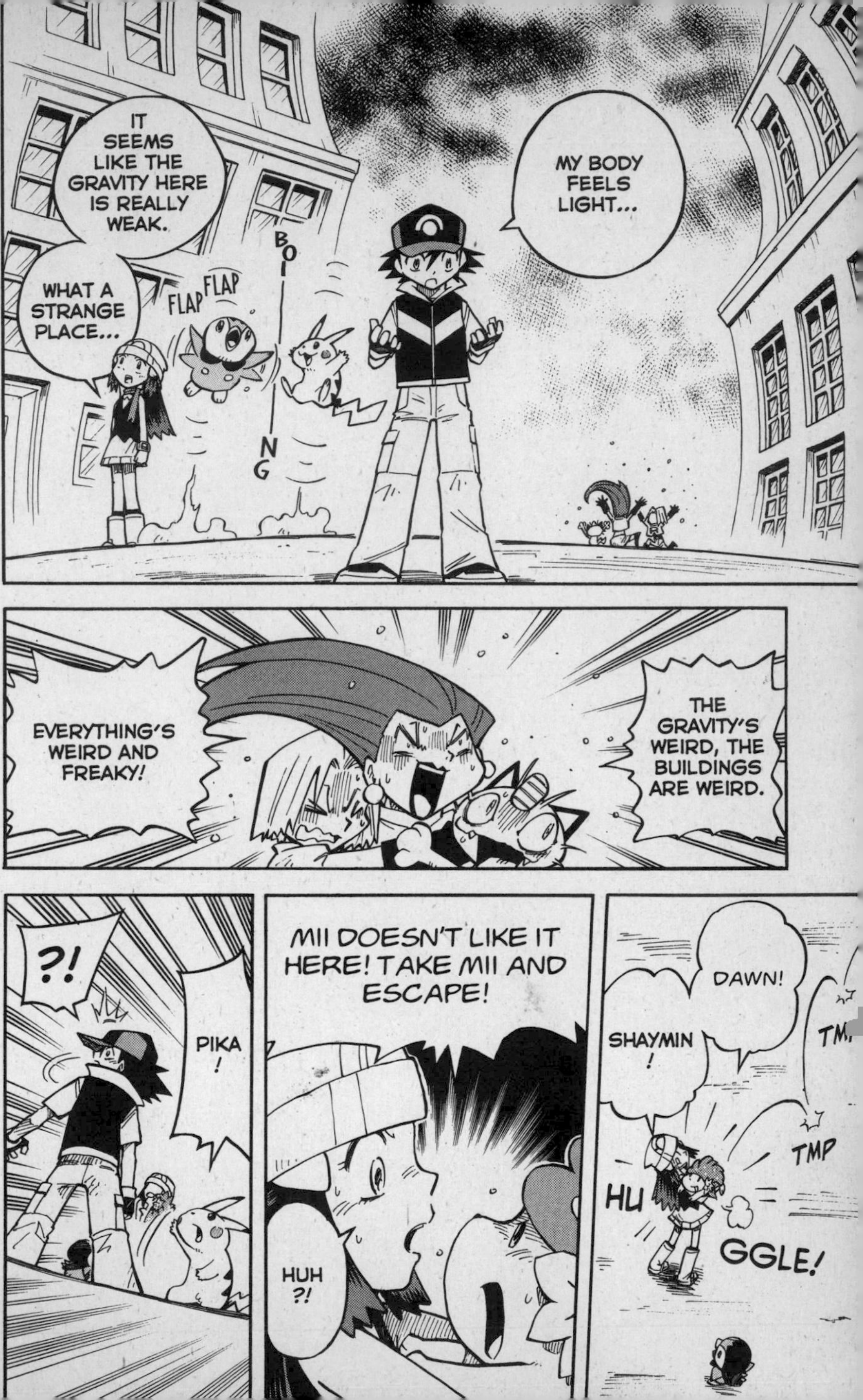

MY BODY FEELS LIGHT...
IT SEEMS LIKE THE GRAVITY HERE IS REALLY WEAK.
BOING
FLAP FLAP
WHAT A STRANGE PLACE...
THE GRAVITY'S WEIRD, THE BUILDINGS ARE WEIRD.
EVERYTHING'S WEIRD AND FREAKY!
DAWN!
SHAYMIN!
TMP
HU
GGLE!
MII DOESN'T LIKE IT HERE! TAKE MII AND ESCAPE!
HUH?!
?!
PIKA!

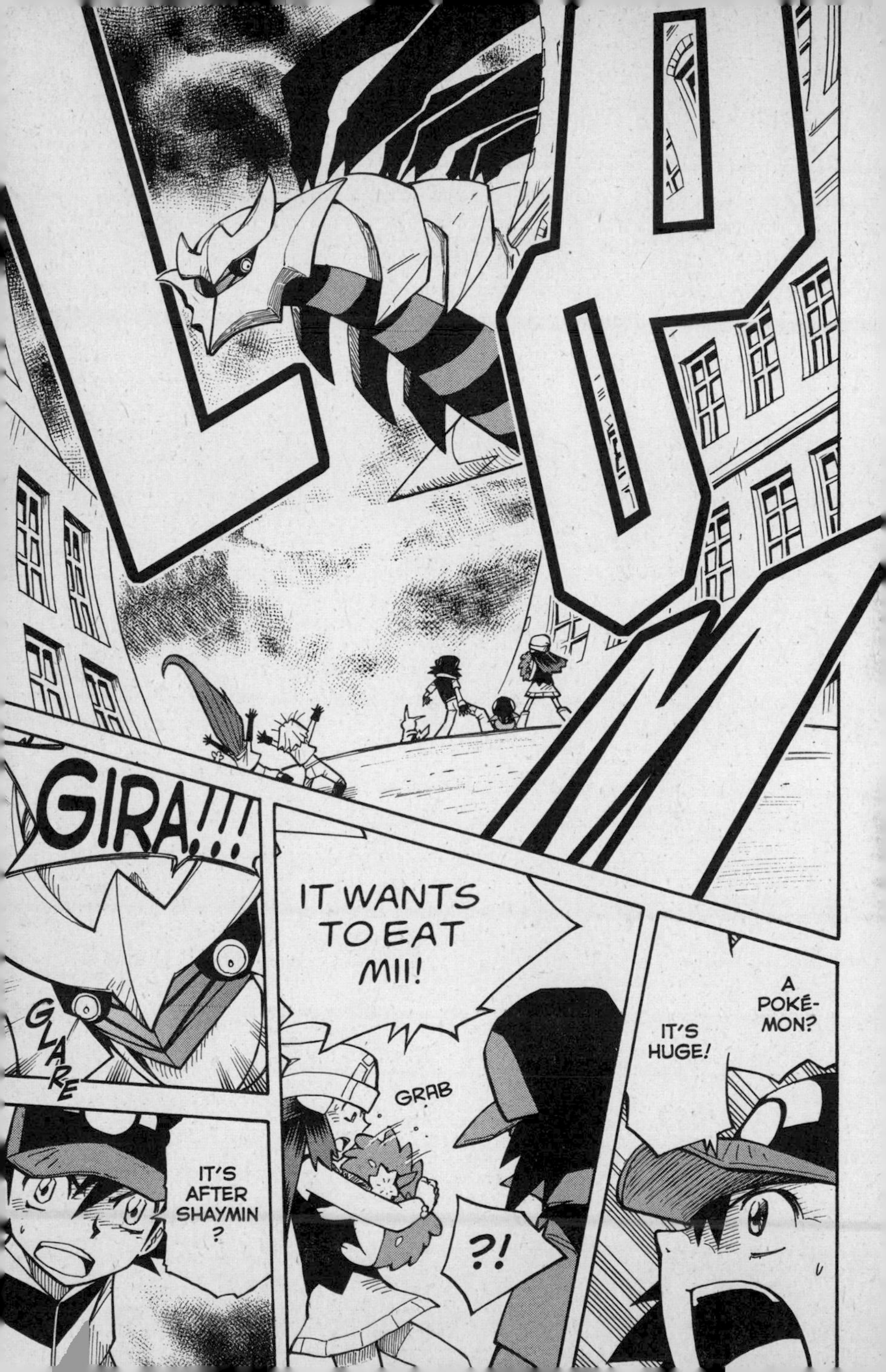
GIRA!!!
A POKÉ-MON?
IT'S HUGE!
?!
GRAB
IT WANTS TO EAT MII!
GLARE
IT'S AFTER SHAYMIN ?

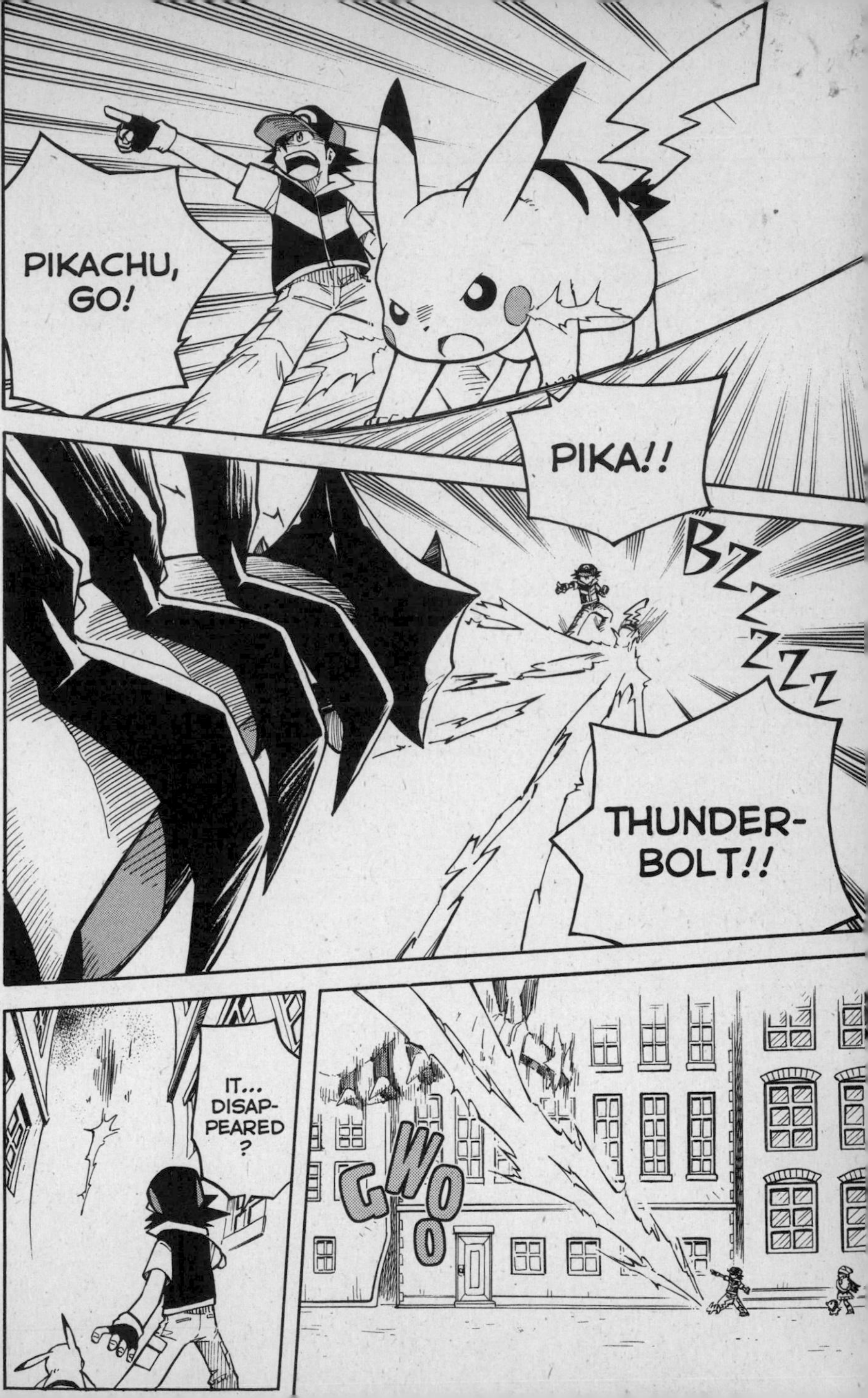
PIKACHU, GO!
PIKA!!
BZZZZZ
THUNDER-BOLT!!
GWOO
IT... DISAP-PEARED?

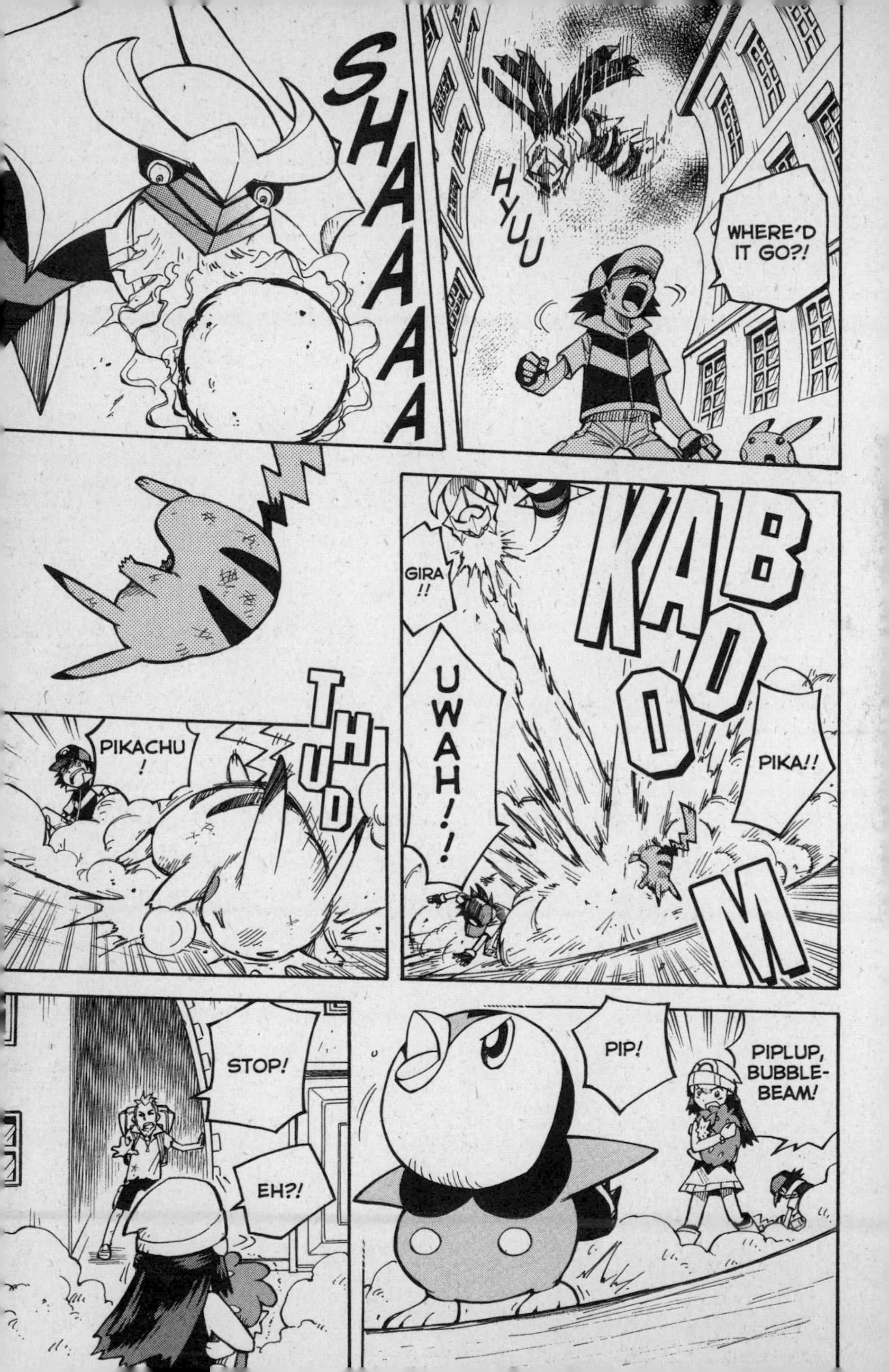
HYUU
WHERE'D IT GO?!
SHAAAAA
KABOOM
GIRA!!
PIKA!!
UWAH!!!
PIKACHU!
THUD
PIPLUP, BUBBLE-BEAM!
PIP!
STOP!
EH?!

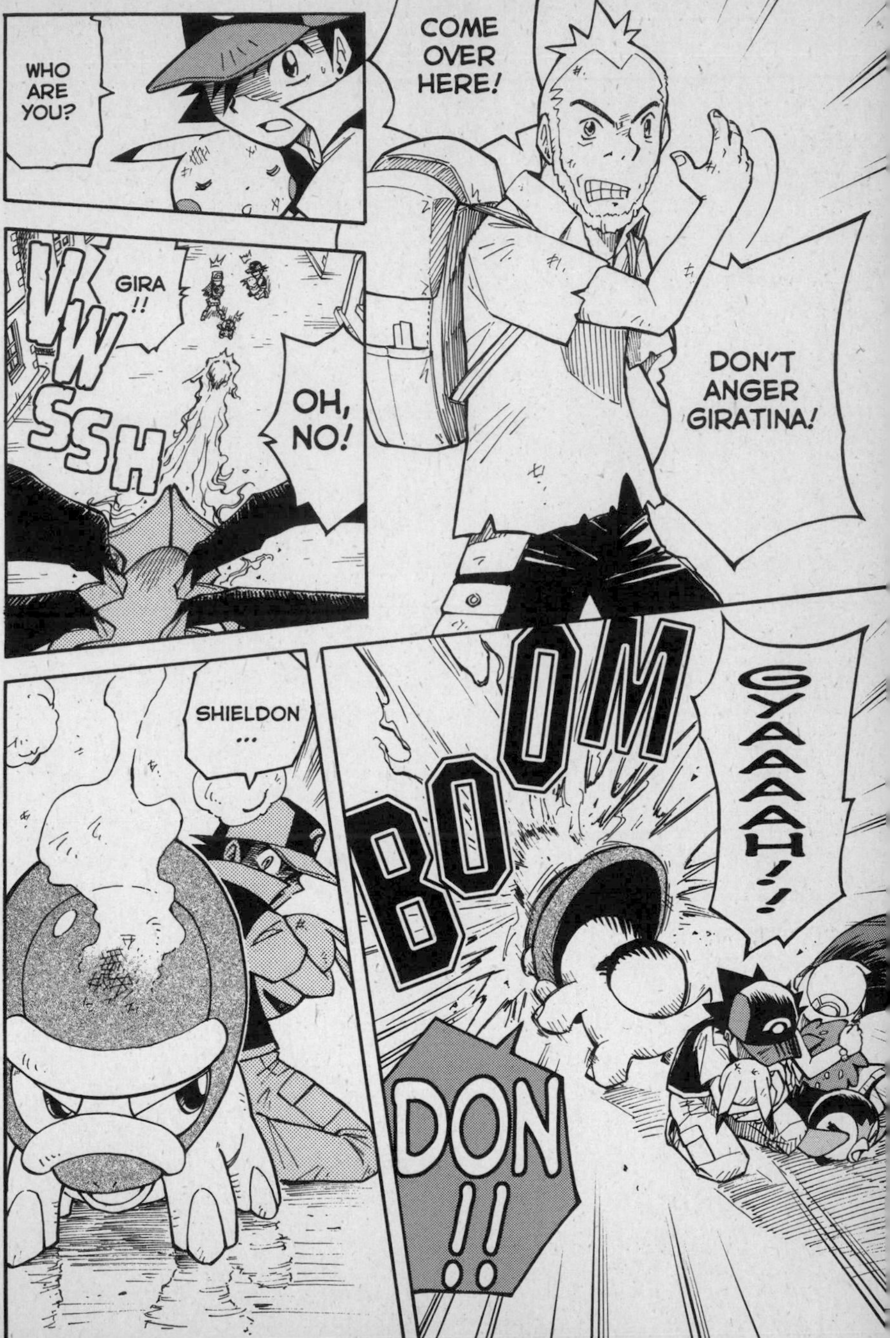
COME OVER HERE!
DON'T ANGER GIRATINA!
WHO ARE YOU?
GIRA !!
OH, NO!
VWSSH
GYAAAAH!!
BOOM
DON !!
SHIELDON ...

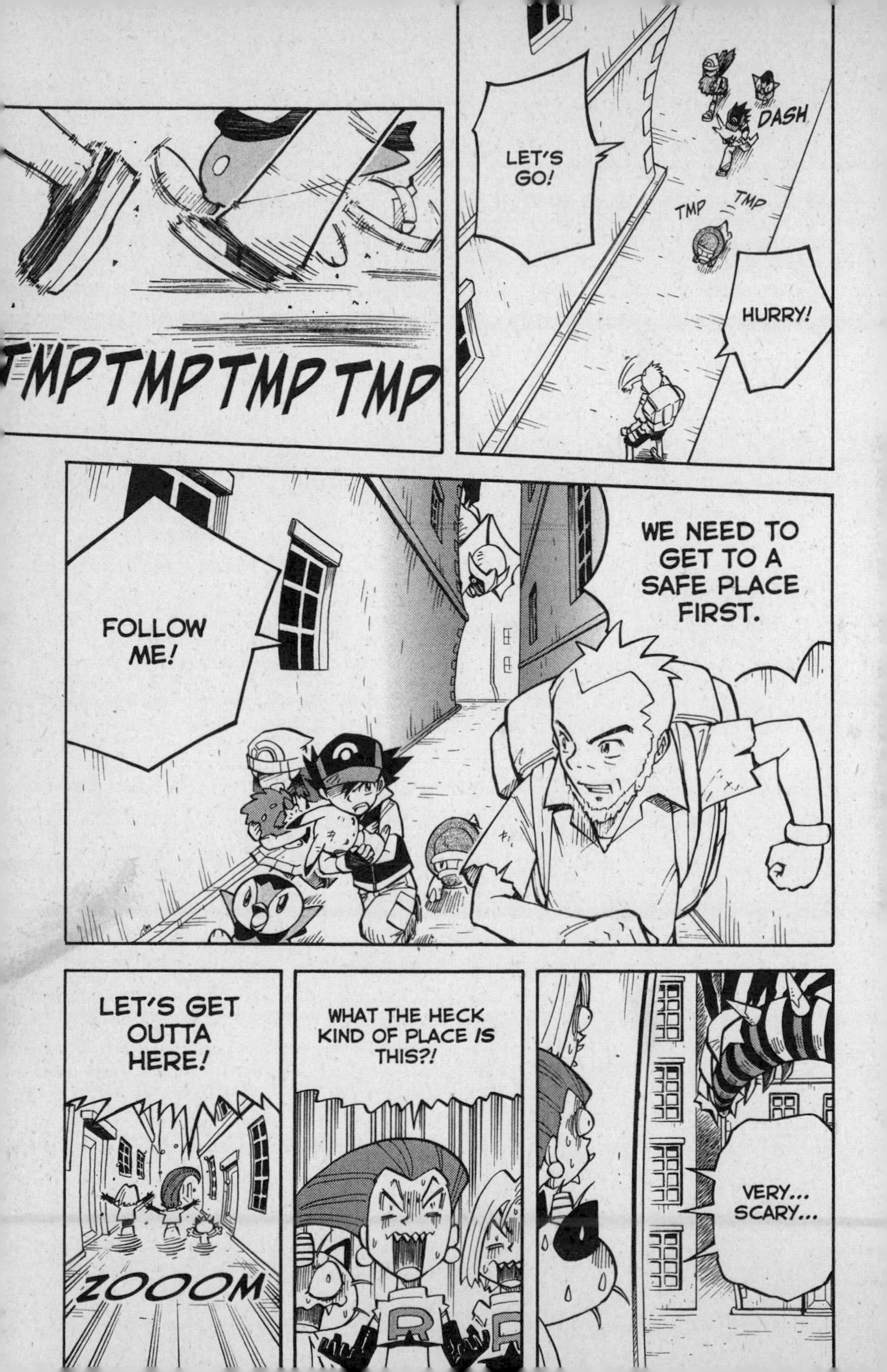
DASH
LET'S GO!
TMP TMP
HURRY!
TMP TMP TMP TMP
WE NEED TO GET TO A SAFE PLACE FIRST.
FOLLOW ME!
VERY... SCARY...
WHAT THE HECK KIND OF PLACE IS THIS?!
LET'S GET OUTTA HERE!
ZOOOM

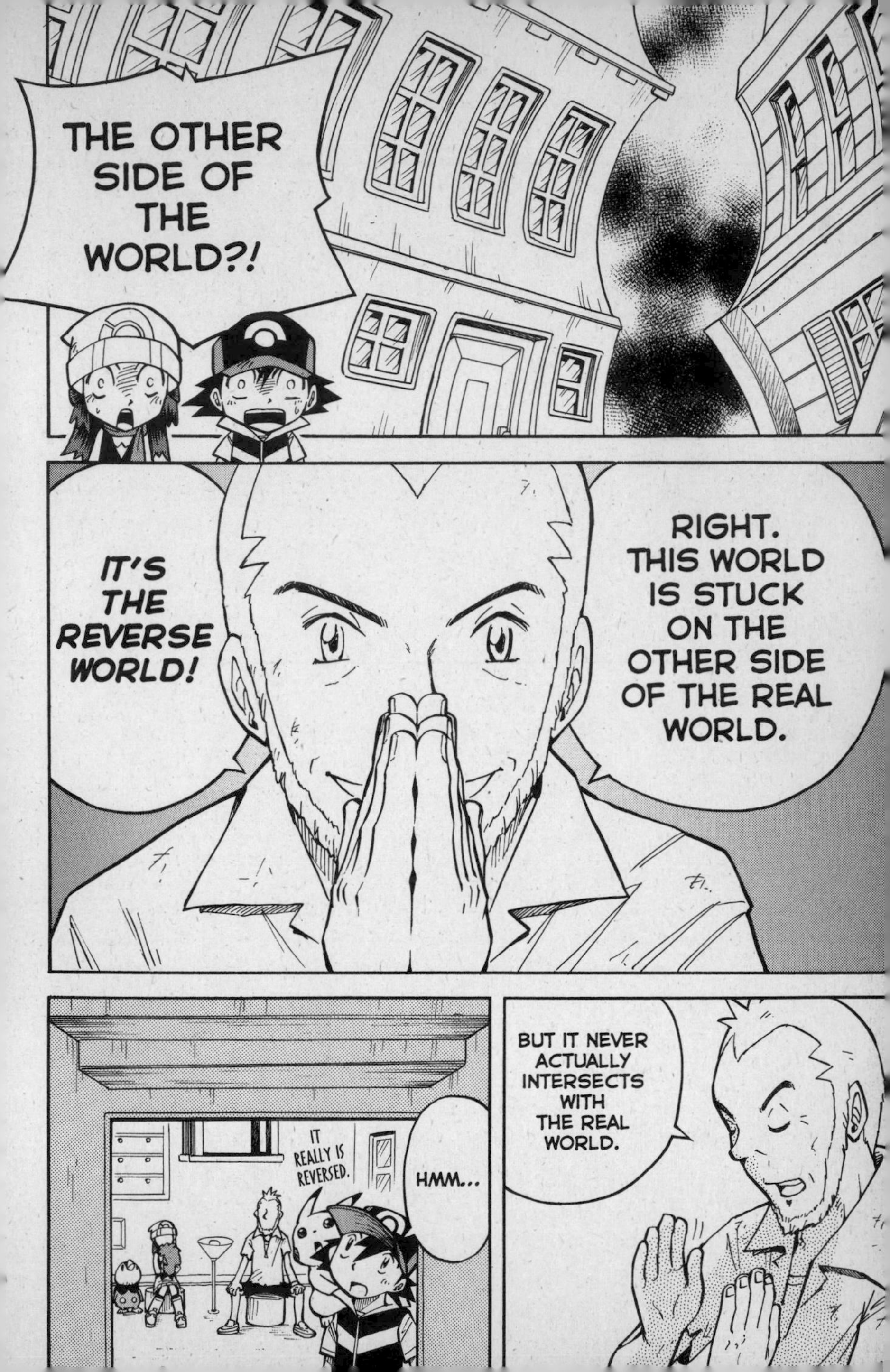
THE OTHER SIDE OF THE WORLD?!
RIGHT. THIS WORLD IS STUCK ON THE OTHER SIDE OF THE REAL WORLD.
IT'S THE REVERSE WORLD!
BUT IT NEVER ACTUALLY INTERSECTS WITH THE REAL WORLD.
HMM...
IT REALLY IS REVERSED.

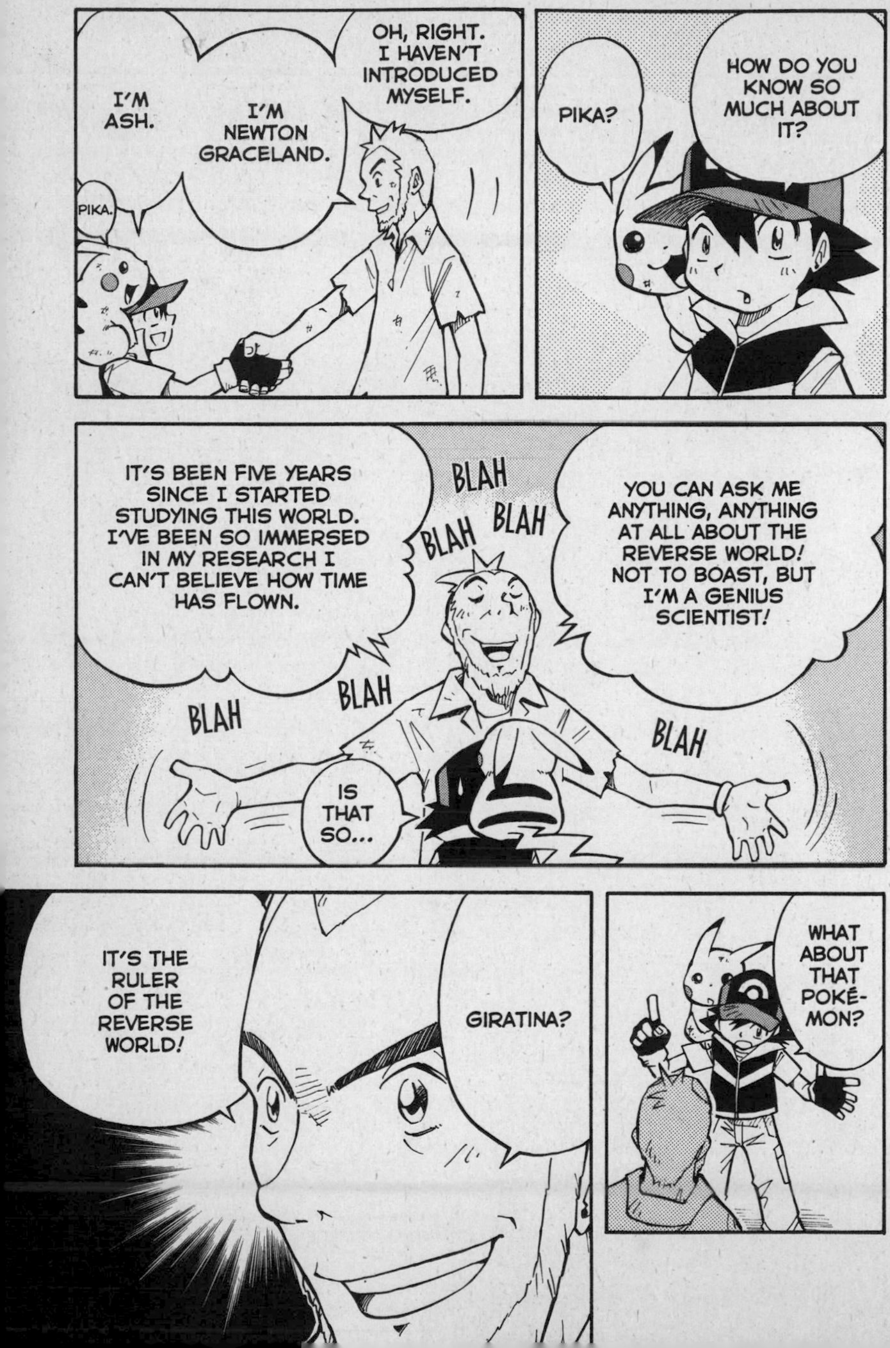
HOW DO YOU KNOW SO MUCH ABOUT IT?
PIKA?
OH, RIGHT. I HAVEN'T INTRODUCED MYSELF.
I'M NEWTON GRACELAND.
I'M ASH.
PIKA.
YOU CAN ASK ME ANYTHING, ANYTHING AT ALL ABOUT THE REVERSE WORLD! NOT TO BOAST, BUT I'M A GENIUS SCIENTIST!
BLAH
BLAH
BLAH
IT'S BEEN FIVE YEARS SINCE I STARTED STUDYING THIS WORLD. I'VE BEEN SO IMMERSED IN MY RESEARCH I CAN'T BELIEVE HOW TIME HAS FLOWN.
BLAH
BLAH
BLAH
IS THAT SO...
WHAT ABOUT THAT POKÉMON?
GIRATINA?
IT'S THE RULER OF THE REVERSE WORLD!

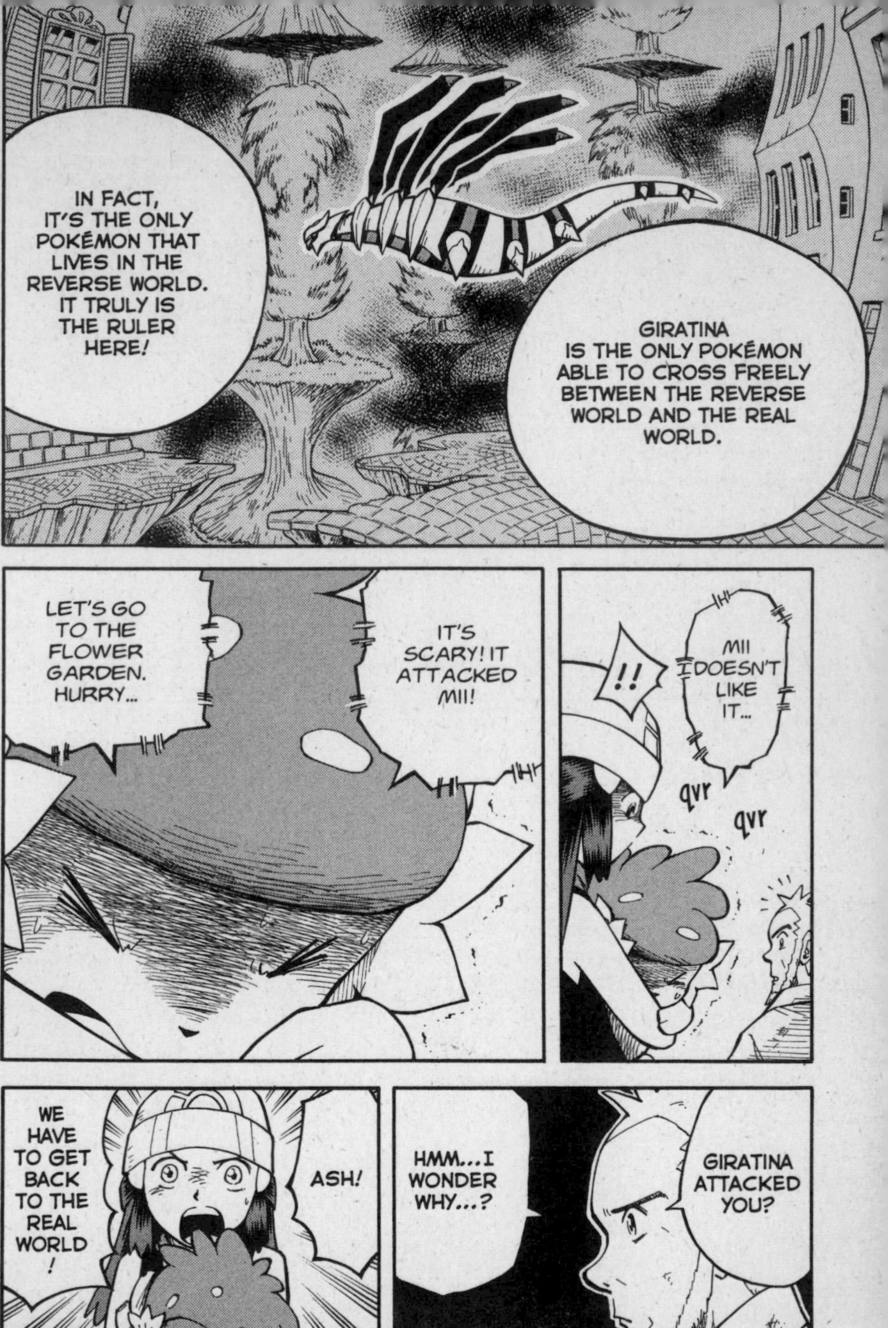
GIRATINA IS THE ONLY POKÉMON ABLE TO CROSS FREELY BETWEEN THE REVERSE WORLD AND THE REAL WORLD.
IN FACT, IT'S THE ONLY POKÉMON THAT LIVES IN THE REVERSE WORLD. IT TRULY IS THE RULER HERE!
!!
MII DOESN'T LIKE IT...
qvr
qvr
IT'S SCARY! IT ATTACKED MII!
LET'S GO TO THE FLOWER GARDEN. HURRY...
GIRATINA ATTACKED YOU?
HMM...I WONDER WHY...?
ASH!
WE HAVE TO GET BACK TO THE REAL WORLD!

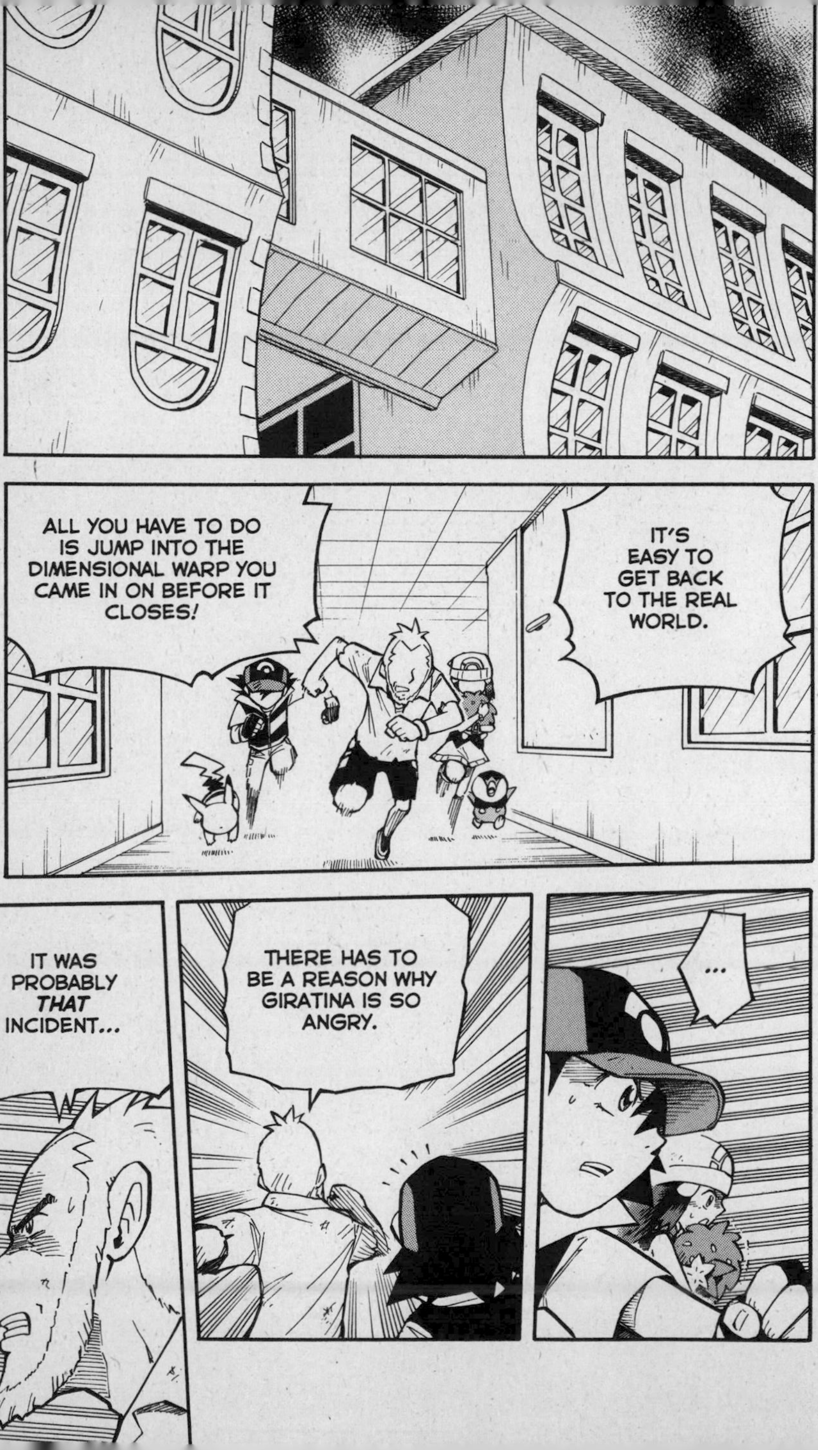
IT'S EASY TO GET BACK TO THE REAL WORLD.
ALL YOU HAVE TO DO IS JUMP INTO THE DIMENSIONAL WARP YOU CAME IN ON BEFORE IT CLOSES!
...
THERE HAS TO BE A REASON WHY GIRATINA IS SO ANGRY.
IT WAS PROBABLY *THAT* INCIDENT...

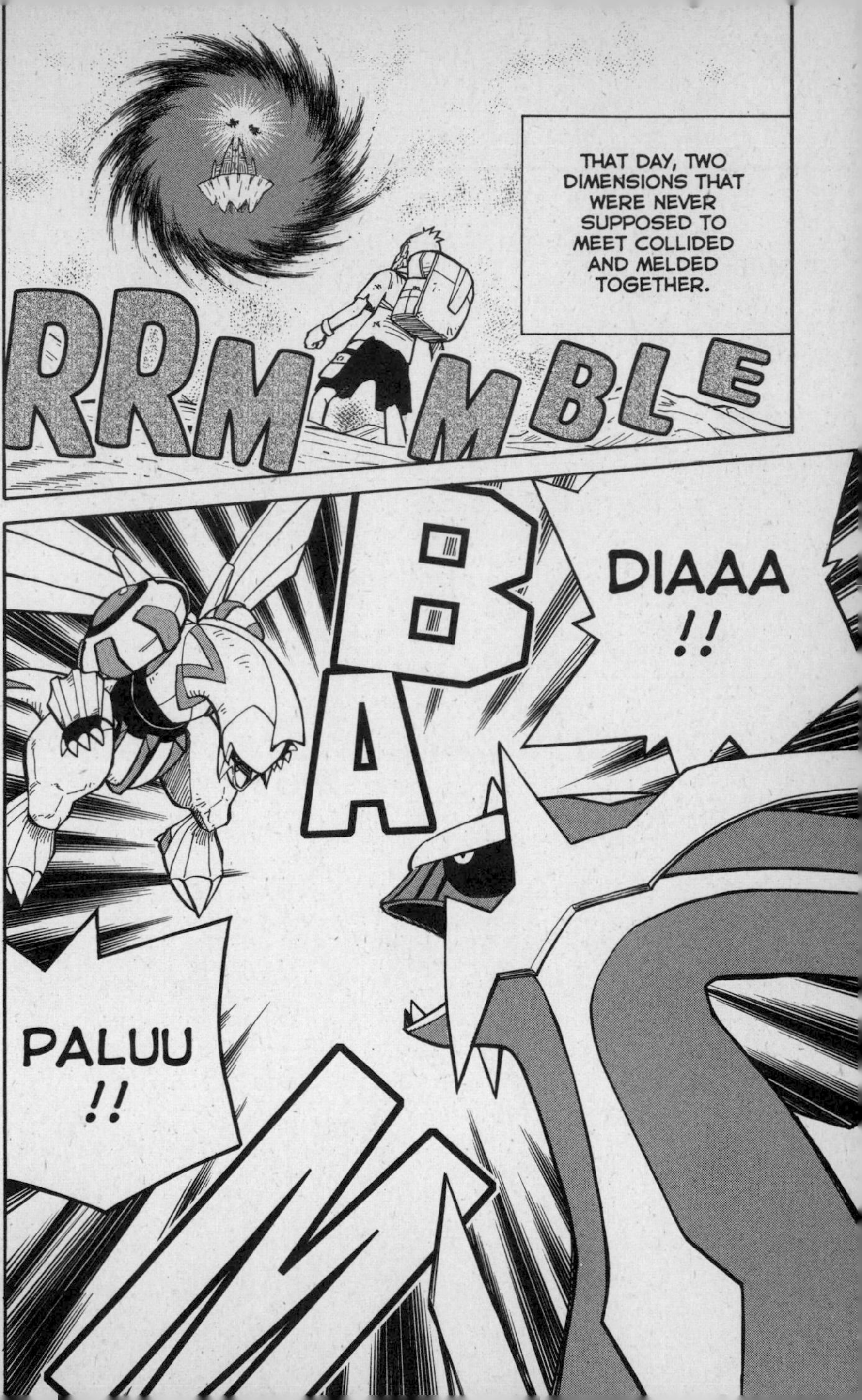
THAT DAY, TWO DIMENSIONS THAT WERE NEVER SUPPOSED TO MEET COLLIDED AND MELDED TOGETHER.
RRMMBLE
DIAAA !!
BAM
PALUU !!

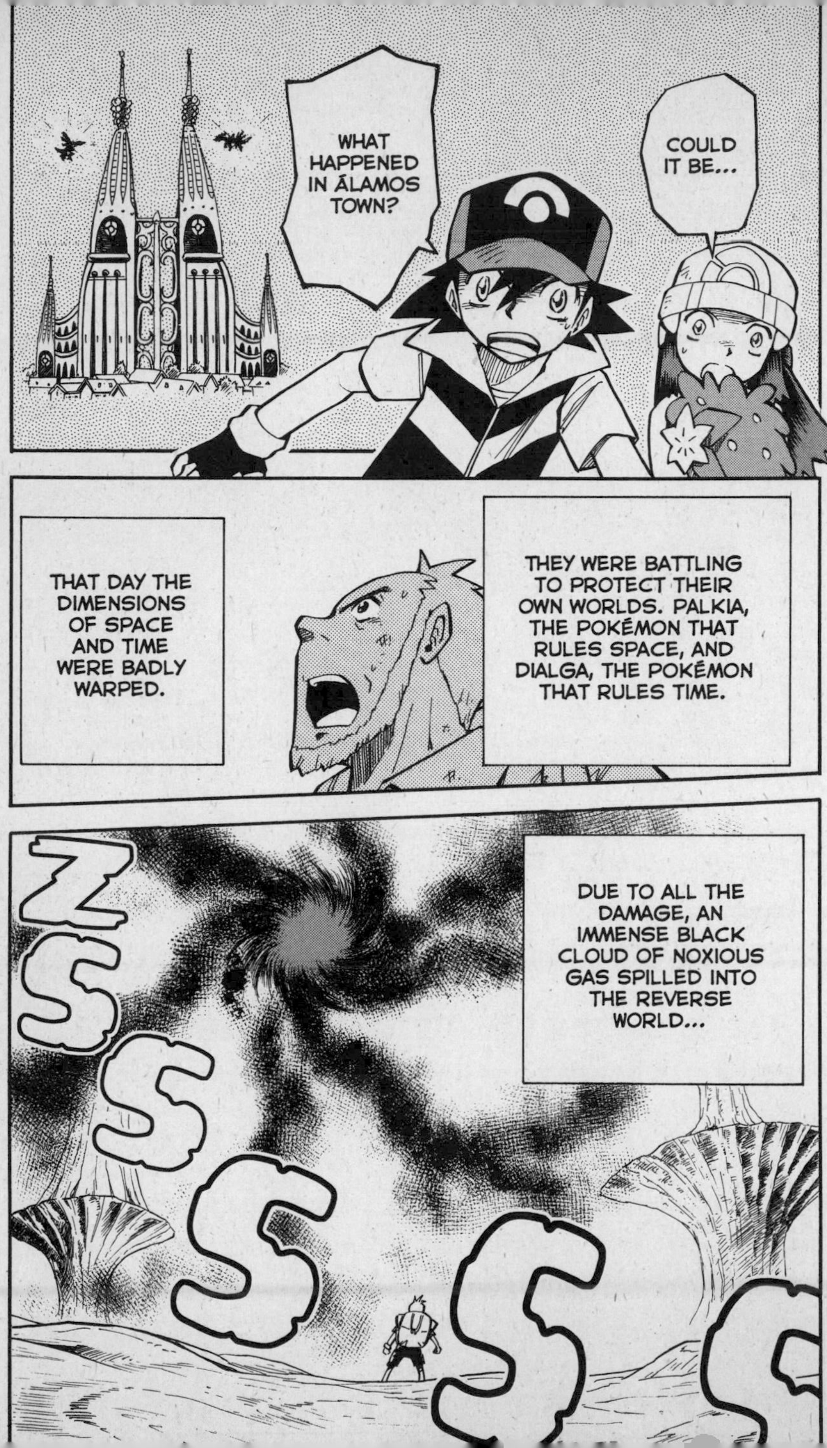
WHAT HAPPENED IN ÁLAMOS TOWN?
COULD IT BE...
THAT DAY THE DIMENSIONS OF SPACE AND TIME WERE BADLY WARPED.
THEY WERE BATTLING TO PROTECT THEIR OWN WORLDS. PALKIA, THE POKÉMON THAT RULES SPACE, AND DIALGA, THE POKÉMON THAT RULES TIME.
DUE TO ALL THE DAMAGE, AN IMMENSE BLACK CLOUD OF NOXIOUS GAS SPILLED INTO THE REVERSE WORLD...
ZSSSSS

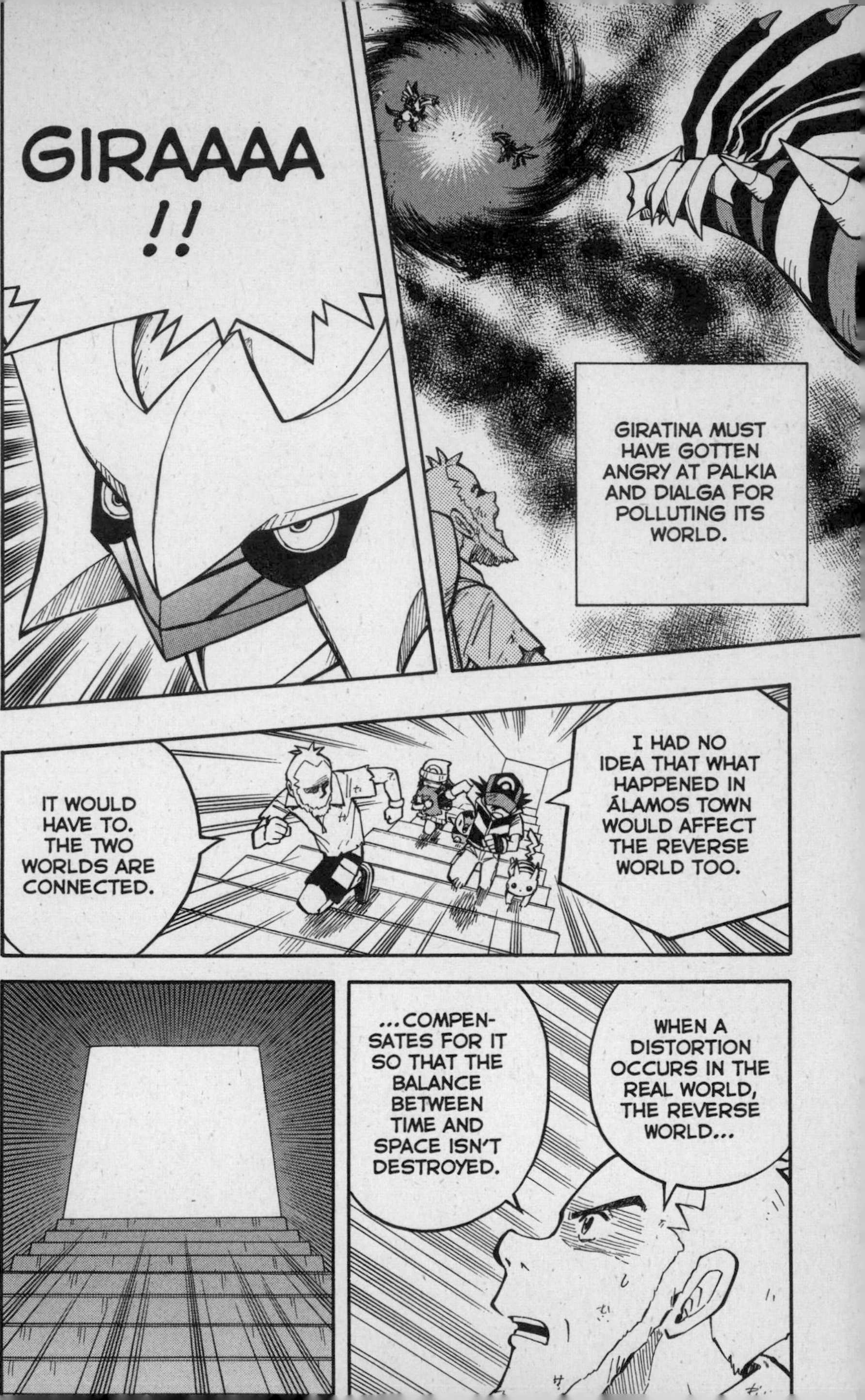
GIRATINA MUST HAVE GOTTEN ANGRY AT PALKIA AND DIALGA FOR POLLUTING ITS WORLD.
GIRAAAA !!
I HAD NO IDEA THAT WHAT HAPPENED IN ÁLAMOS TOWN WOULD AFFECT THE REVERSE WORLD TOO.
IT WOULD HAVE TO. THE TWO WORLDS ARE CONNECTED.
WHEN A DISTORTION OCCURS IN THE REAL WORLD, THE REVERSE WORLD...
...COMPENSATES FOR IT SO THAT THE BALANCE BETWEEN TIME AND SPACE ISN'T DESTROYED.

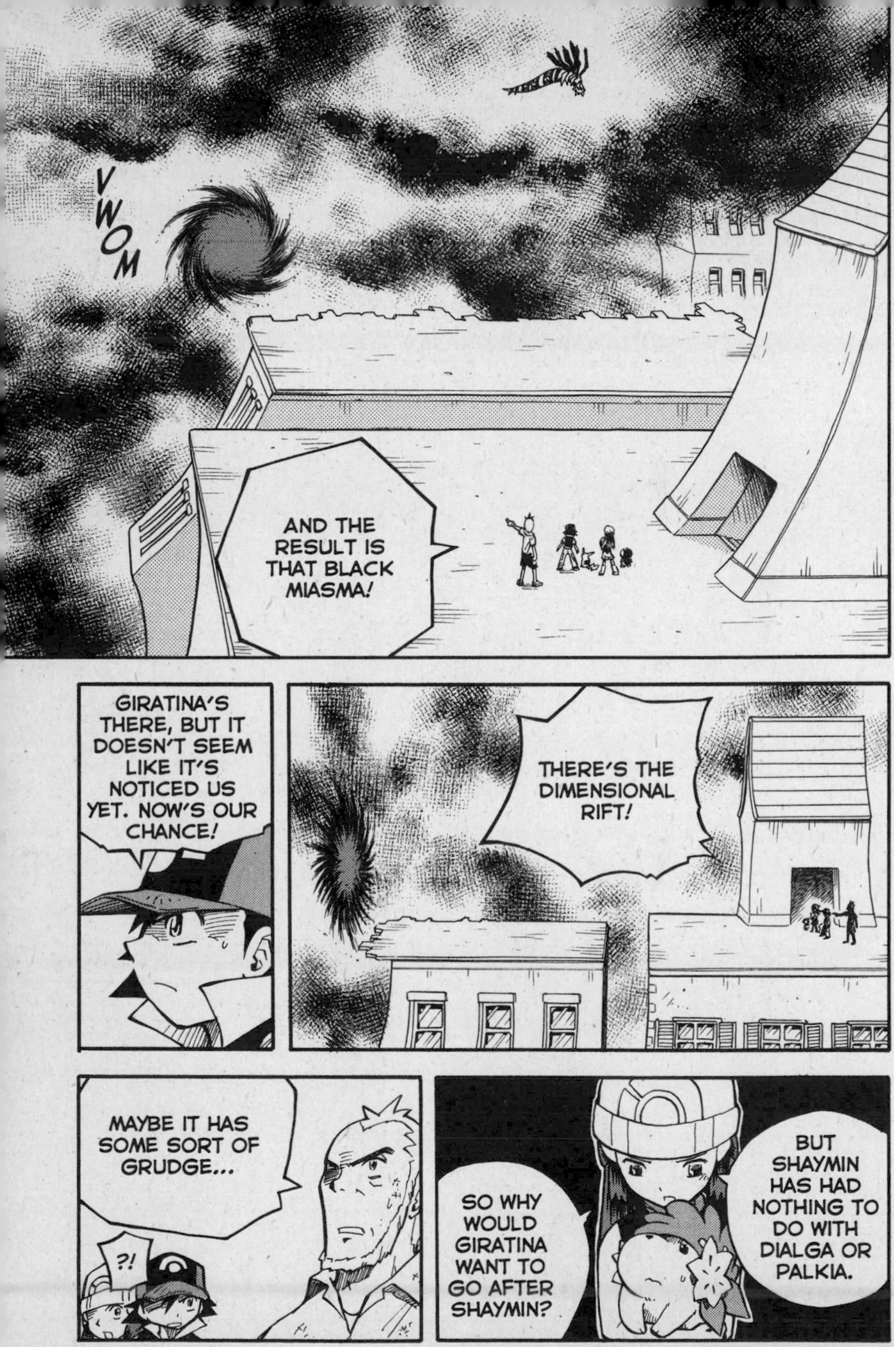
VWOM
AND THE RESULT IS THAT BLACK MIASMA!
THERE'S THE DIMENSIONAL RIFT!
GIRATINA'S THERE, BUT IT DOESN'T SEEM LIKE IT'S NOTICED US YET. NOW'S OUR CHANCE!
BUT SHAYMIN HAS HAD NOTHING TO DO WITH DIALGA OR PALKIA.
SO WHY WOULD GIRATINA WANT TO GO AFTER SHAYMIN?
MAYBE IT HAS SOME SORT OF GRUDGE...
?!

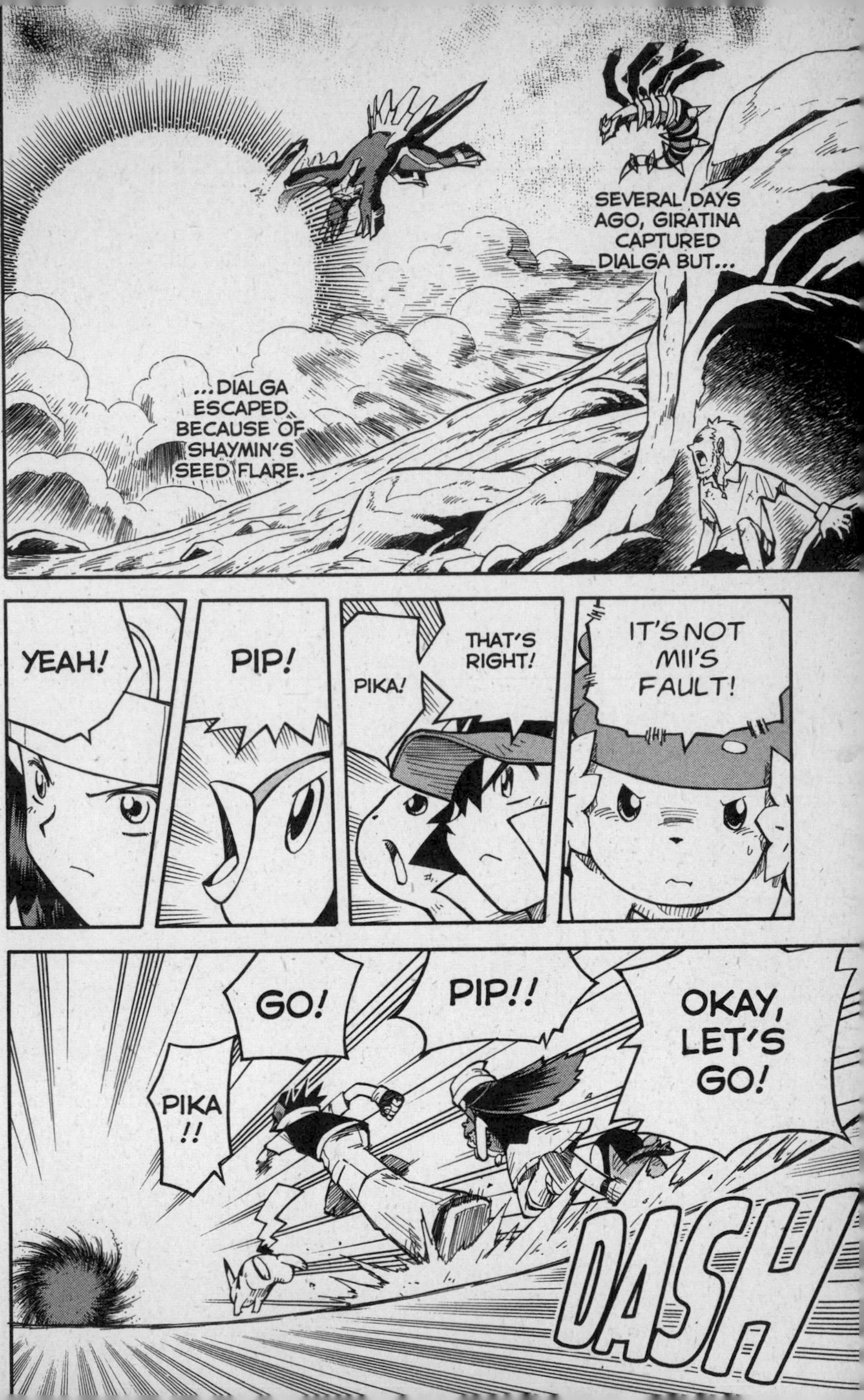
SEVERAL DAYS AGO, GIRATINA CAPTURED DIALGA BUT...
...DIALGA ESCAPED BECAUSE OF SHAYMIN'S SEED FLARE.
IT'S NOT MII'S FAULT!
THAT'S RIGHT!
PIKA!
PIP!
YEAH!
OKAY, LET'S GO!
PIP!!
GO!
PIKA !!
DASH

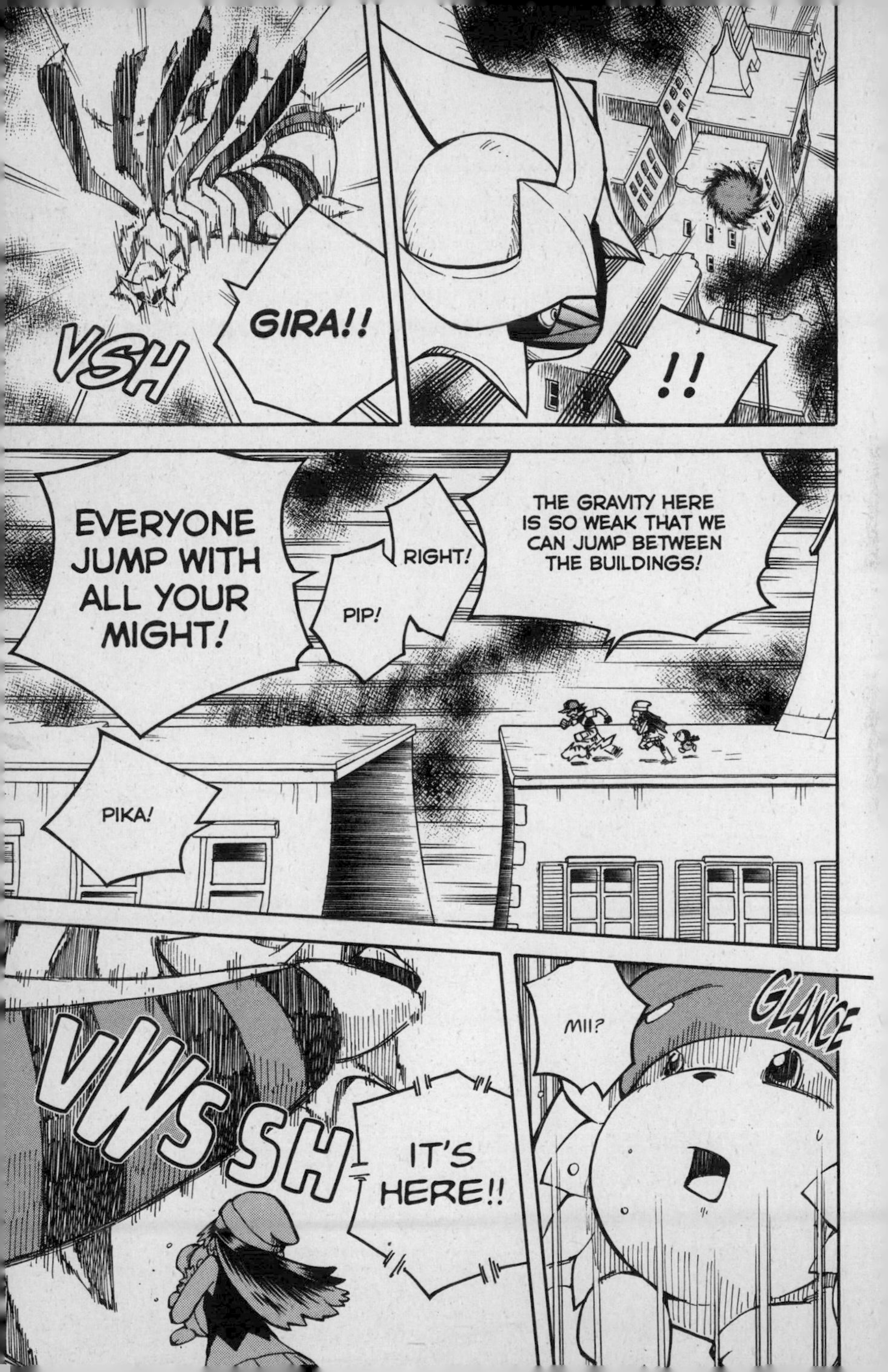
!!
GIRA!!
VSH
THE GRAVITY HERE IS SO WEAK THAT WE CAN JUMP BETWEEN THE BUILDINGS!
RIGHT!
PIP!
EVERYONE JUMP WITH ALL YOUR MIGHT!
PIKA!
GLANCE
MII?
IT'S HERE!!
VWSSH

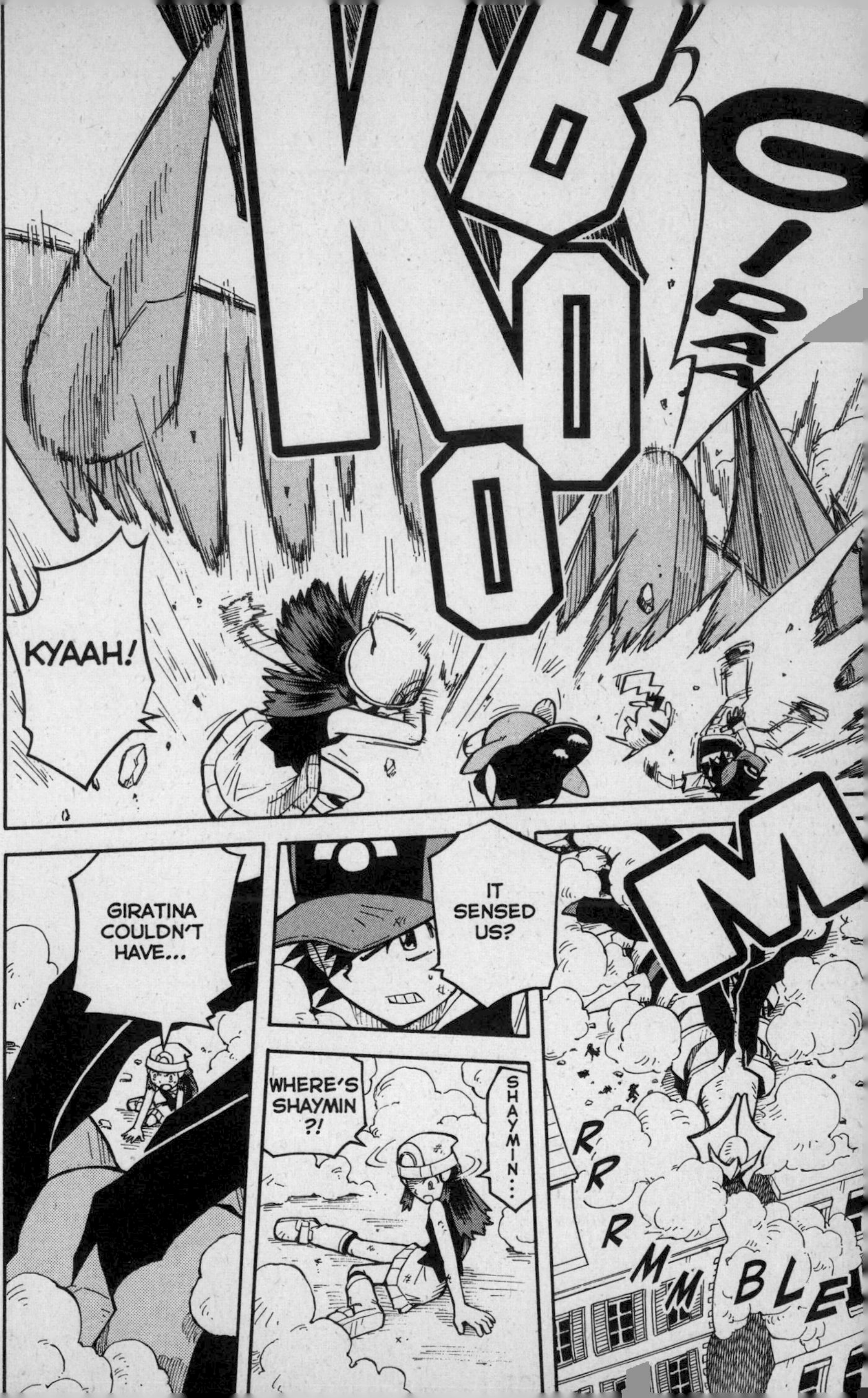
KYAAH!
RRRMMMBLE
IT SENSED US?
SHAYMIN...
WHERE'S SHAYMIN?!
GIRATINA COULDN'T HAVE...

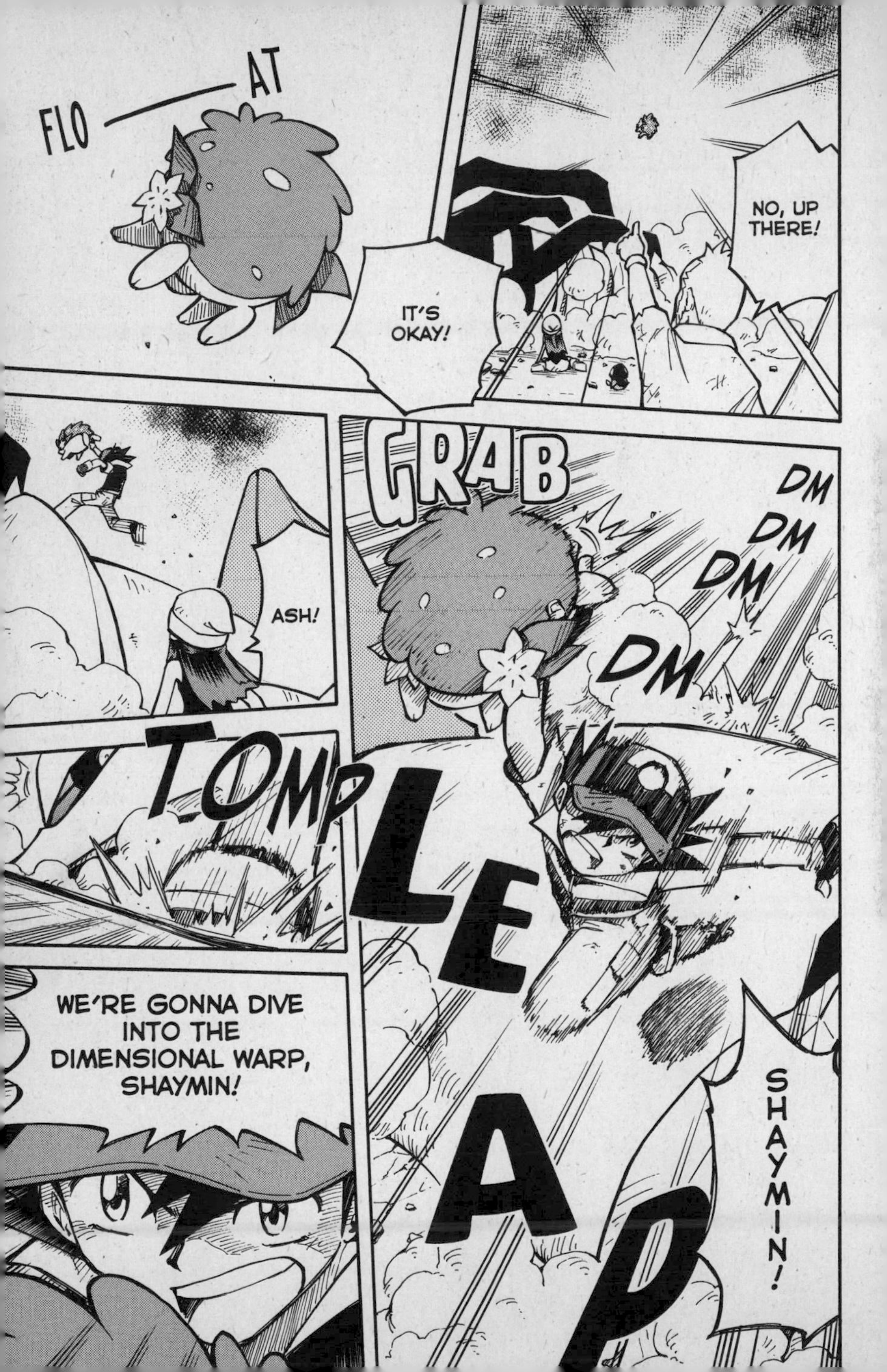
NO, UP THERE!
IT'S OKAY!
FLO—AT
GRAB
DM DM DM DM
DM
LEAP
SHAYMIN!
ASH!
TOMP
WE'RE GONNA DIVE INTO THE DIMENSIONAL WARP, SHAYMIN!

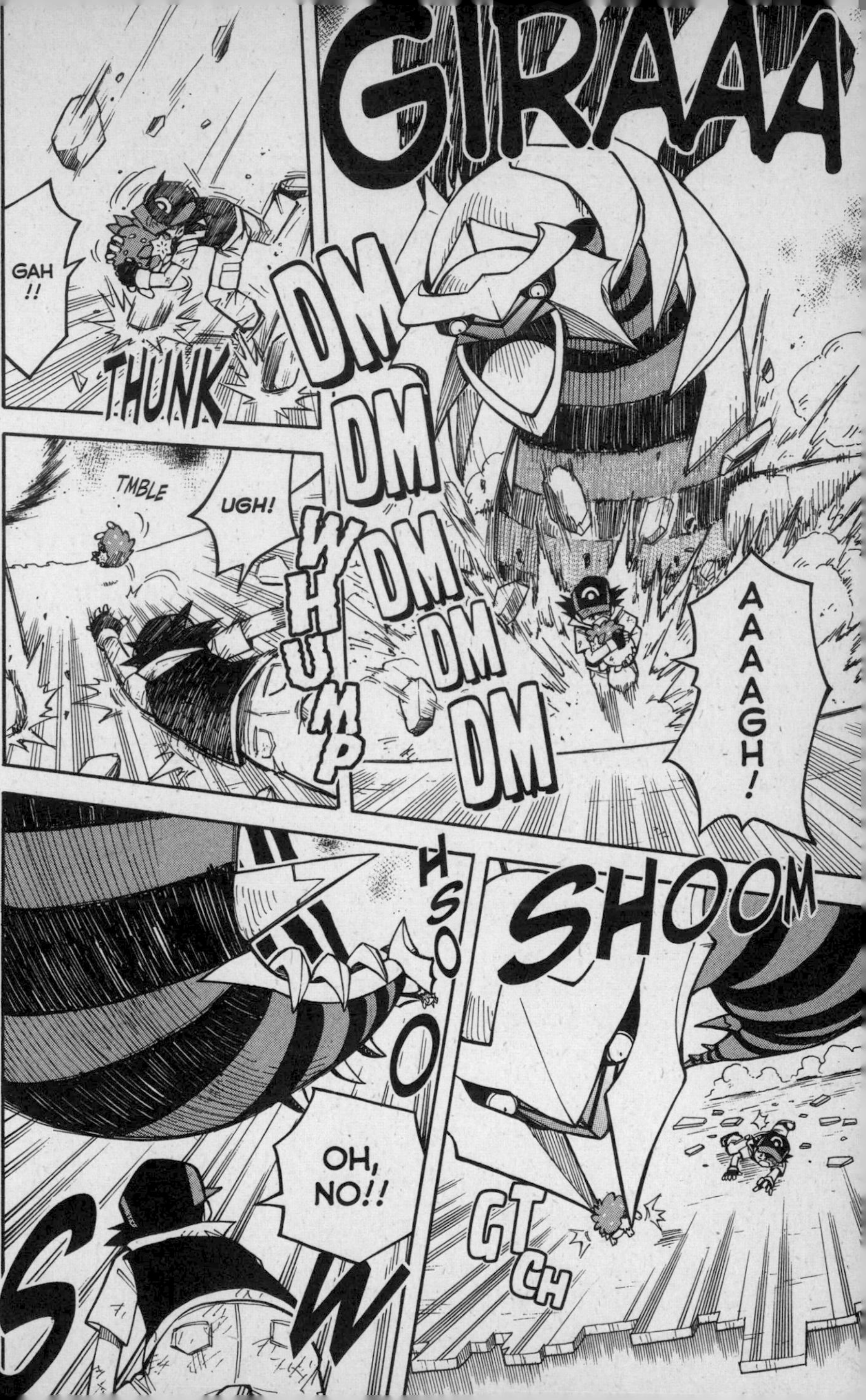
GIRAAA
DM DM DM DM DM DM
AAAAGH!
GAH!!
THUNK
TMBLE
UGH!
WHUMP
SHOOM
GTCH
OH, NO!!
SWOOSH

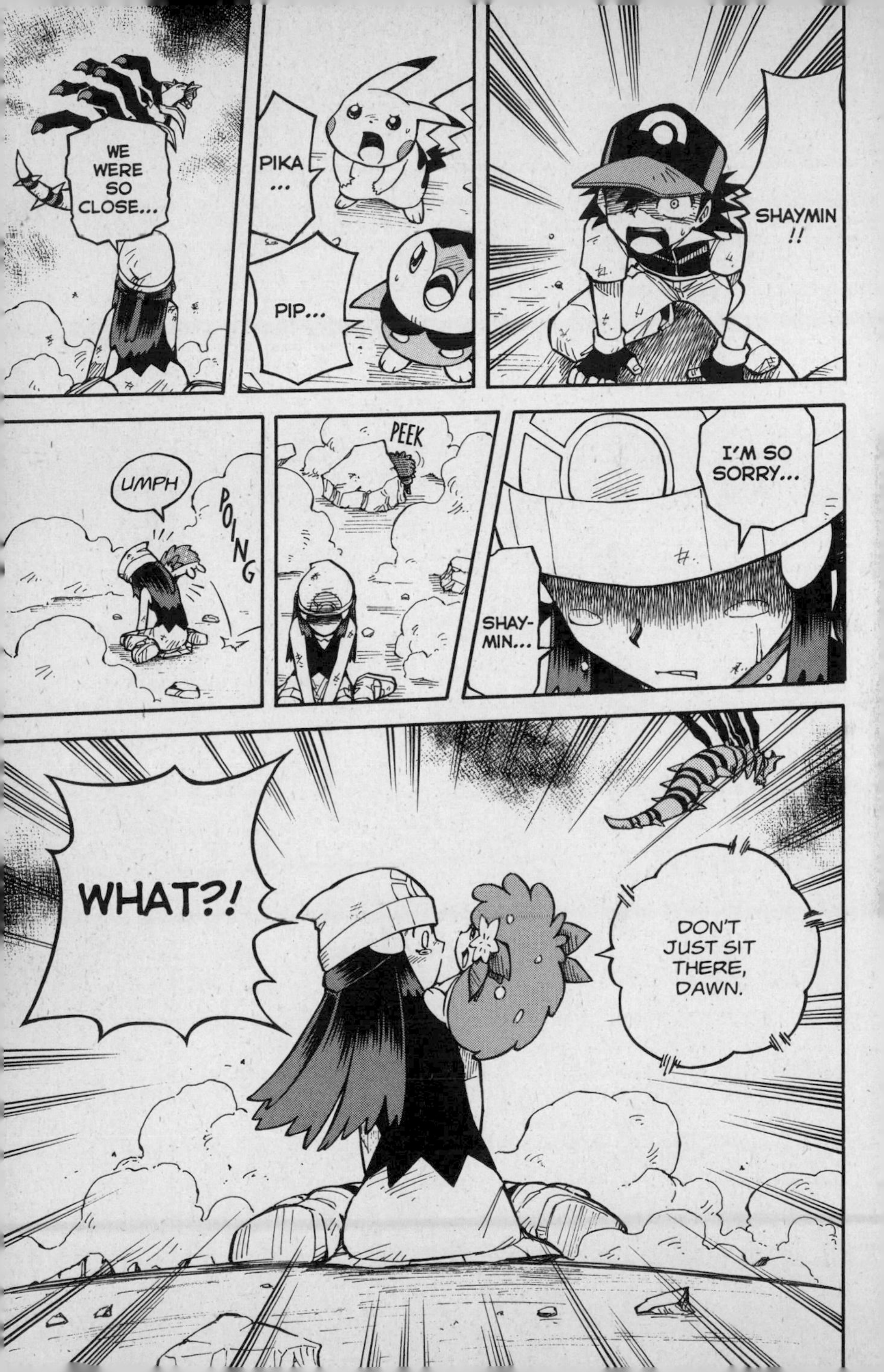
WE WERE SO CLOSE...
PIKA ...
PIP...
SHAYMIN !!
UMPH
POING
PEEK
I'M SO SORRY...
SHAY-MIN...
WHAT?!
DON'T JUST SIT THERE, DAWN.

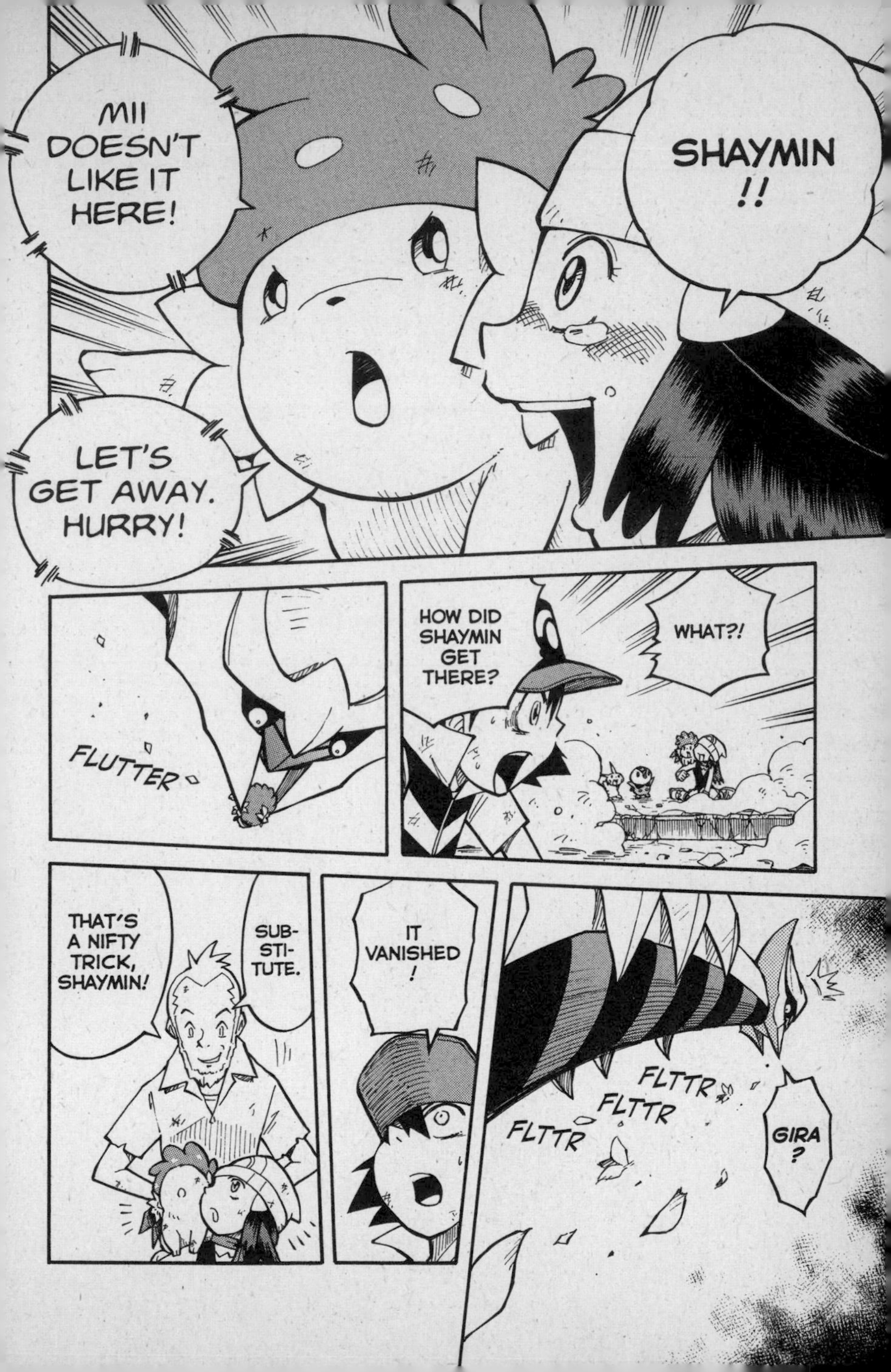
SHAYMIN!!
MII DOESN'T LIKE IT HERE!
LET'S GET AWAY. HURRY!
WHAT?!
HOW DID SHAYMIN GET THERE?
FLUTTER
FLTTR
FLTTR
FLTTR
GIRA?
IT VANISHED!
SUB-STI-TUTE.
THAT'S A NIFTY TRICK, SHAYMIN!

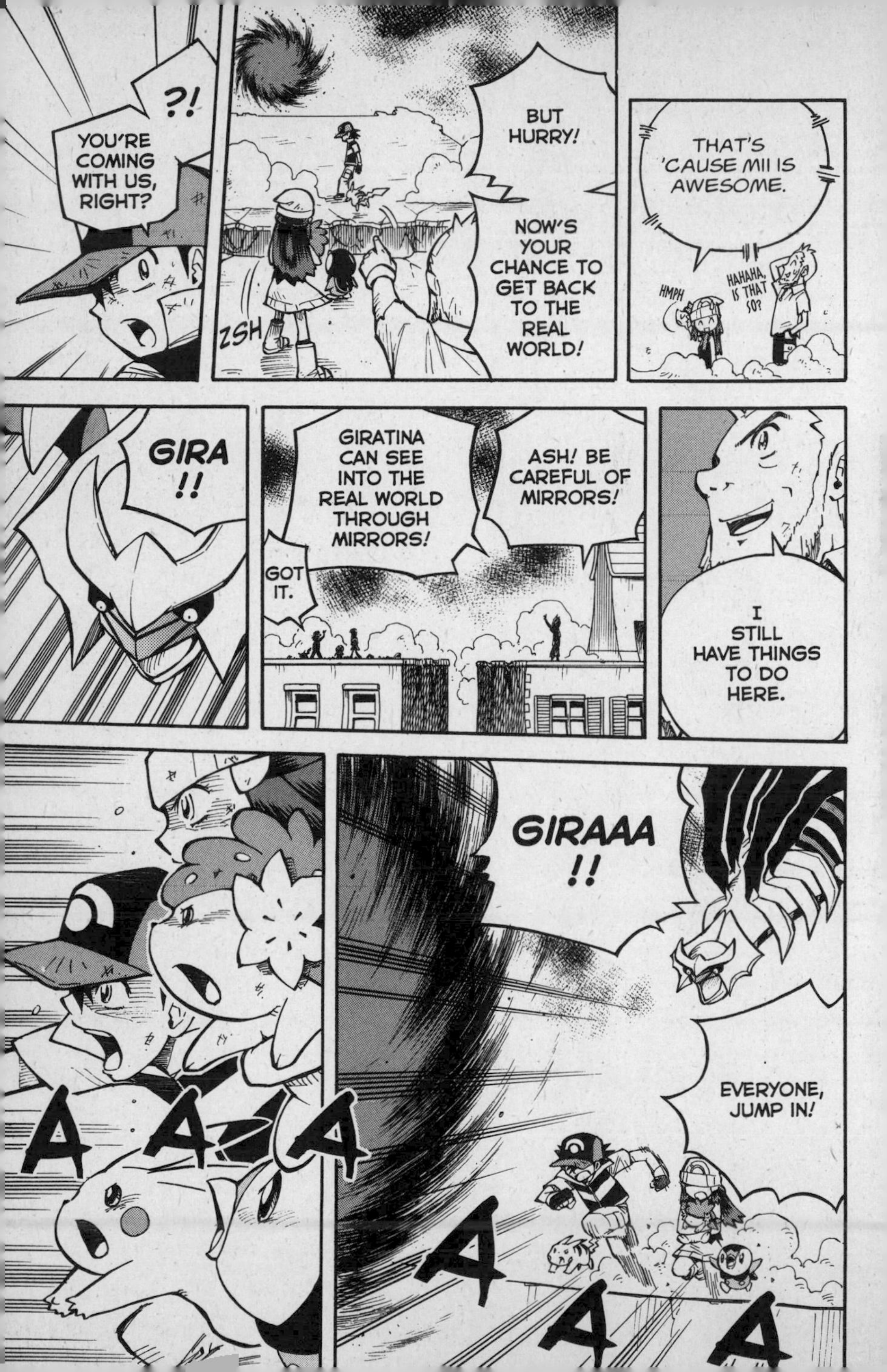
THAT'S 'CAUSE MII IS AWESOME.
HAHAHA, IS THAT SO?
HMPH
BUT HURRY!
NOW'S YOUR CHANCE TO GET BACK TO THE REAL WORLD!
ZSH
?!
YOU'RE COMING WITH US, RIGHT?
I STILL HAVE THINGS TO DO HERE.
ASH! BE CAREFUL OF MIRRORS!
GIRATINA CAN SEE INTO THE REAL WORLD THROUGH MIRRORS!
GOT IT.
GIRA !!
GIRAAA !!
EVERYONE, JUMP IN!
A A A
A A A

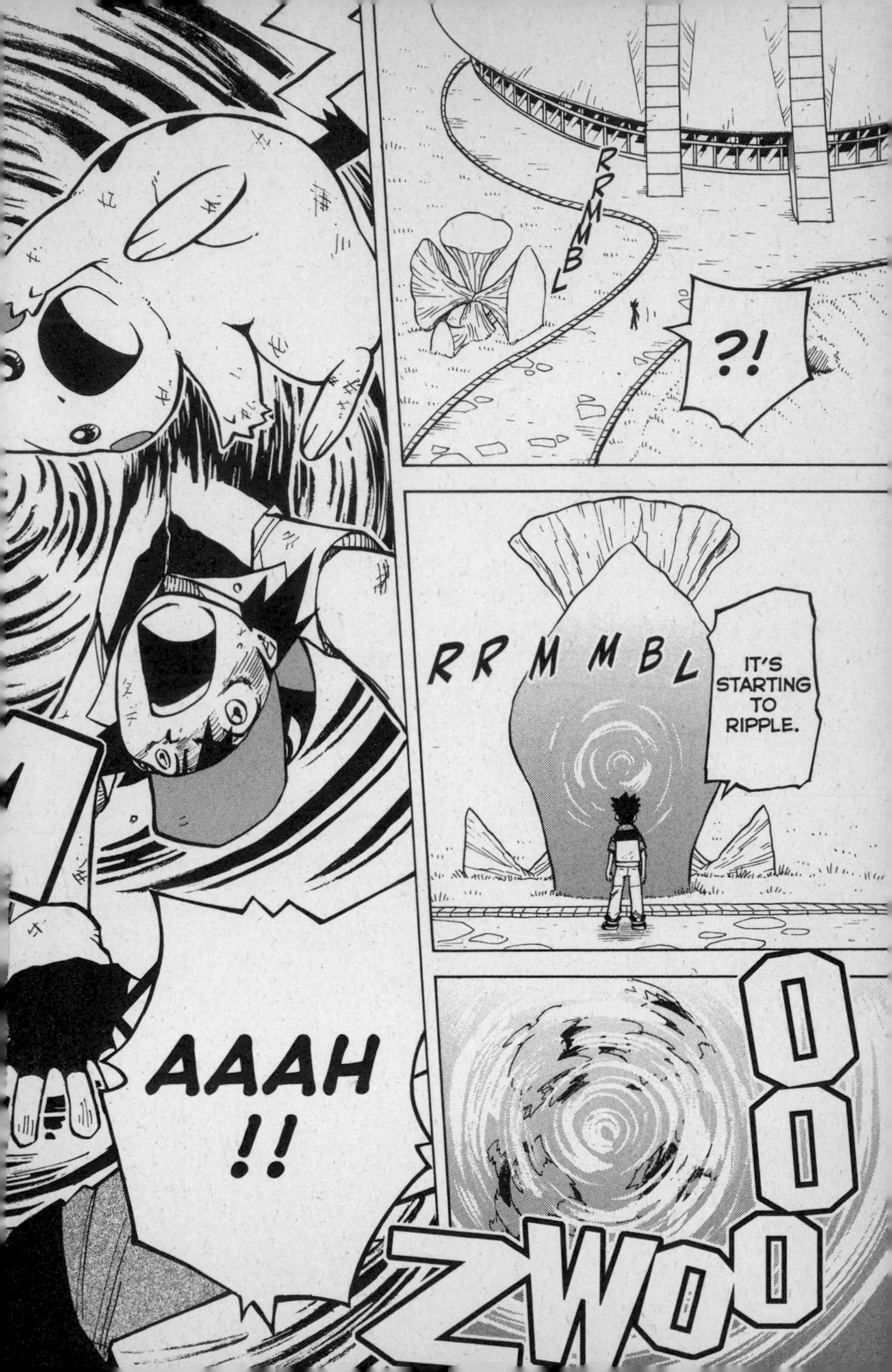
RRMMBL
?!
RRMMBL
IT'S STARTING TO RIPPLE.
ZWOOO
AAAH!!

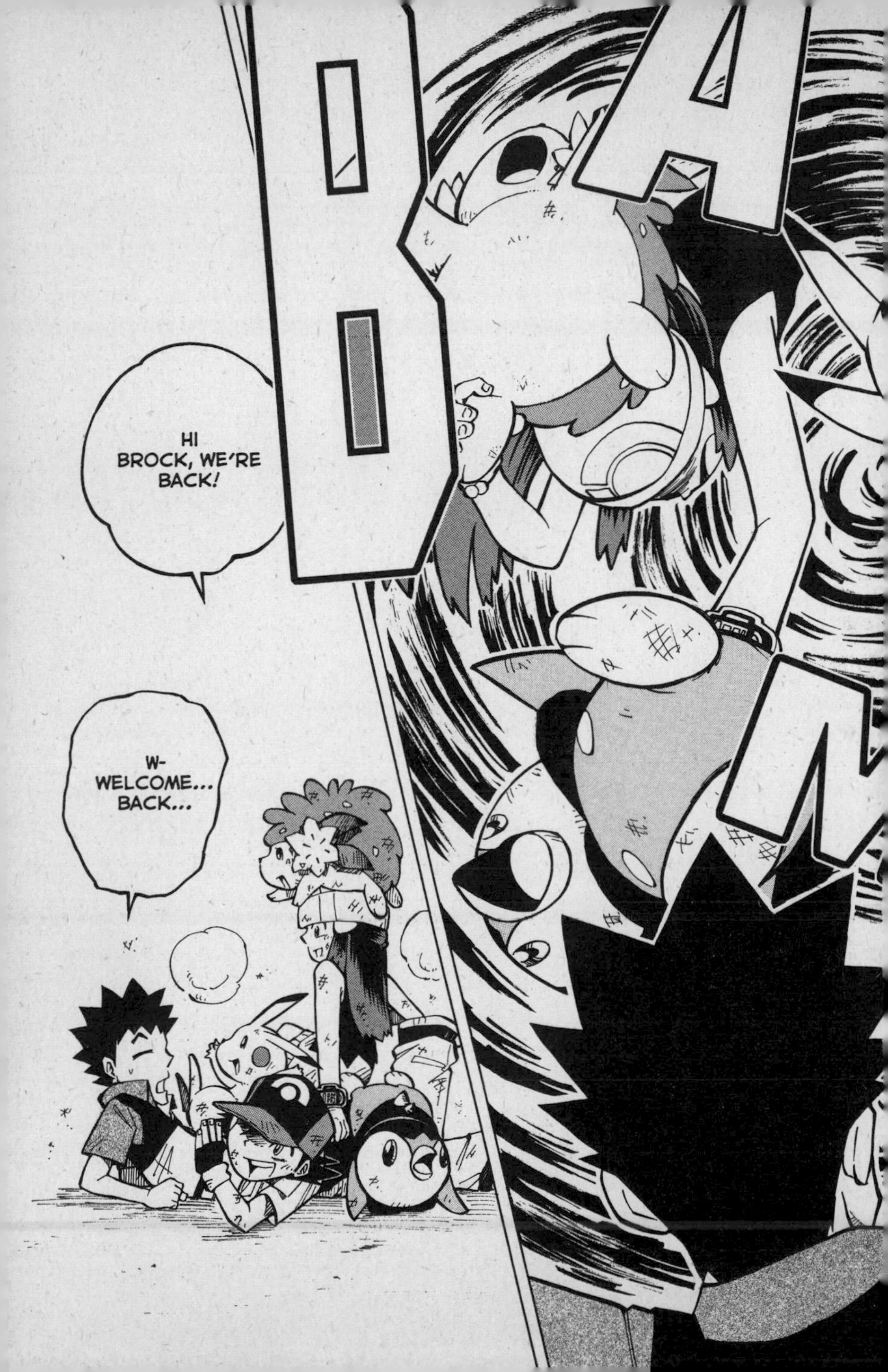
HI BROCK, WE'RE BACK!
W- WELCOME... BACK...

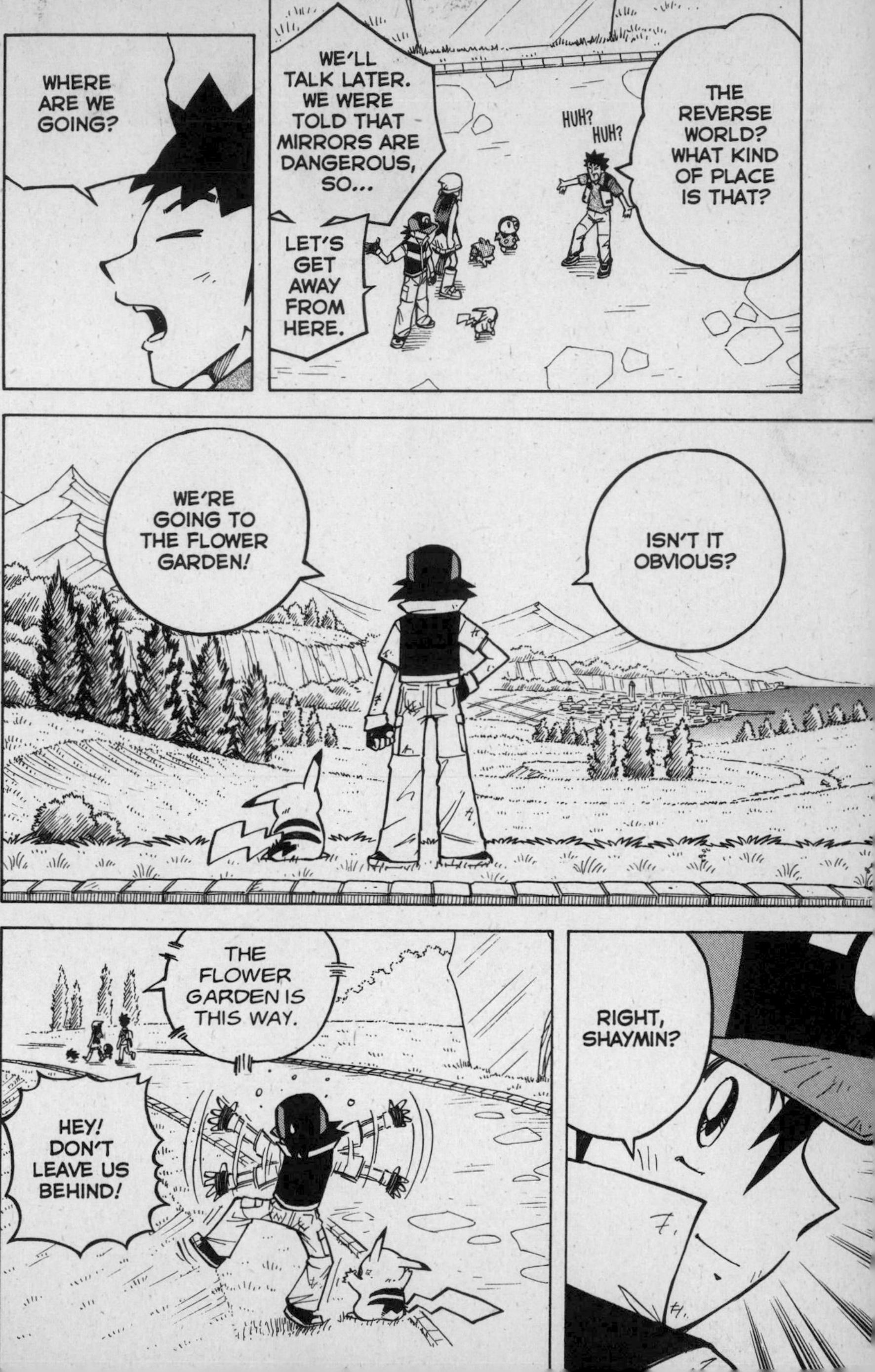
THE REVERSE WORLD? WHAT KIND OF PLACE IS THAT?
HUH? HUH?
WE'LL TALK LATER. WE WERE TOLD THAT MIRRORS ARE DANGEROUS, SO...
LET'S GET AWAY FROM HERE.
WHERE ARE WE GOING?
WE'RE GOING TO THE FLOWER GARDEN!
ISN'T IT OBVIOUS?
RIGHT, SHAYMIN?
THE FLOWER GARDEN IS THIS WAY.
HEY! DON'T LEAVE US BEHIND!

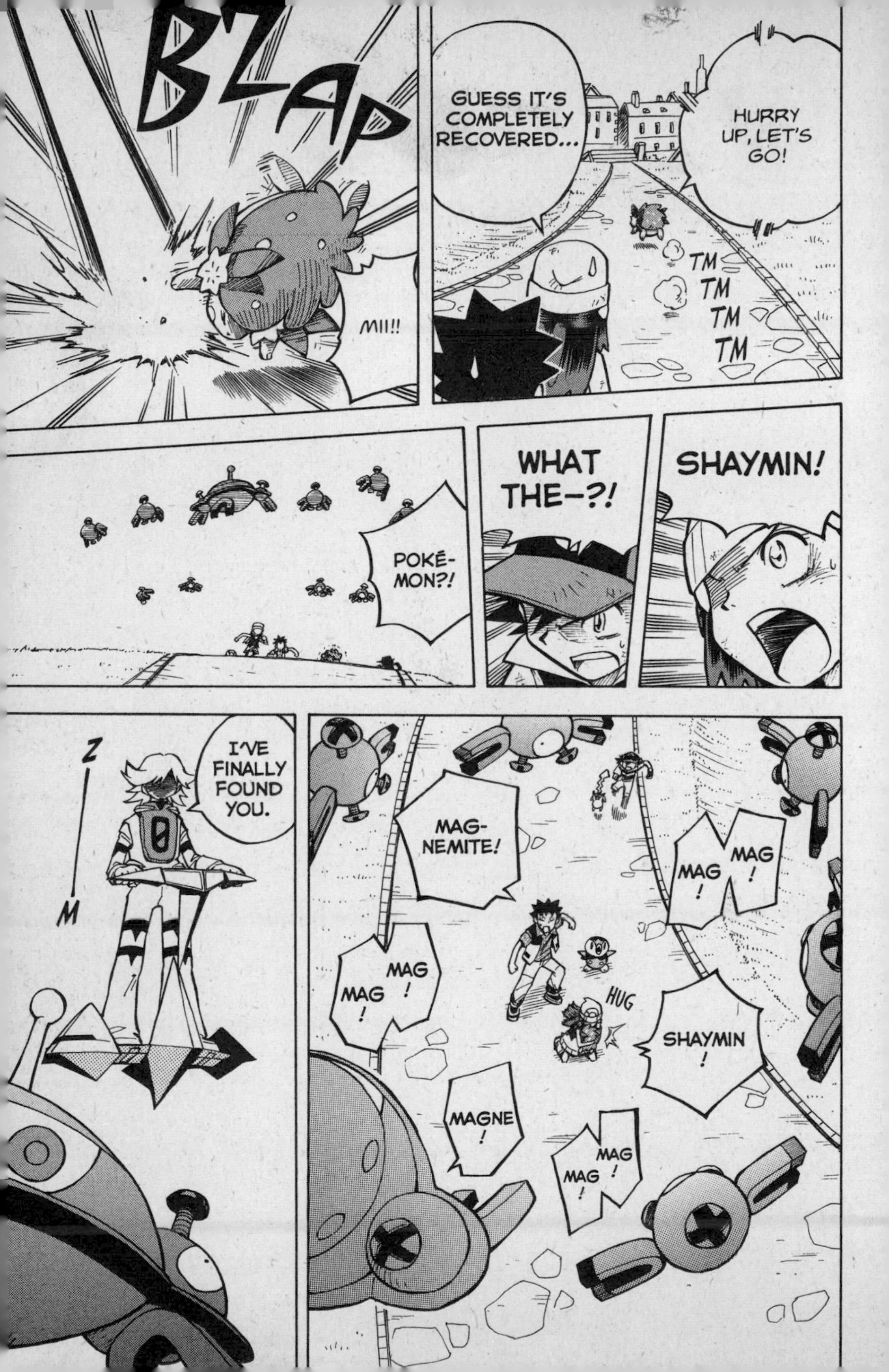
HURRY UP, LET'S GO!
GUESS IT'S COMPLETELY RECOVERED...
TM TM TM TM
B'ZLAP
MII!!
SHAYMIN!
WHAT THE-?!
POKÉ-MON?!
MAG! MAG!
MAG-NEMITE!
SHAYMIN!
HUG
MAG! MAG!
MAGNE!
MAG! MAG!
I'VE FINALLY FOUND YOU.
ZM

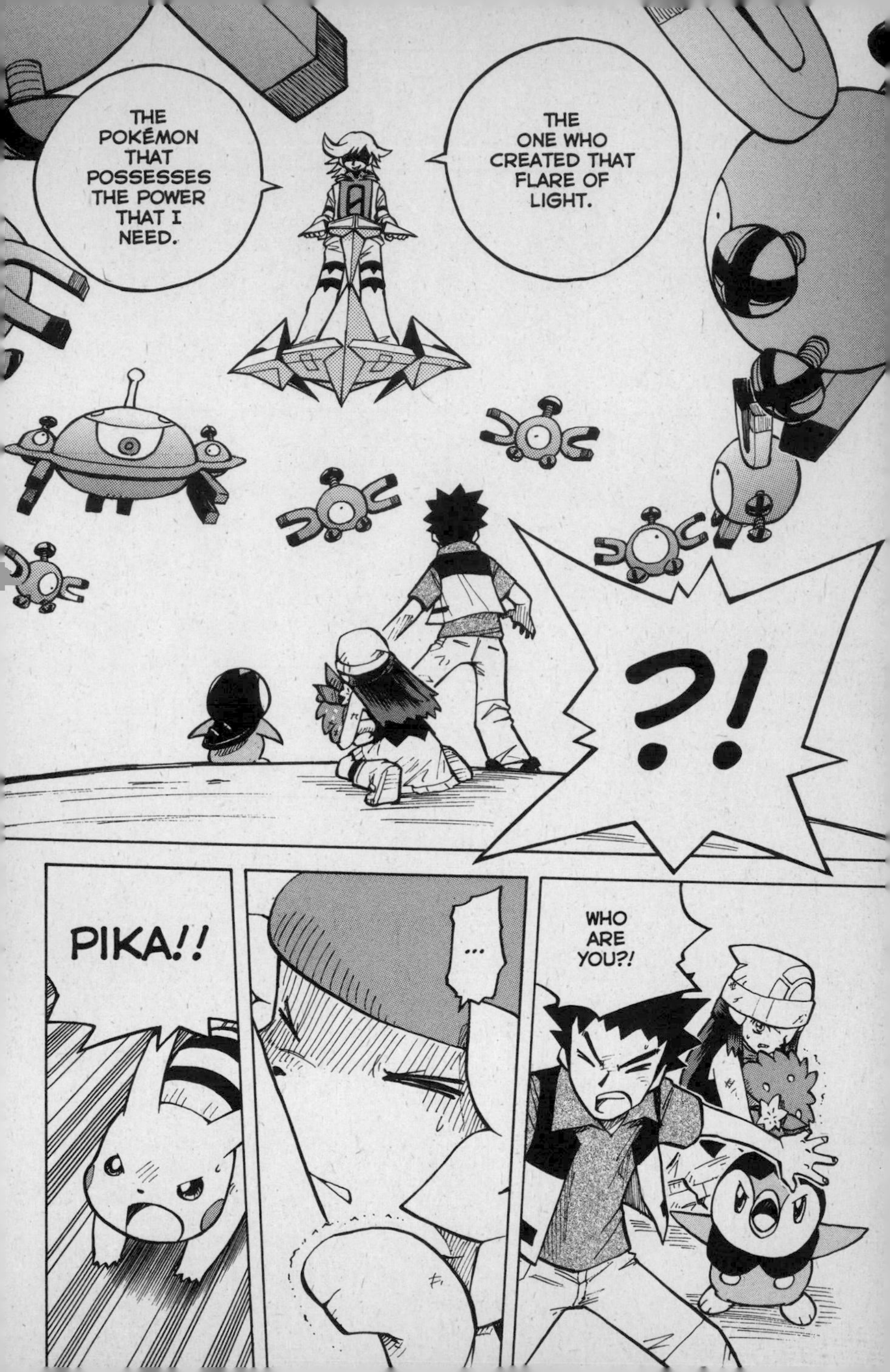
THE ONE WHO CREATED THAT FLARE OF LIGHT.
THE POKÉMON THAT POSSESSES THE POWER THAT I NEED.
?!
WHO ARE YOU?!
...
PIKA!!

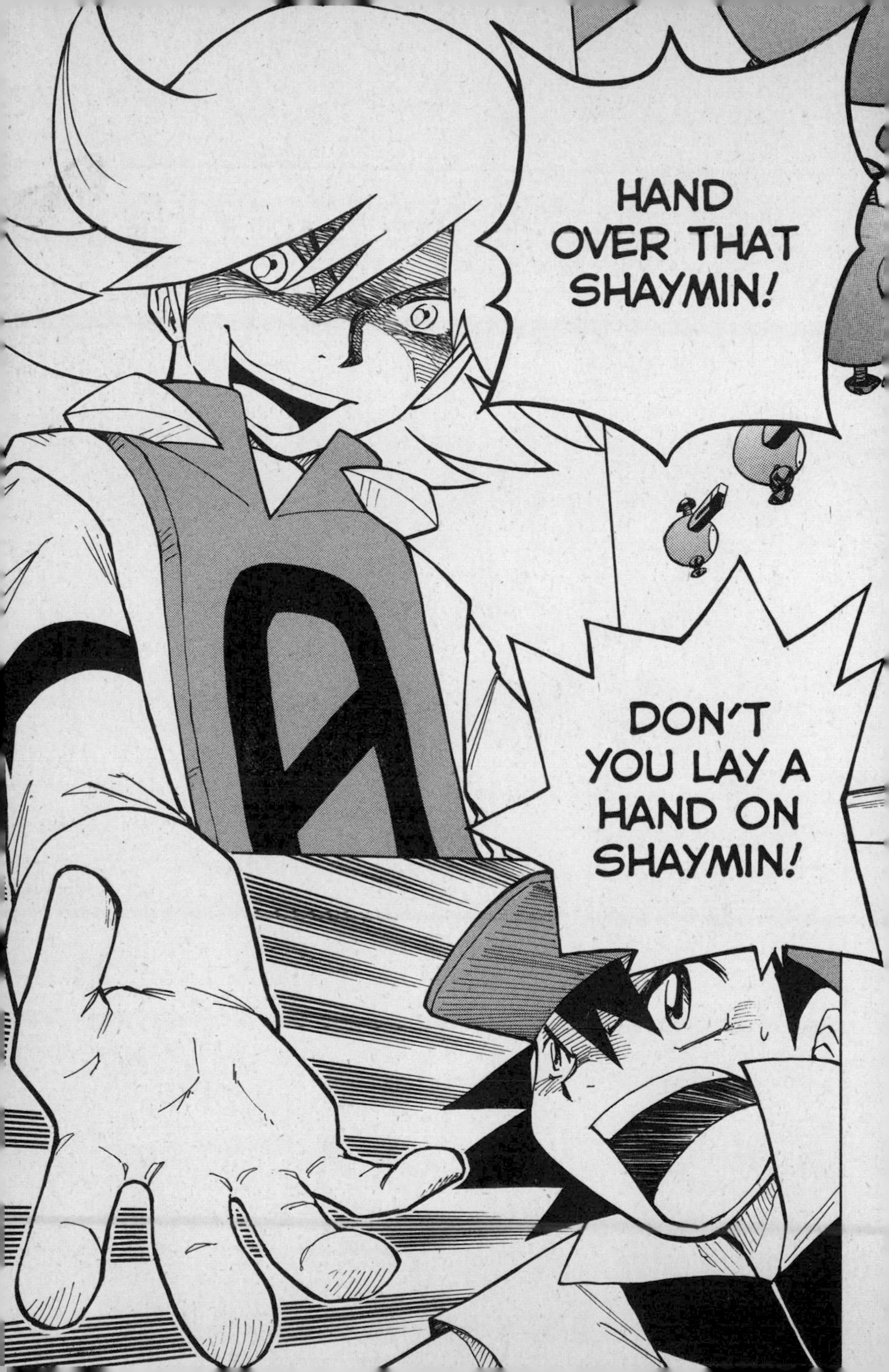
HAND OVER THAT SHAYMIN!
DON'T YOU LAY A HAND ON SHAYMIN!

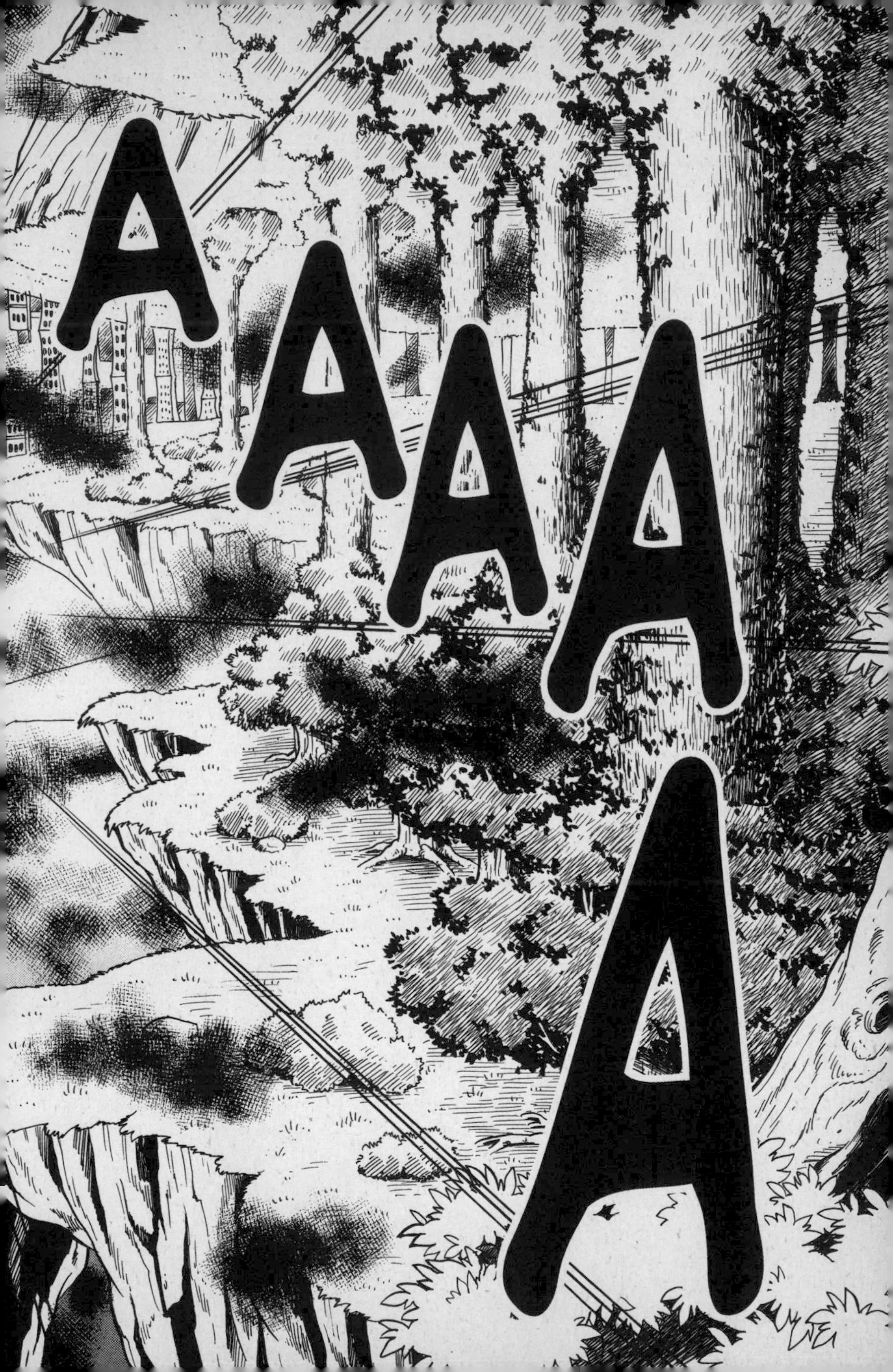
AAAAA

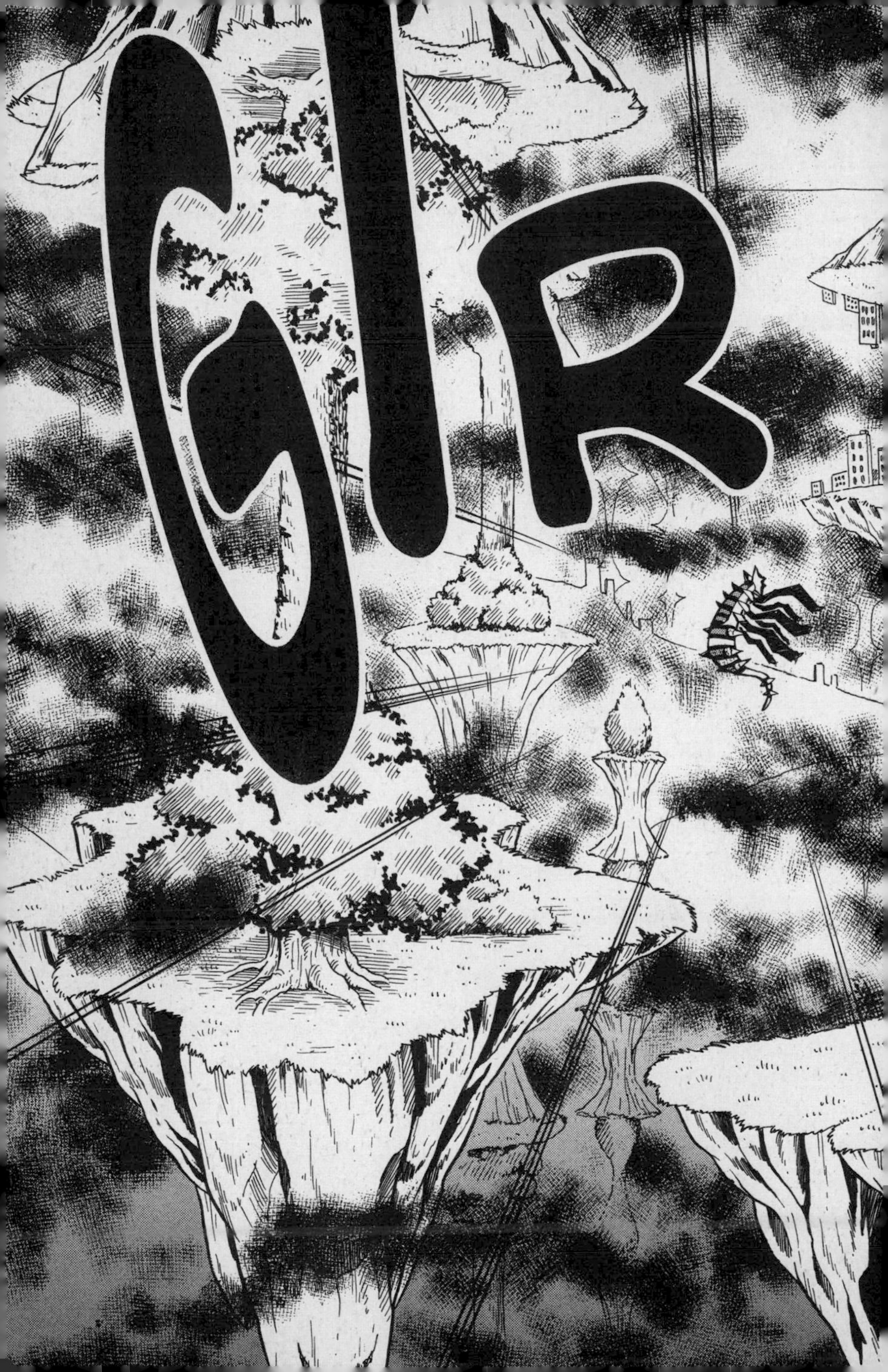
GIR

Chapter 2
Target: Shaymin!

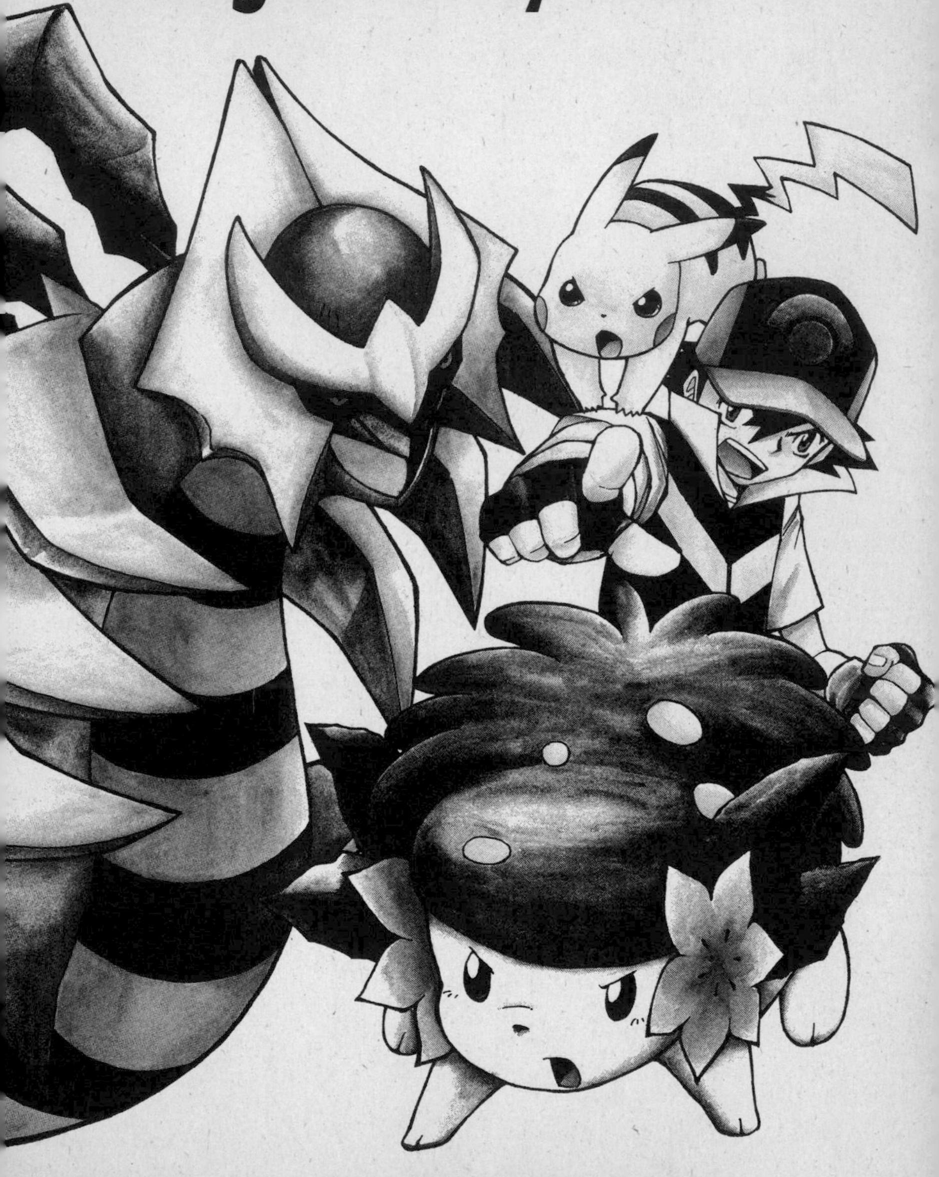

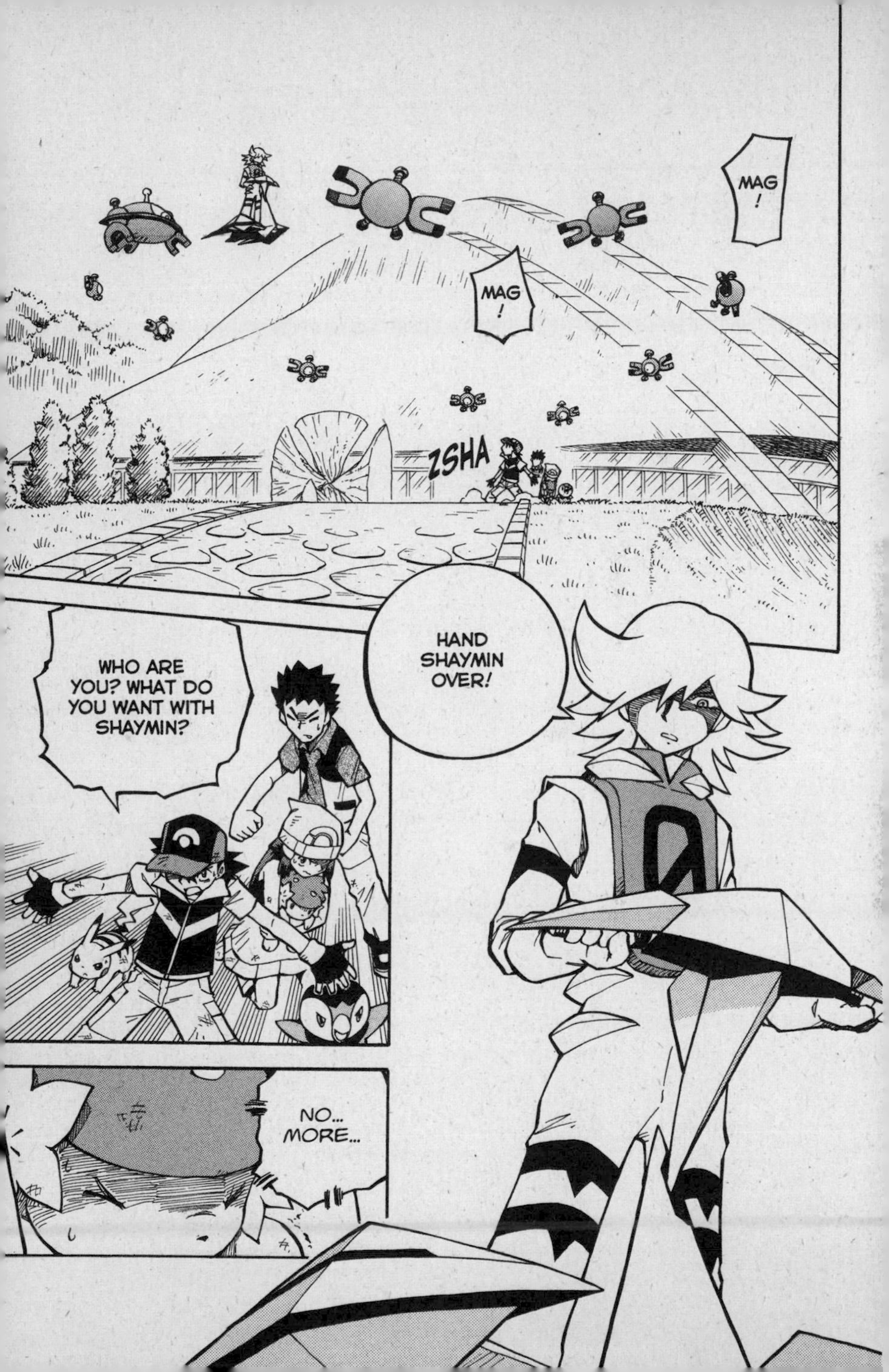
MAG!
MAG!
ZSHA
HAND SHAYMIN OVER!
WHO ARE YOU? WHAT DO YOU WANT WITH SHAYMIN?
NO... MORE...

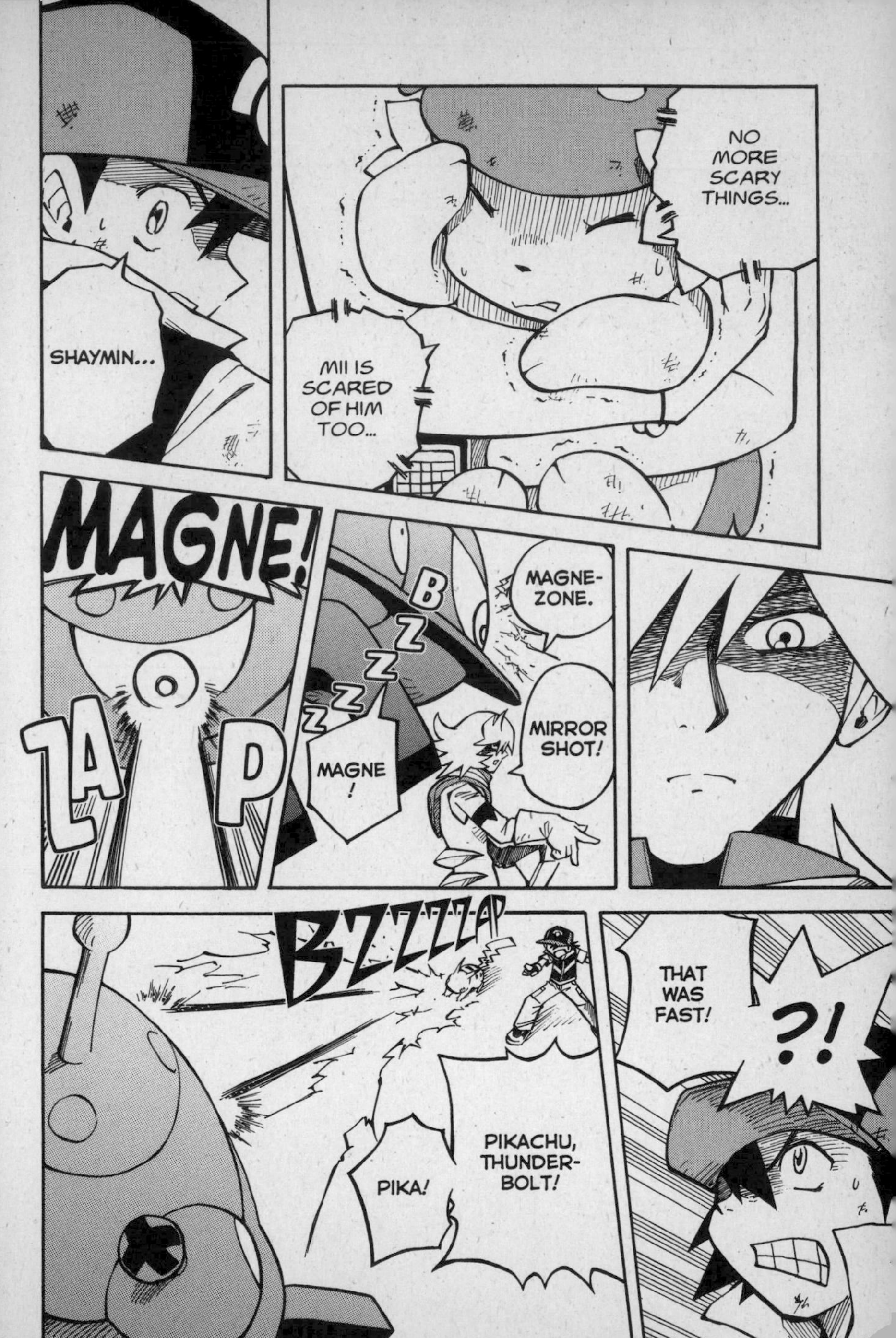
NO MORE SCARY THINGS...
MII IS SCARED OF HIM TOO...
SHAYMIN...
MAGNE-ZONE.
BZZZZZ
MIRROR SHOT!
MAGNE!
MAGNE!
ZAP
THAT WAS FAST!
?!
BZZZZZAP
PIKACHU, THUNDERBOLT!
PIKA!

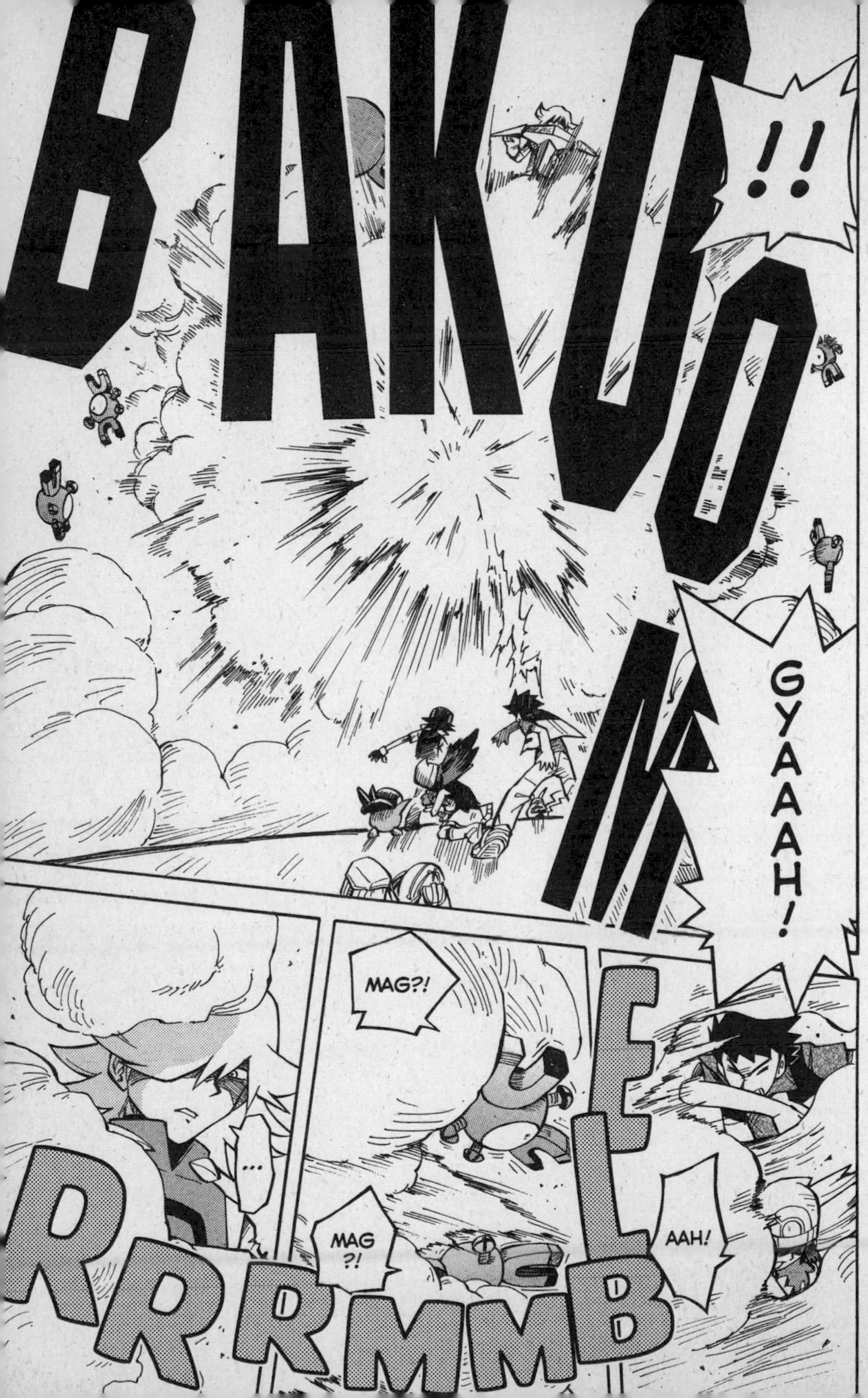
BAKOOM
!!
GYAAAH!
AAH!
MAG?!
MAG ?!
...
RRRMMBLE

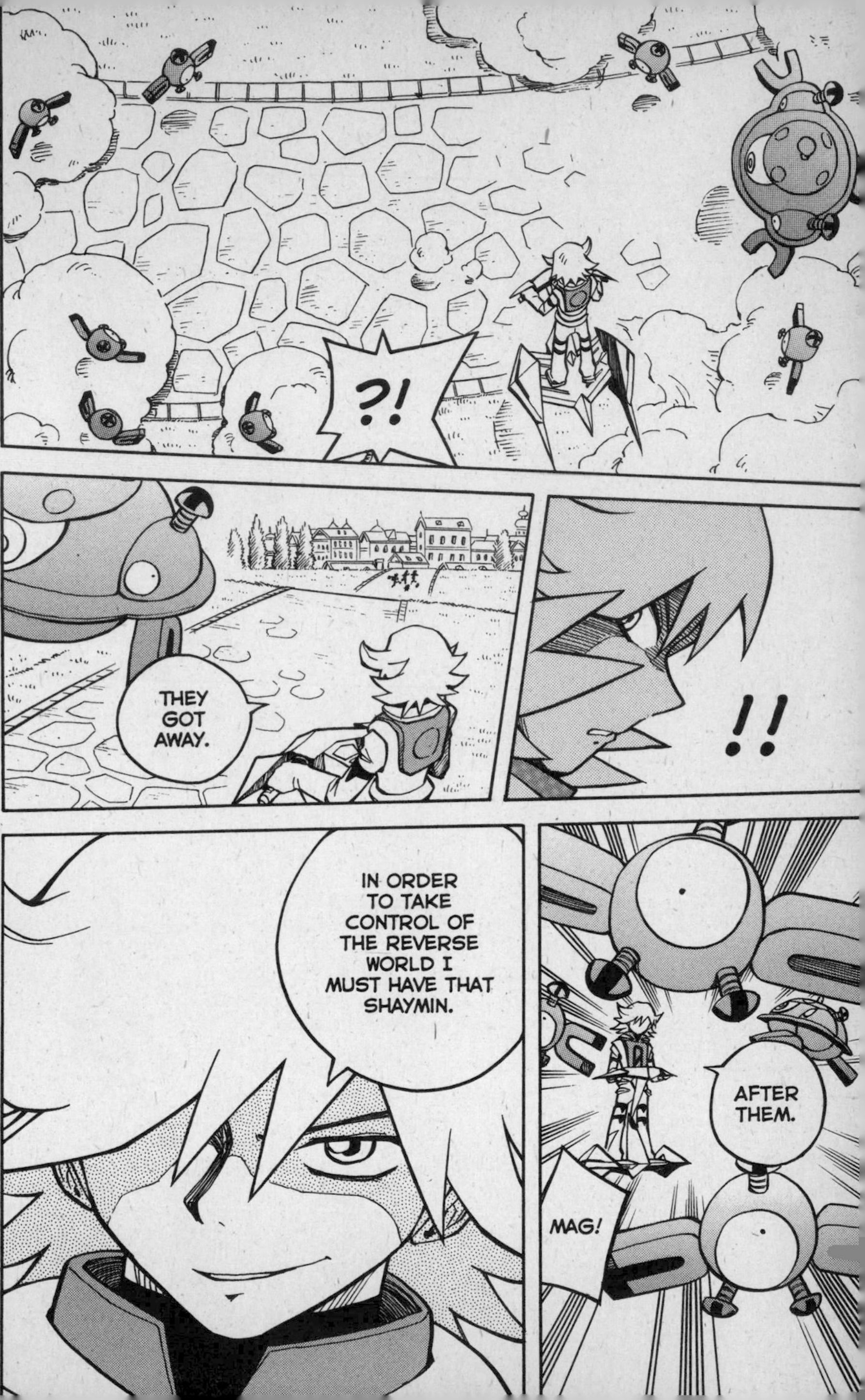
?!
!!
THEY GOT AWAY.
AFTER THEM.
MAG!
IN ORDER TO TAKE CONTROL OF THE REVERSE WORLD I MUST HAVE THAT SHAYMIN.

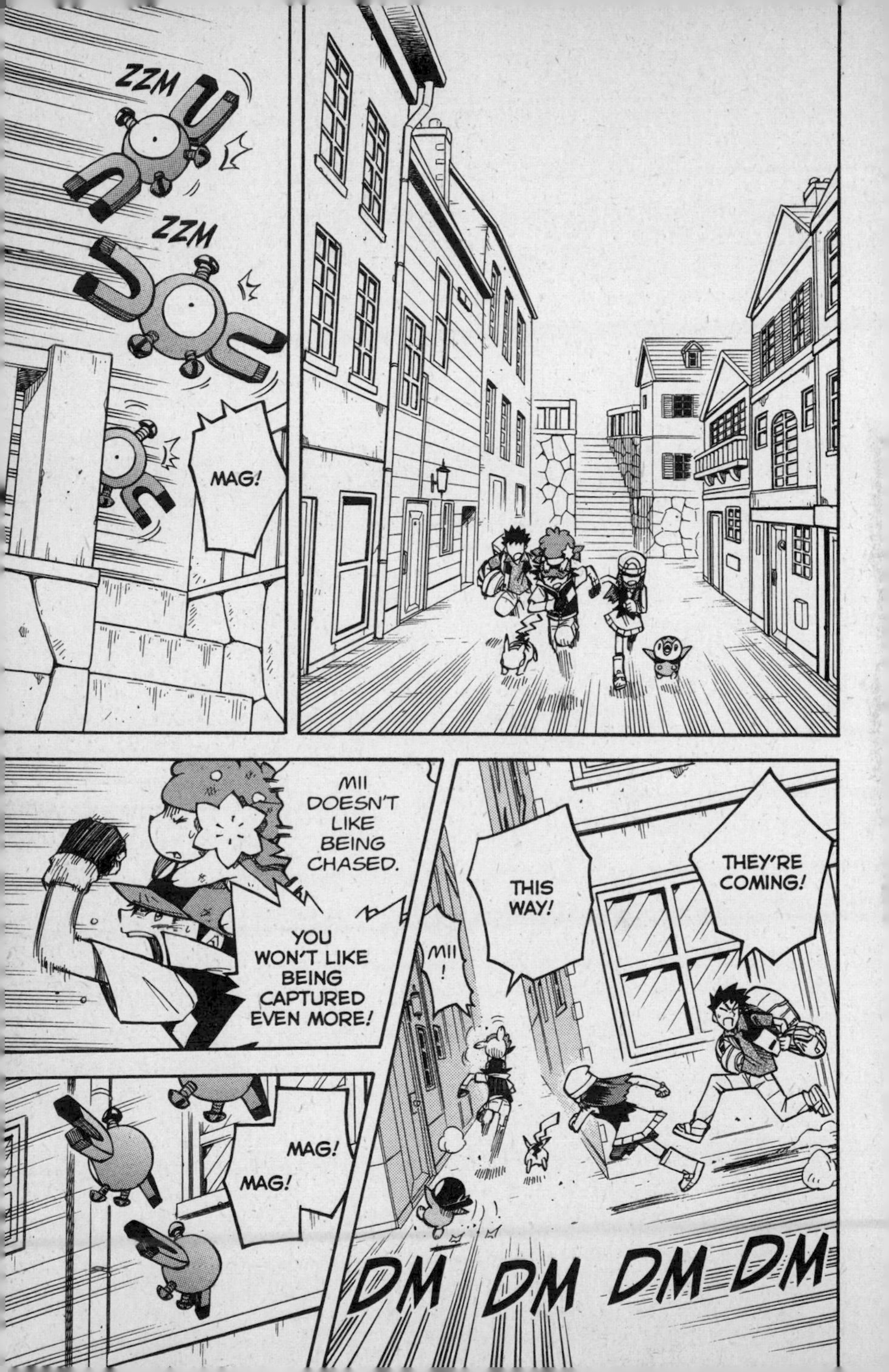
ZZM
ZZM
MAG!
THEY'RE COMING!
THIS WAY!
MII!
DM DM DM DM
MII DOESN'T LIKE BEING CHASED.
YOU WON'T LIKE BEING CAPTURED EVEN MORE!
MAG!
MAG!

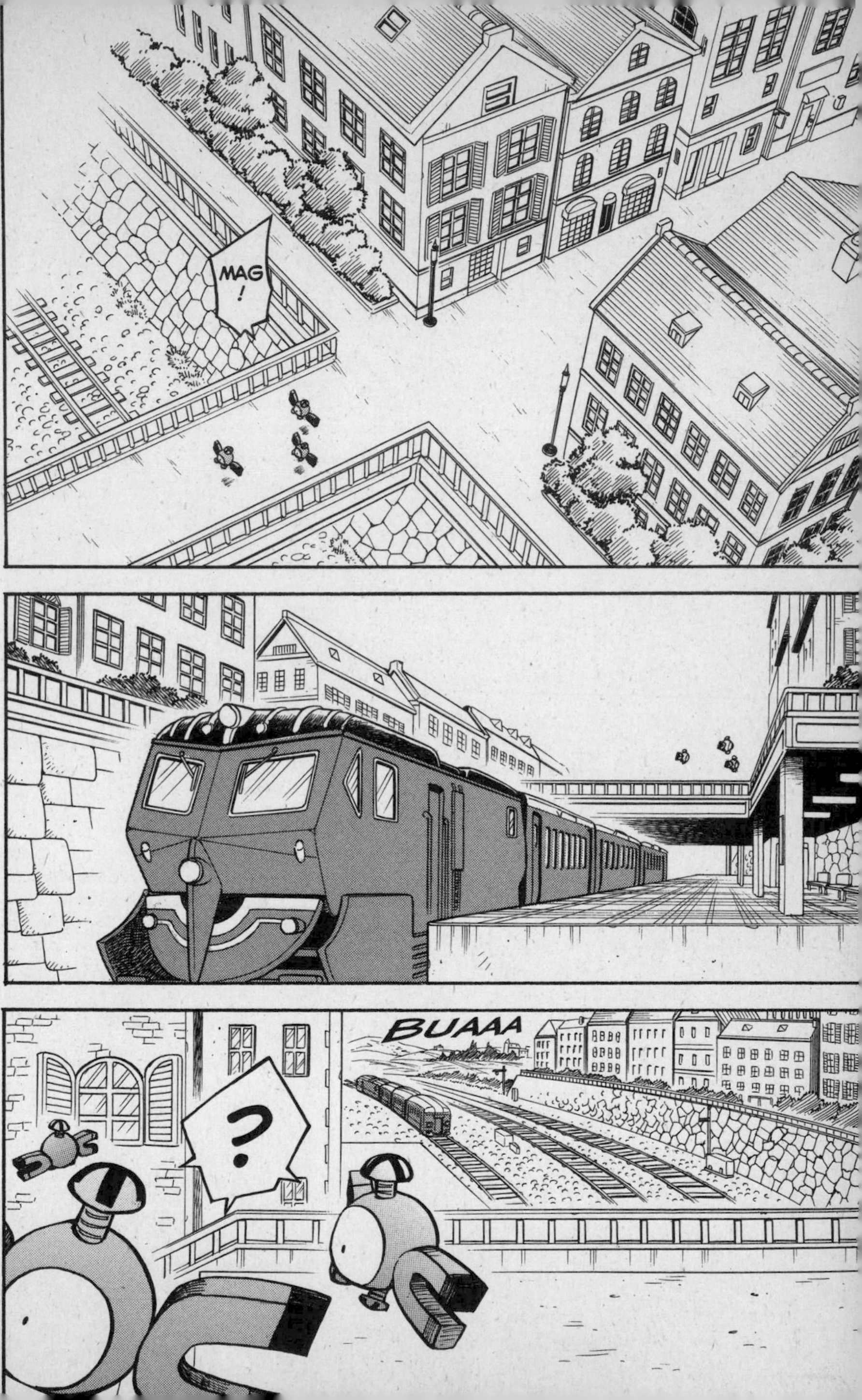
MAG
!
BUAAA
?

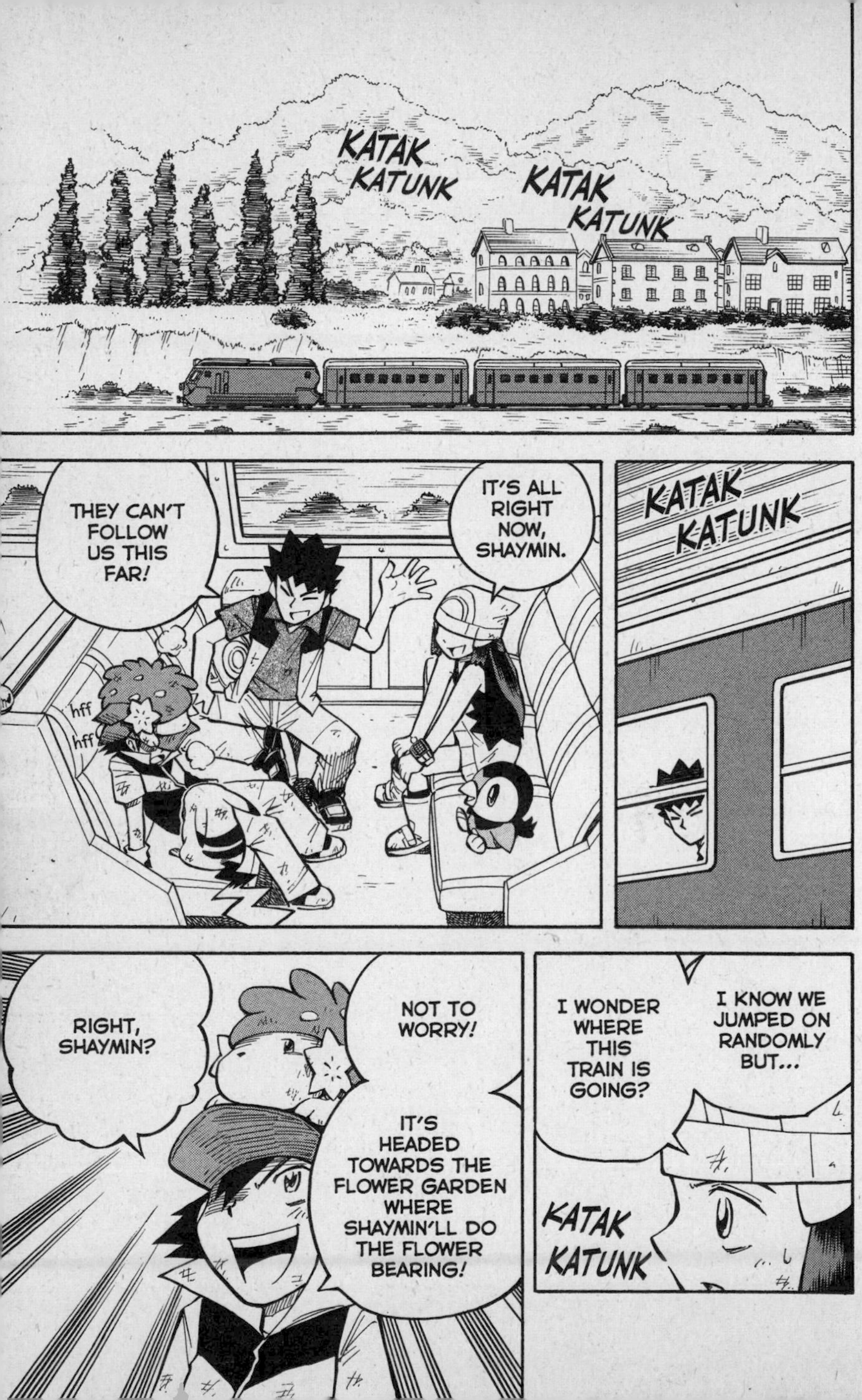
KATAK
KATUNK
KATAK
KATUNK
KATAK
KATUNK
IT'S ALL RIGHT NOW, SHAYMIN.
THEY CAN'T FOLLOW US THIS FAR!
hff
hff
I KNOW WE JUMPED ON RANDOMLY BUT...
I WONDER WHERE THIS TRAIN IS GOING?
KATAK
KATUNK
NOT TO WORRY!
IT'S HEADED TOWARDS THE FLOWER GARDEN WHERE SHAYMIN'LL DO THE FLOWER BEARING!
RIGHT, SHAYMIN?

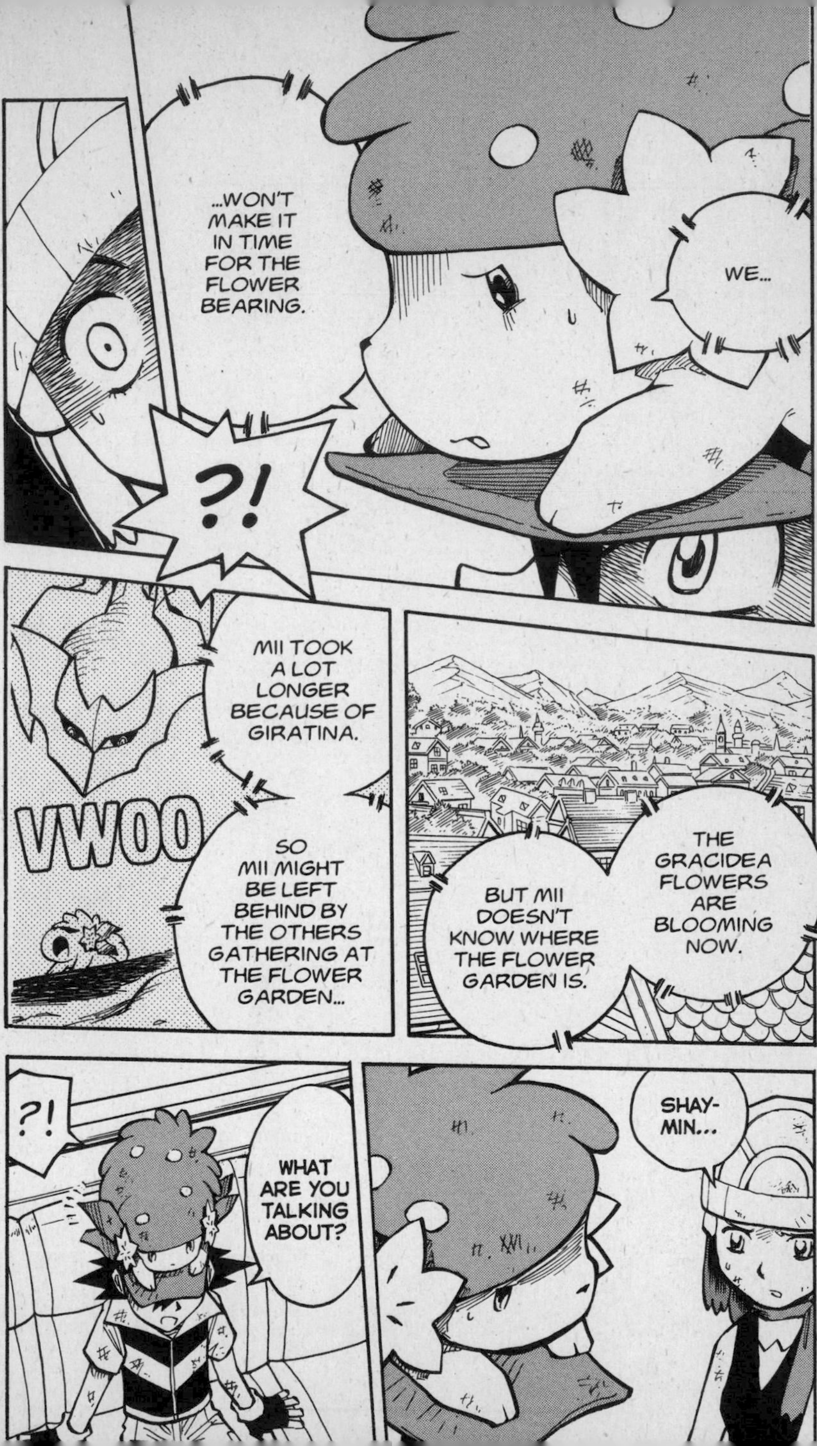
WE...
...WON'T MAKE IT IN TIME FOR THE FLOWER BEARING.
?!
THE GRACIDEA FLOWERS ARE BLOOMING NOW.
BUT MII DOESN'T KNOW WHERE THE FLOWER GARDEN IS.
MII TOOK A LOT LONGER BECAUSE OF GIRATINA.
VWOO
SO MII MIGHT BE LEFT BEHIND BY THE OTHERS GATHERING AT THE FLOWER GARDEN...
SHAY-MIN...
?!
WHAT ARE YOU TALKING ABOUT?

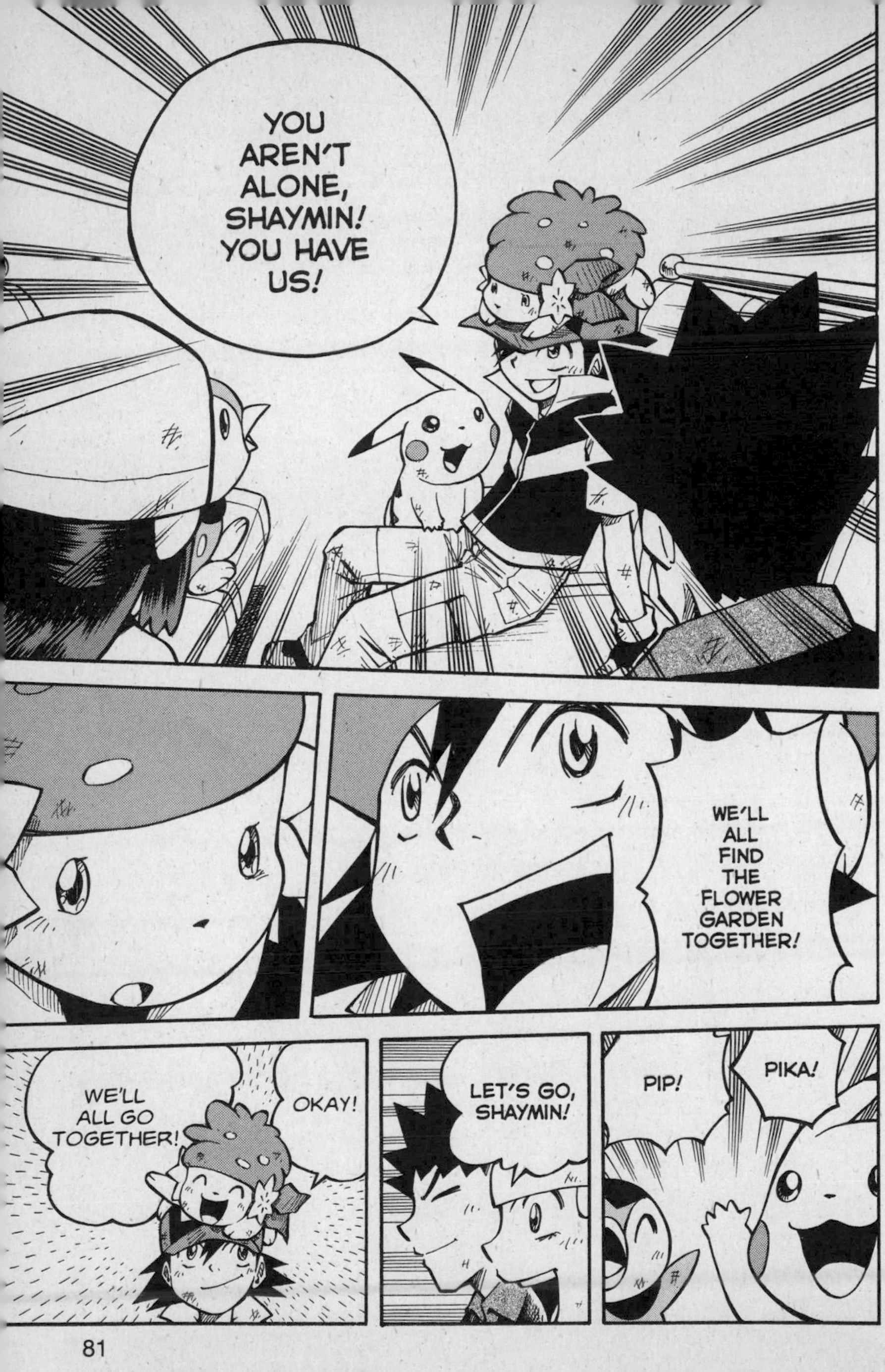
YOU AREN'T ALONE, SHAYMIN! YOU HAVE US!
WE'LL ALL FIND THE FLOWER GARDEN TOGETHER!
PIKA!
PIP!
LET'S GO, SHAYMIN!
OKAY!
WE'LL ALL GO TOGETHER!

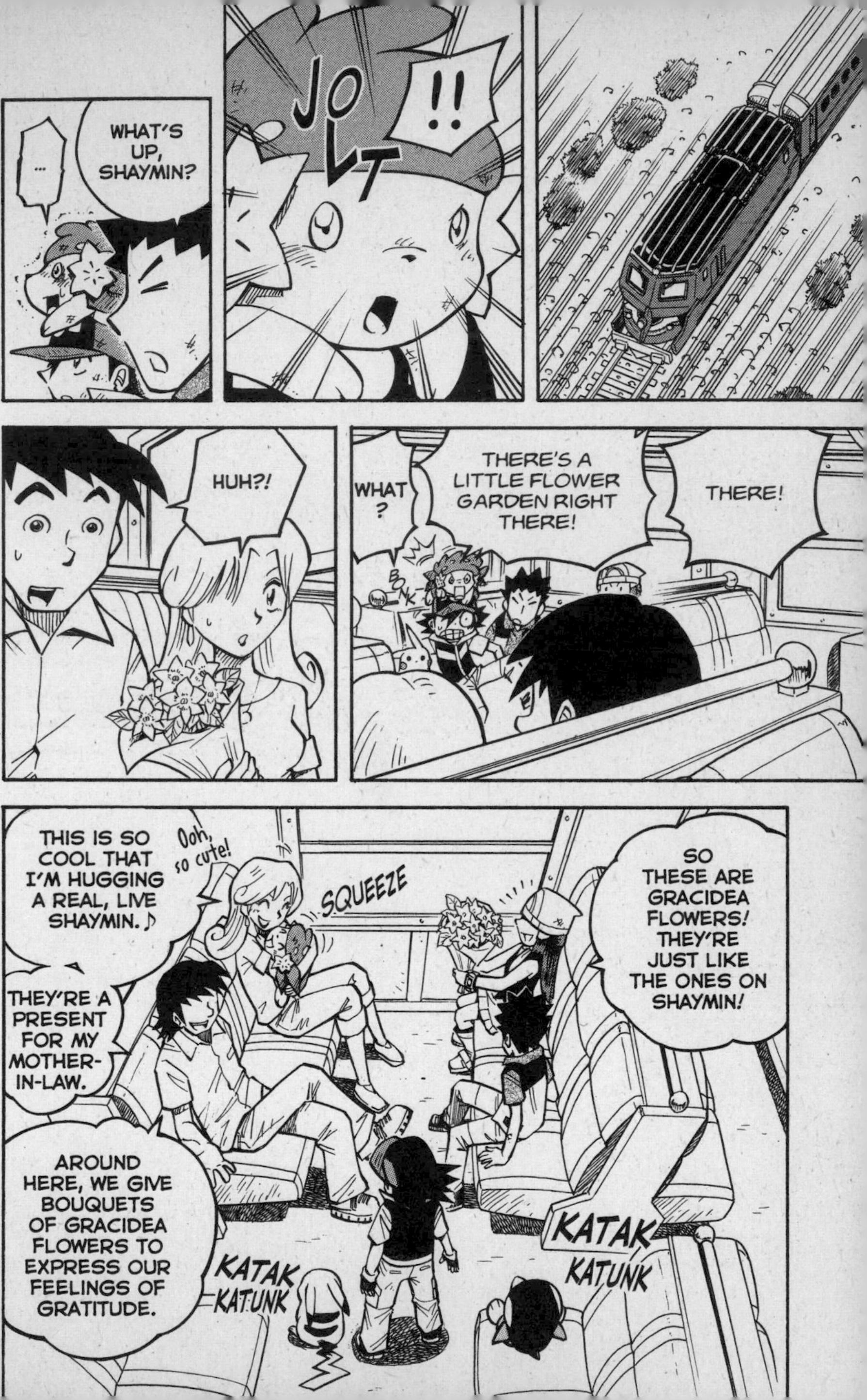
JOLT
!!
WHAT'S UP, SHAYMIN?
...
THERE!
THERE'S A LITTLE FLOWER GARDEN RIGHT THERE!
WHAT?
BONK
HUH?!
SO THESE ARE GRACIDEA FLOWERS! THEY'RE JUST LIKE THE ONES ON SHAYMIN!
SQUEEZE
Ooh, so cute!
THIS IS SO COOL THAT I'M HUGGING A REAL, LIVE SHAYMIN. ♪
THEY'RE A PRESENT FOR MY MOTHER-IN-LAW.
KATAK
KATUNK
AROUND HERE, WE GIVE BOUQUETS OF GRACIDEA FLOWERS TO EXPRESS OUR FEELINGS OF GRATITUDE.
KATAK
KATUNK

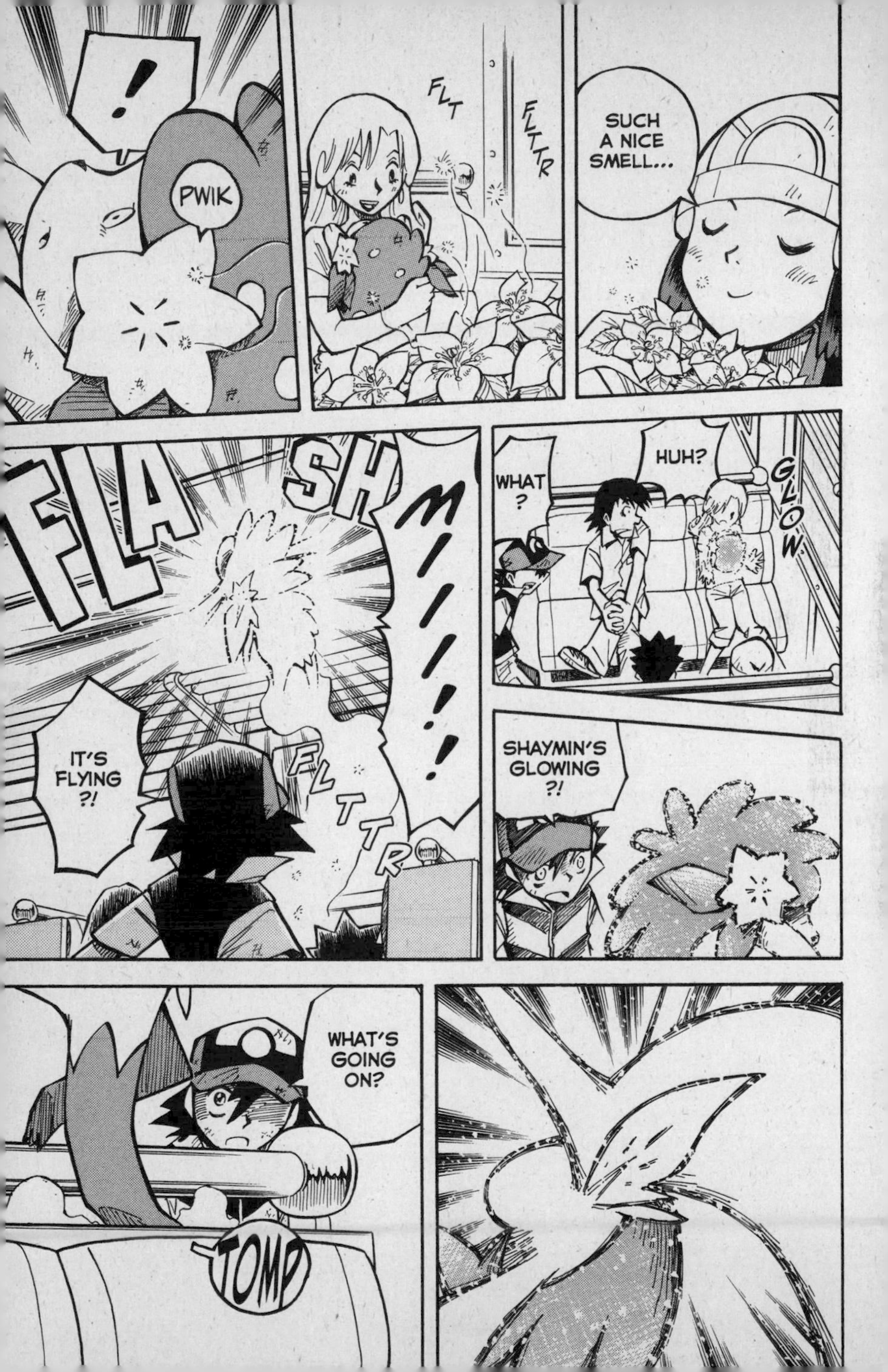
!
PWIK
FLT
FLTTR
SUCH A NICE SMELL...
FLASH
M!!!!!
IT'S FLYING ?!
FLTTR
WHAT ?
HUH?
GLOW
SHAYMIN'S GLOWING ?!
WHAT'S GOING ON?
TOMP

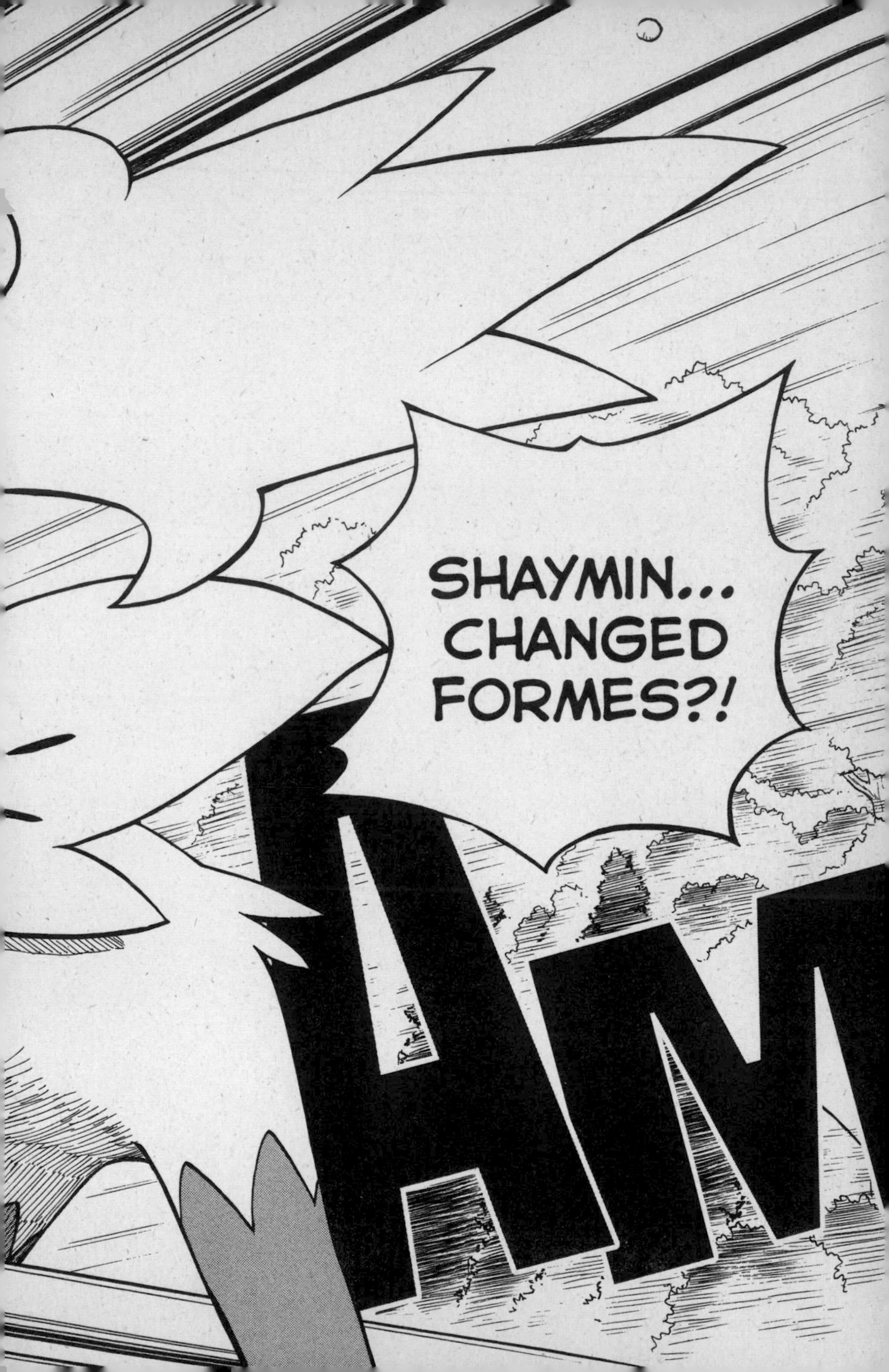
SHAYMIN... CHANGED FORMES?!

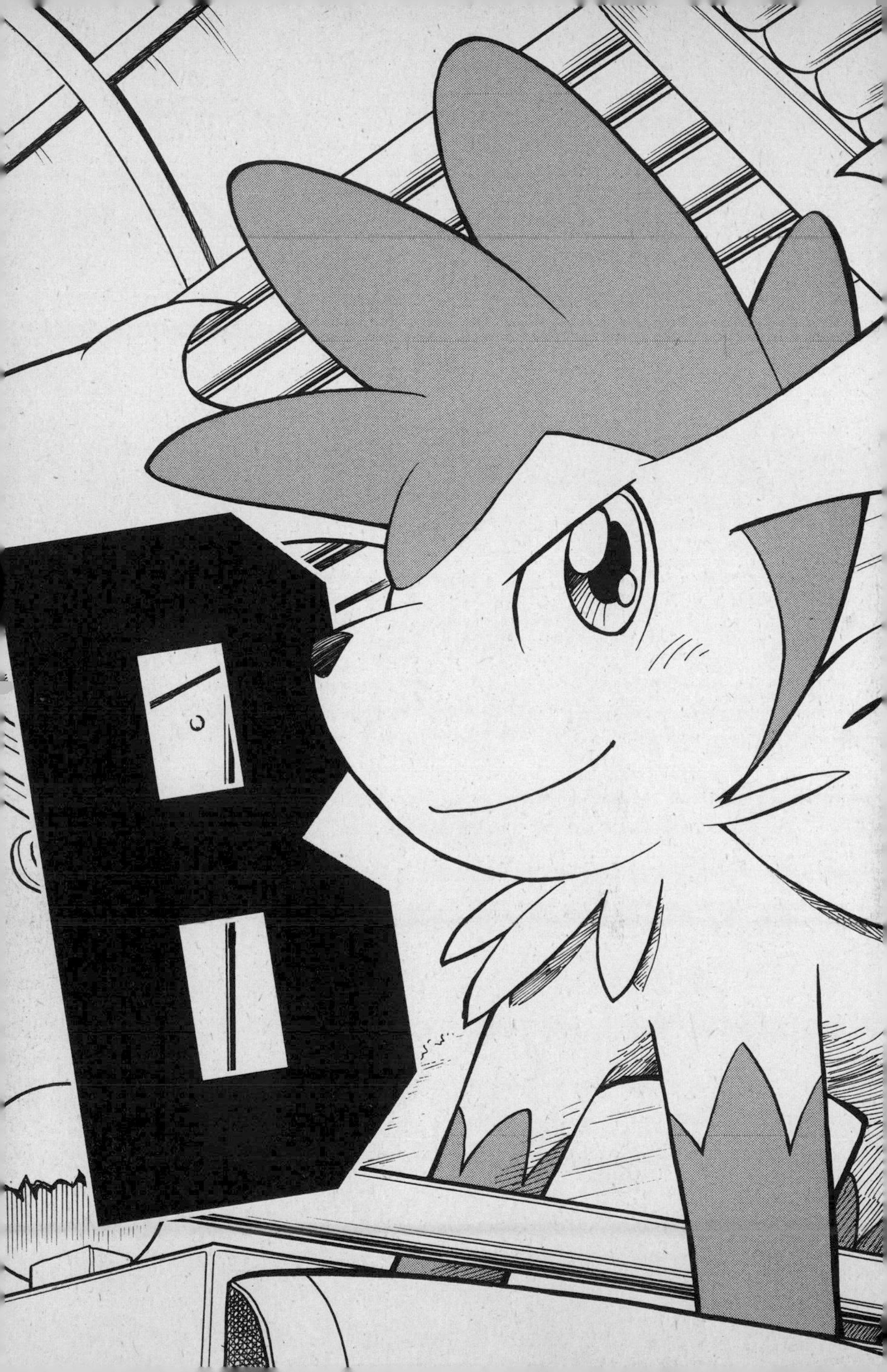

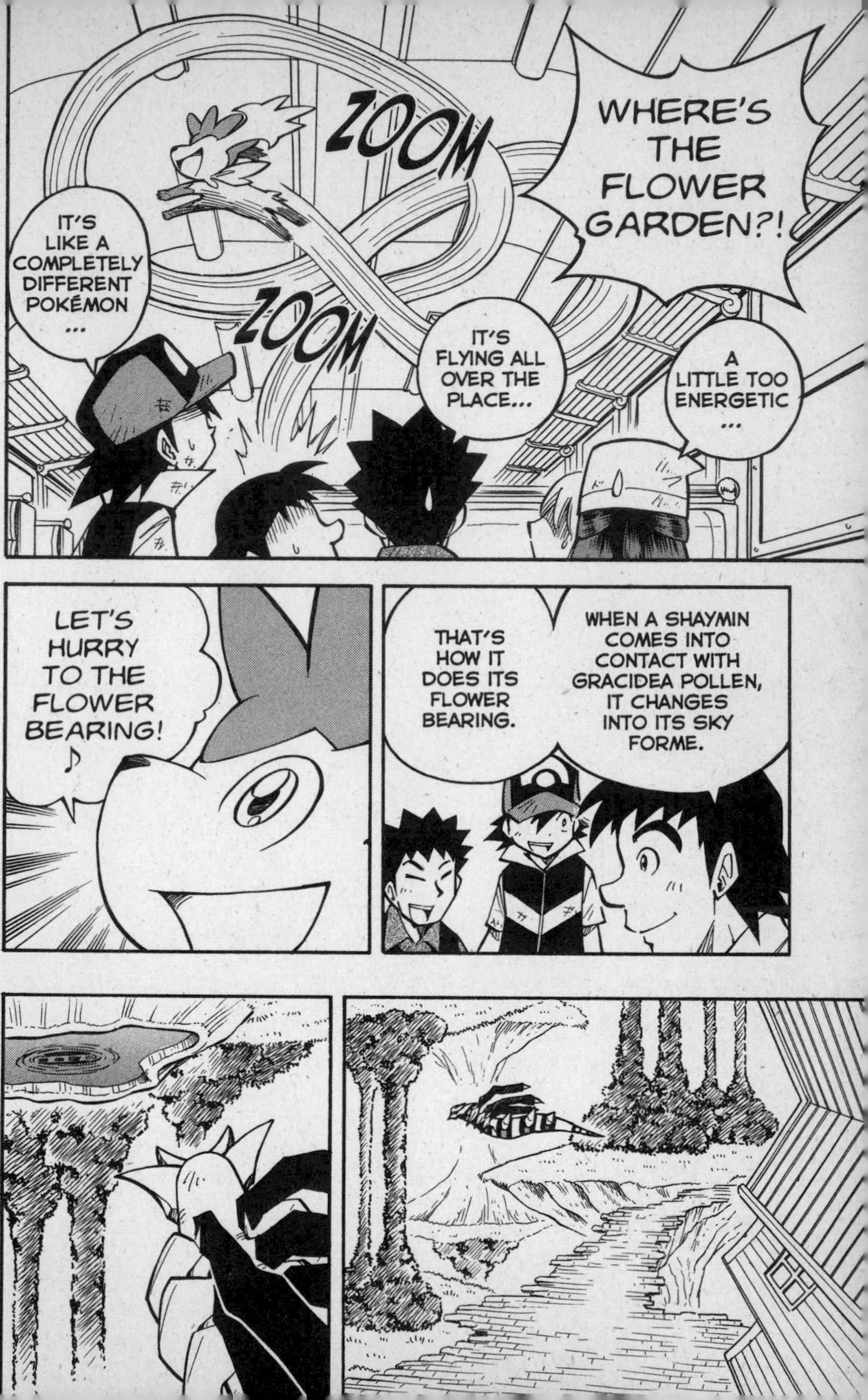
WHERE'S THE FLOWER GARDEN?!
ZOOM
ZOOM
A LITTLE TOO ENERGETIC...
IT'S FLYING ALL OVER THE PLACE...
IT'S LIKE A COMPLETELY DIFFERENT POKÉMON...
WHEN A SHAYMIN COMES INTO CONTACT WITH GRACIDEA POLLEN, IT CHANGES INTO ITS SKY FORME.
THAT'S HOW IT DOES ITS FLOWER BEARING.
LET'S HURRY TO THE FLOWER BEARING! ♪

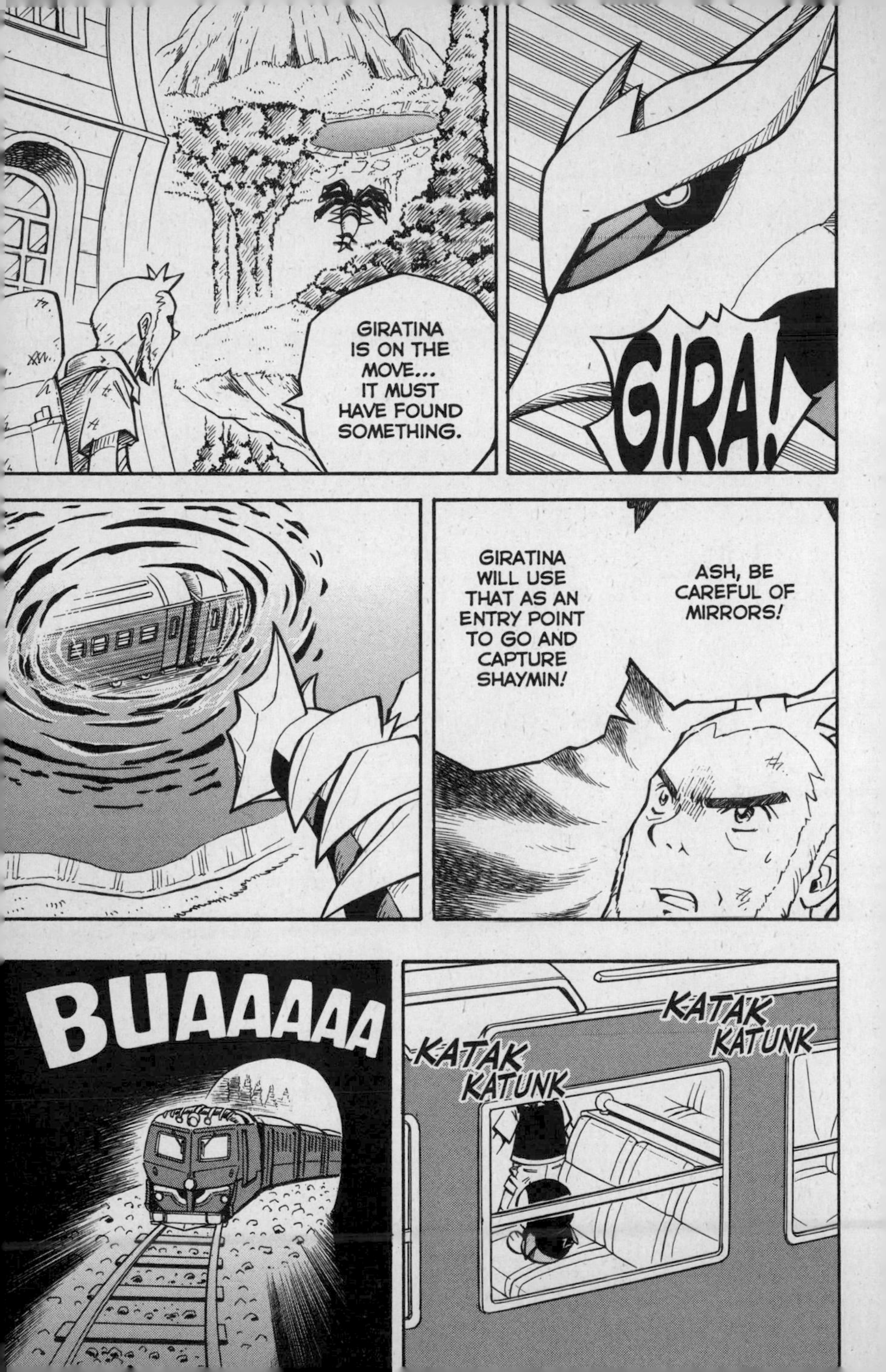
GIRA!
GIRATINA IS ON THE MOVE... IT MUST HAVE FOUND SOMETHING.
ASH, BE CAREFUL OF MIRRORS!
GIRATINA WILL USE THAT AS AN ENTRY POINT TO GO AND CAPTURE SHAYMIN!
KATAK KATUNK
KATAK KATUNK
BUAAAAA

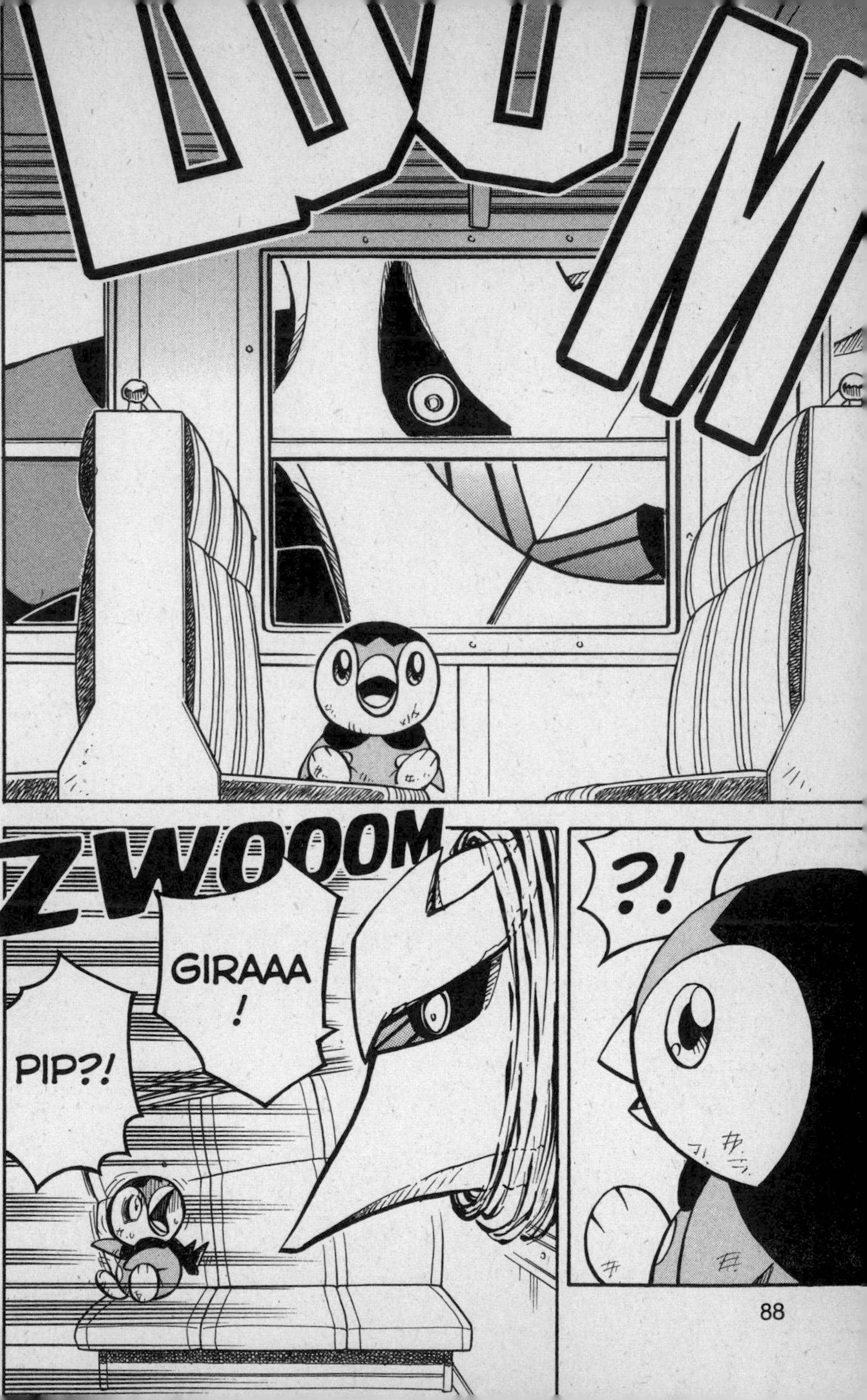
?!
ZWOOOM
GIRAAA!
PIP?!

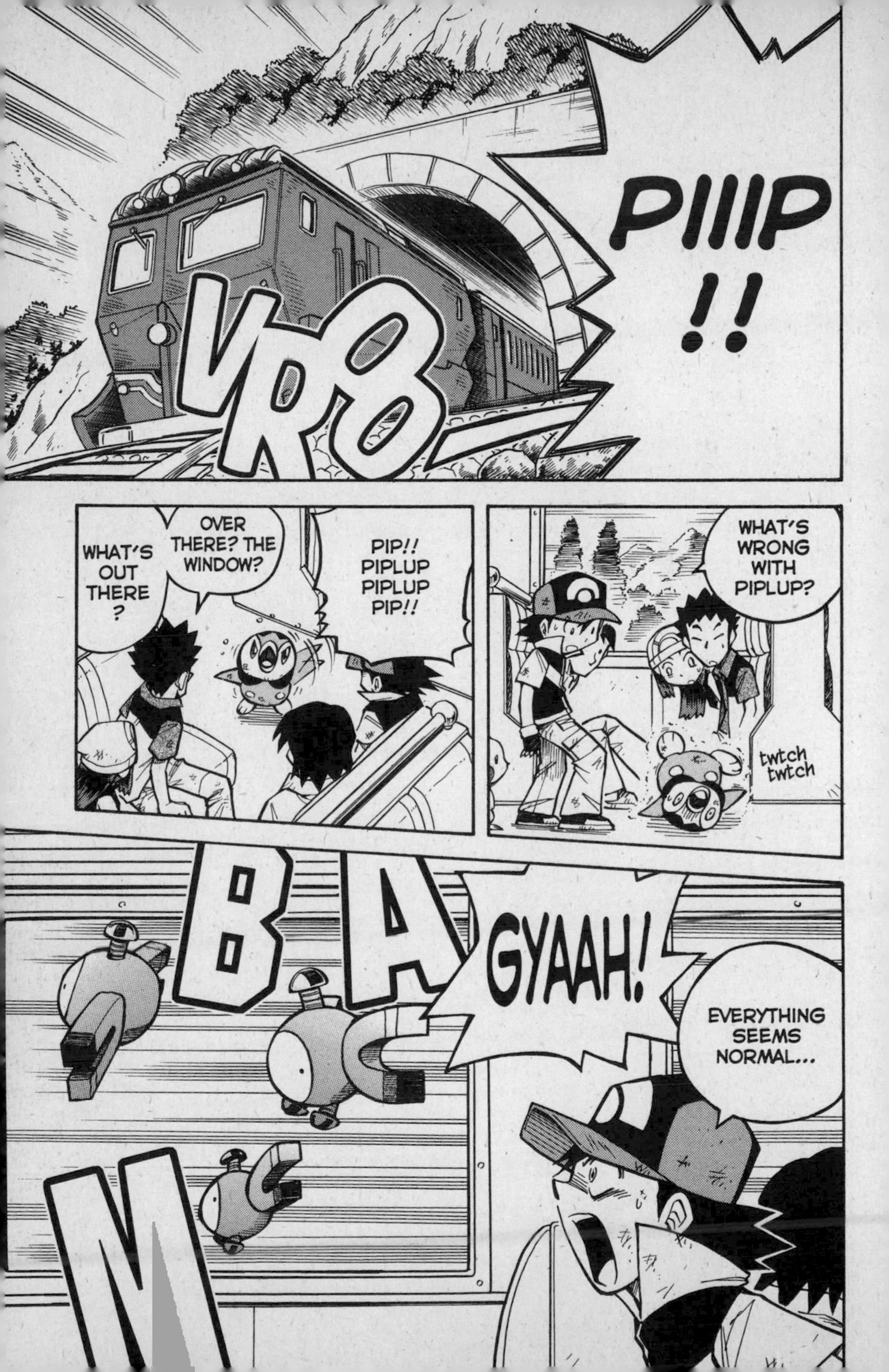
PIIIP!!
VRB
WHAT'S WRONG WITH PIPLUP?
twtch twtch
PIP!! PIPLUP PIPLUP PIP!!
OVER THERE? THE WINDOW?
WHAT'S OUT THERE ?
EVERYTHING SEEMS NORMAL...
GYAAH!
BAM

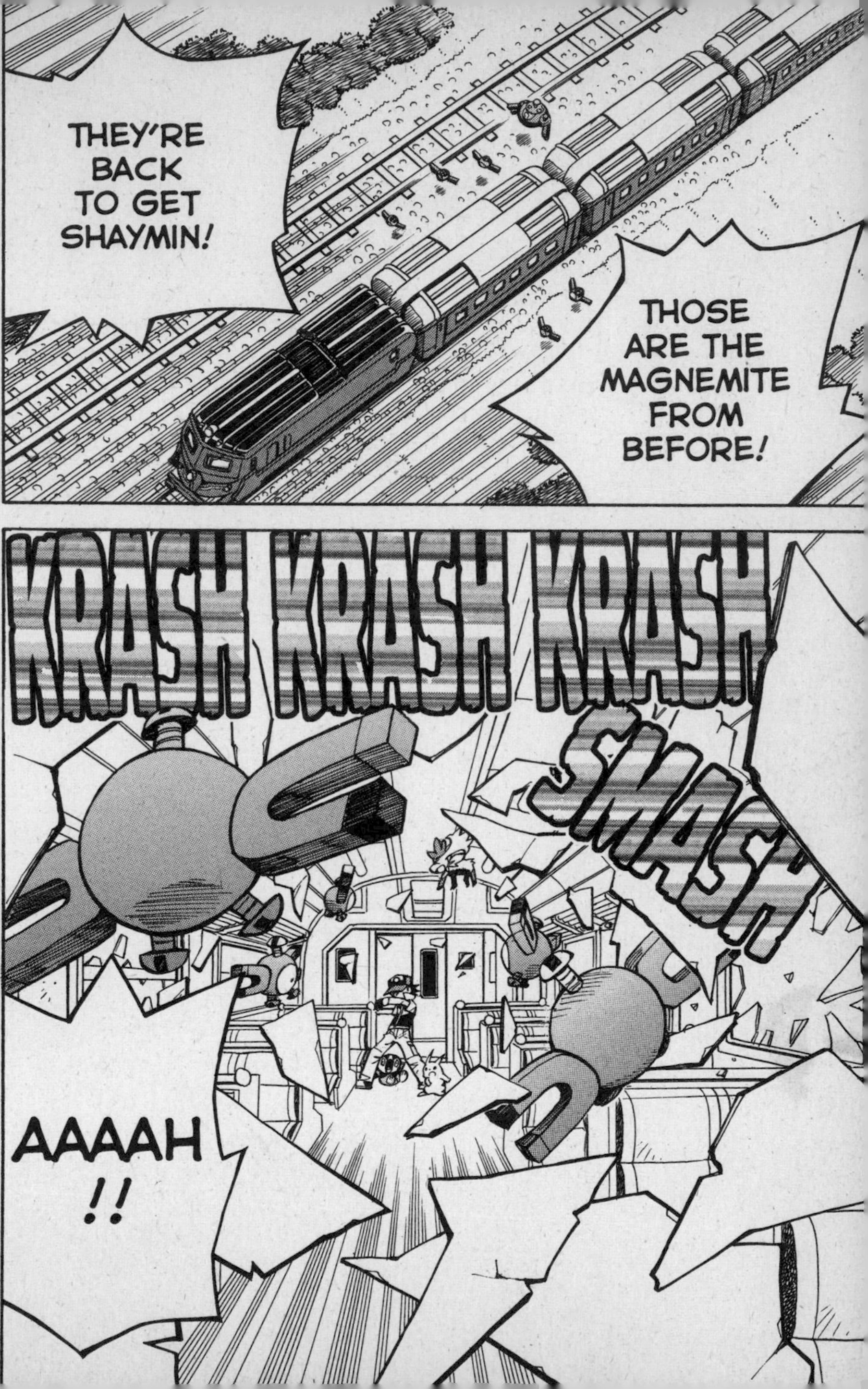
THOSE ARE THE MAGNEMITE FROM BEFORE!
THEY'RE BACK TO GET SHAYMIN!
KRASH KRASH KRASH
SMASH
AAAAH !!

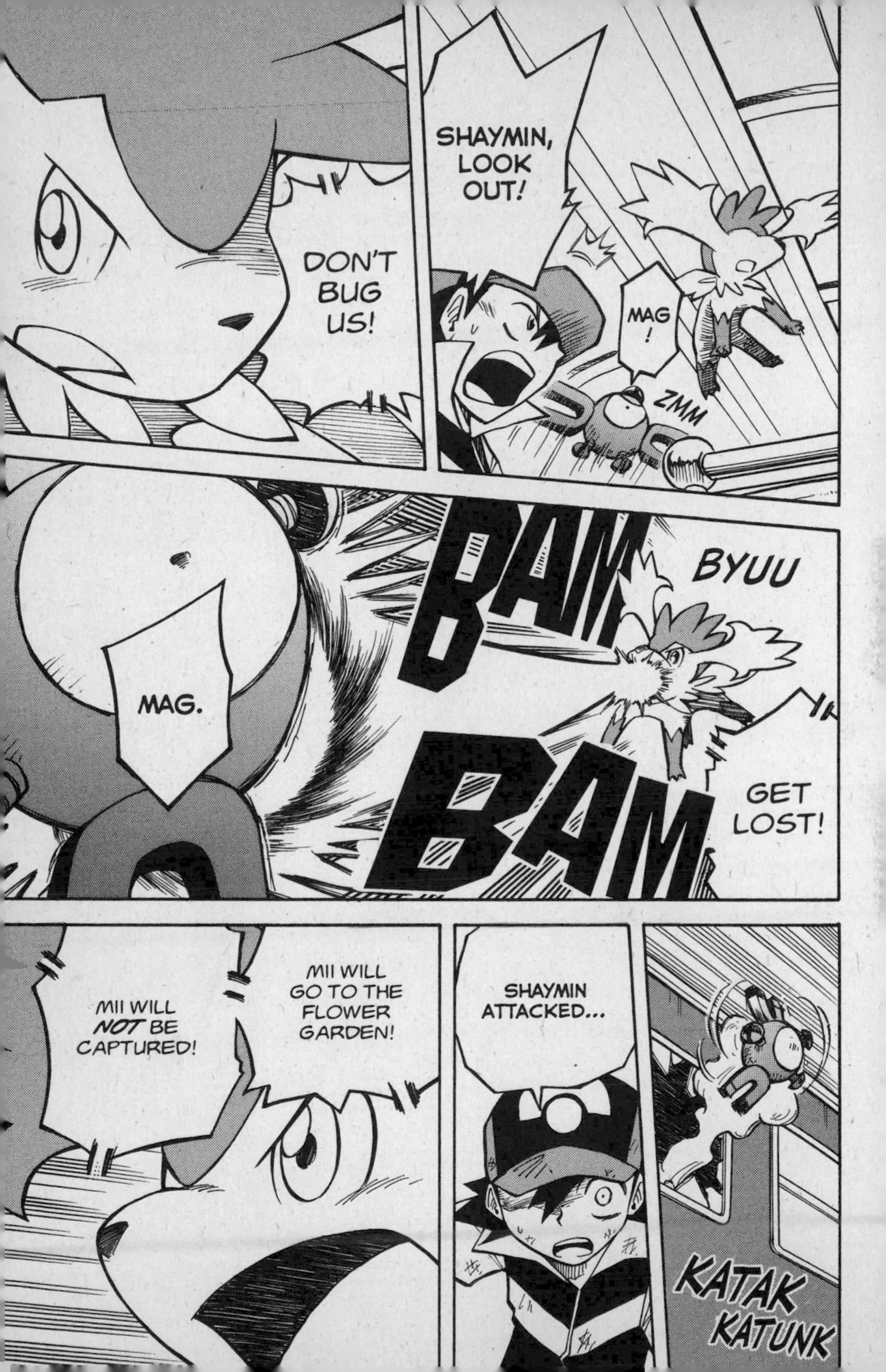
SHAYMIN, LOOK OUT!
MAG!
ZMM
DON'T BUG US!
BYUU
BAM
BAM
GET LOST!
MAG.
KATAK KATUNK
SHAYMIN ATTACKED...
MII WILL GO TO THE FLOWER GARDEN!
MII WILL *NOT* BE CAPTURED!

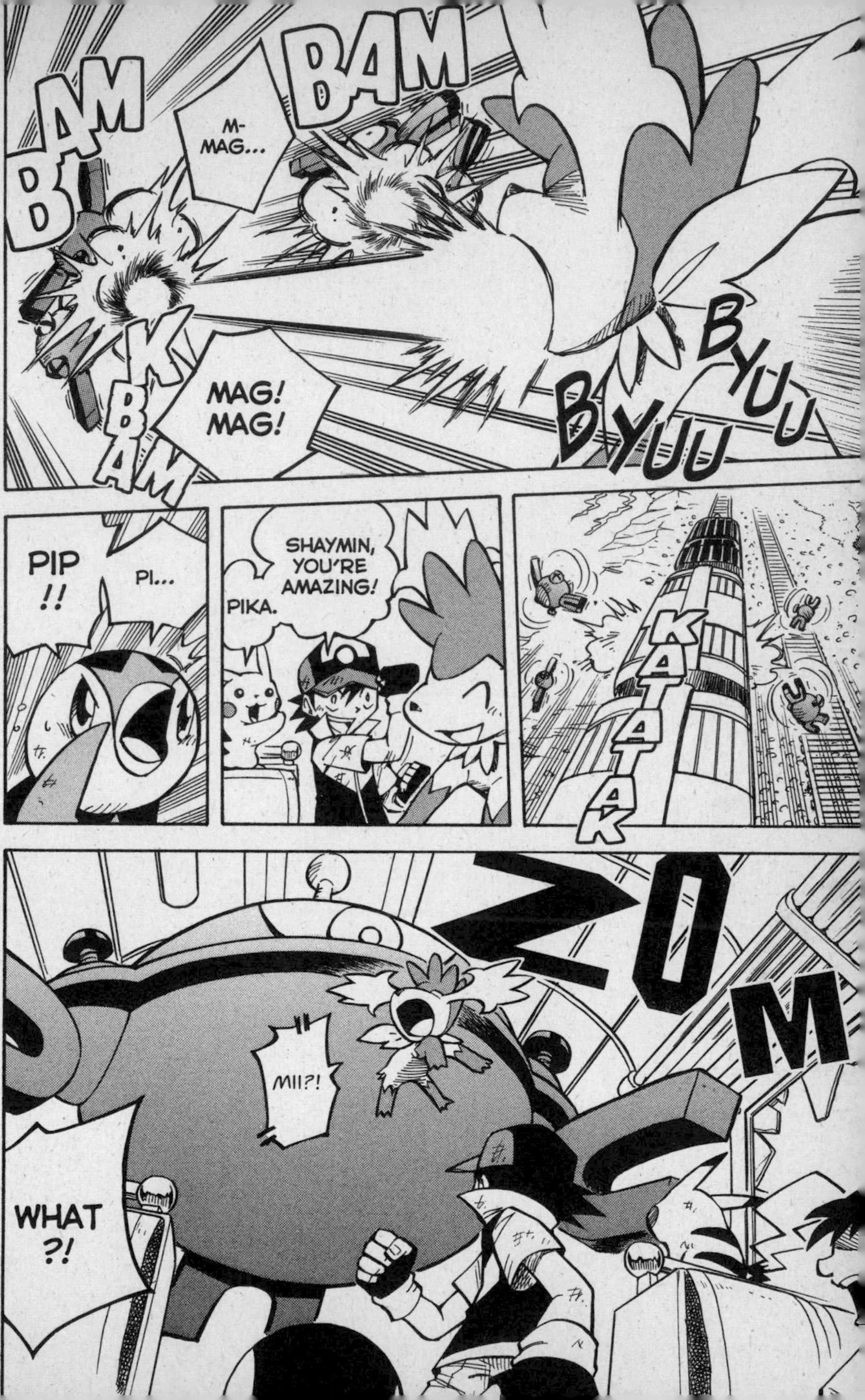
BYUU
BYUU
BAM
M-
MAG...
BAM
MAG!
MAG!
KBAM
KATATAK
SHAYMIN, YOU'RE AMAZING!
PIKA.
PI...
PIP !!
ZOM
MII?!
WHAT ?!

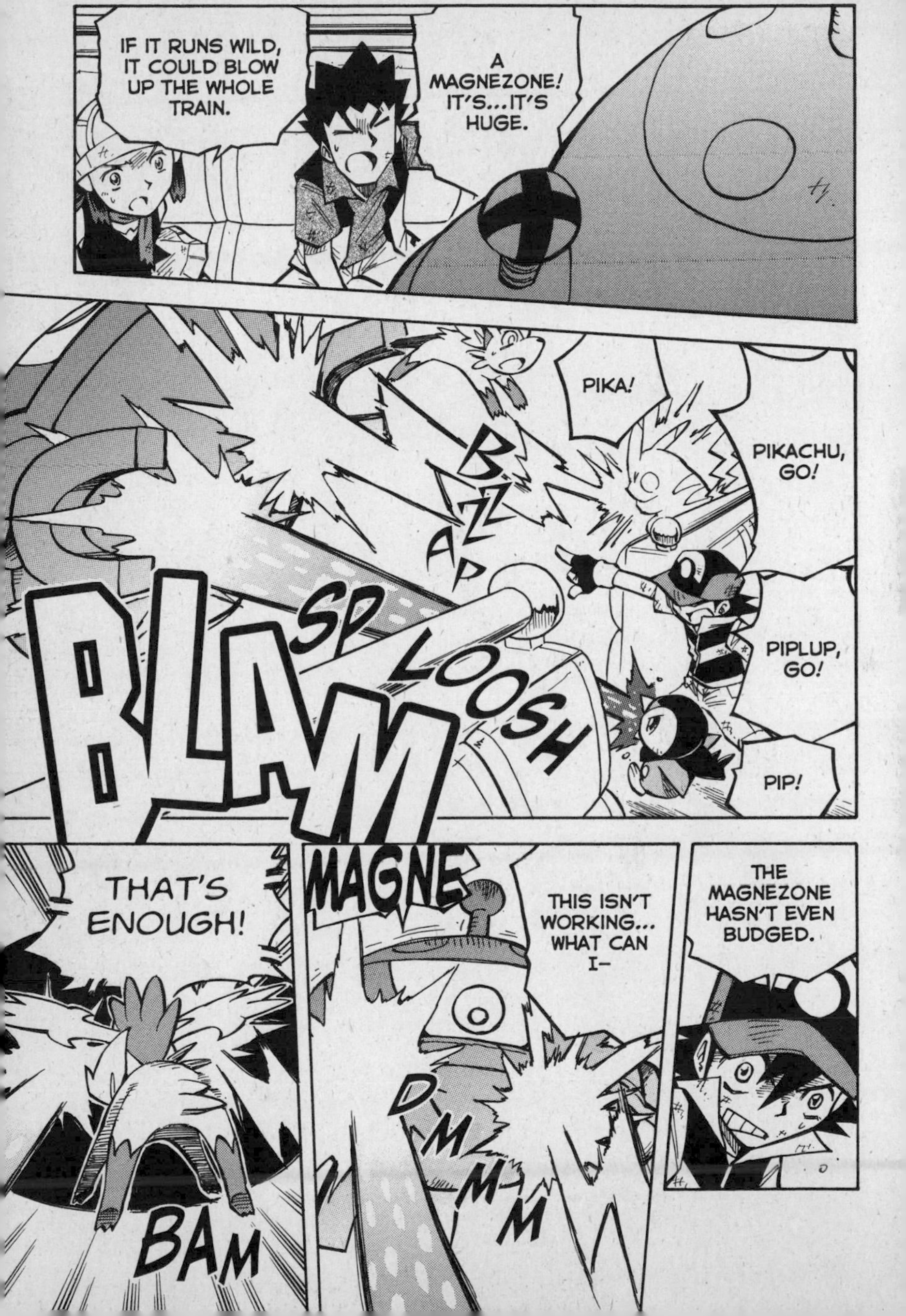
A MAGNEZONE! IT'S...IT'S HUGE.
IF IT RUNS WILD, IT COULD BLOW UP THE WHOLE TRAIN.
PIKA!
PIKACHU, GO!
BZZAP
PIPLUP, GO!
PIP!
SPLOOSH
BLAM
THE MAGNEZONE HASN'T EVEN BUDGED.
THIS ISN'T WORKING... WHAT CAN I–
MAGNE
DMMMM
THAT'S ENOUGH!
BAM

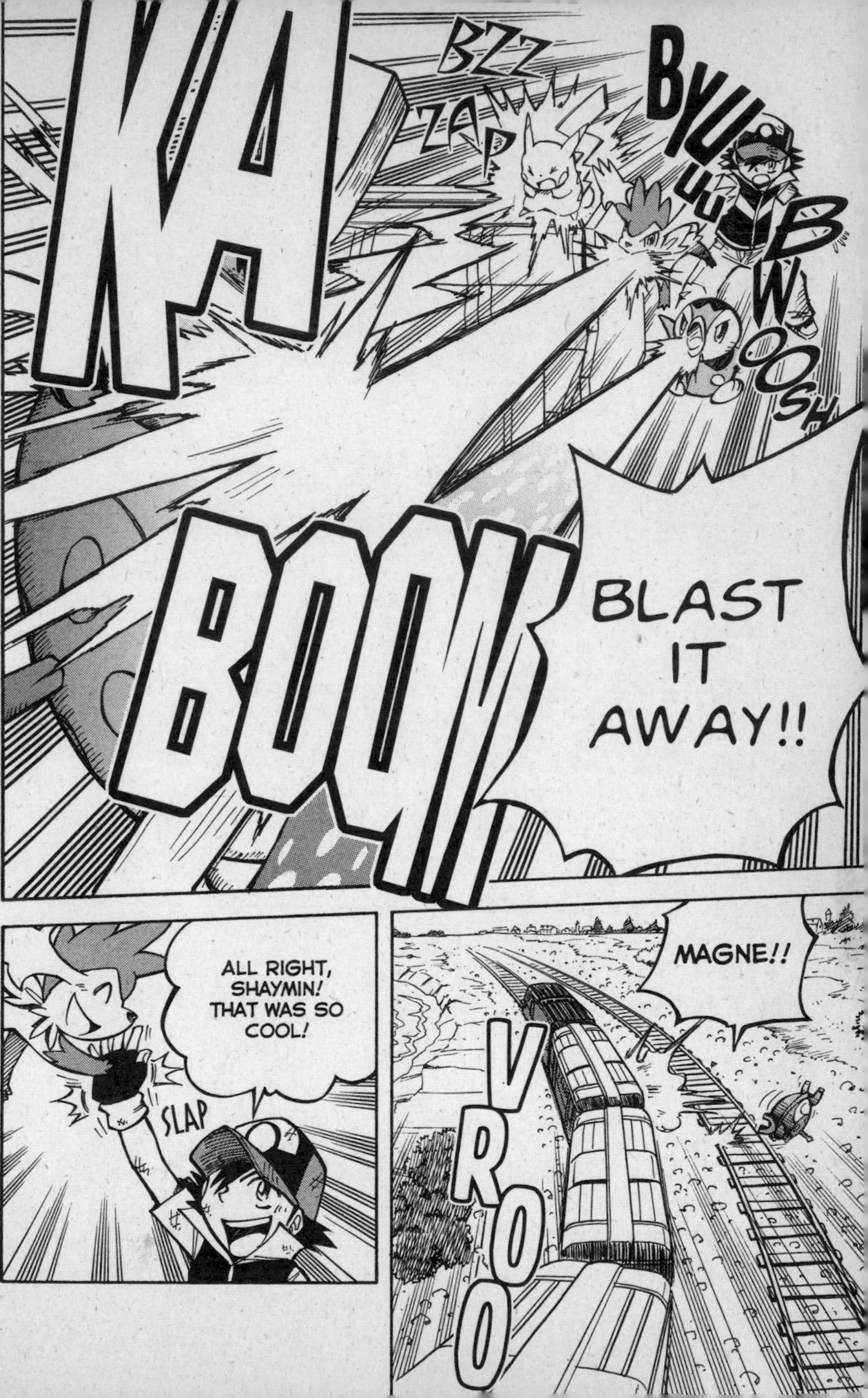
BYUUUU
BWOOOSH
BZZZ
ZAP
KA
BLAST IT AWAY!!
BOOM
MAGNE!!
VROOO
ALL RIGHT, SHAYMIN! THAT WAS SO COOL!
SLAP

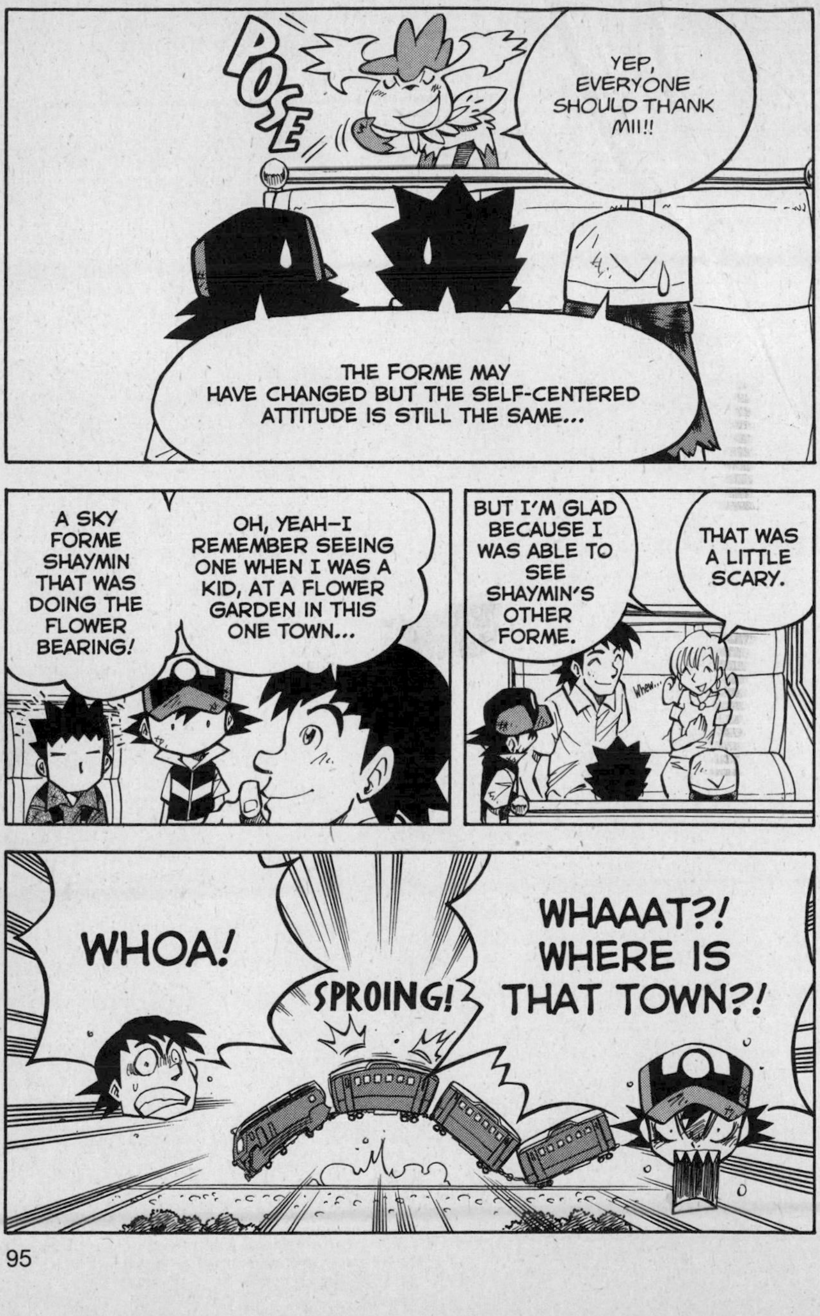
YEP, EVERYONE SHOULD THANK MII!!
POSE
THE FORME MAY HAVE CHANGED BUT THE SELF-CENTERED ATTITUDE IS STILL THE SAME...
THAT WAS A LITTLE SCARY.
BUT I'M GLAD BECAUSE I WAS ABLE TO SEE SHAYMIN'S OTHER FORME.
Whew...
OH, YEAH—I REMEMBER SEEING ONE WHEN I WAS A KID, AT A FLOWER GARDEN IN THIS ONE TOWN...
A SKY FORME SHAYMIN THAT WAS DOING THE FLOWER BEARING!
WHAAAT?! WHERE IS THAT TOWN?!
SPROING!
WHOA!

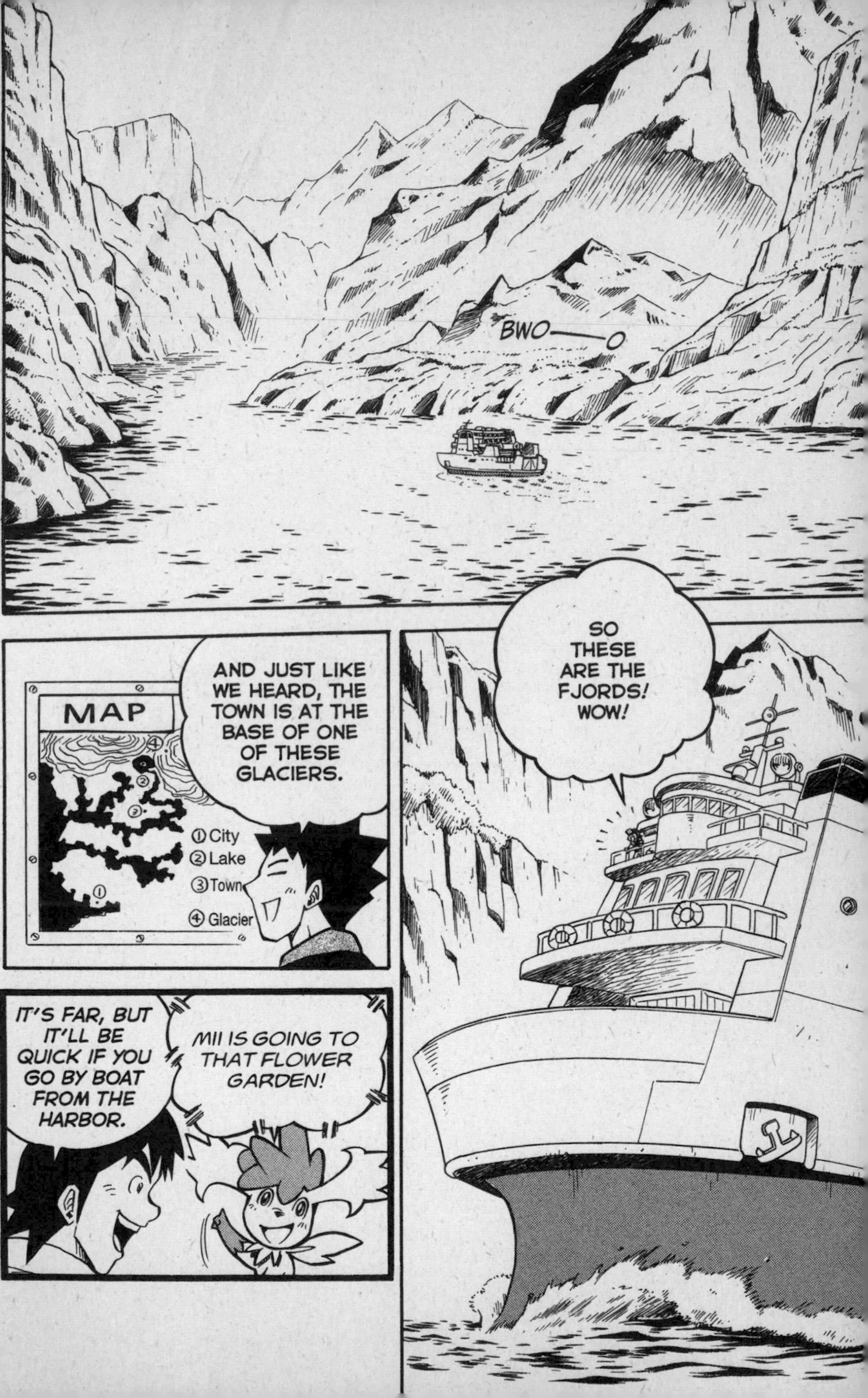
BWO—O
SO THESE ARE THE FJORDS! WOW!
AND JUST LIKE WE HEARD, THE TOWN IS AT THE BASE OF ONE OF THESE GLACIERS.
MAP
① City
② Lake
③ Town
④ Glacier
MII IS GOING TO THAT FLOWER GARDEN!
IT'S FAR, BUT IT'LL BE QUICK IF YOU GO BY BOAT FROM THE HARBOR.

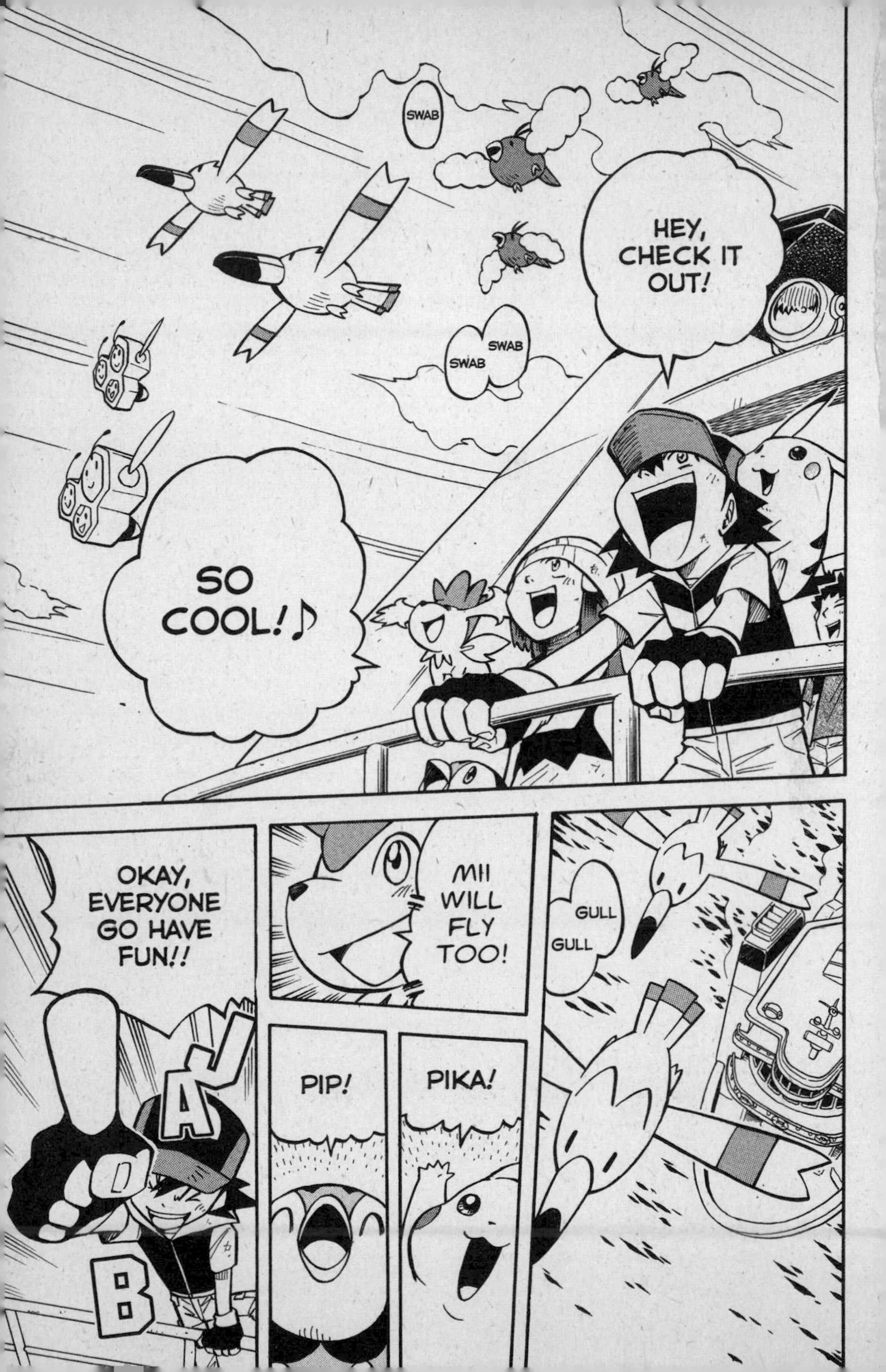

HEY, CHECK IT OUT!
SWAB
SWAB SWAB
SO COOL!♪
GULL GULL
MII WILL FLY TOO!
PIKA!
PIP!
OKAY, EVERYONE GO HAVE FUN!!

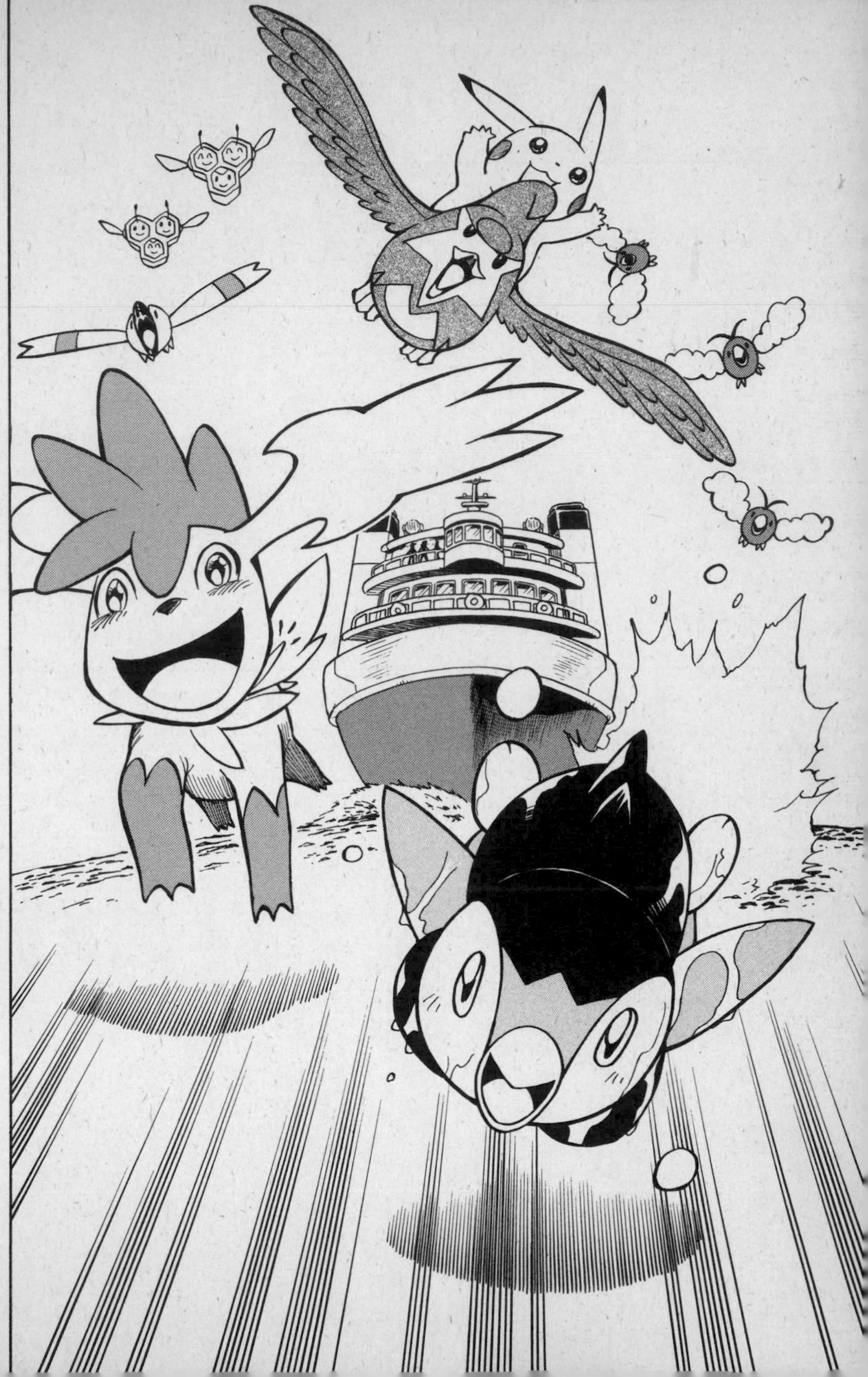

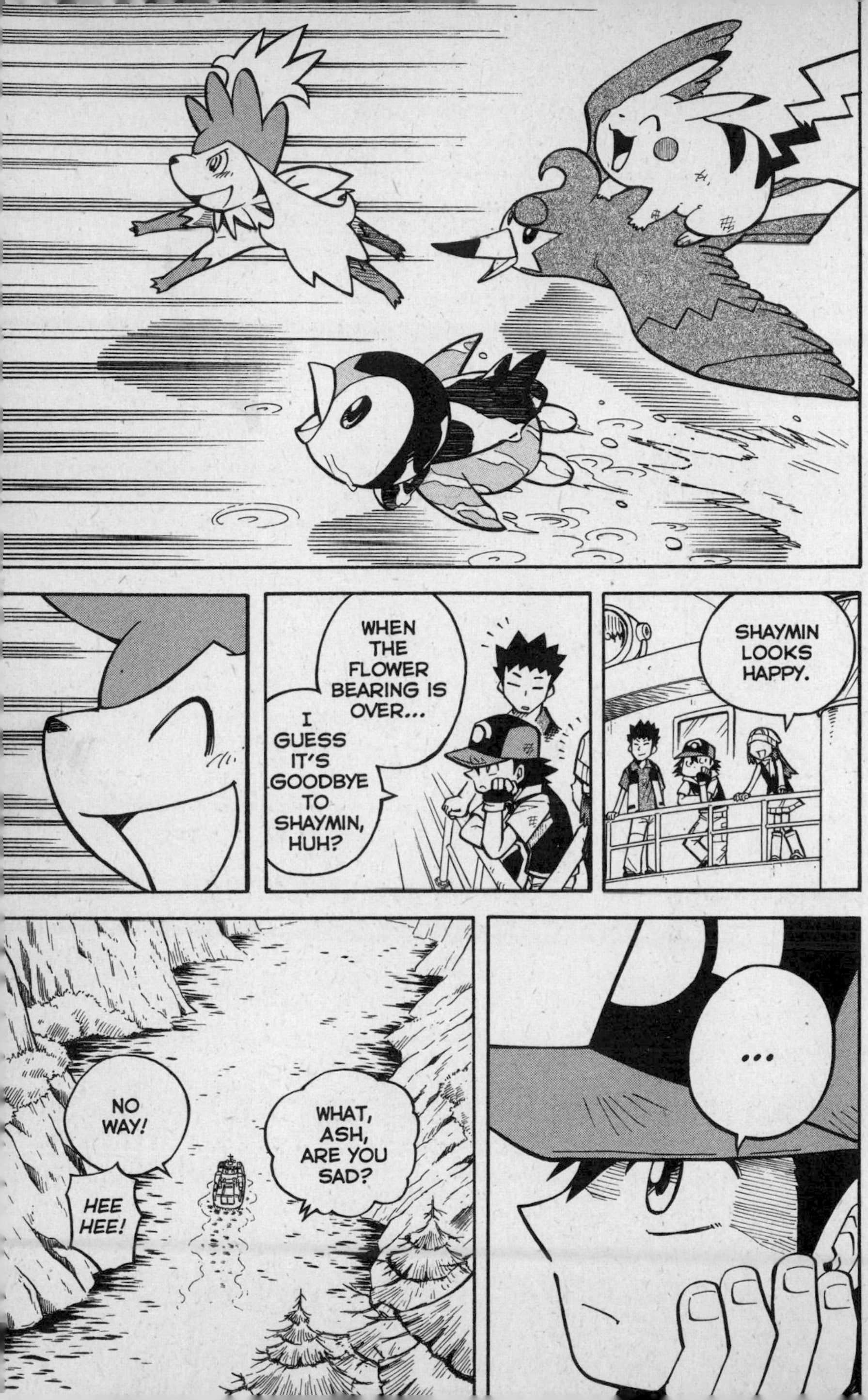
SHAYMIN LOOKS HAPPY.
WHEN THE FLOWER BEARING IS OVER...
I GUESS IT'S GOODBYE TO SHAYMIN, HUH?
...
WHAT, ASH, ARE YOU SAD?
NO WAY!
HEE HEE!

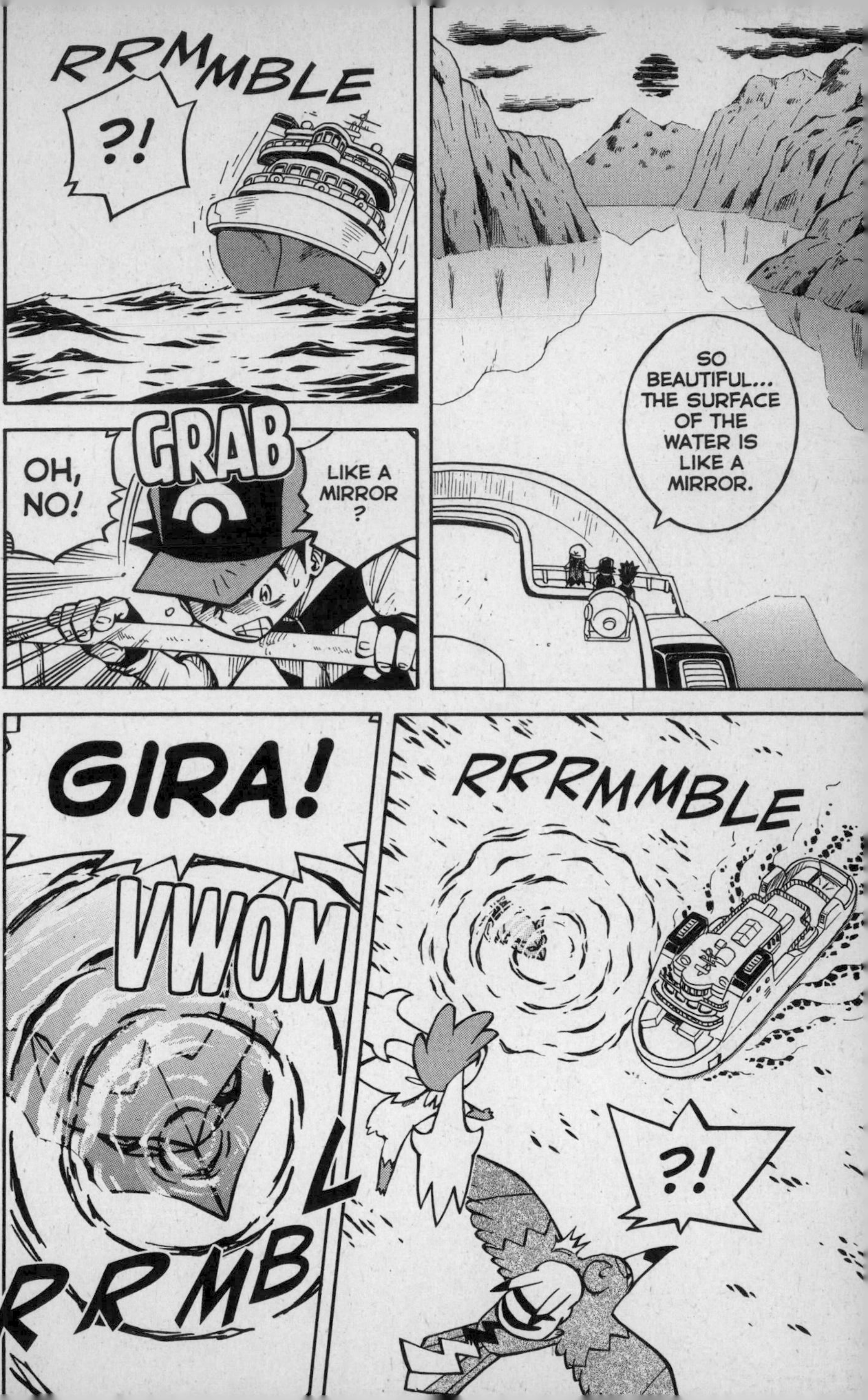
SO BEAUTIFUL... THE SURFACE OF THE WATER IS LIKE A MIRROR.
RRMMBLE
?!
LIKE A MIRROR ?
GRAB
OH, NO!
RRRMMBLE
?!
GIRA!
VWOM
RRMBL

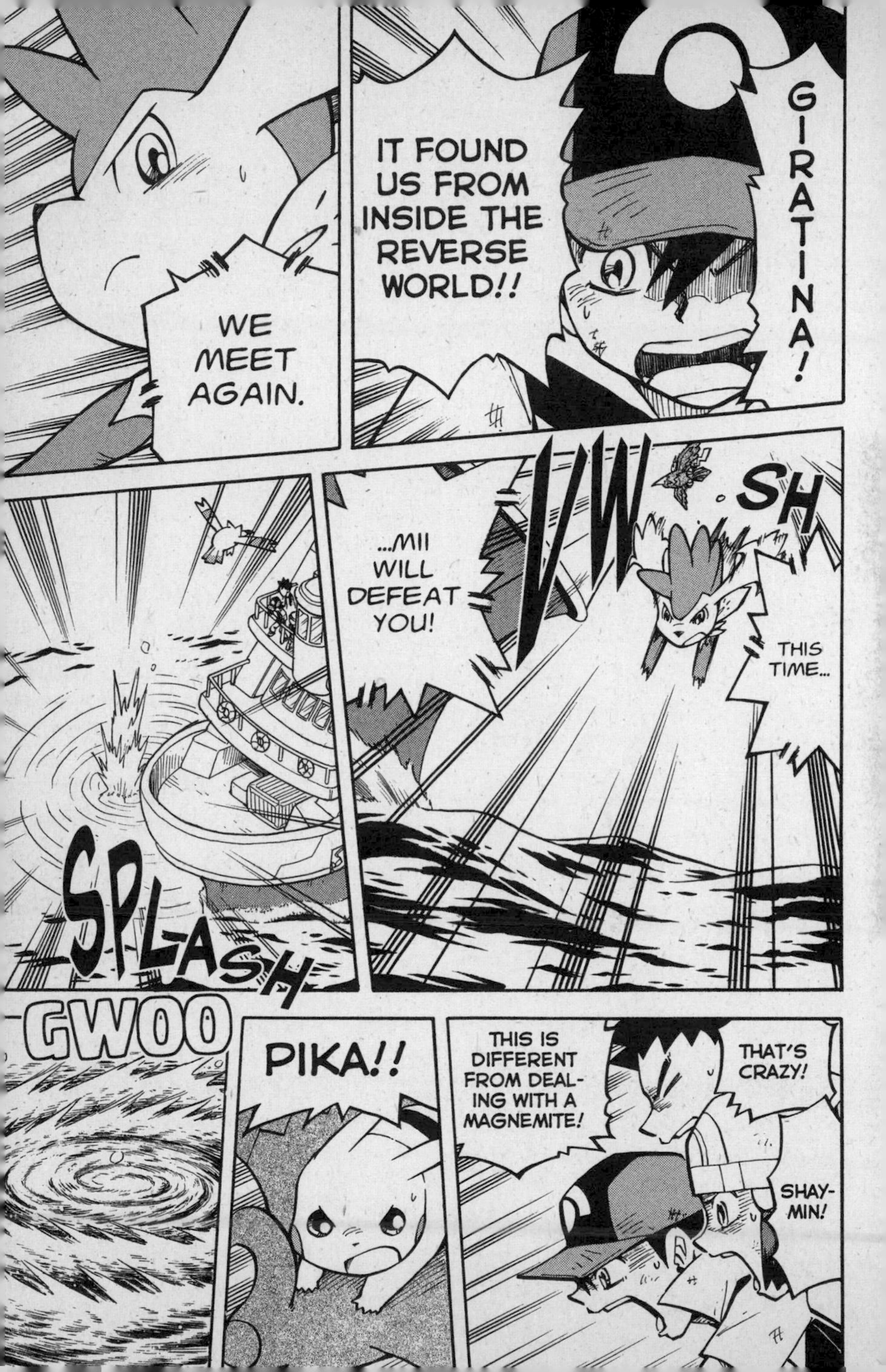
GIRATINA!
IT FOUND US FROM INSIDE THE REVERSE WORLD!!
WE MEET AGAIN.
VW
SH
THIS TIME...
...MII WILL DEFEAT YOU!
SPLASH
THAT'S CRAZY!
THIS IS DIFFERENT FROM DEALING WITH A MAGNEMITE!
SHAY-MIN!
PIKA!!
GWOO

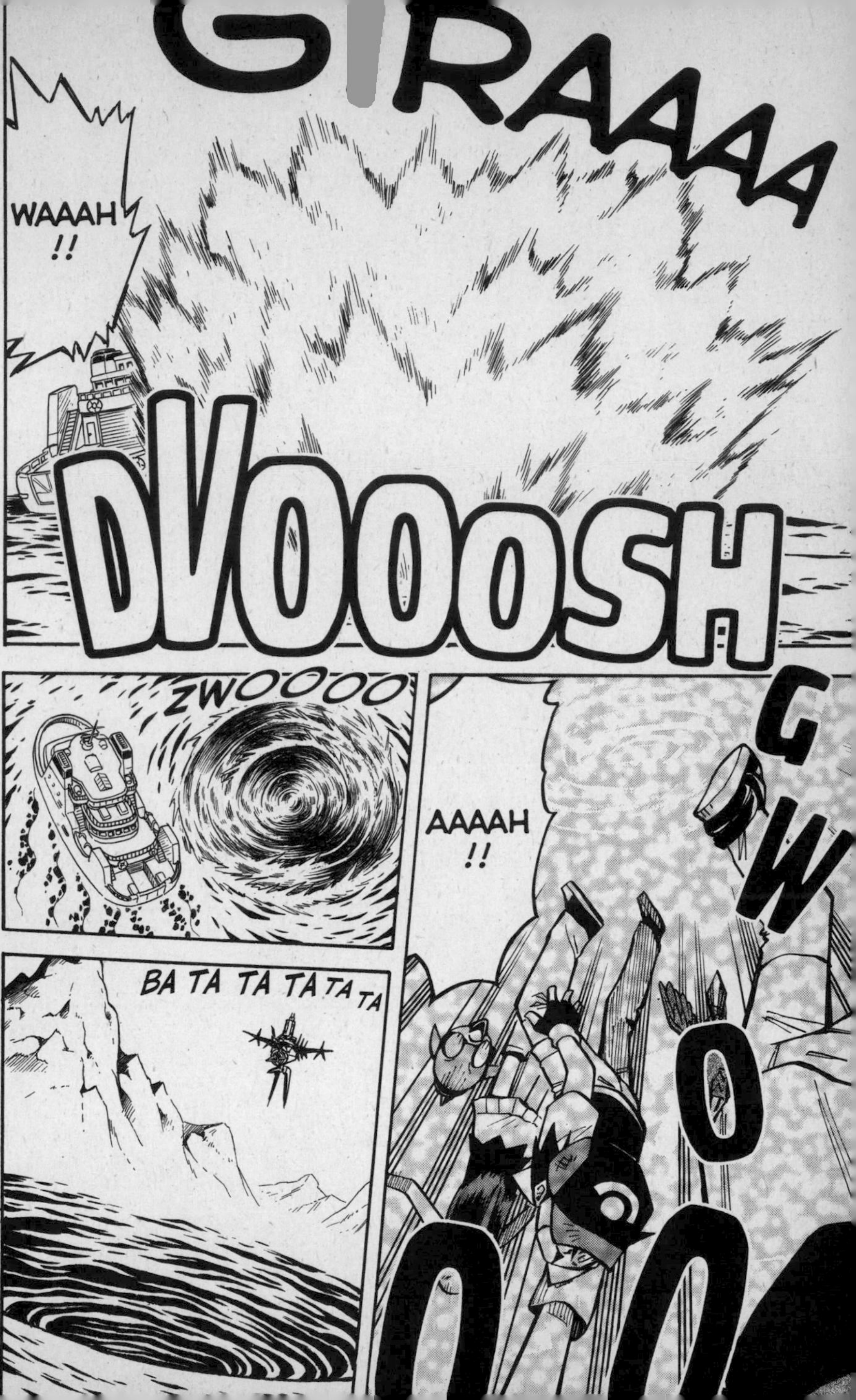
GRAAAA
WAAAH!!
DVOOOSH
AAAAH!!
GWOOO
ZWOOOO
BA TA TA TA TA TA

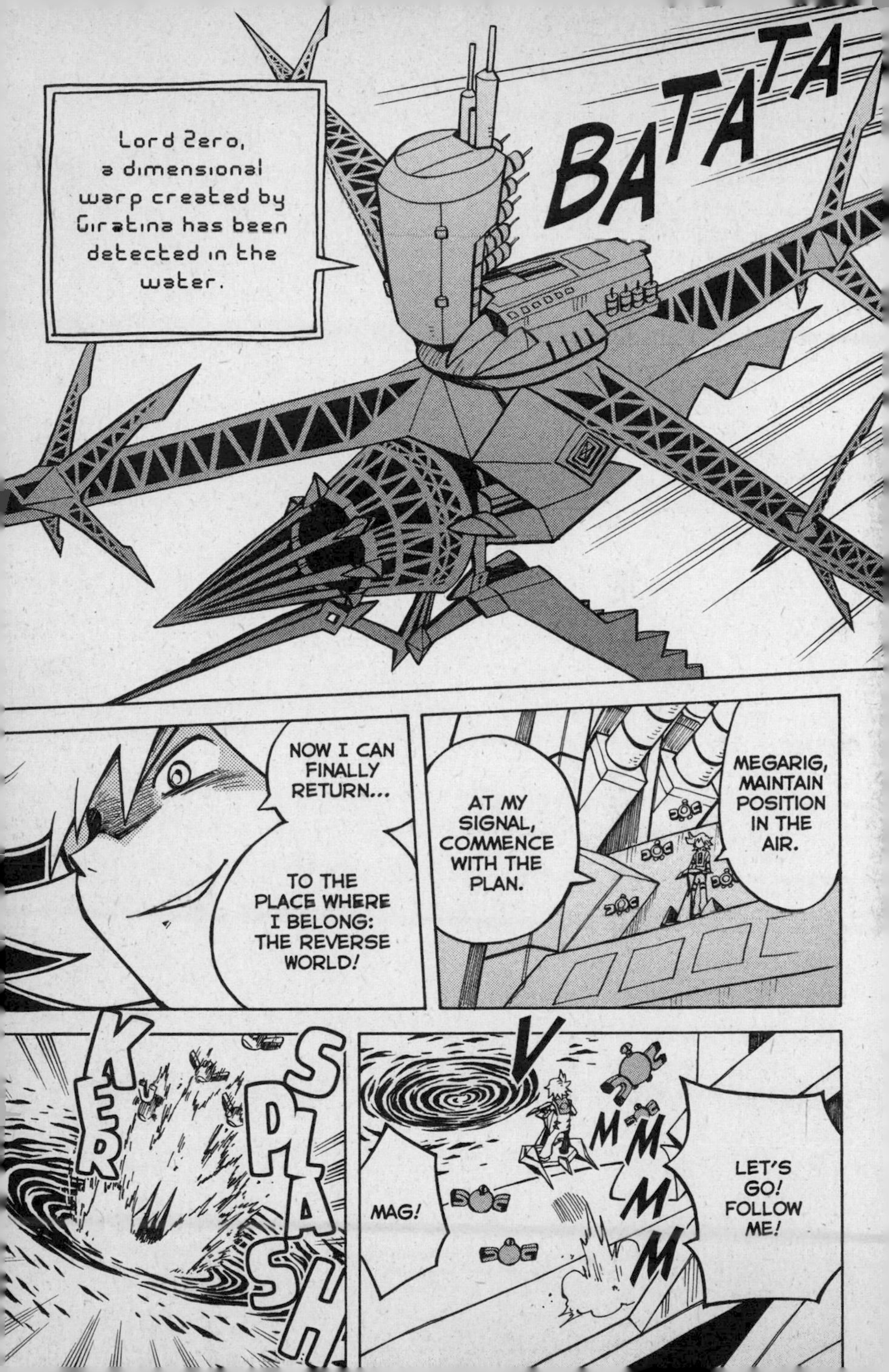
BATATA
Lord Zero, a dimensional warp created by Giratina has been detected in the water.
MEGARIG, MAINTAIN POSITION IN THE AIR.
AT MY SIGNAL, COMMENCE WITH THE PLAN.
NOW I CAN FINALLY RETURN...
TO THE PLACE WHERE I BELONG: THE REVERSE WORLD!
V
LET'S GO! FOLLOW ME!
MMMMM
MAG!
KERSPLASH

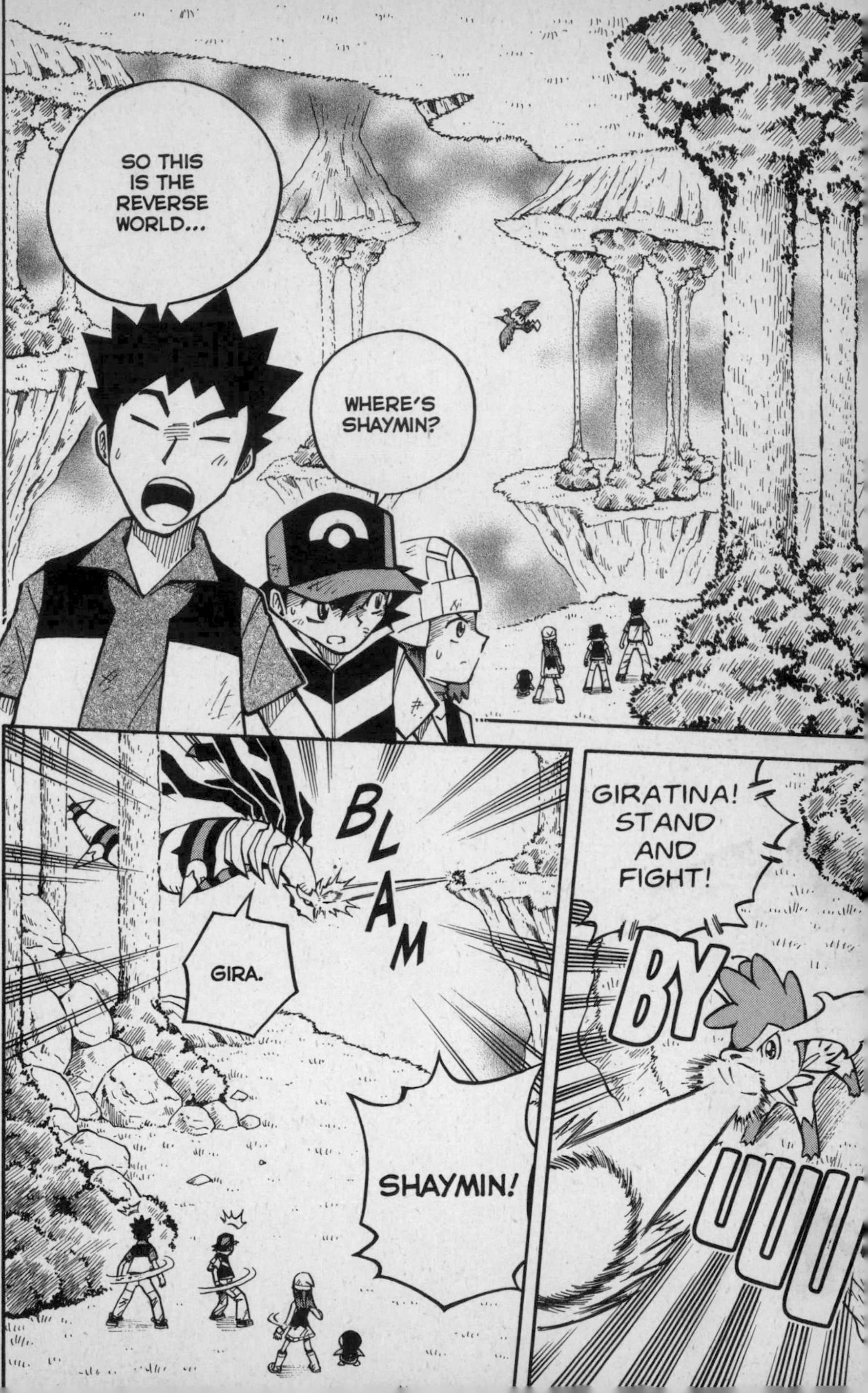
SO THIS IS THE REVERSE WORLD...
WHERE'S SHAYMIN?
GIRATINA! STAND AND FIGHT!
BLAM
GIRA.
SHAYMIN!
BYUUU

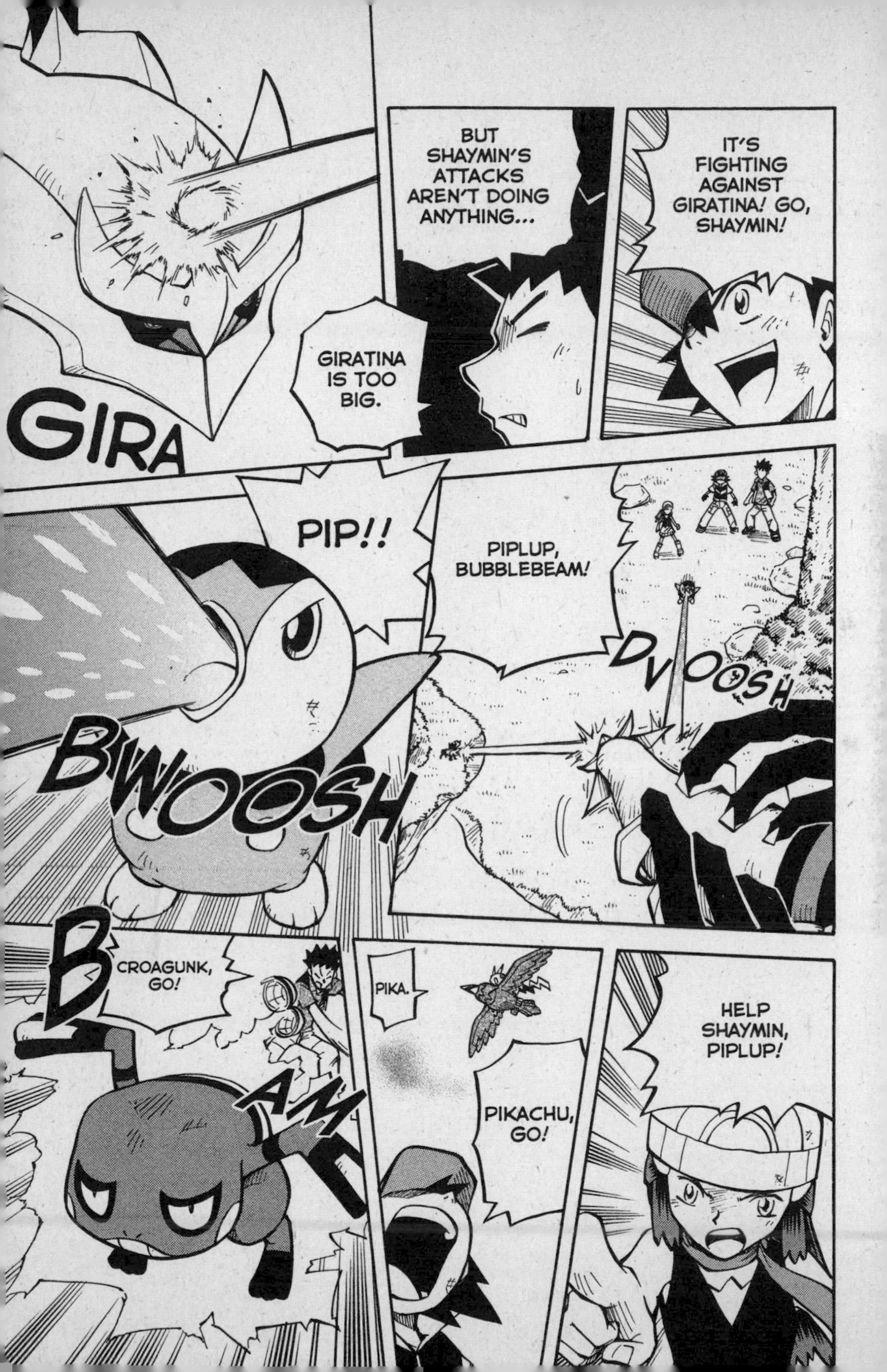
IT'S FIGHTING AGAINST GIRATINA! GO, SHAYMIN!
BUT SHAYMIN'S ATTACKS AREN'T DOING ANYTHING...
GIRATINA IS TOO BIG.
GIRA
PIPLUP, BUBBLEBEAM!
DVOOSH
PIP!!
BWOOSH
HELP SHAYMIN, PIPLUP!
PIKACHU, GO!
PIKA.
CROAGUNK, GO!
BAM

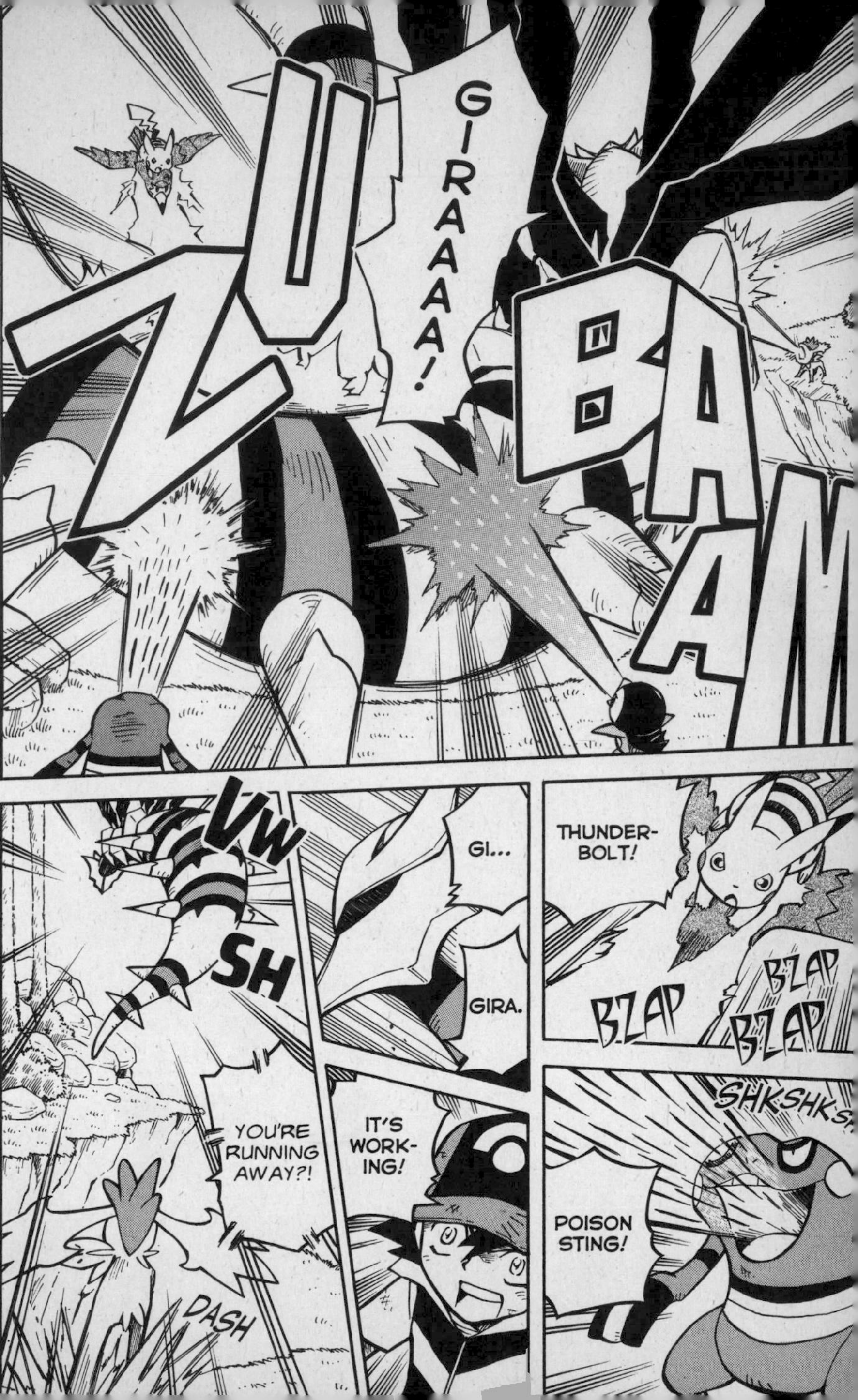
BAM
GIRAAAA!
ZU
THUNDER-BOLT!
BZAP
BZAP
BZAP
GI...
GIRA.
SHKSHK
POISON STING!
IT'S WORK-ING!
VW
SH
YOU'RE RUNNING AWAY?!
DASH

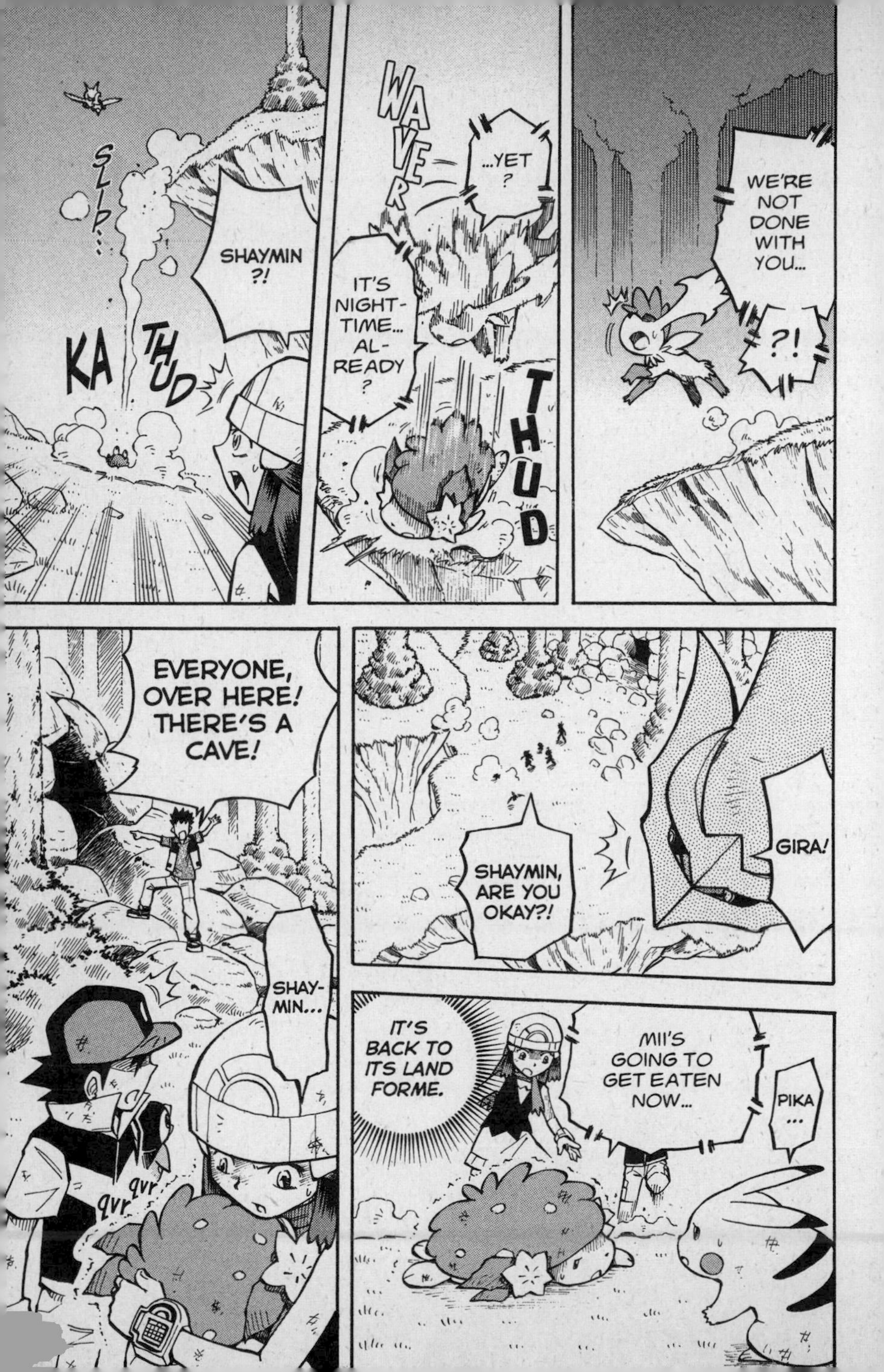
WE'RE NOT DONE WITH YOU...
?!
WAVER
...YET?
IT'S NIGHT-TIME... AL-READY?
THUD
SLIP...
SHAYMIN?!
KA THUD
GIRA!
SHAYMIN, ARE YOU OKAY?!
PIKA...
MII'S GOING TO GET EATEN NOW...
IT'S BACK TO ITS LAND FORME.
EVERYONE, OVER HERE! THERE'S A CAVE!
SHAY-MIN...
qvr
qvr

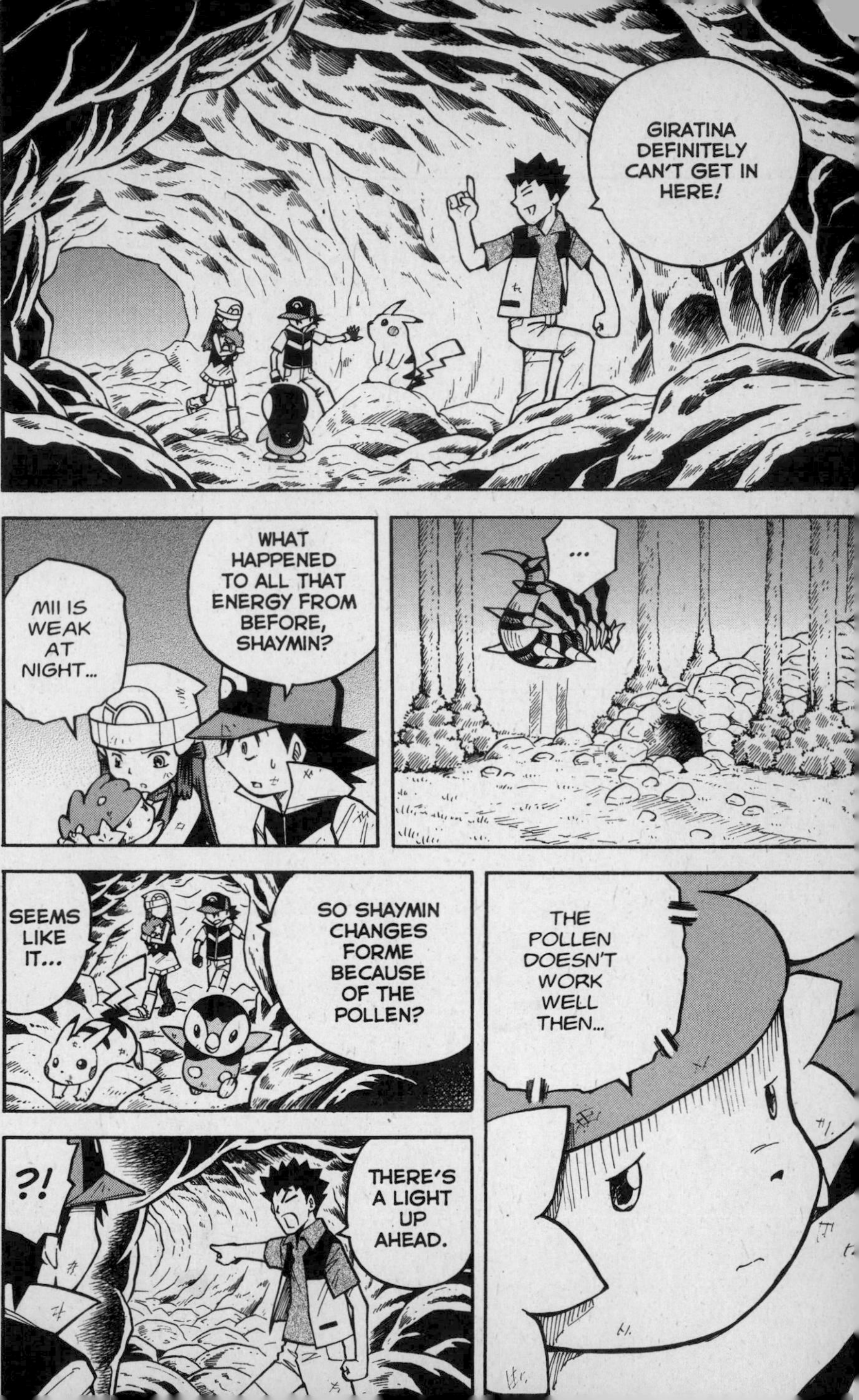
GIRATINA DEFINITELY CAN'T GET IN HERE!
...
WHAT HAPPENED TO ALL THAT ENERGY FROM BEFORE, SHAYMIN?
MII IS WEAK AT NIGHT...
THE POLLEN DOESN'T WORK WELL THEN...
SO SHAYMIN CHANGES FORME BECAUSE OF THE POLLEN?
SEEMS LIKE IT...
THERE'S A LIGHT UP AHEAD.
?!

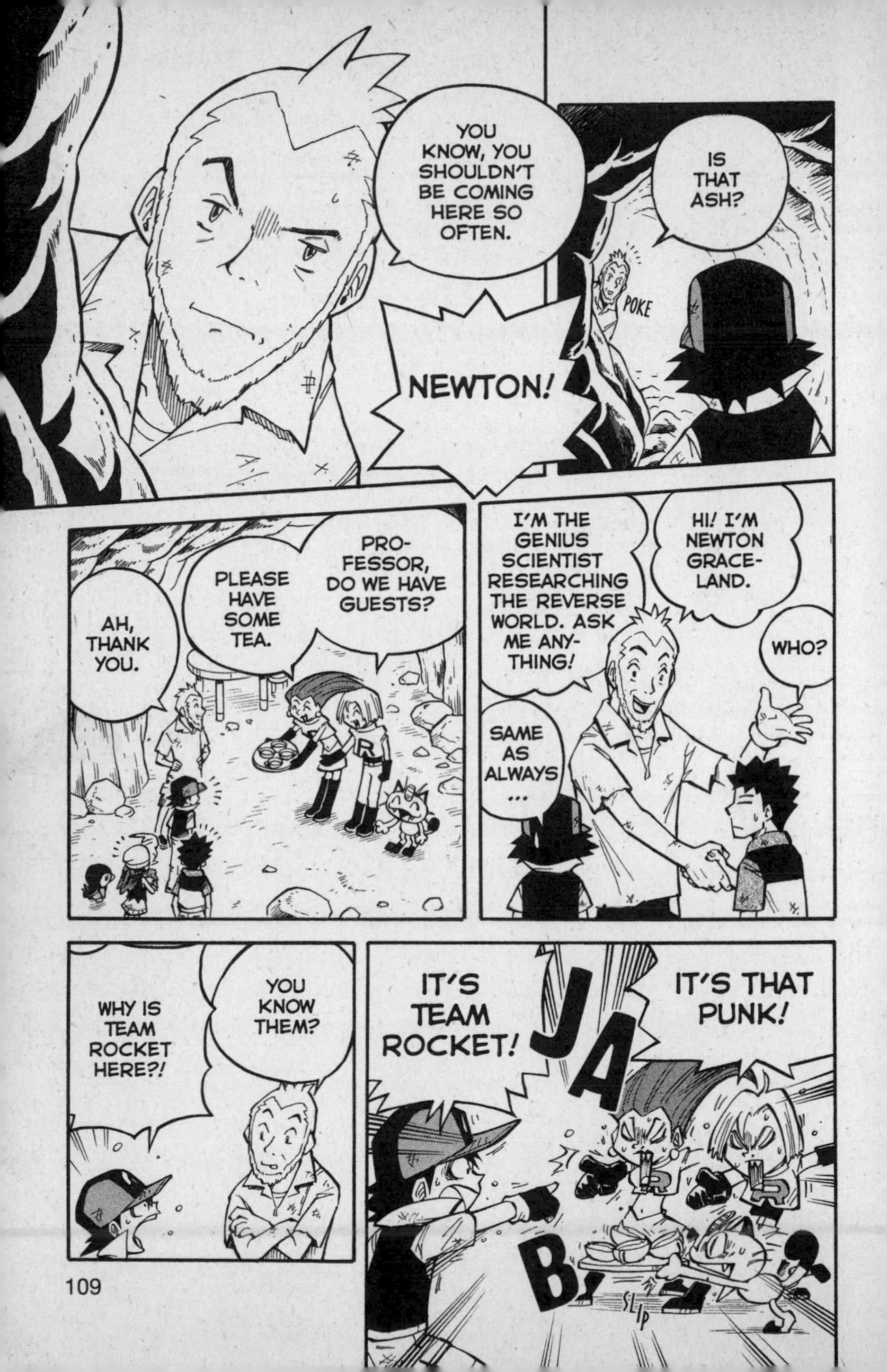
IS THAT ASH?
POKE
NEWTON!
YOU KNOW, YOU SHOULDN'T BE COMING HERE SO OFTEN.
HI! I'M NEWTON GRACE-LAND.
I'M THE GENIUS SCIENTIST RESEARCHING THE REVERSE WORLD. ASK ME ANY-THING!
WHO?
SAME AS ALWAYS...
PRO-FESSOR, DO WE HAVE GUESTS?
PLEASE HAVE SOME TEA.
AH, THANK YOU.
IT'S THAT PUNK!
IT'S TEAM ROCKET!
JAB
SLIP
YOU KNOW THEM?
WHY IS TEAM ROCKET HERE?!

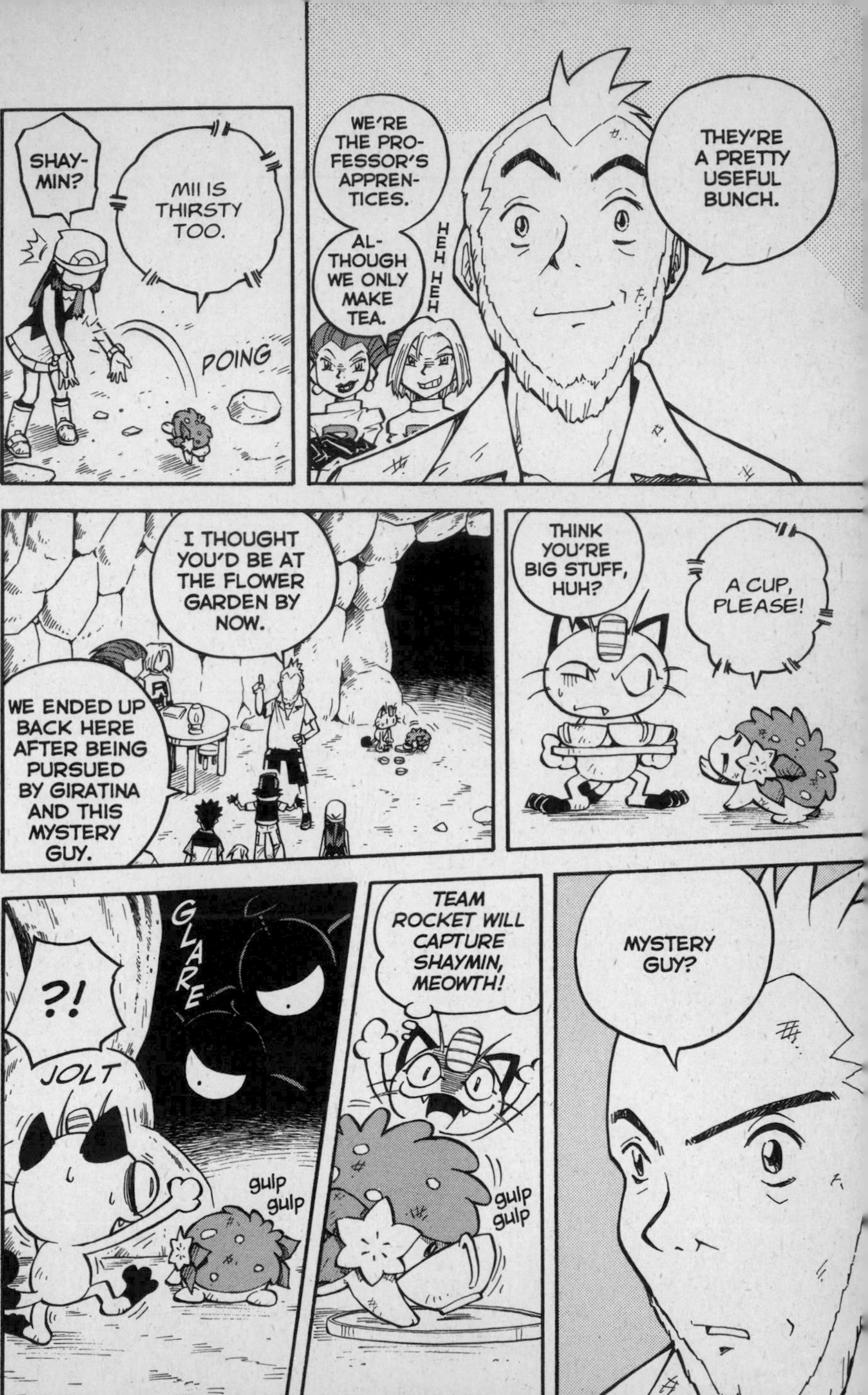
THEY'RE A PRETTY USEFUL BUNCH.
WE'RE THE PROFESSOR'S APPRENTICES.
HEH HEH
ALTHOUGH WE ONLY MAKE TEA.
MII IS THIRSTY TOO.
SHAYMIN?
POING
A CUP, PLEASE!
THINK YOU'RE BIG STUFF, HUH?
I THOUGHT YOU'D BE AT THE FLOWER GARDEN BY NOW.
WE ENDED UP BACK HERE AFTER BEING PURSUED BY GIRATINA AND THIS MYSTERY GUY.
MYSTERY GUY?
TEAM ROCKET WILL CAPTURE SHAYMIN, MEOWTH!
gulp gulp
GLARE
?!
JOLT
gulp gulp

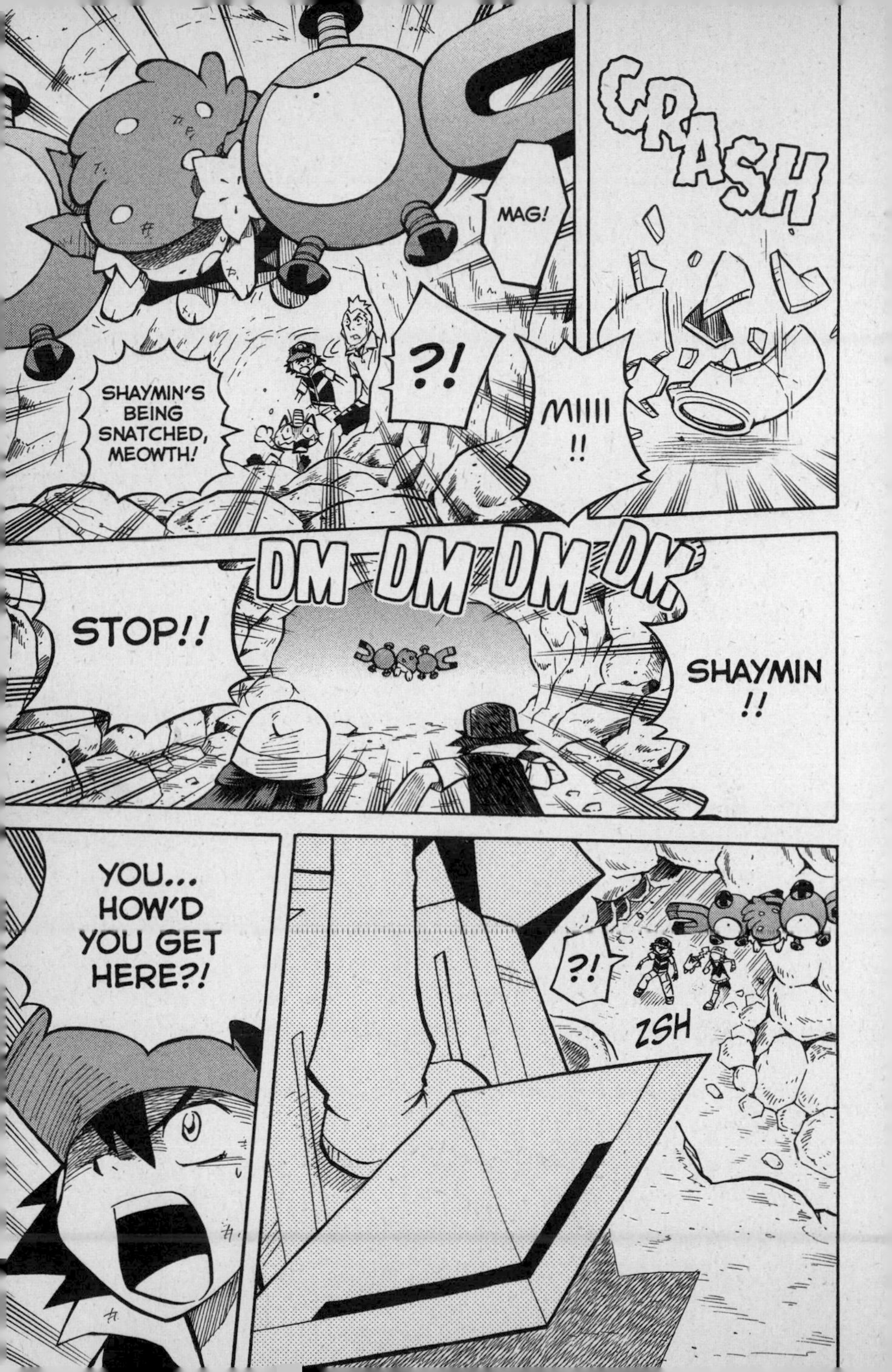
CRASH
MAG!
MIIII !!
?!
SHAYMIN'S BEING SNATCHED, MEOWTH!
DM DM DM DK
SHAYMIN !!
STOP!!
?!
ZSH
YOU... HOW'D YOU GET HERE?!

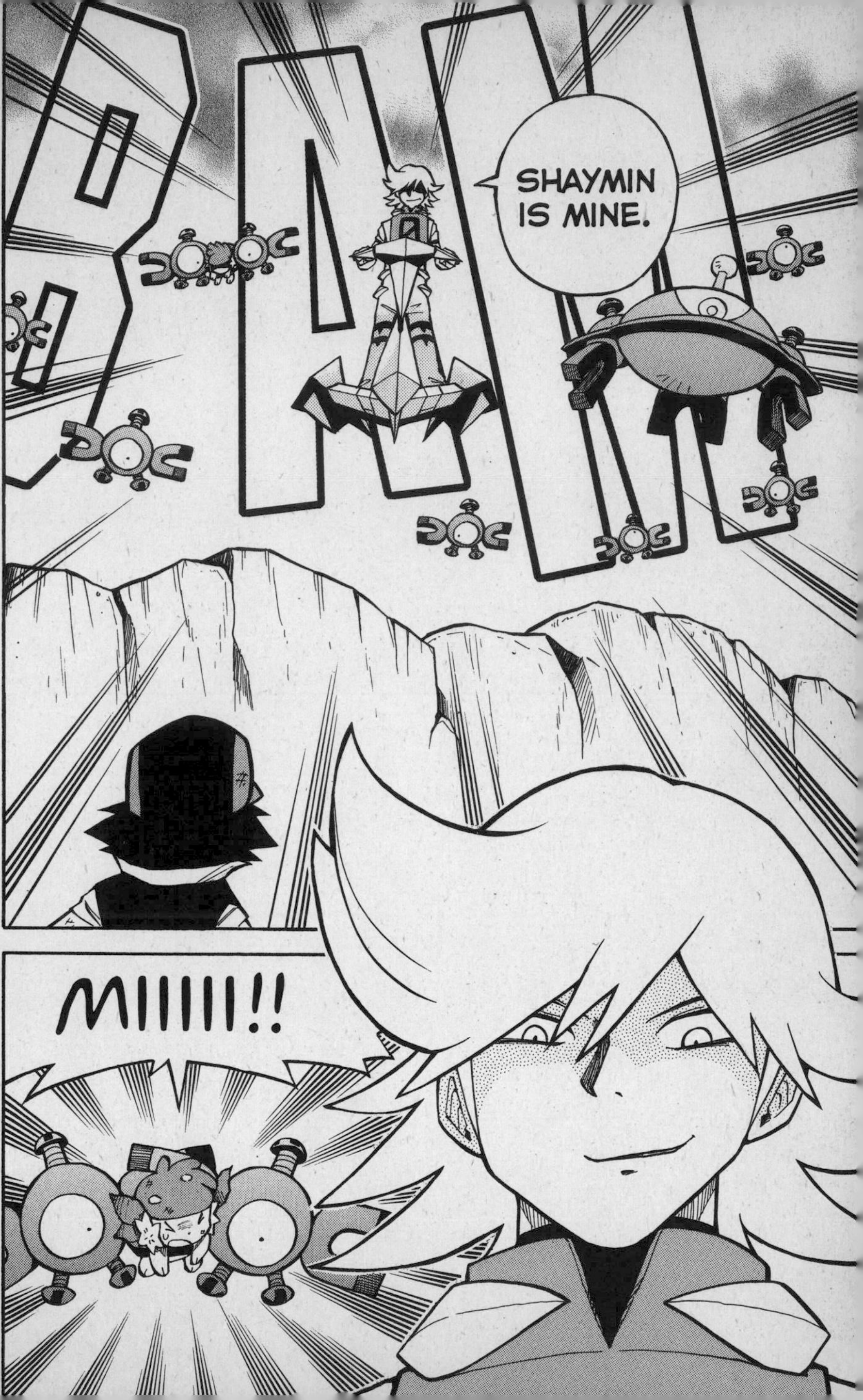
BAM
SHAYMIN IS MINE.
MIIIII!!

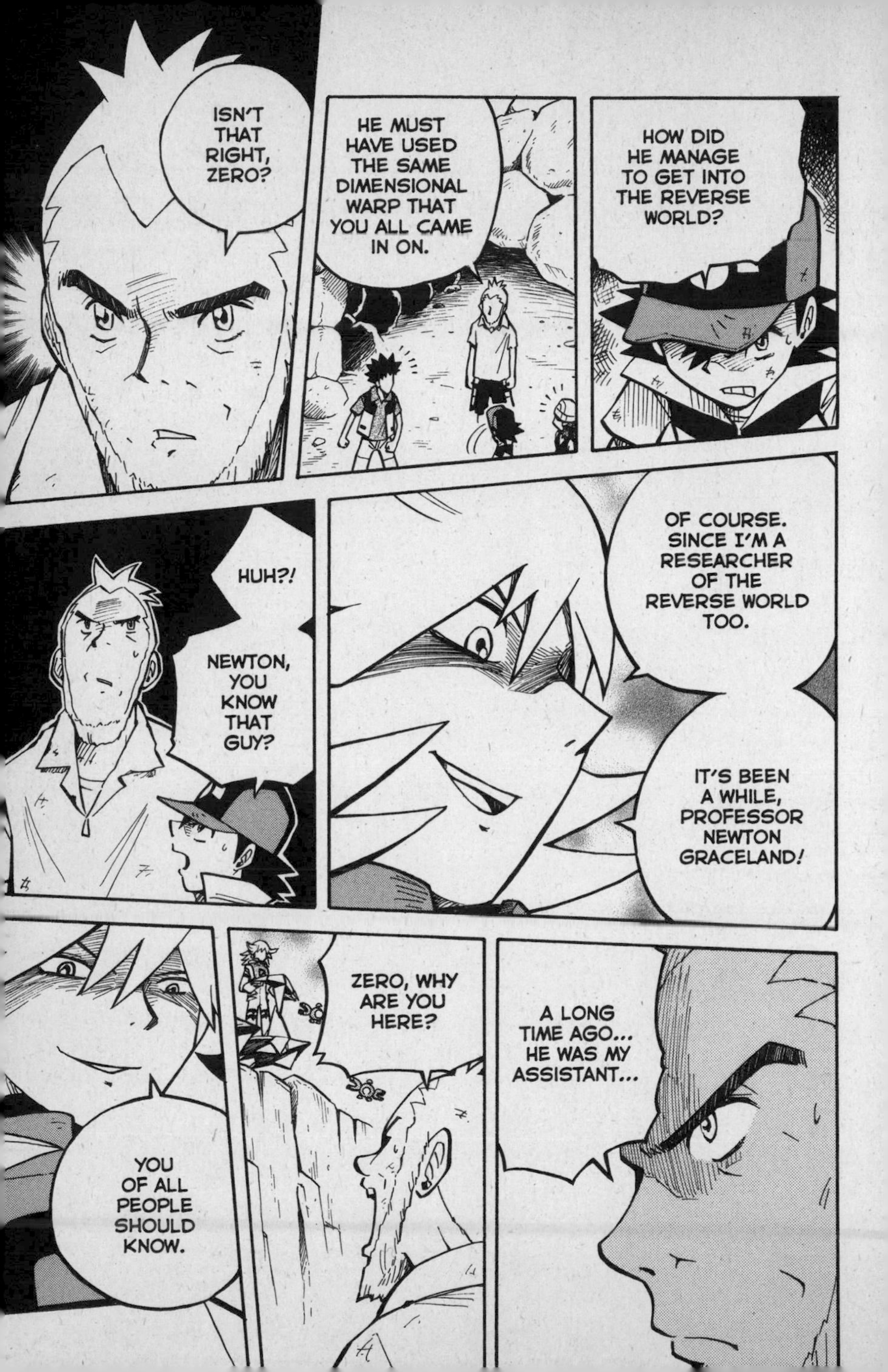
HOW DID HE MANAGE TO GET INTO THE REVERSE WORLD?
HE MUST HAVE USED THE SAME DIMENSIONAL WARP THAT YOU ALL CAME IN ON.
ISN'T THAT RIGHT, ZERO?
OF COURSE. SINCE I'M A RESEARCHER OF THE REVERSE WORLD TOO.
IT'S BEEN A WHILE, PROFESSOR NEWTON GRACELAND!
HUH?!
NEWTON, YOU KNOW THAT GUY?
A LONG TIME AGO... HE WAS MY ASSISTANT...
ZERO, WHY ARE YOU HERE?
YOU OF ALL PEOPLE SHOULD KNOW.

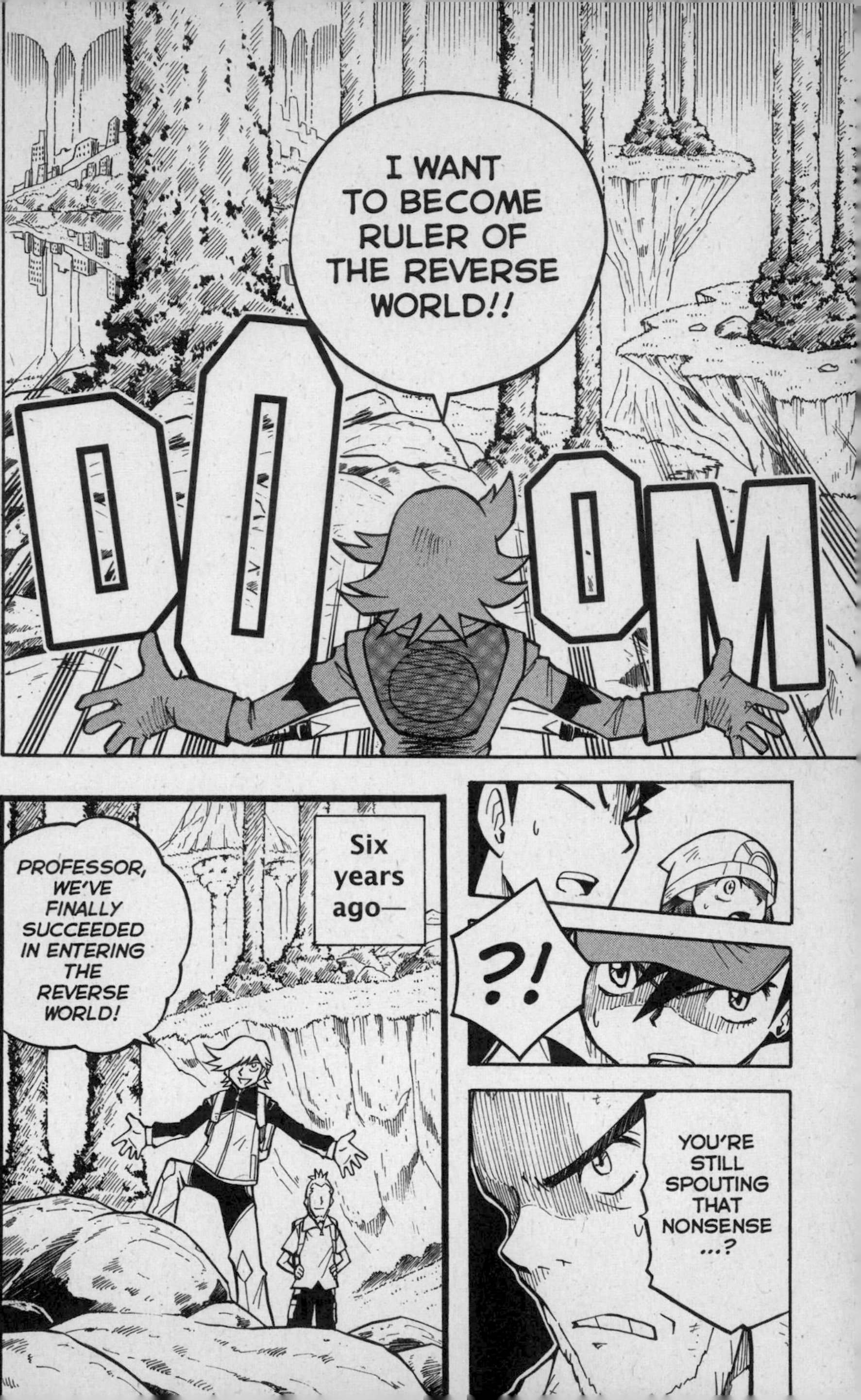
I WANT TO BECOME RULER OF THE REVERSE WORLD!!
DOOM
?!
YOU'RE STILL SPOUTING THAT NONSENSE ...?
Six years ago—
PROFESSOR, WE'VE FINALLY SUCCEEDED IN ENTERING THE REVERSE WORLD!

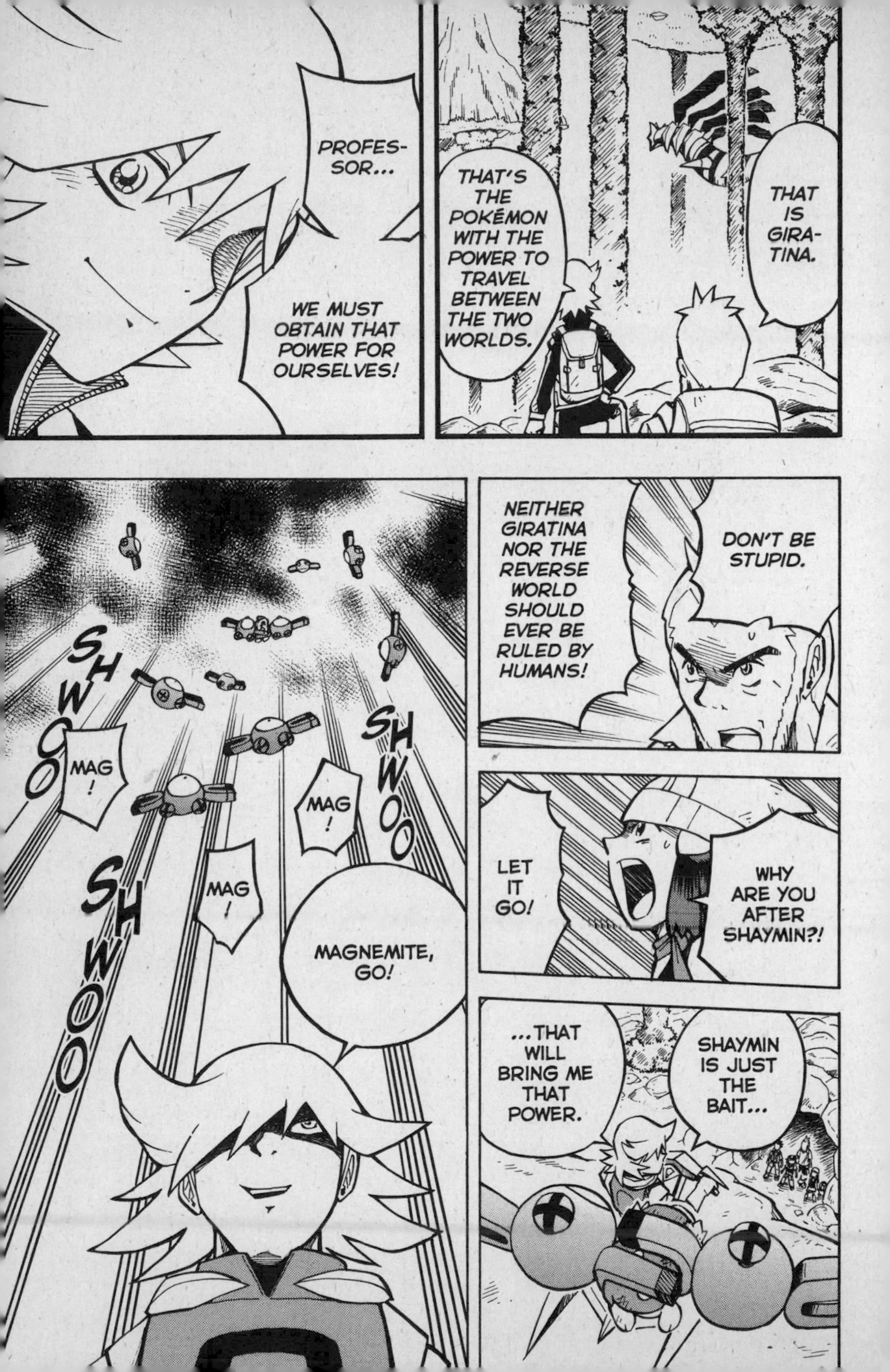
THAT IS GIRA-TINA.
THAT'S THE POKÉMON WITH THE POWER TO TRAVEL BETWEEN THE TWO WORLDS.
PROFES-SOR...
WE MUST OBTAIN THAT POWER FOR OURSELVES!
DON'T BE STUPID.
NEITHER GIRATINA NOR THE REVERSE WORLD SHOULD EVER BE RULED BY HUMANS!
WHY ARE YOU AFTER SHAYMIN?!
LET IT GO!
SHAYMIN IS JUST THE BAIT...
...THAT WILL BRING ME THAT POWER.
SHWOO
MAG!
SHWOO
MAG!
MAG!
SHWOOO
MAGNEMITE, GO!

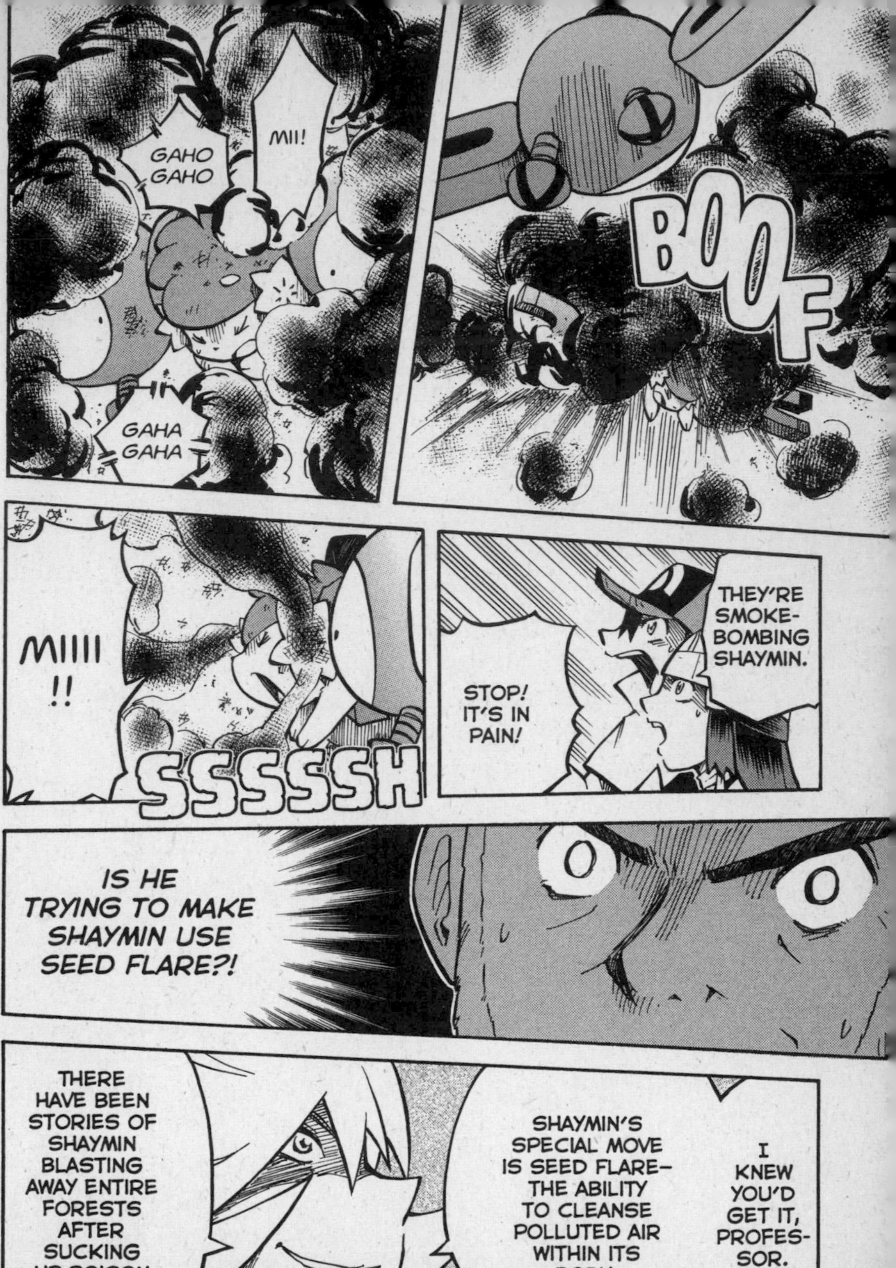
BOOF
MII!
GAHO GAHO
GAHA GAHA
THEY'RE SMOKE-BOMBING SHAYMIN.
STOP! IT'S IN PAIN!
MIIII!!
SSSSSH
IS HE TRYING TO MAKE SHAYMIN USE SEED FLARE?!
I KNEW YOU'D GET IT, PROFESSOR.
SHAYMIN'S SPECIAL MOVE IS SEED FLARE—THE ABILITY TO CLEANSE POLLUTED AIR WITHIN ITS BODY.
THERE HAVE BEEN STORIES OF SHAYMIN BLASTING AWAY ENTIRE FORESTS AFTER SUCKING UP POISON GAS.

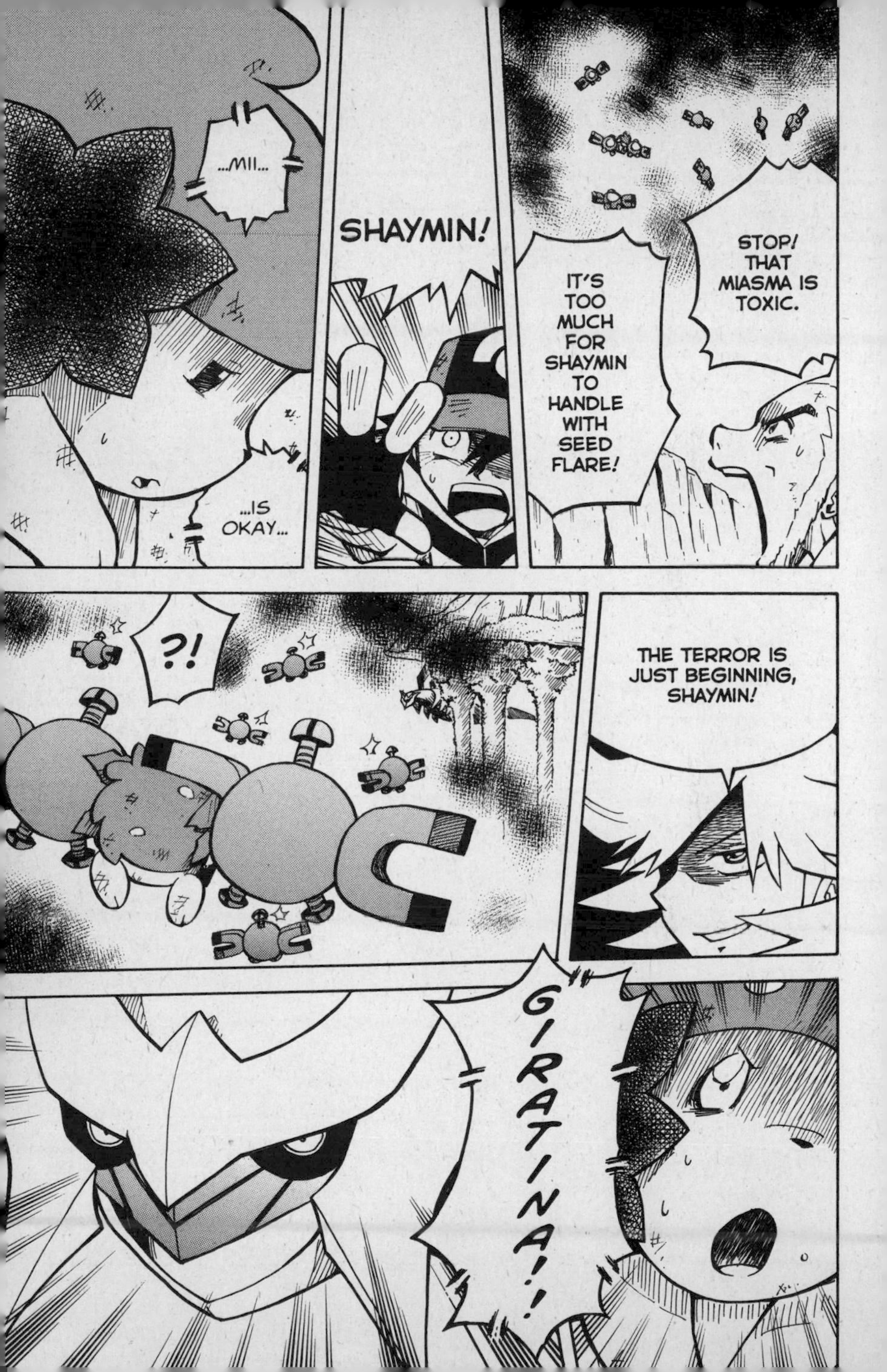
STOP! THAT MIASMA IS TOXIC.
IT'S TOO MUCH FOR SHAYMIN TO HANDLE WITH SEED FLARE!
SHAYMIN!
...MII...
...IS OKAY...
THE TERROR IS JUST BEGINNING, SHAYMIN!
?!
GIRATINA!!

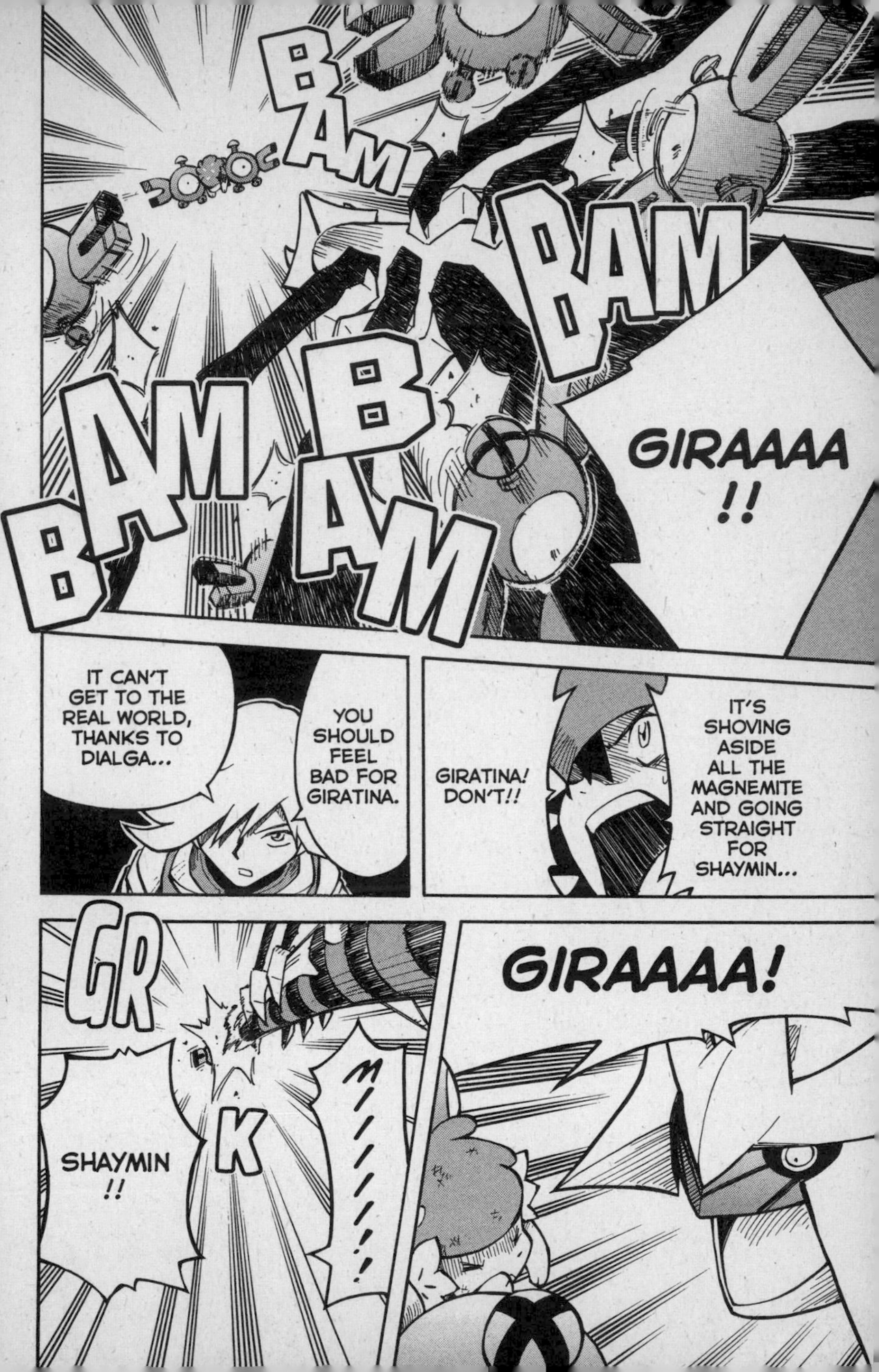
GIRAAAA !!
BAM
BAM
BAM
BAM
IT'S SHOVING ASIDE ALL THE MAGNEMITE AND GOING STRAIGHT FOR SHAYMIN...
GIRATINA! DON'T!!
YOU SHOULD FEEL BAD FOR GIRATINA.
IT CAN'T GET TO THE REAL WORLD, THANKS TO DIALGA...
GIRAAAA!
GRK
SHAYMIN !!

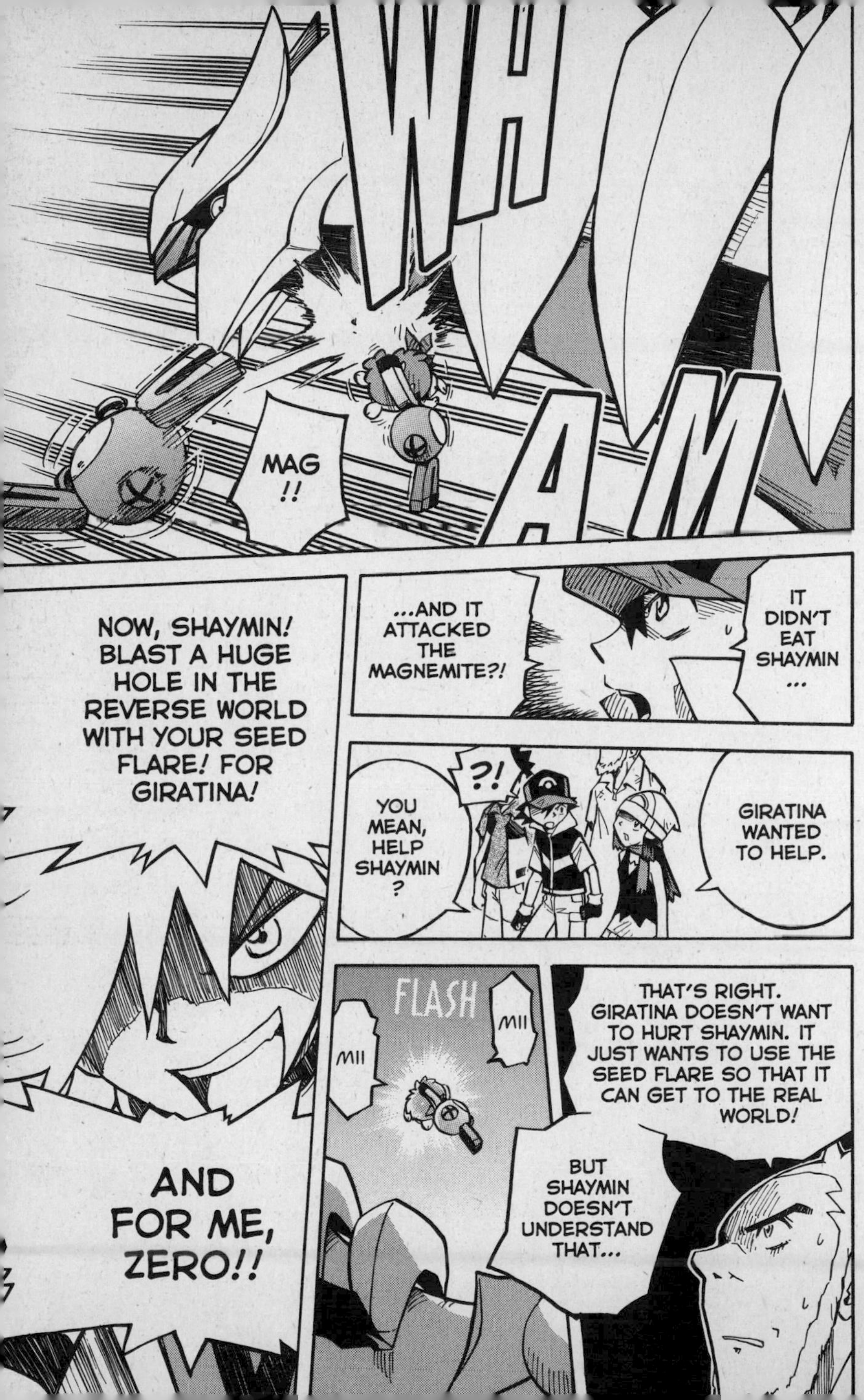
WHAM
MAG !!
IT DIDN'T EAT SHAYMIN...
...AND IT ATTACKED THE MAGNEMITE?!
GIRATINA WANTED TO HELP.
?!
YOU MEAN, HELP SHAYMIN?
THAT'S RIGHT. GIRATINA DOESN'T WANT TO HURT SHAYMIN. IT JUST WANTS TO USE THE SEED FLARE SO THAT IT CAN GET TO THE REAL WORLD!
FLASH
MII
MII
BUT SHAYMIN DOESN'T UNDERSTAND THAT...
NOW, SHAYMIN! BLAST A HUGE HOLE IN THE REVERSE WORLD WITH YOUR SEED FLARE! FOR GIRATINA!
AND FOR ME, ZERO!!

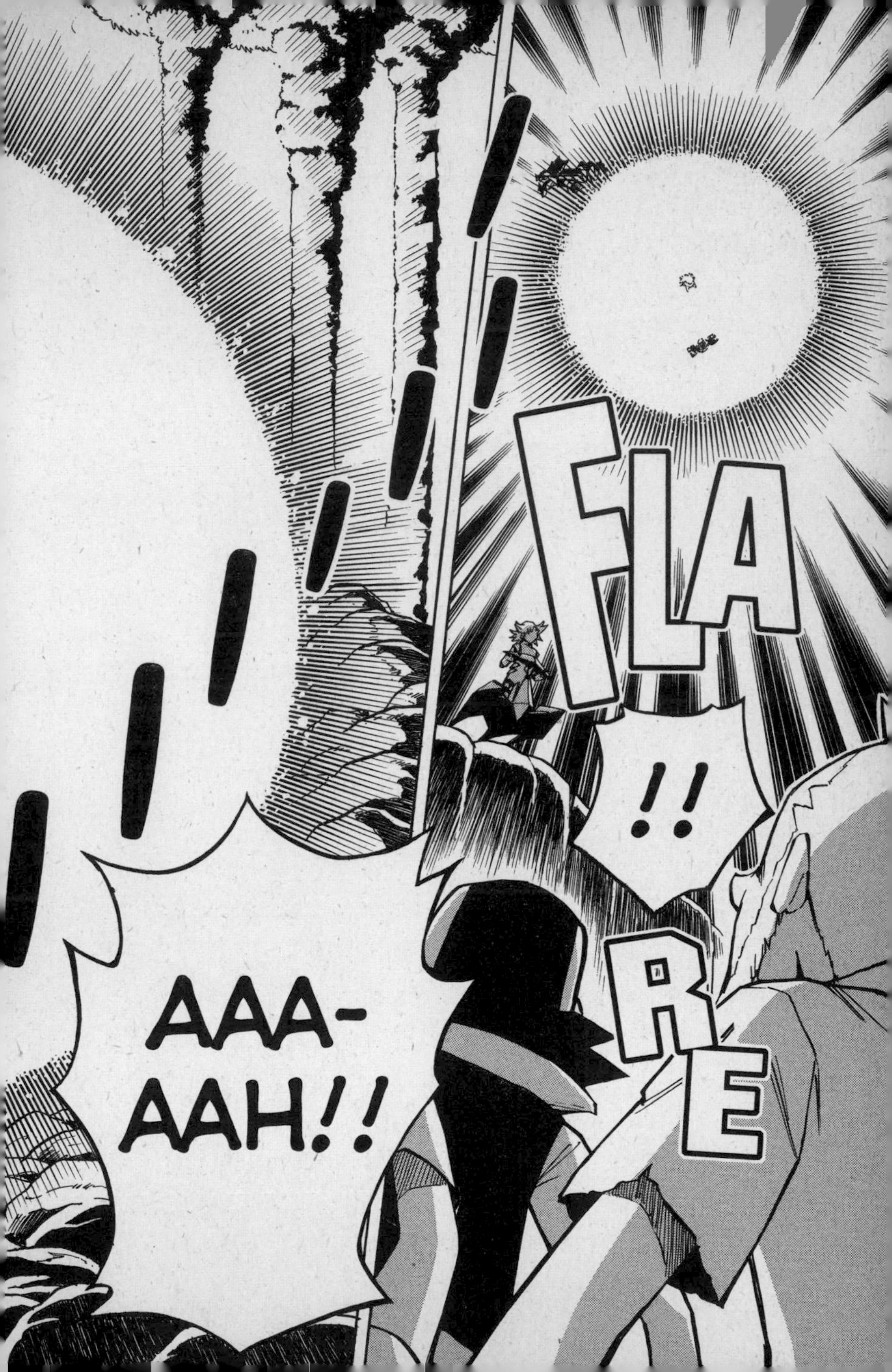
FLA
!!
RE
AAA-
AAH!!

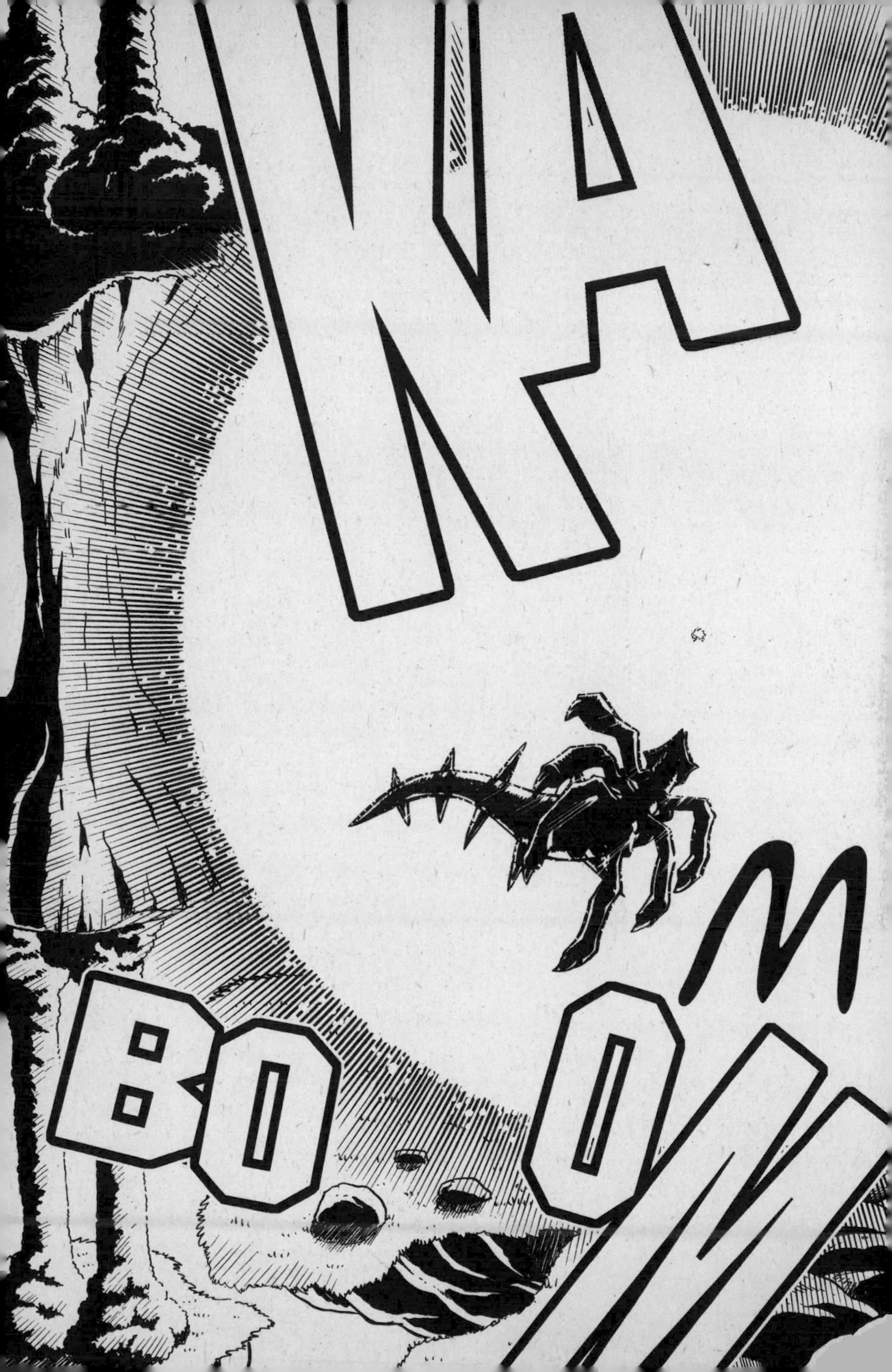
KA
BOOM

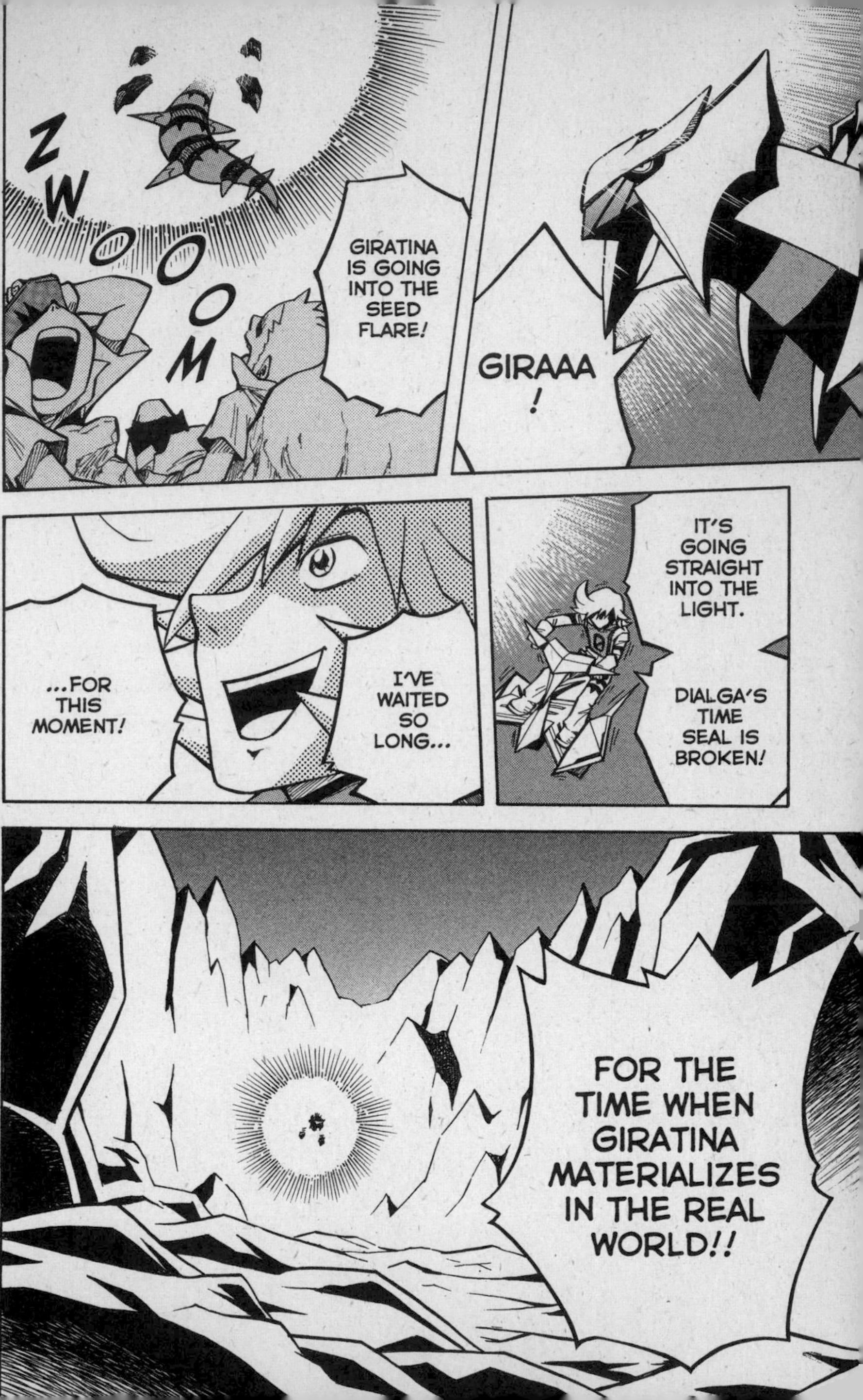
GIRAAA!
GIRATINA IS GOING INTO THE SEED FLARE!
ZWOOOM
IT'S GOING STRAIGHT INTO THE LIGHT.
DIALGA'S TIME SEAL IS BROKEN!
I'VE WAITED SO LONG...
...FOR THIS MOMENT!
FOR THE TIME WHEN GIRATINA MATERIALIZES IN THE REAL WORLD!!

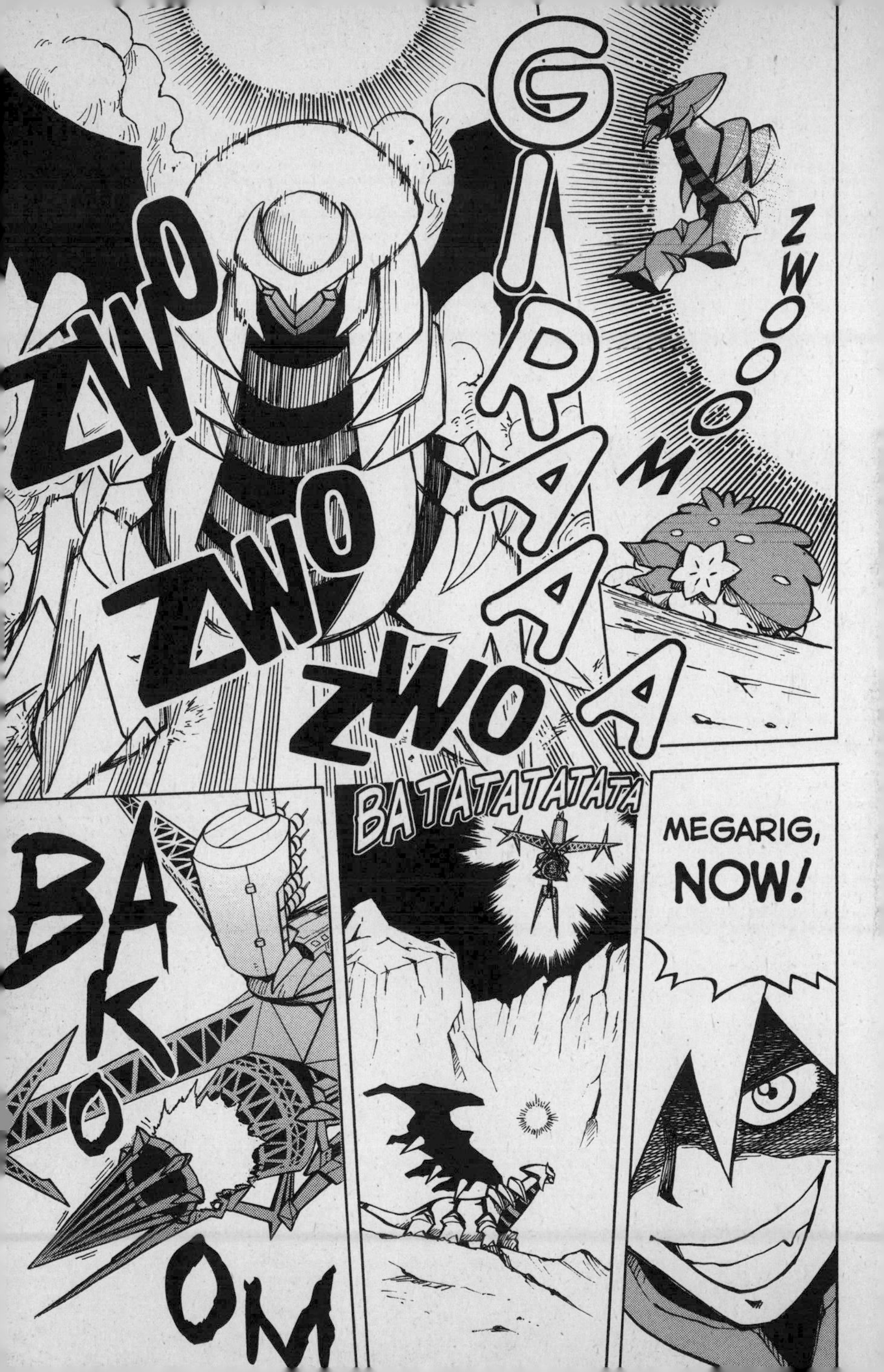
ZWOOOOM
GIRAAAA
ZWO ZWO ZWO ZWO
MEGARIG, NOW!
BATATATATATA
BAKOOM

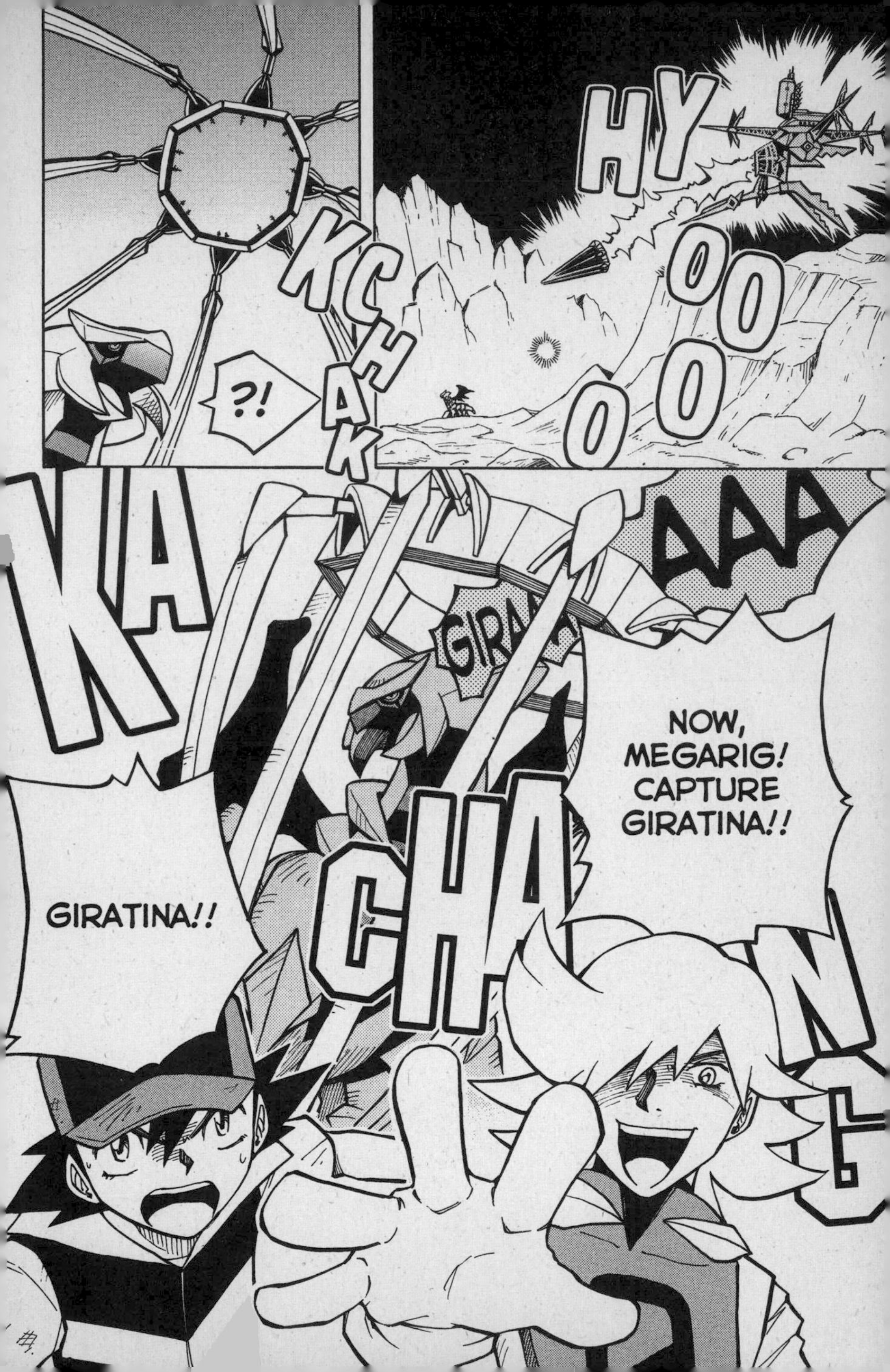
HYOOOO
KCHAK
?!
AAA
GIRAA
NOW, MEGARIG! CAPTURE GIRATINA!!
KA
CHA
N
GIRATINA!!

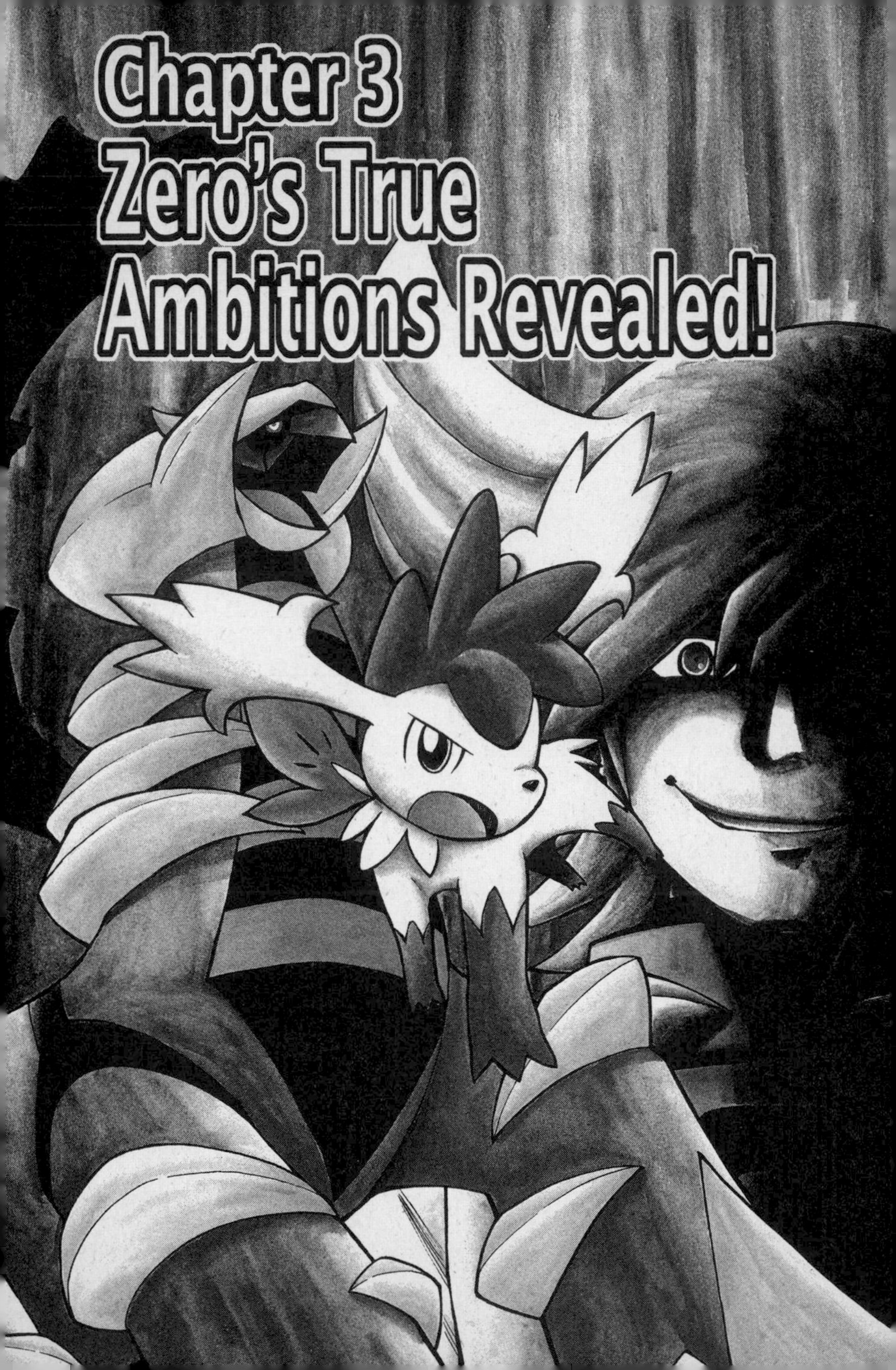
Chapter 3
Zero's True
Ambitions Revealed!

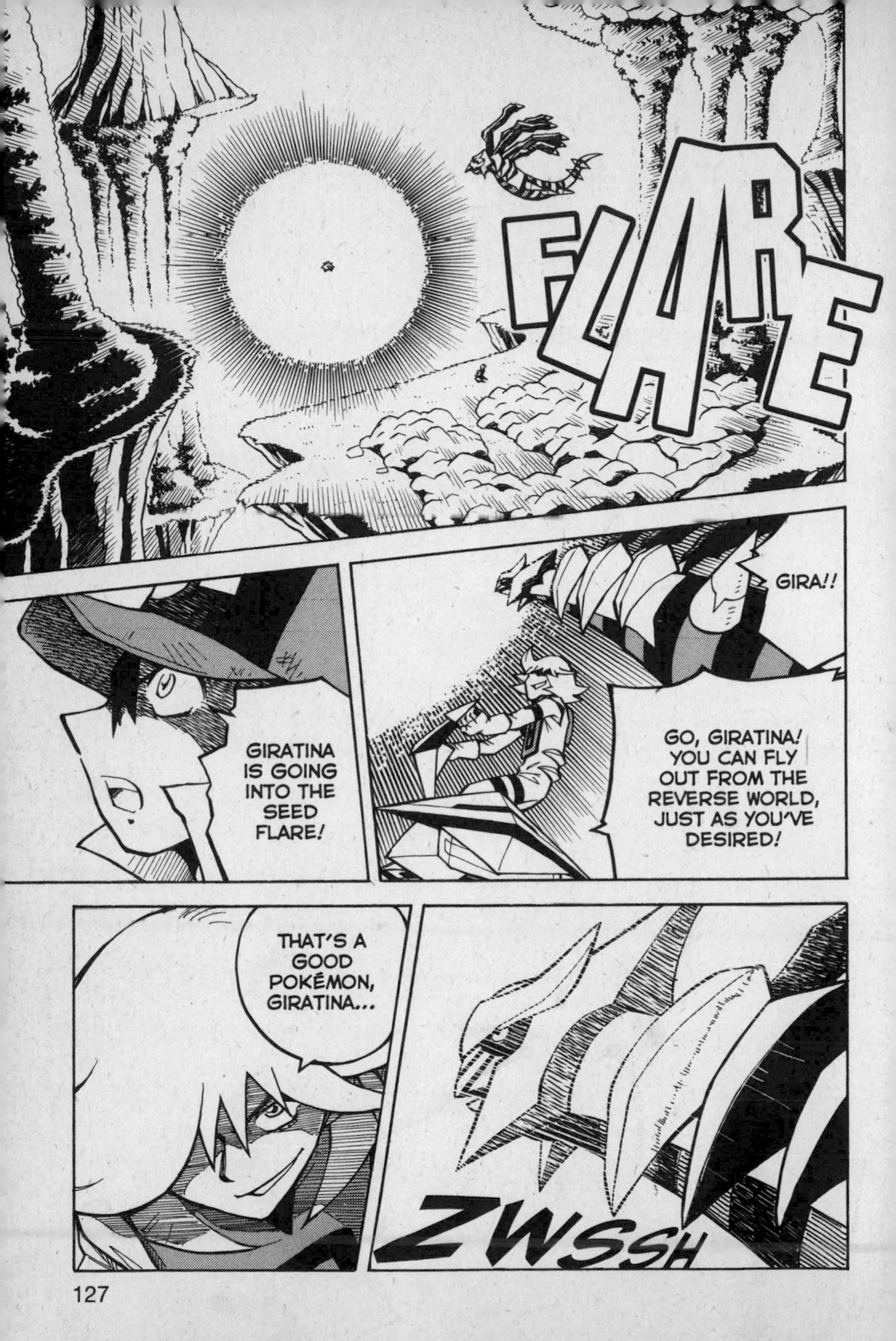
FLARE
GIRA!!
GO, GIRATINA! YOU CAN FLY OUT FROM THE REVERSE WORLD, JUST AS YOU'VE DESIRED!
GIRATINA IS GOING INTO THE SEED FLARE!
ZWSSH
THAT'S A GOOD POKÉMON, GIRATINA...

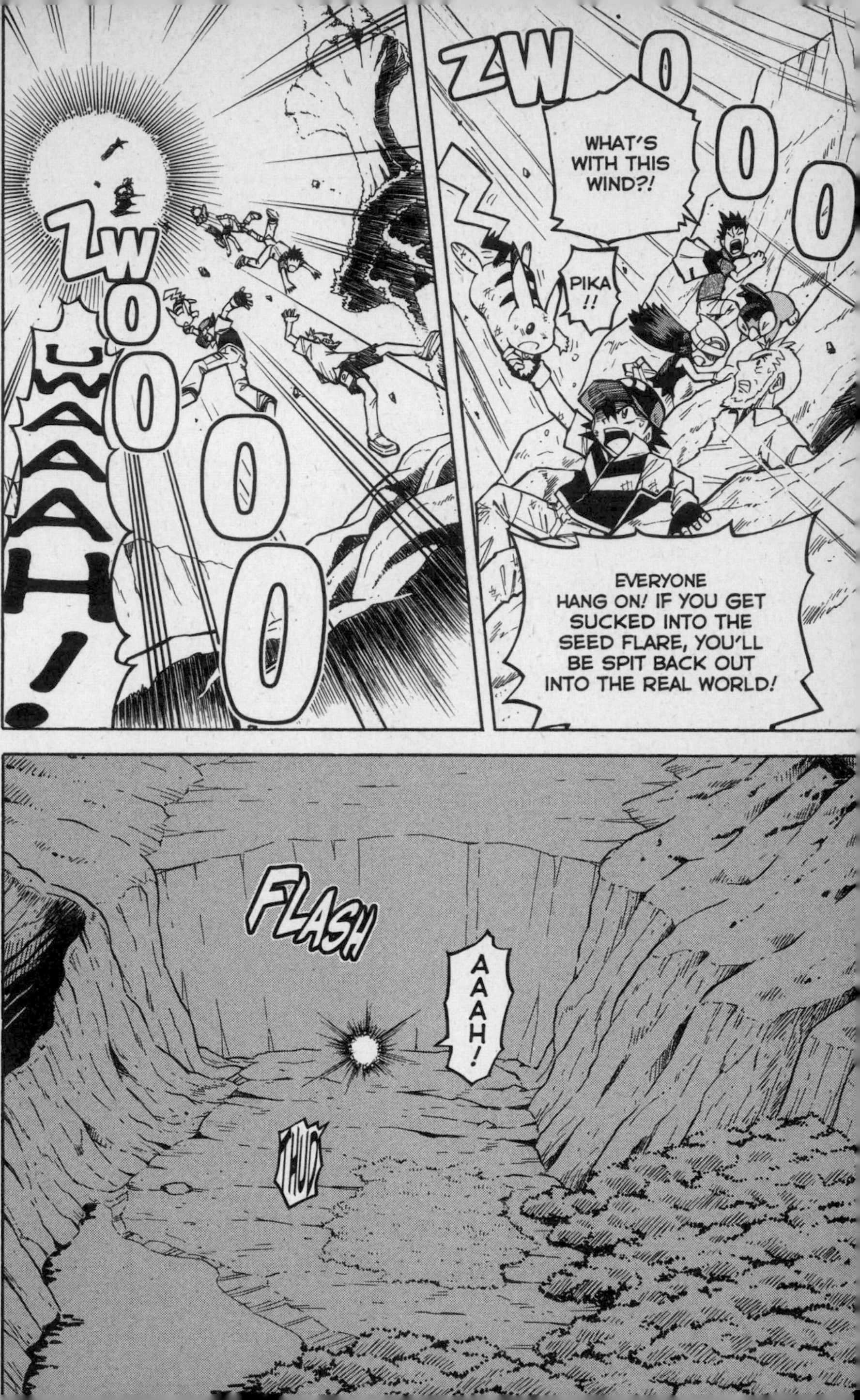
ZWOOOOO
WHAT'S WITH THIS WIND?!
PIKA!!
EVERYONE HANG ON! IF YOU GET SUCKED INTO THE SEED FLARE, YOU'LL BE SPIT BACK OUT INTO THE REAL WORLD!
ZWOOOOO
UWAAAAH!
FLASH
AAAH!
THUD

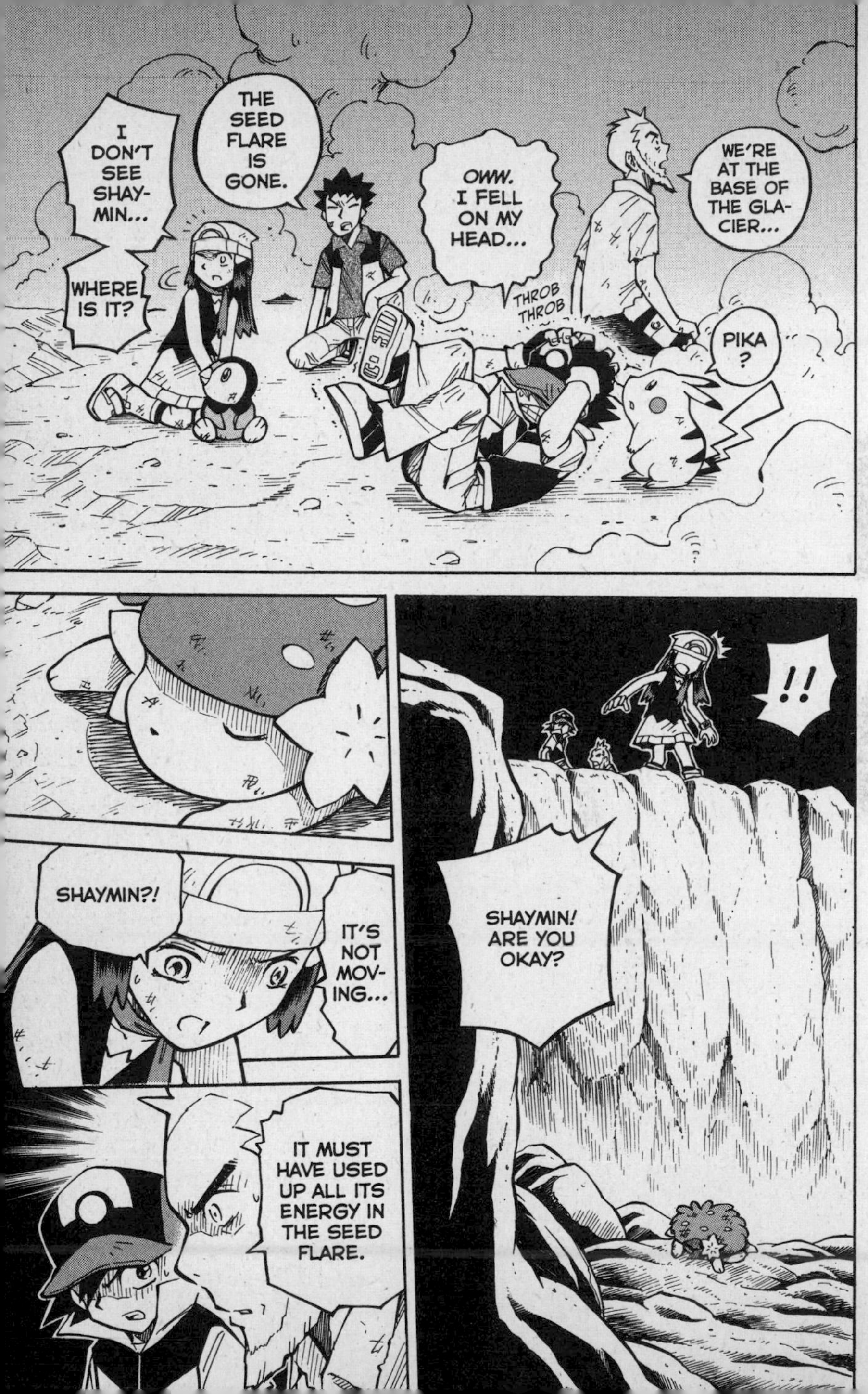

WE'RE AT THE BASE OF THE GLA-CIER...
PIKA ?
OWW. I FELL ON MY HEAD...
THROB THROB
THE SEED FLARE IS GONE.
I DON'T SEE SHAY-MIN...
WHERE IS IT?
!!
SHAYMIN! ARE YOU OKAY?
SHAYMIN?!
IT'S NOT MOV-ING...
IT MUST HAVE USED UP ALL ITS ENERGY IN THE SEED FLARE.

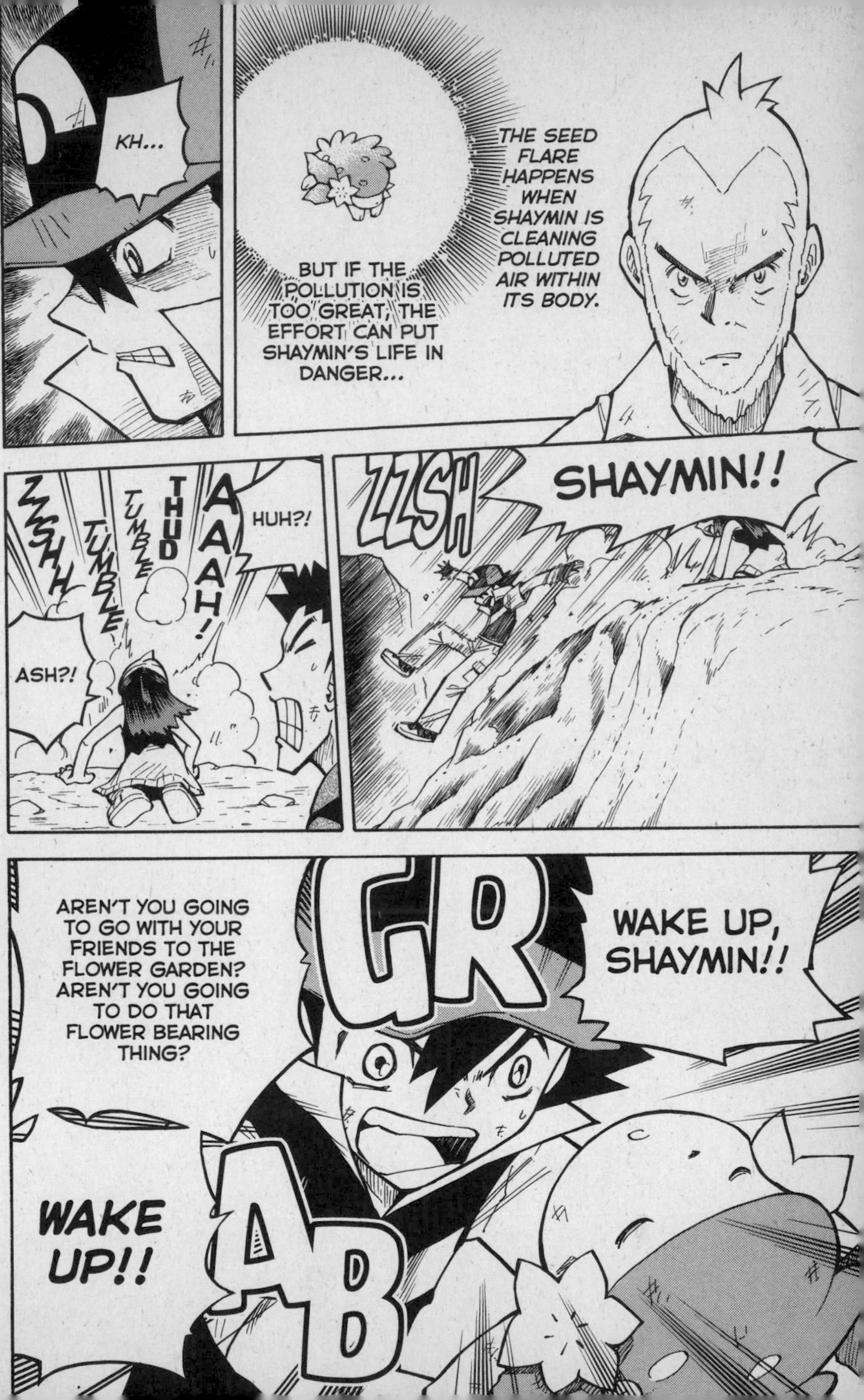
THE SEED FLARE HAPPENS WHEN SHAYMIN IS CLEANING POLLUTED AIR WITHIN ITS BODY.
BUT IF THE POLLUTION IS TOO GREAT, THE EFFORT CAN PUT SHAYMIN'S LIFE IN DANGER...
KH...
SHAYMIN!!
ZZSH
HUH?!
AAAAH!
THUD
TUMBLE
TUMBLE
ZZSHHH
ASH?!
WAKE UP, SHAYMIN!!
CR
AREN'T YOU GOING TO GO WITH YOUR FRIENDS TO THE FLOWER GARDEN? AREN'T YOU GOING TO DO THAT FLOWER BEARING THING?
WAKE UP!!
AB

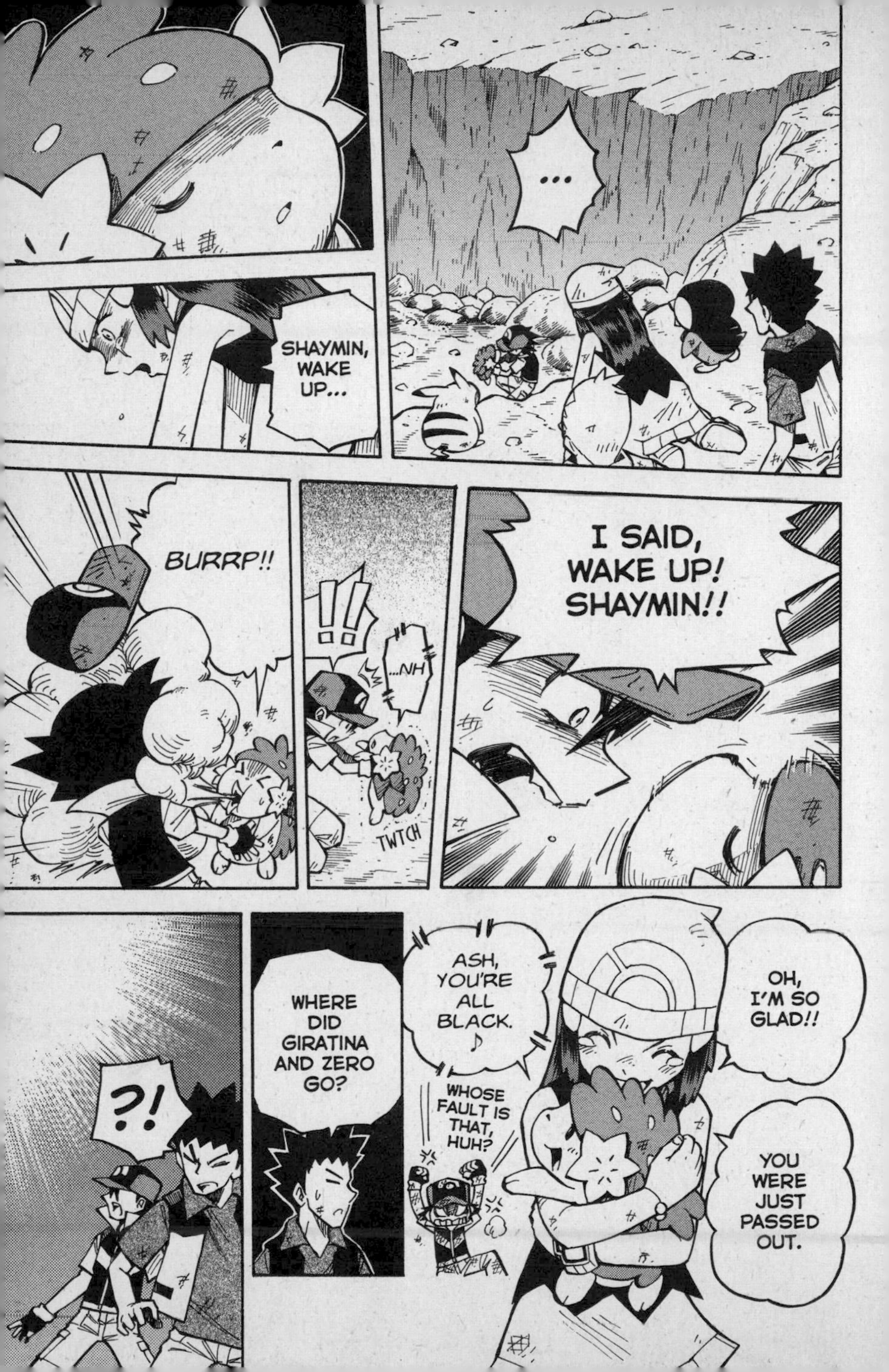
...
SHAYMIN, WAKE UP...
I SAID, WAKE UP! SHAYMIN!!
!!
...NH
TWTCH
BURRP!!
OH, I'M SO GLAD!!
YOU WERE JUST PASSED OUT.
ASH, YOU'RE ALL BLACK. ♪
WHOSE FAULT IS THAT, HUH?
WHERE DID GIRATINA AND ZERO GO?
?!

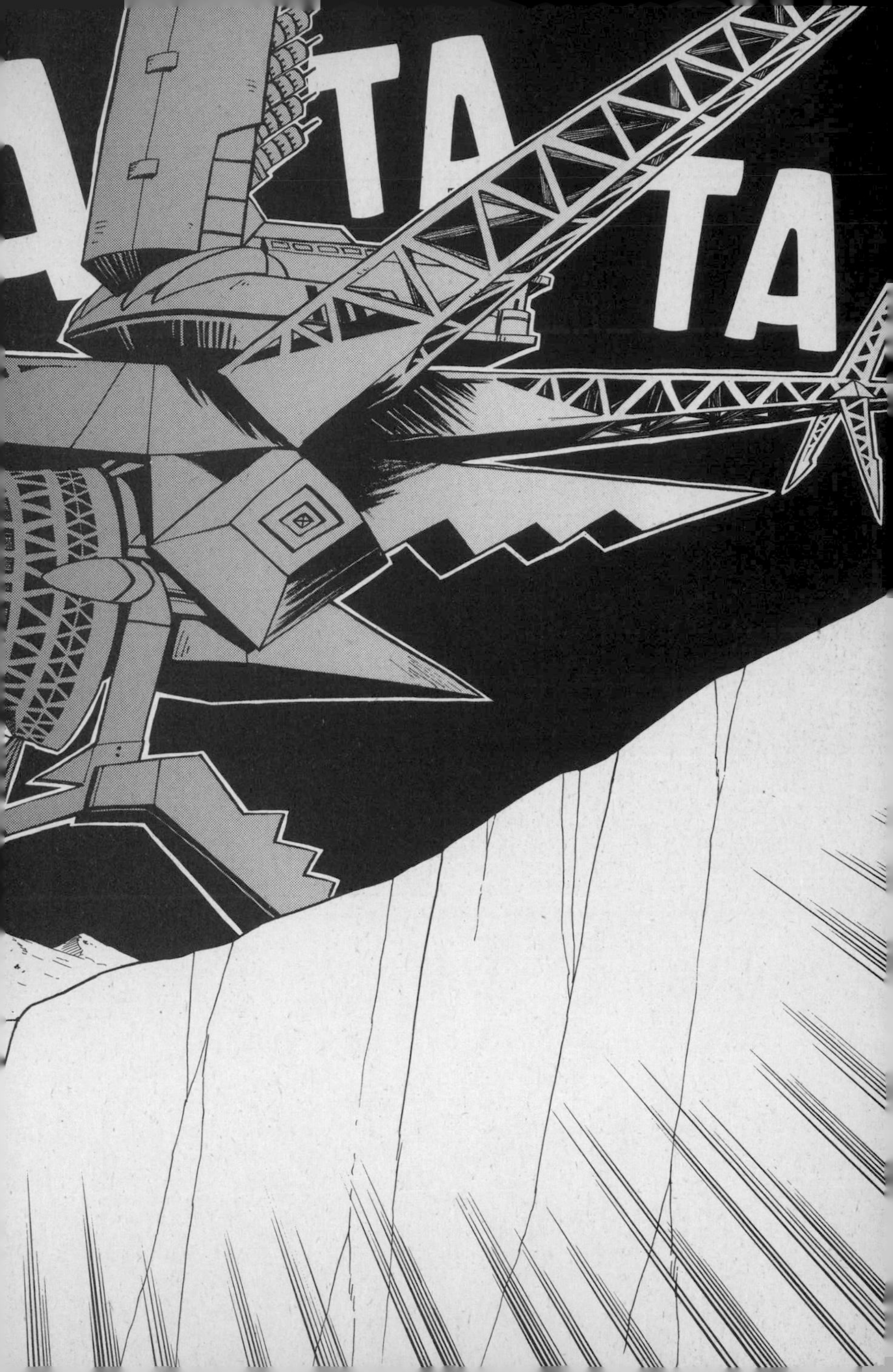
TA TA

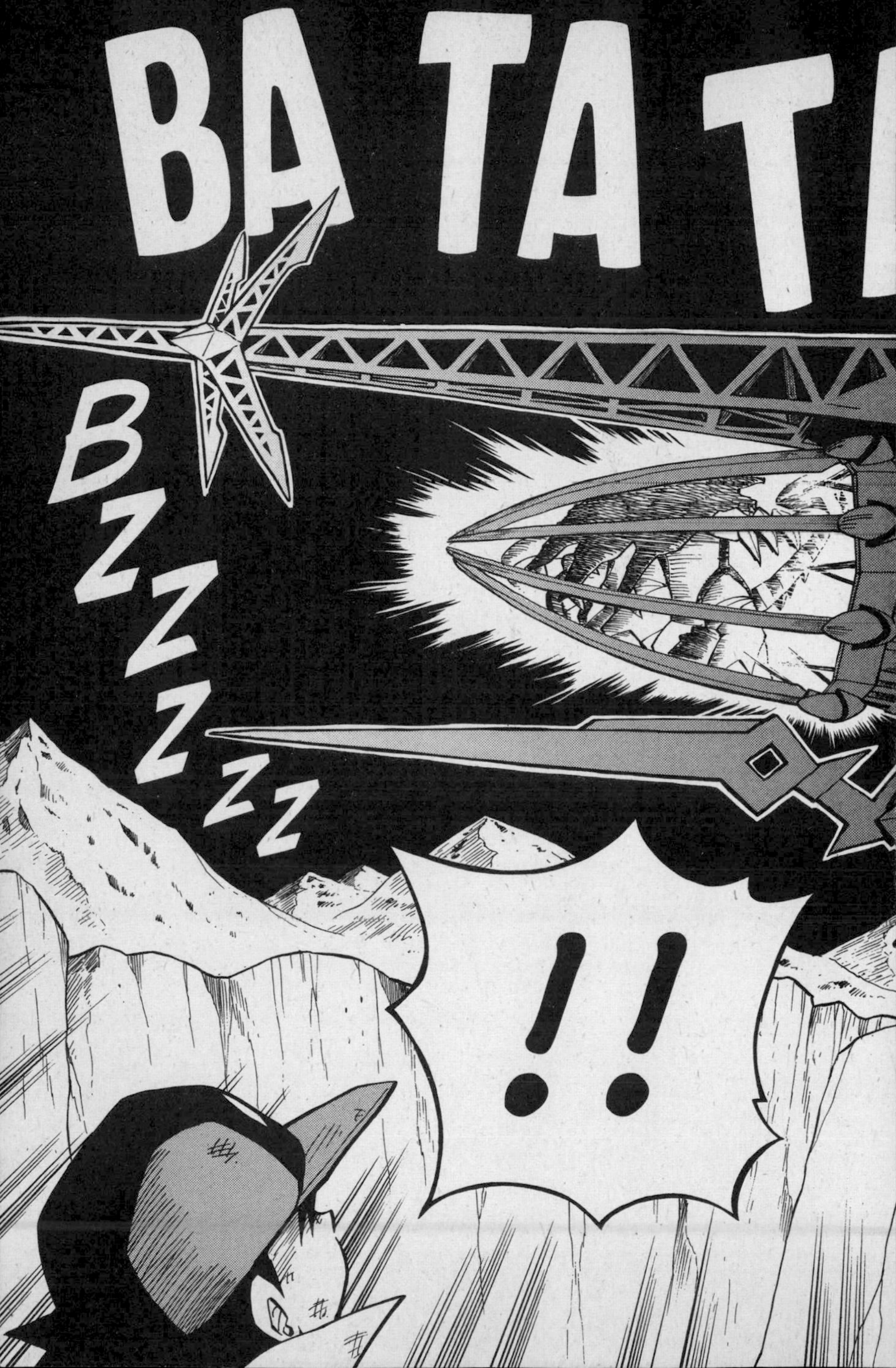
BA TA TA
BZZZZZZ
!!

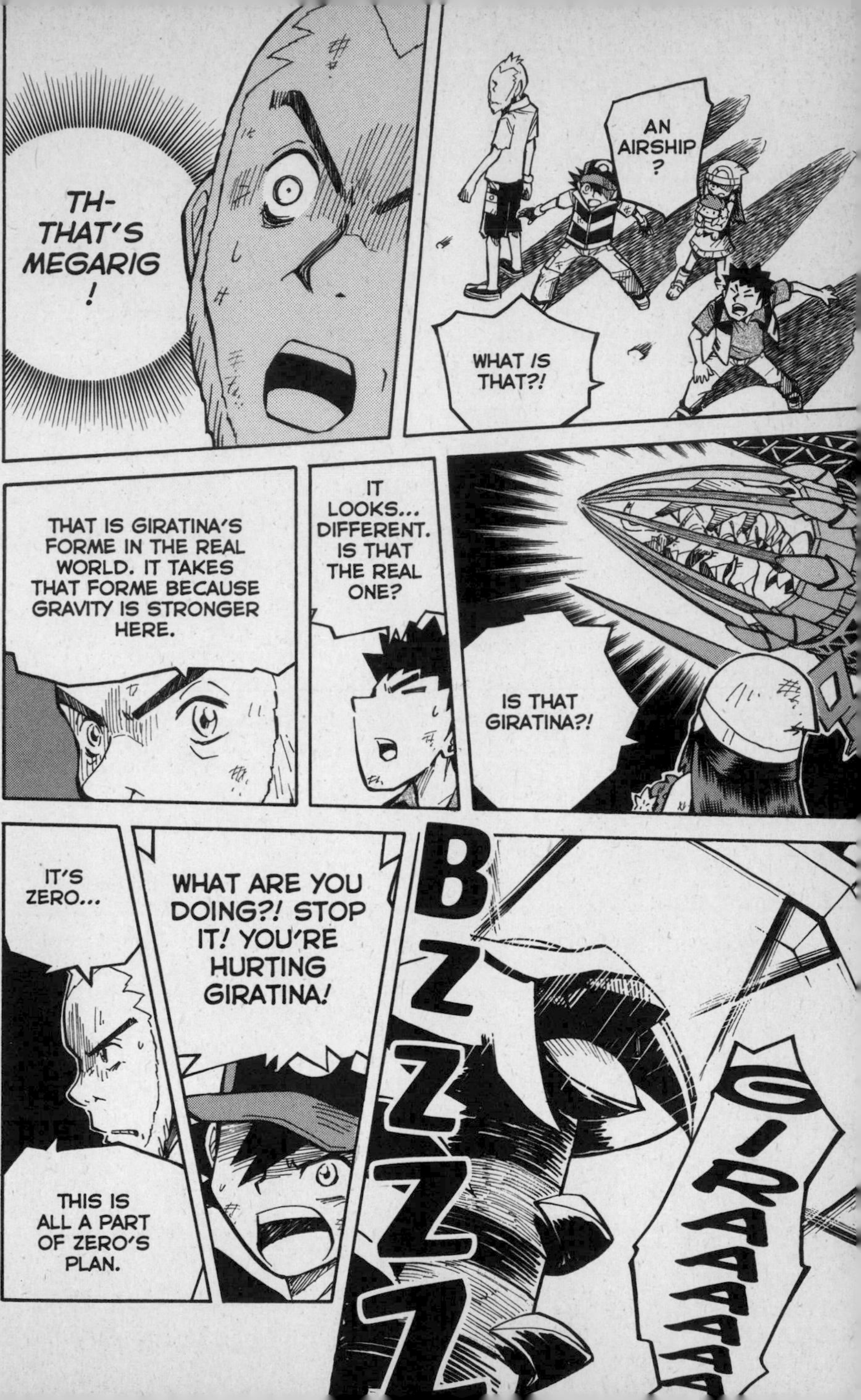
AN AIRSHIP?
WHAT IS THAT?!
TH-THAT'S MEGARIG!
IS THAT GIRATINA?!
IT LOOKS... DIFFERENT. IS THAT THE REAL ONE?
THAT IS GIRATINA'S FORME IN THE REAL WORLD. IT TAKES THAT FORME BECAUSE GRAVITY IS STRONGER HERE.
GIRAAAAAAA
BZZZZZ
WHAT ARE YOU DOING?! STOP IT! YOU'RE HURTING GIRATINA!
IT'S ZERO...
THIS IS ALL A PART OF ZERO'S PLAN.

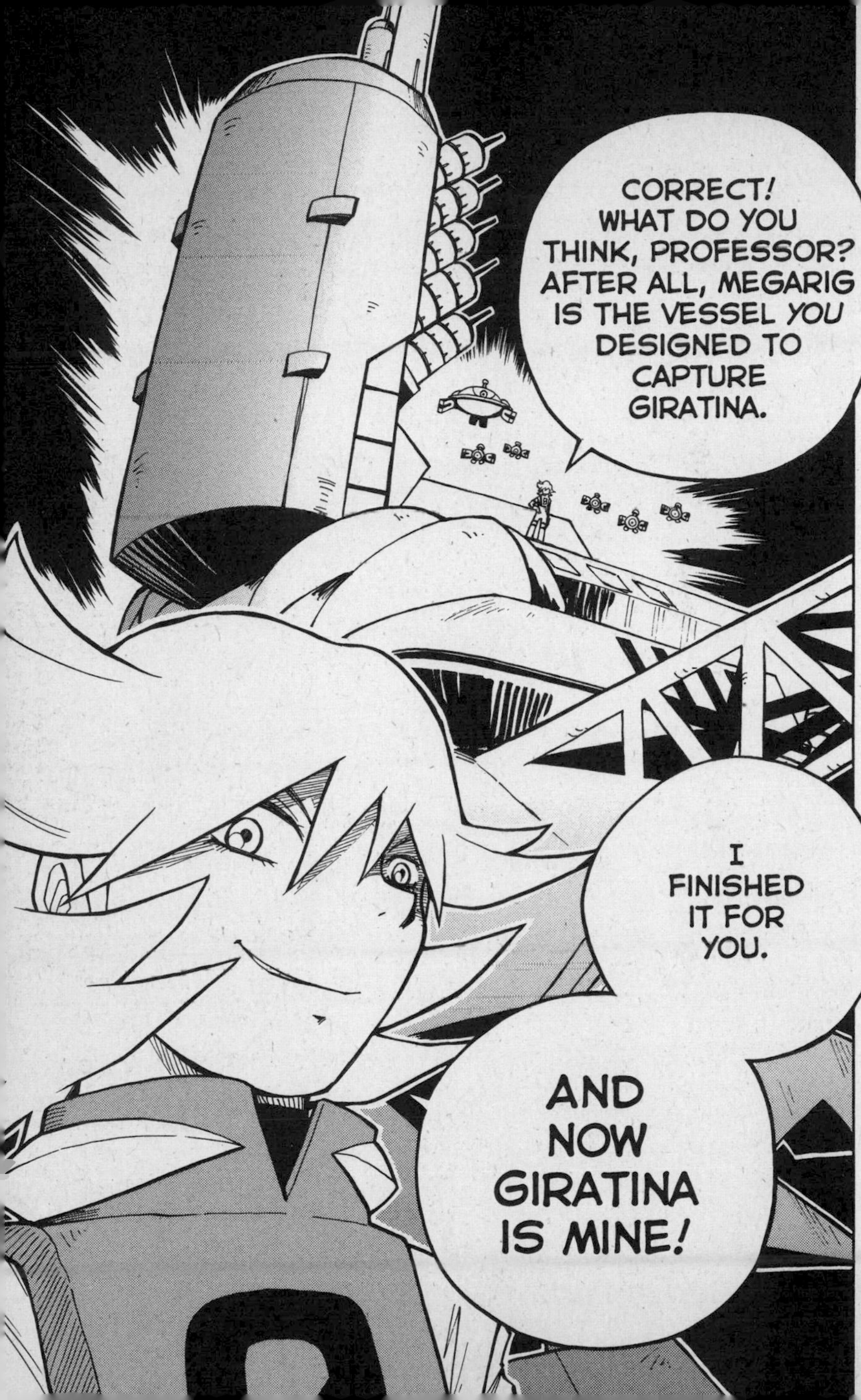
CORRECT! WHAT DO YOU THINK, PROFESSOR? AFTER ALL, MEGARIG IS THE VESSEL *YOU* DESIGNED TO CAPTURE GIRATINA.
I FINISHED IT FOR YOU.
AND NOW GIRATINA IS MINE!

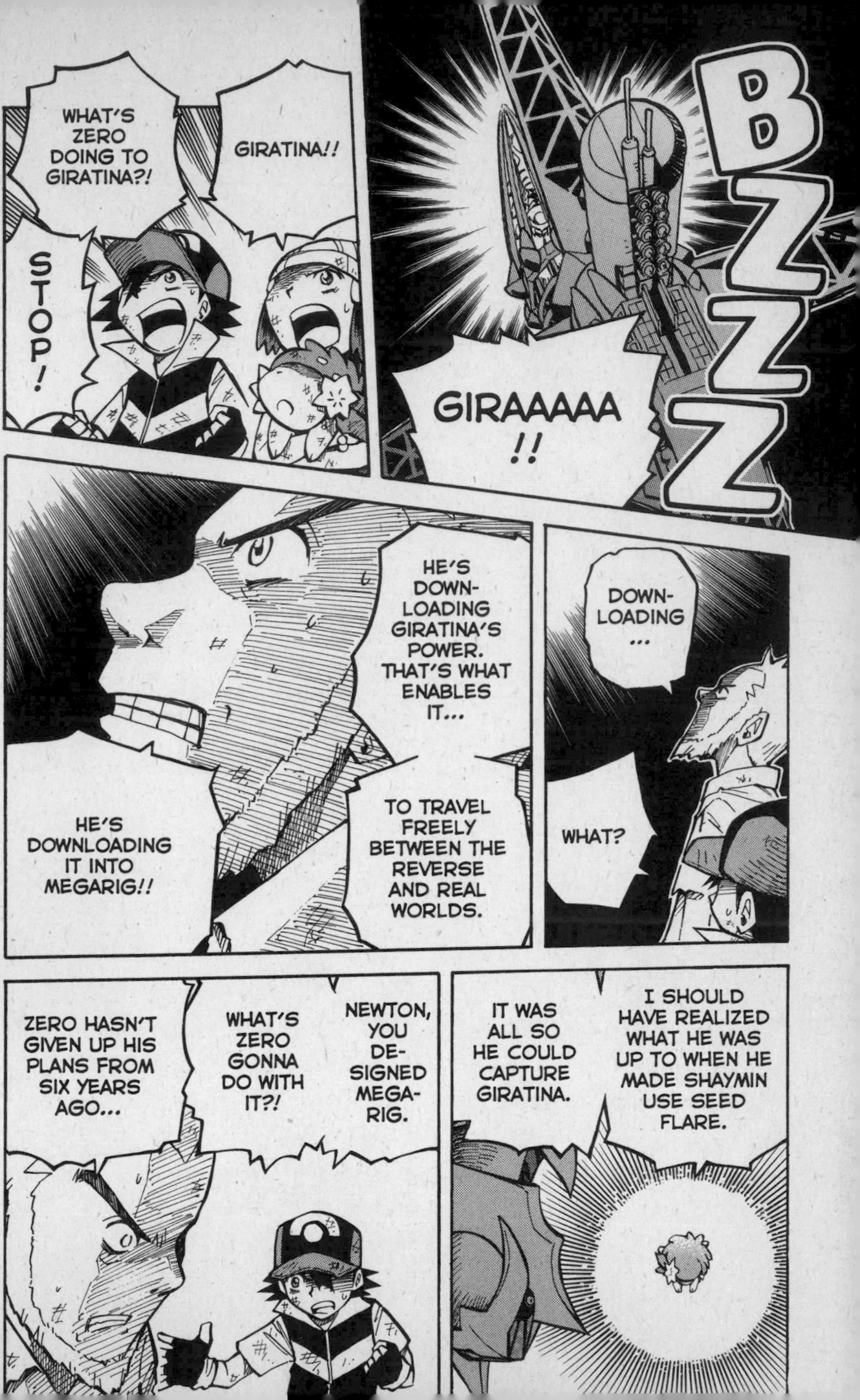

BZZZ
GIRAAAAA!!
GIRATINA!!
WHAT'S ZERO DOING TO GIRATINA?!
STOP!
DOWN-LOADING...
WHAT?
HE'S DOWN-LOADING GIRATINA'S POWER. THAT'S WHAT ENABLES IT...
TO TRAVEL FREELY BETWEEN THE REVERSE AND REAL WORLDS.
HE'S DOWNLOADING IT INTO MEGARIG!!
I SHOULD HAVE REALIZED WHAT HE WAS UP TO WHEN HE MADE SHAYMIN USE SEED FLARE.
IT WAS ALL SO HE COULD CAPTURE GIRATINA.
NEWTON, YOU DE-SIGNED MEGA-RIG.
WHAT'S ZERO GONNA DO WITH IT?!
ZERO HASN'T GIVEN UP HIS PLANS FROM SIX YEARS AGO...

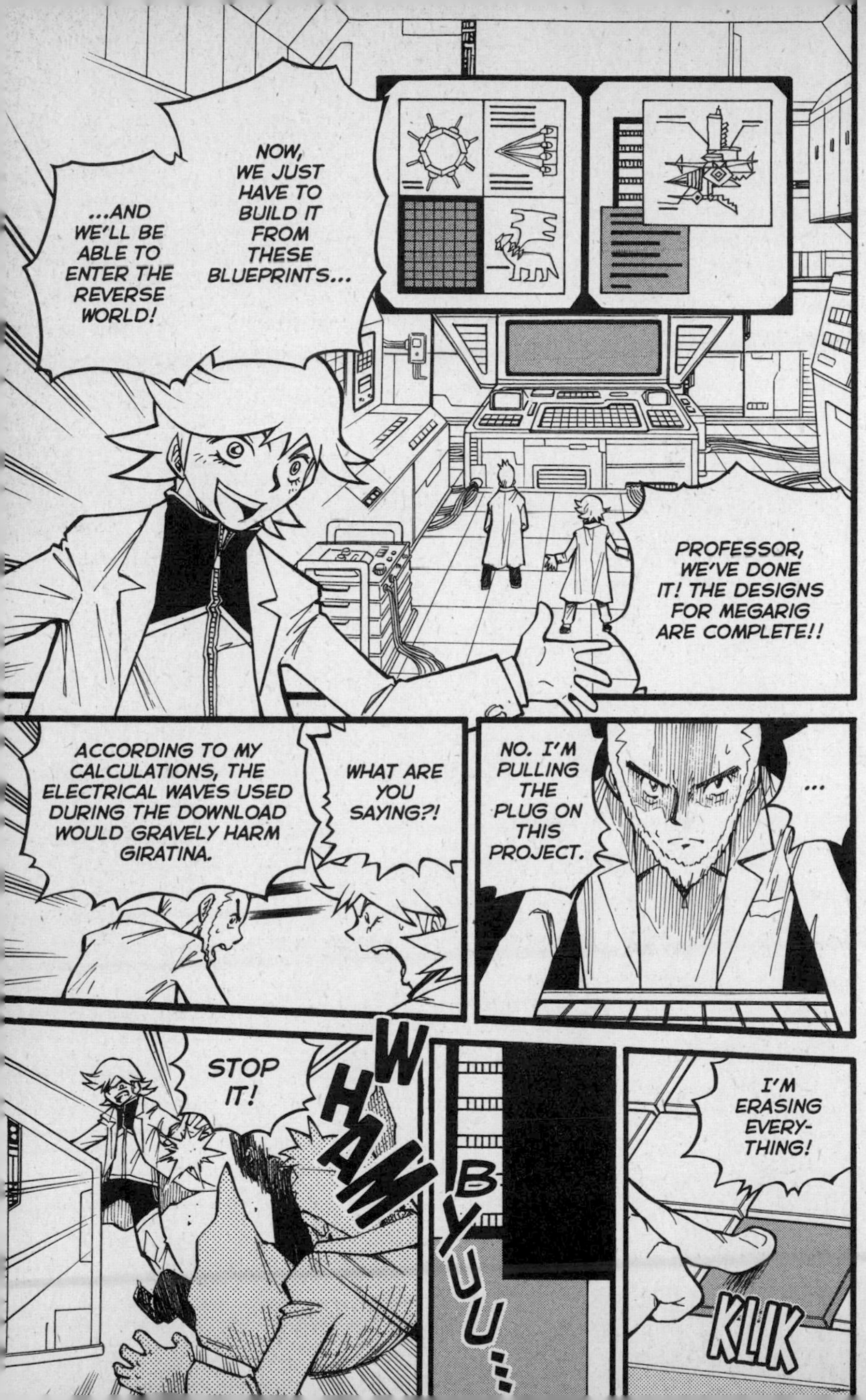
PROFESSOR, WE'VE DONE IT! THE DESIGNS FOR MEGARIG ARE COMPLETE!!
NOW, WE JUST HAVE TO BUILD IT FROM THESE BLUEPRINTS...
...AND WE'LL BE ABLE TO ENTER THE REVERSE WORLD!
...
NO. I'M PULLING THE PLUG ON THIS PROJECT.
WHAT ARE YOU SAYING?!
ACCORDING TO MY CALCULATIONS, THE ELECTRICAL WAVES USED DURING THE DOWNLOAD WOULD GRAVELY HARM GIRATINA.
I'M ERASING EVERY-THING!
KLIK
BYUU...
WHAM
STOP IT!

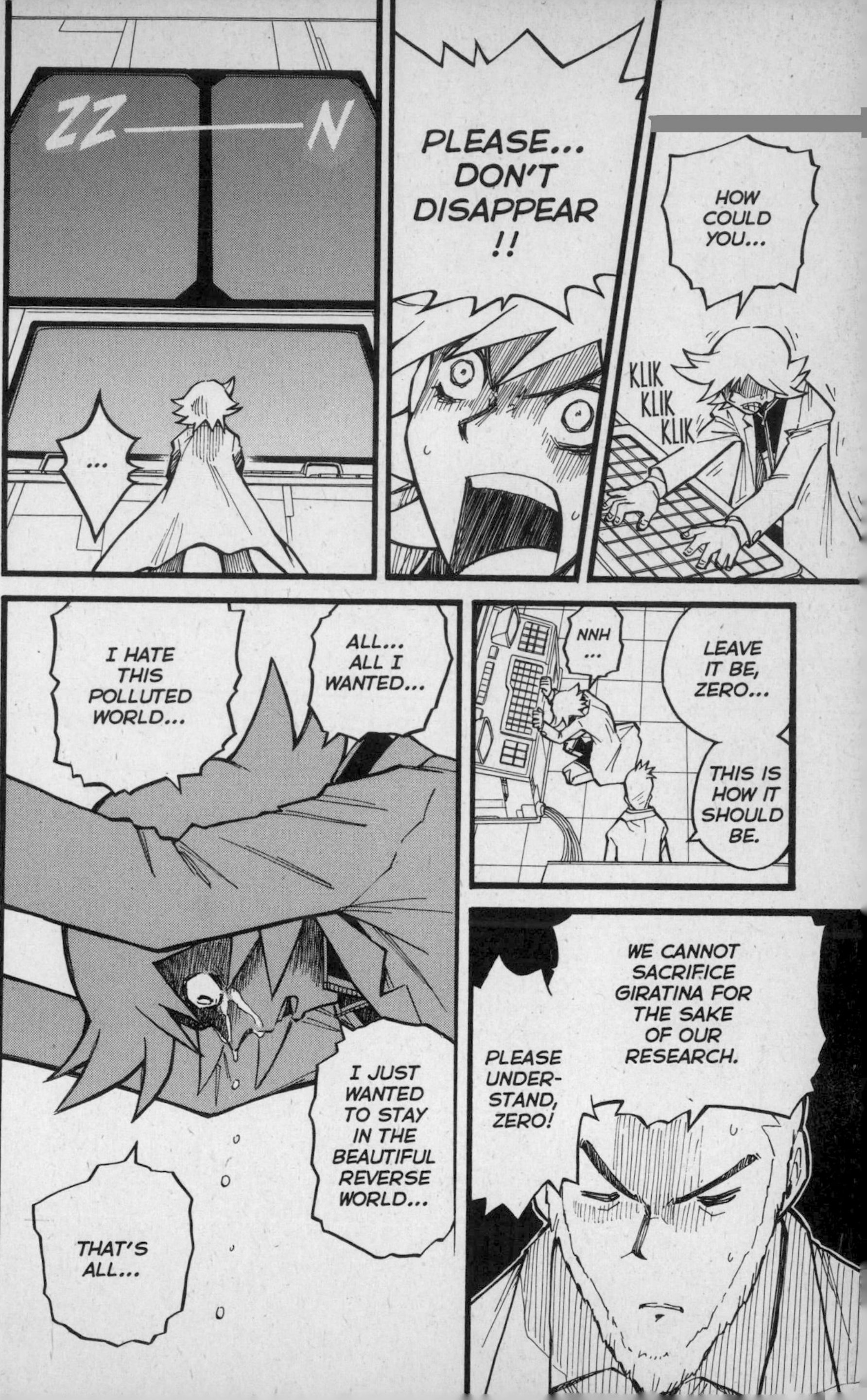
HOW COULD YOU...
KLIK KLIK KLIK
PLEASE... DON'T DISAPPEAR !!
ZZ——N
...
LEAVE IT BE, ZERO...
NNH ...
THIS IS HOW IT SHOULD BE.
WE CANNOT SACRIFICE GIRATINA FOR THE SAKE OF OUR RESEARCH.
PLEASE UNDER-STAND, ZERO!
ALL... ALL I WANTED...
I HATE THIS POLLUTED WORLD...
I JUST WANTED TO STAY IN THE BEAUTIFUL REVERSE WORLD...
THAT'S ALL...

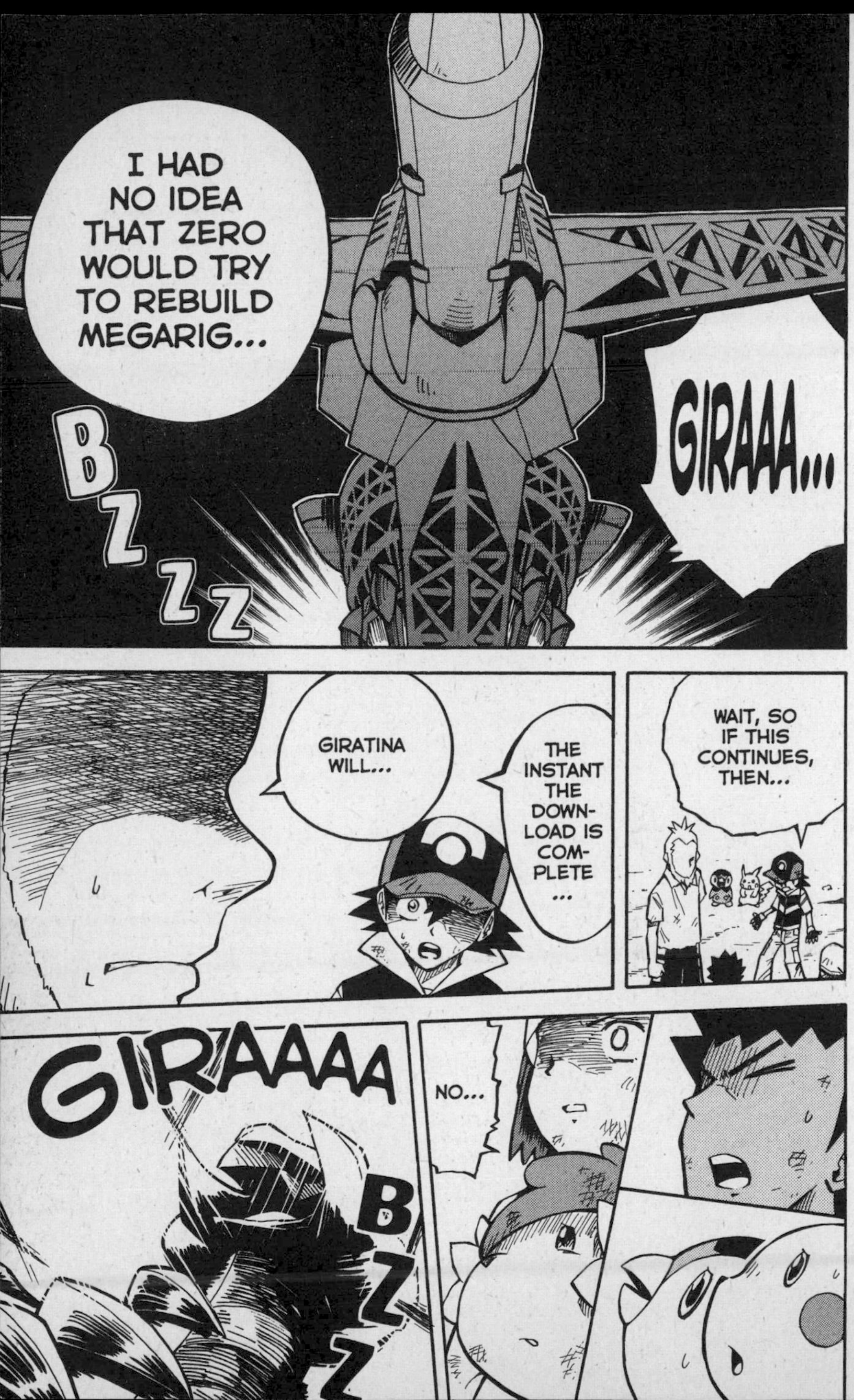
I HAD NO IDEA THAT ZERO WOULD TRY TO REBUILD MEGARIG...
GIRAAA...
BZZZ
WAIT, SO IF THIS CONTINUES, THEN...
THE INSTANT THE DOWNLOAD IS COMPLETE...
GIRATINA WILL...
NO...
GIRAAAA
BZZ

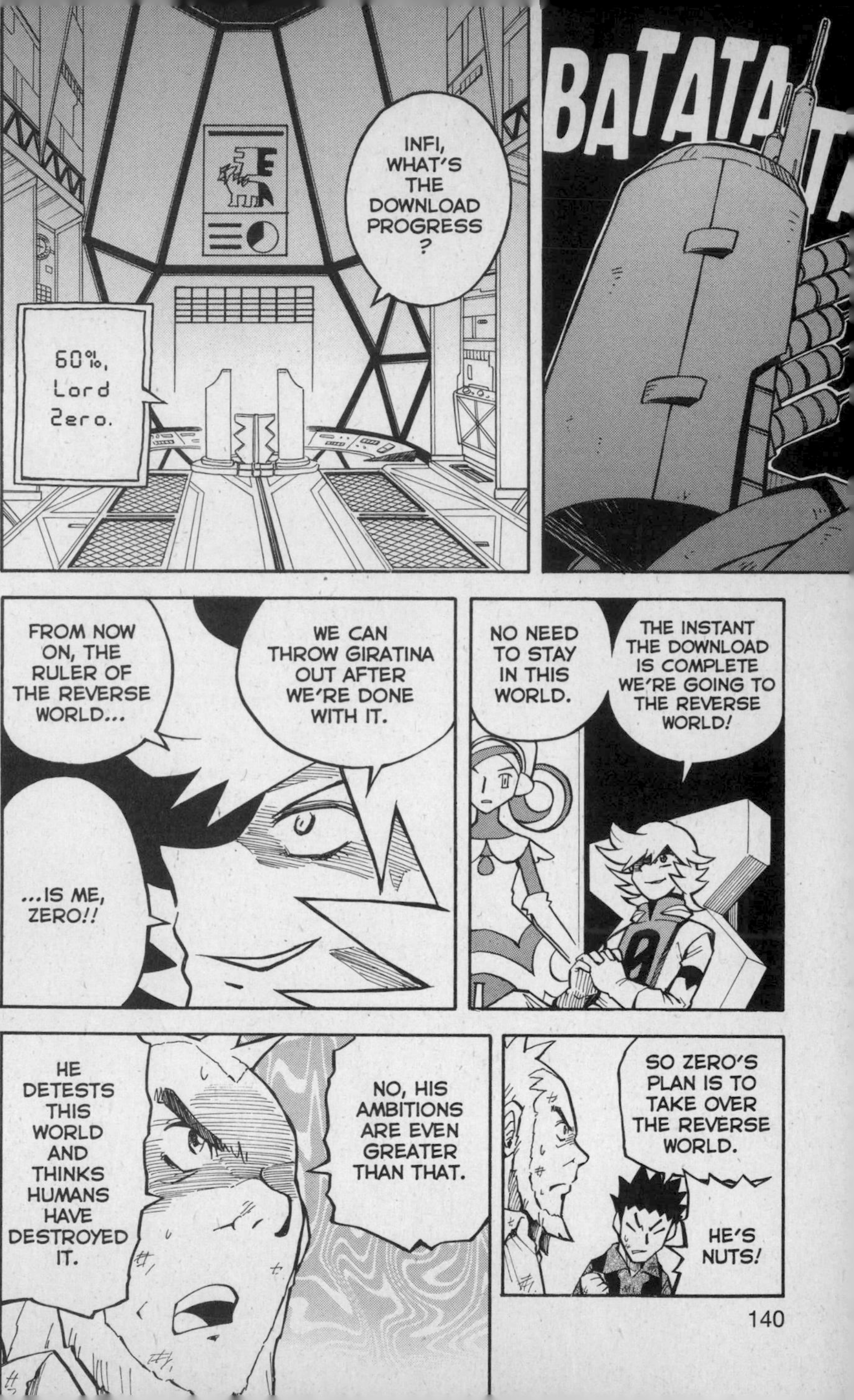
BATATATA
INFI, WHAT'S THE DOWNLOAD PROGRESS?
60%, Lord Zero.
THE INSTANT THE DOWNLOAD IS COMPLETE WE'RE GOING TO THE REVERSE WORLD!
NO NEED TO STAY IN THIS WORLD.
WE CAN THROW GIRATINA OUT AFTER WE'RE DONE WITH IT.
FROM NOW ON, THE RULER OF THE REVERSE WORLD...
...IS ME, ZERO!!
SO ZERO'S PLAN IS TO TAKE OVER THE REVERSE WORLD.
HE'S NUTS!
NO, HIS AMBITIONS ARE EVEN GREATER THAN THAT.
HE DETESTS THIS WORLD AND THINKS HUMANS HAVE DESTROYED IT.

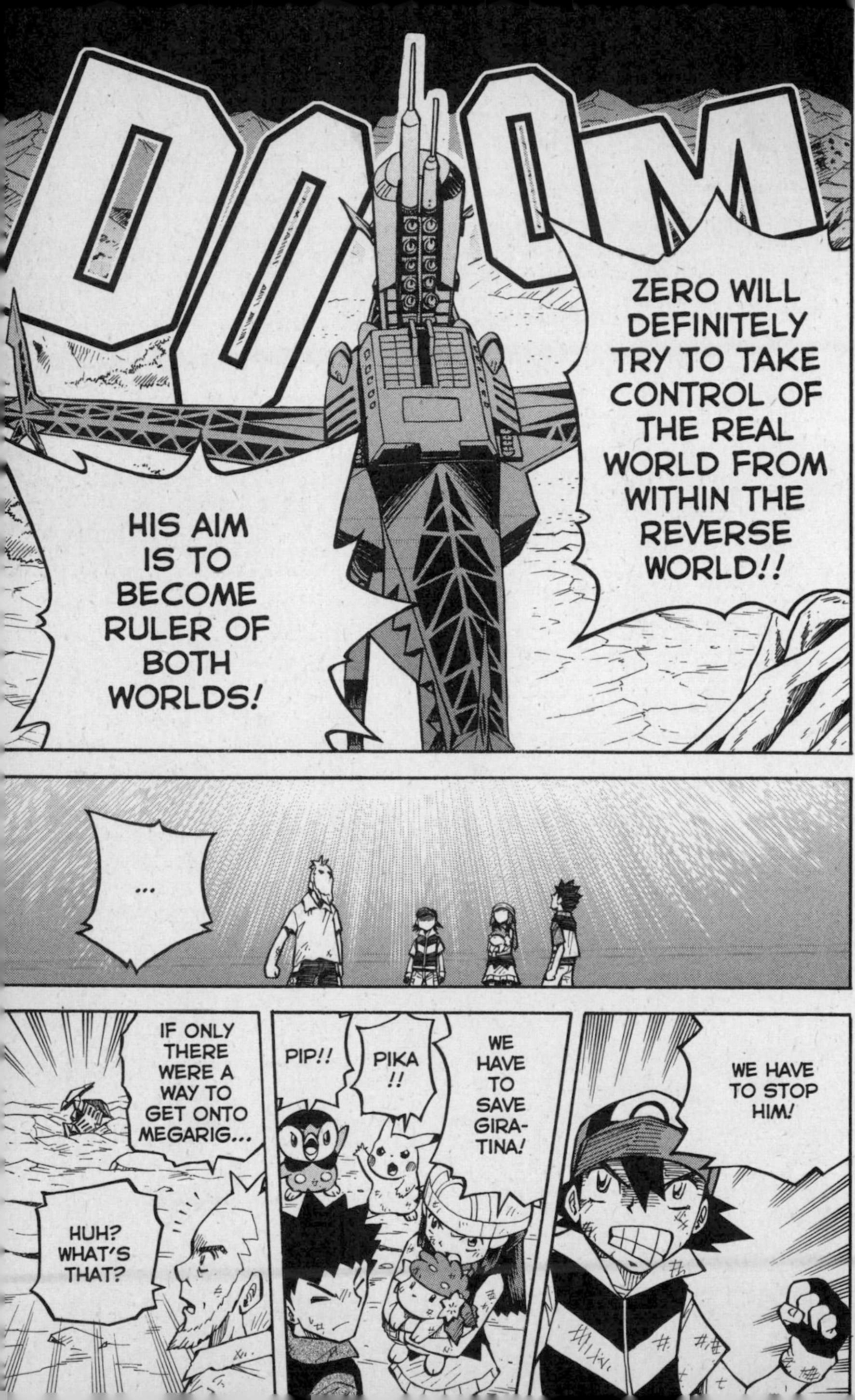
DOOM
ZERO WILL DEFINITELY TRY TO TAKE CONTROL OF THE REAL WORLD FROM WITHIN THE REVERSE WORLD!!
HIS AIM IS TO BECOME RULER OF BOTH WORLDS!
...
WE HAVE TO STOP HIM!
WE HAVE TO SAVE GIRA-TINA!
PIKA!!
PIP!!
IF ONLY THERE WERE A WAY TO GET ONTO MEGARIG...
HUH? WHAT'S THAT?

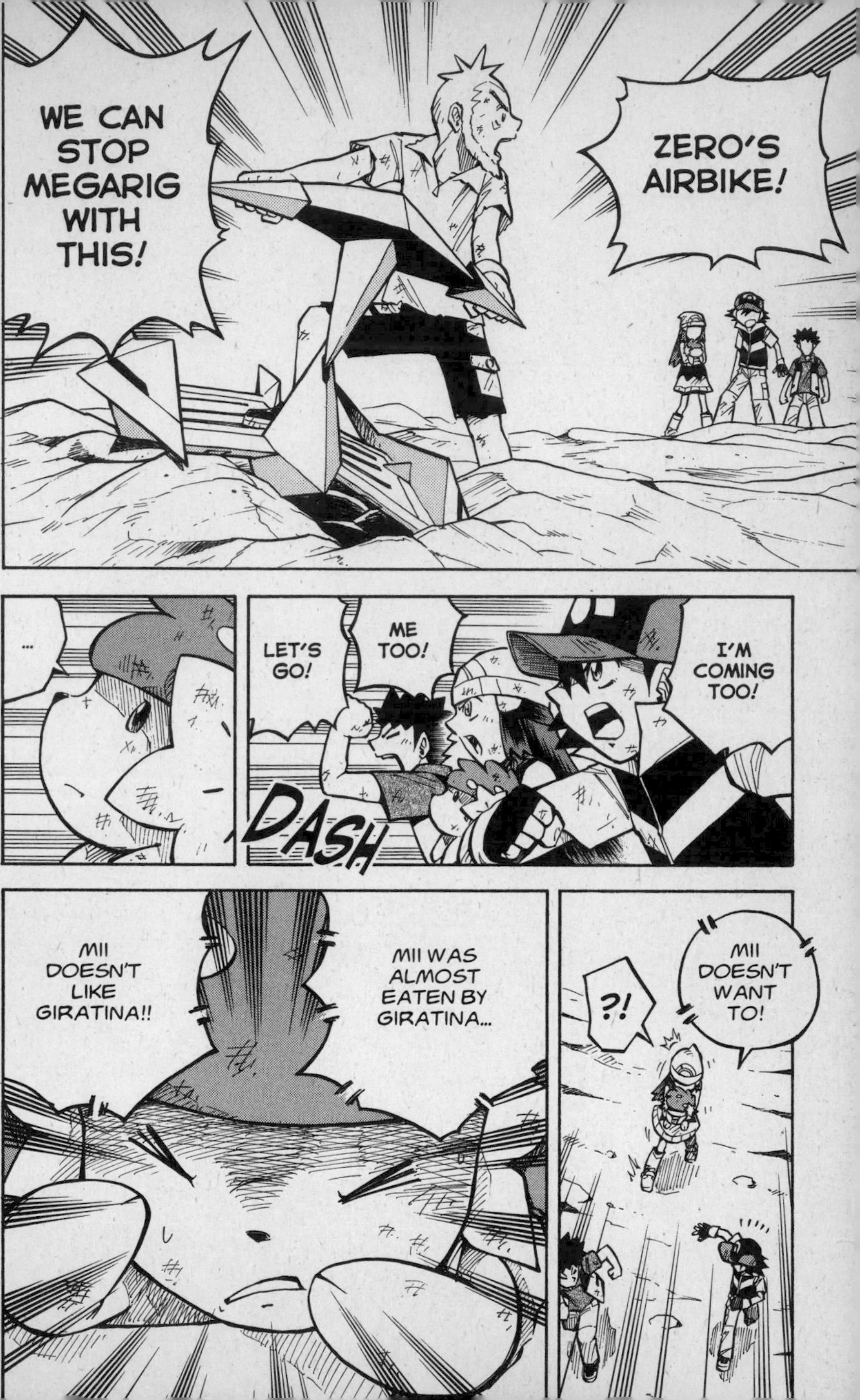
ZERO'S AIRBIKE!
WE CAN STOP MEGARIG WITH THIS!
I'M COMING TOO!
ME TOO!
LET'S GO!
DASH
...
MII DOESN'T WANT TO!
?!
MII WAS ALMOST EATEN BY GIRATINA...
MII DOESN'T LIKE GIRATINA!!

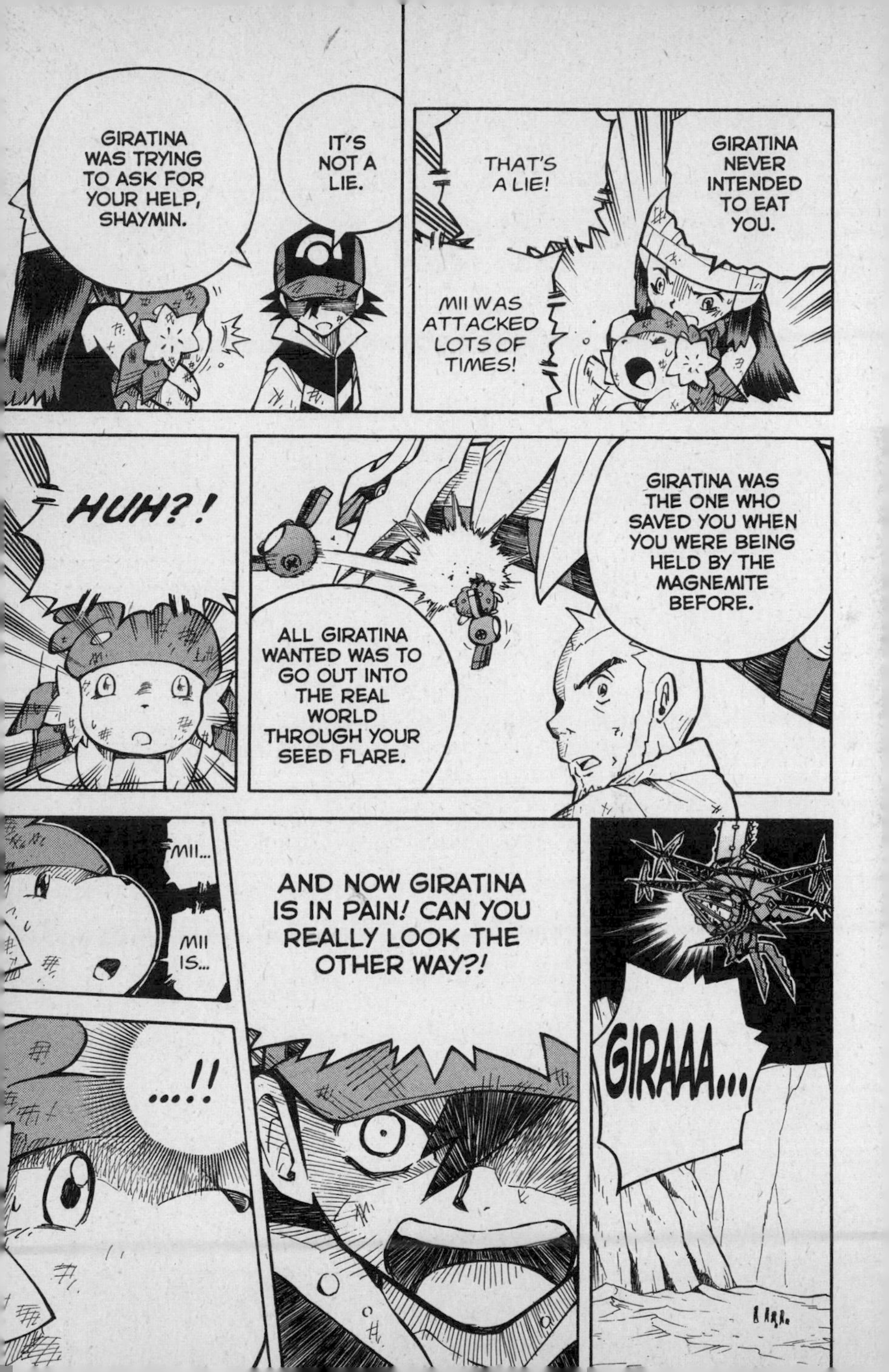
GIRATINA NEVER INTENDED TO EAT YOU.
THAT'S A LIE!
MII WAS ATTACKED LOTS OF TIMES!
IT'S NOT A LIE.
GIRATINA WAS TRYING TO ASK FOR YOUR HELP, SHAYMIN.
GIRATINA WAS THE ONE WHO SAVED YOU WHEN YOU WERE BEING HELD BY THE MAGNEMITE BEFORE.
ALL GIRATINA WANTED WAS TO GO OUT INTO THE REAL WORLD THROUGH YOUR SEED FLARE.
HUH?!
GIRAAA...
AND NOW GIRATINA IS IN PAIN! CAN YOU REALLY LOOK THE OTHER WAY?!
MII...
MII IS...
....!!

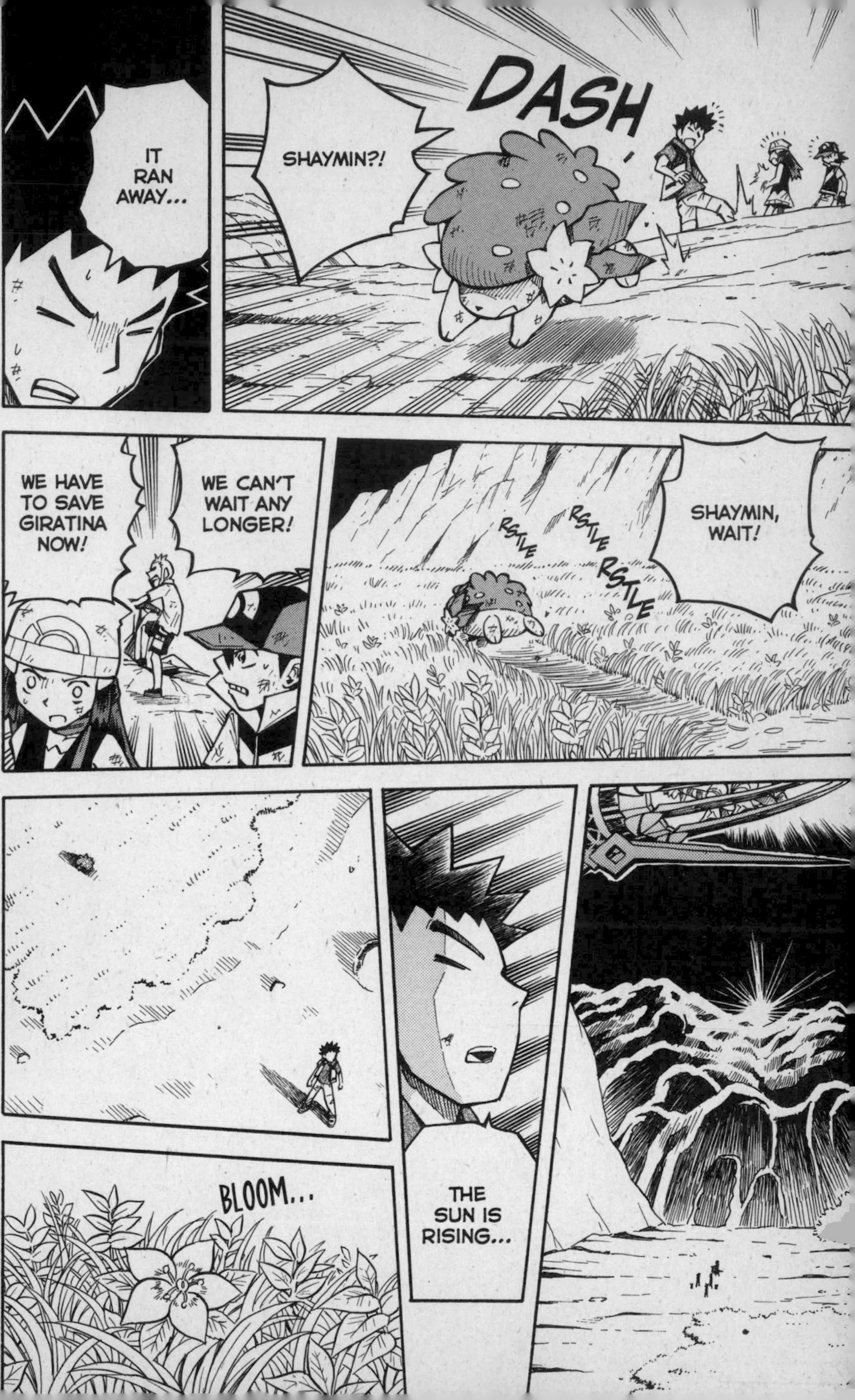
DASH
SHAYMIN?!
IT RAN AWAY...
SHAYMIN, WAIT!
RSTLE
RSTLE
RSTLE
WE CAN'T WAIT ANY LONGER!
WE HAVE TO SAVE GIRATINA NOW!
THE SUN IS RISING...
BLOOM...

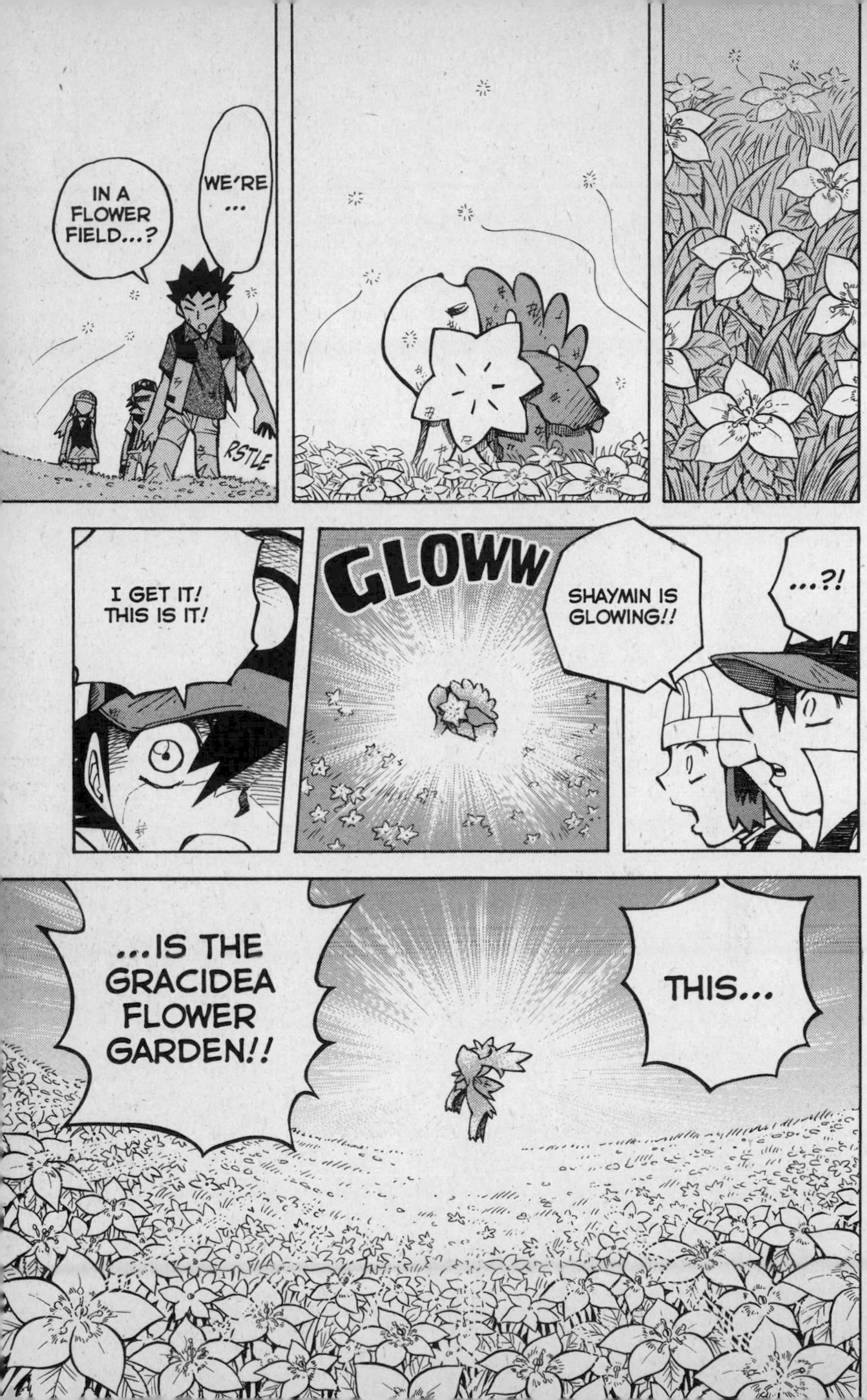

WE'RE ...
IN A FLOWER FIELD...?
RSTLE
...?!
SHAYMIN IS GLOWING!!
GLOWW
I GET IT! THIS IS IT!
THIS...
...IS THE GRACIDEA FLOWER GARDEN!!

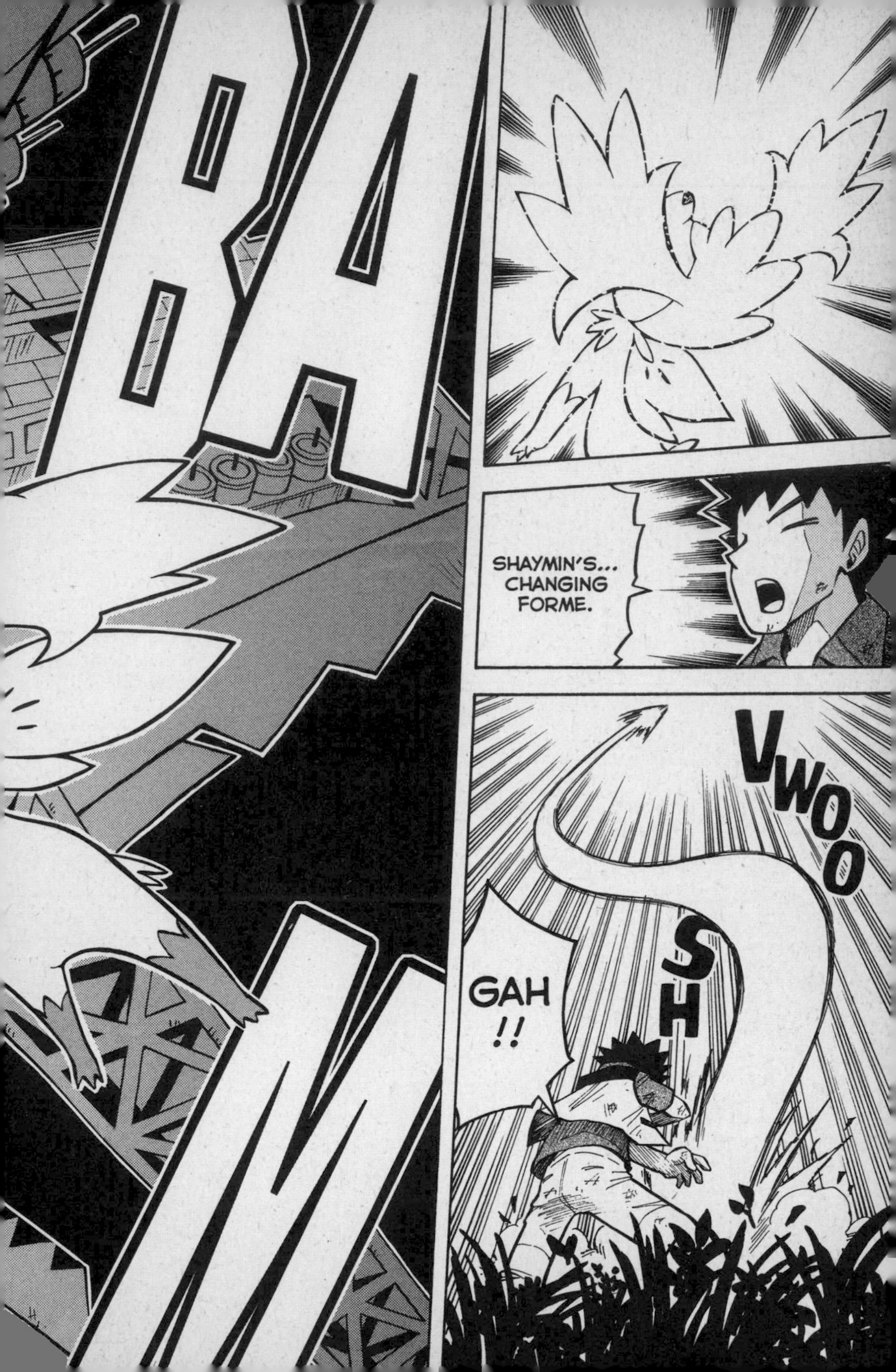
SHAYMIN'S... CHANGING FORME.
VWOOSH
GAH!!
BA

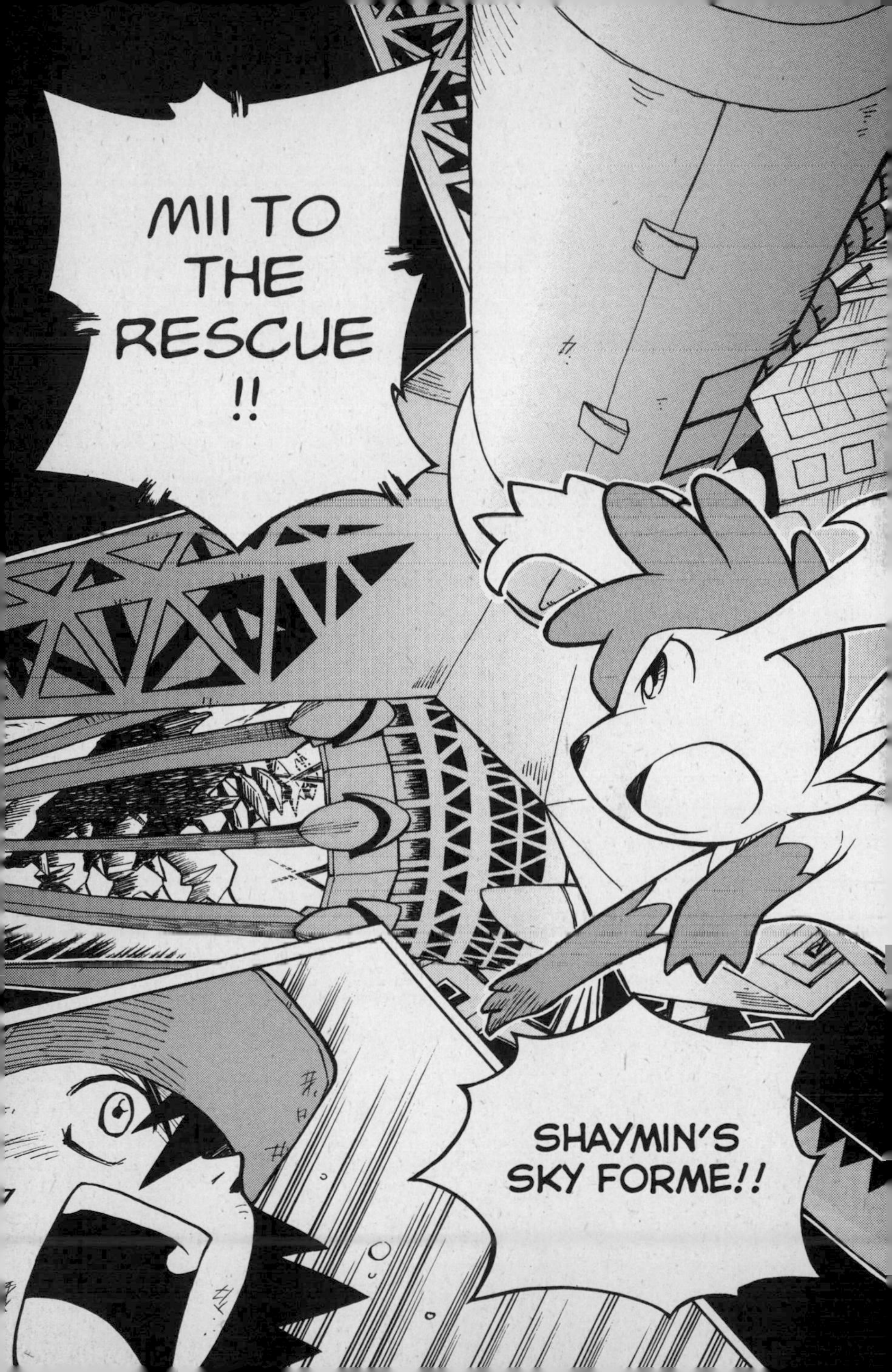
MII TO THE RESCUE !!
SHAYMIN'S SKY FORME!!

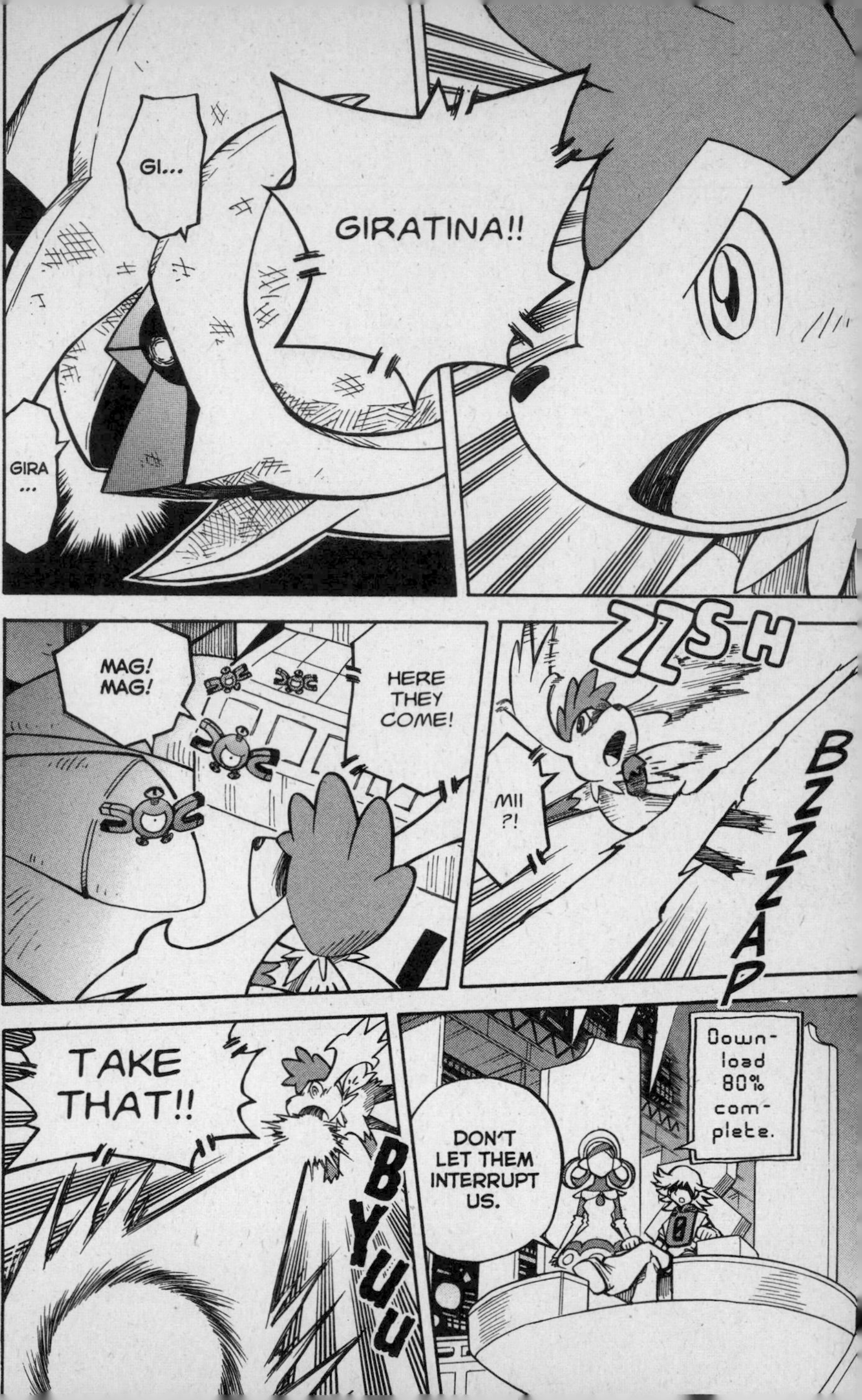
GIRATINA!!
GI...
GIRA ...
ZZSH
MII ?!
BZZZZAP
HERE THEY COME!
MAG! MAG!
Down-load 80% com-plete.
DON'T LET THEM INTERRUPT US.
BYUU
TAKE THAT!!

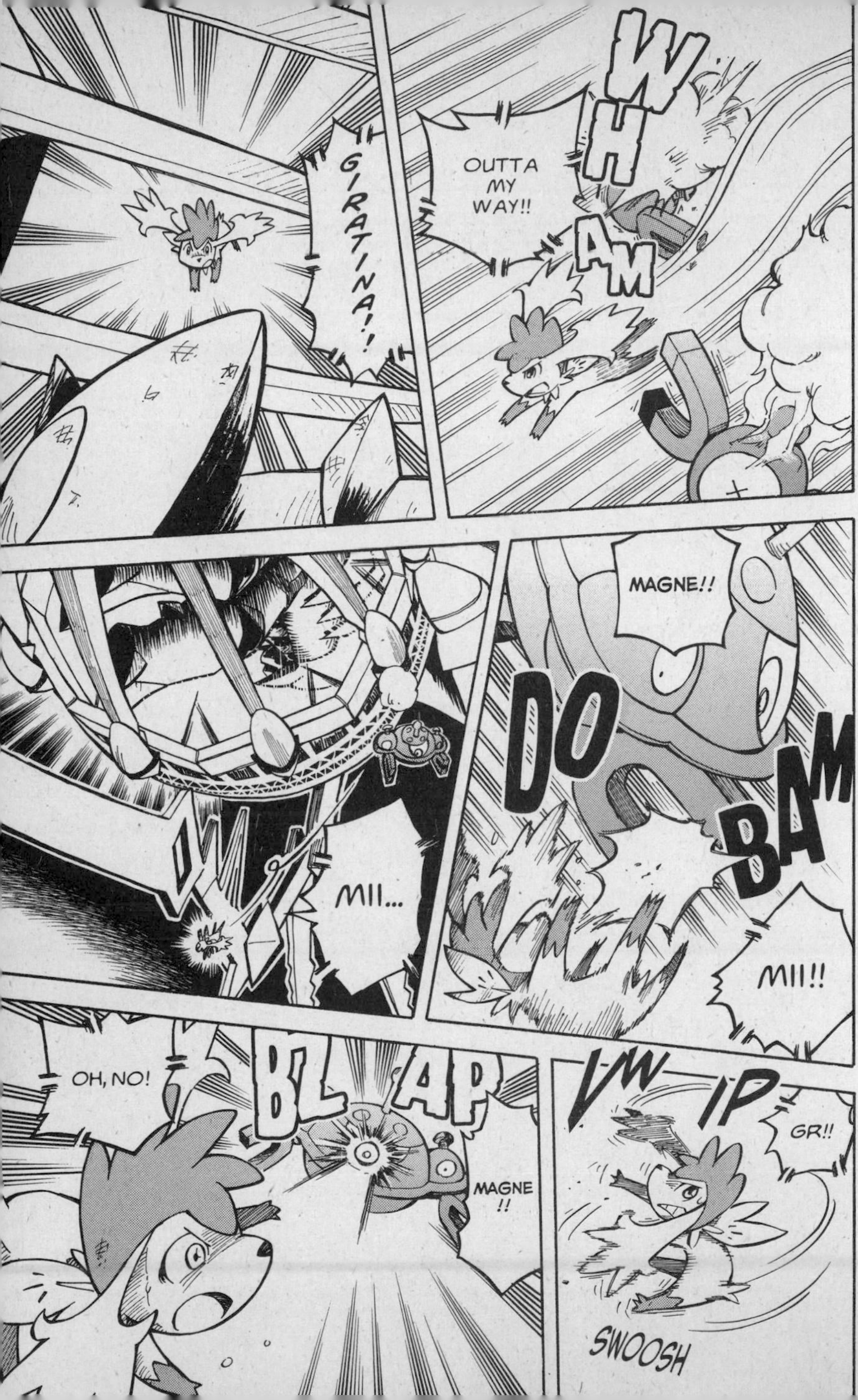
WHAM
OUTTA MY WAY!!
GIRATINA!!
MAGNE!!
DOBAM
MII!!
MII...
VWIP
GR!!
SWOOSH
OH, NO!
BLAP
MAGNE !!

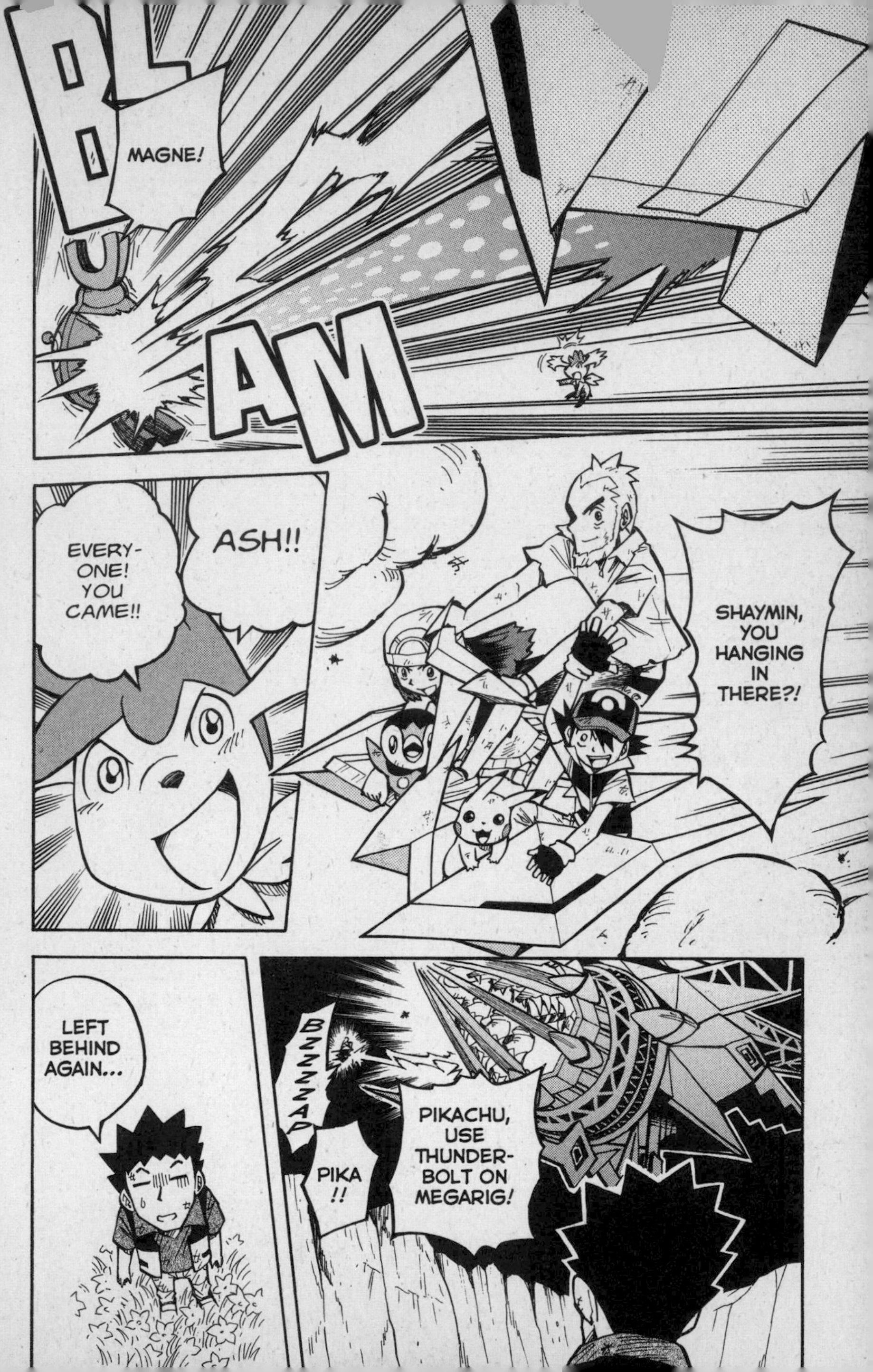
BLAM
MAGNE!
SHAYMIN, YOU HANGING IN THERE?!
ASH!!
EVERY-ONE! YOU CAME!!
BZZZZAP
PIKACHU, USE THUNDER-BOLT ON MEGARIG!
PIKA!!
LEFT BEHIND AGAIN...

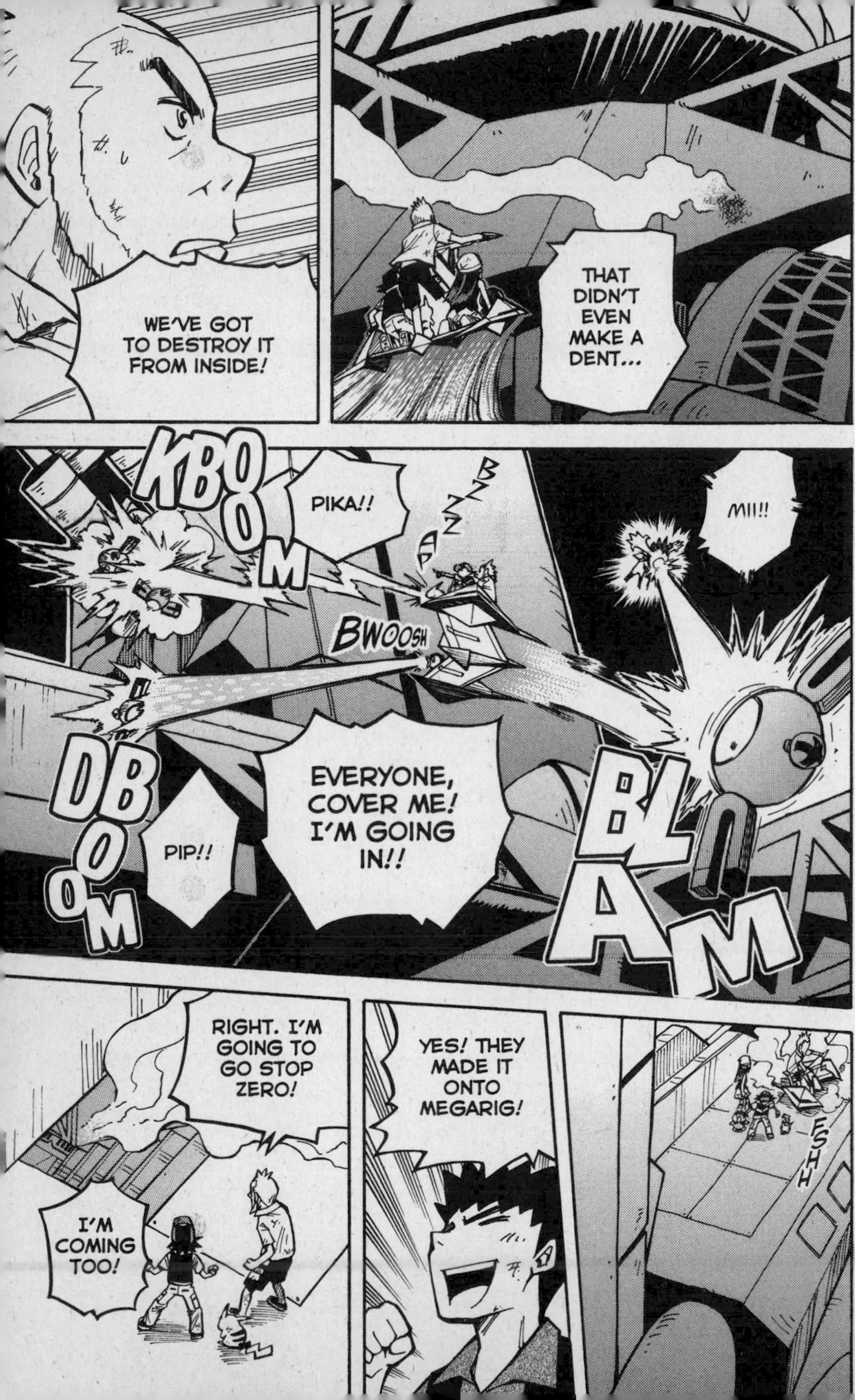
THAT DIDN'T EVEN MAKE A DENT...
WE'VE GOT TO DESTROY IT FROM INSIDE!
MII!!
BZZZT
PIKA!!
KBOOM
BWOOSH
BLAM
EVERYONE, COVER ME! I'M GOING IN!!
PIP!!
DBOOOM
FSHH
YES! THEY MADE IT ONTO MEGARIG!
RIGHT. I'M GOING TO GO STOP ZERO!
I'M COMING TOO!

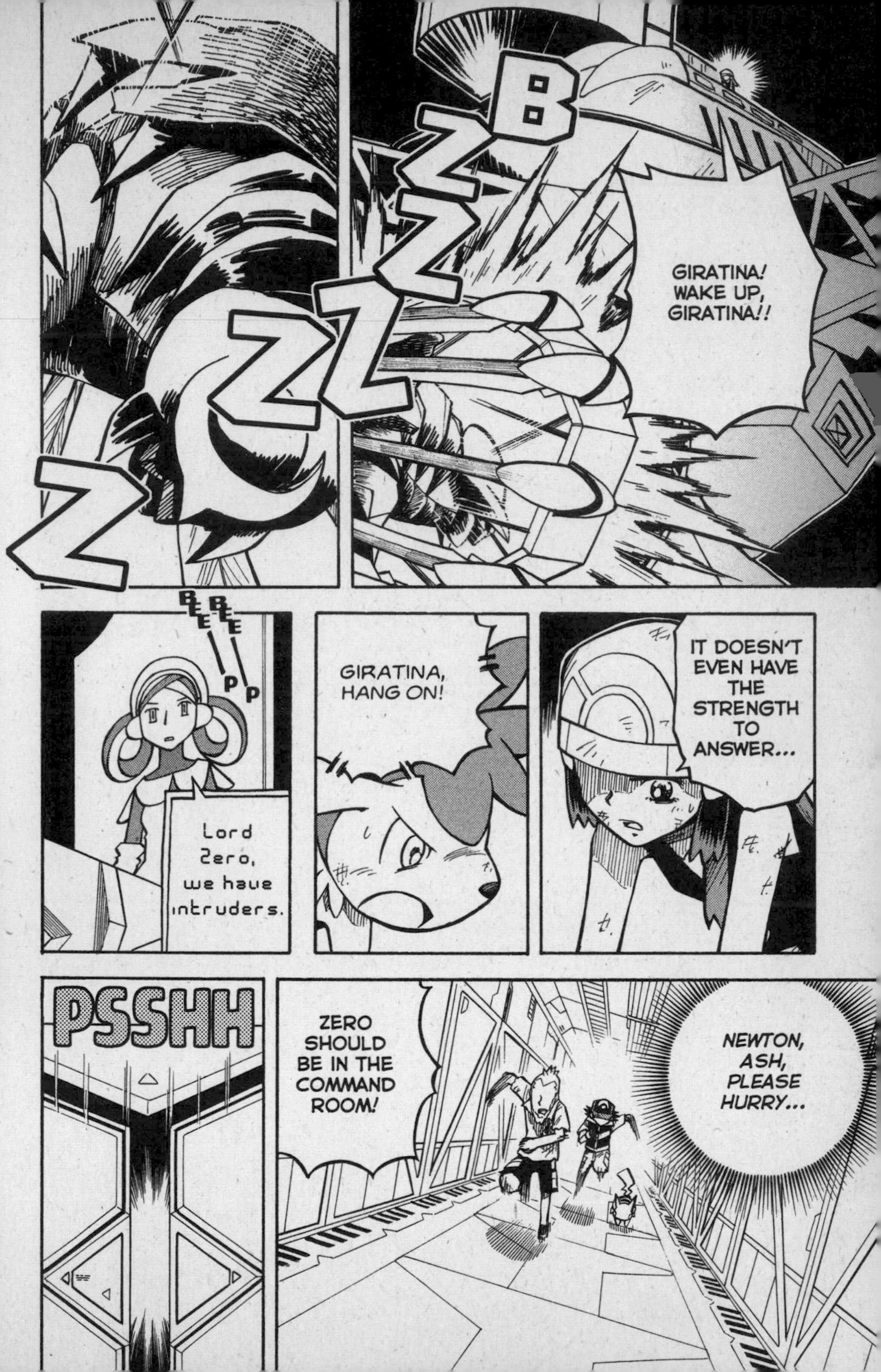
BZZZZZZ
GIRATINA! WAKE UP, GIRATINA!!
IT DOESN'T EVEN HAVE THE STRENGTH TO ANSWER...
GIRATINA, HANG ON!
BEEP BEEP
Lord Zero, we have intruders.
NEWTON, ASH, PLEASE HURRY...
ZERO SHOULD BE IN THE COMMAND ROOM!
PSSHH

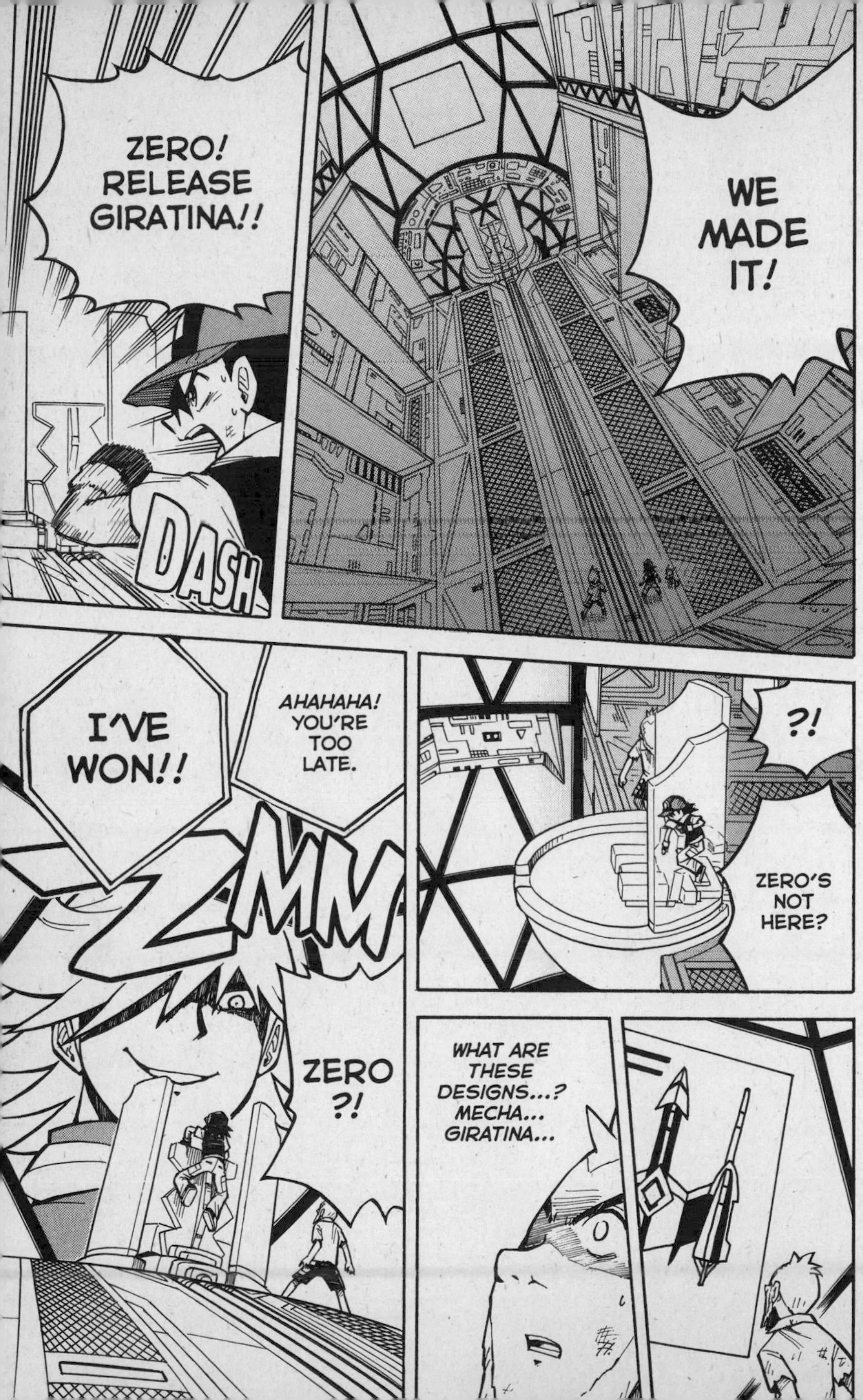
WE MADE IT!
ZERO! RELEASE GIRATINA!!
DASH
?!
ZERO'S NOT HERE?
WHAT ARE THESE DESIGNS...? MECHA... GIRATINA...
AHAHAHA! YOU'RE TOO LATE.
I'VE WON!!
MM
ZERO ?!

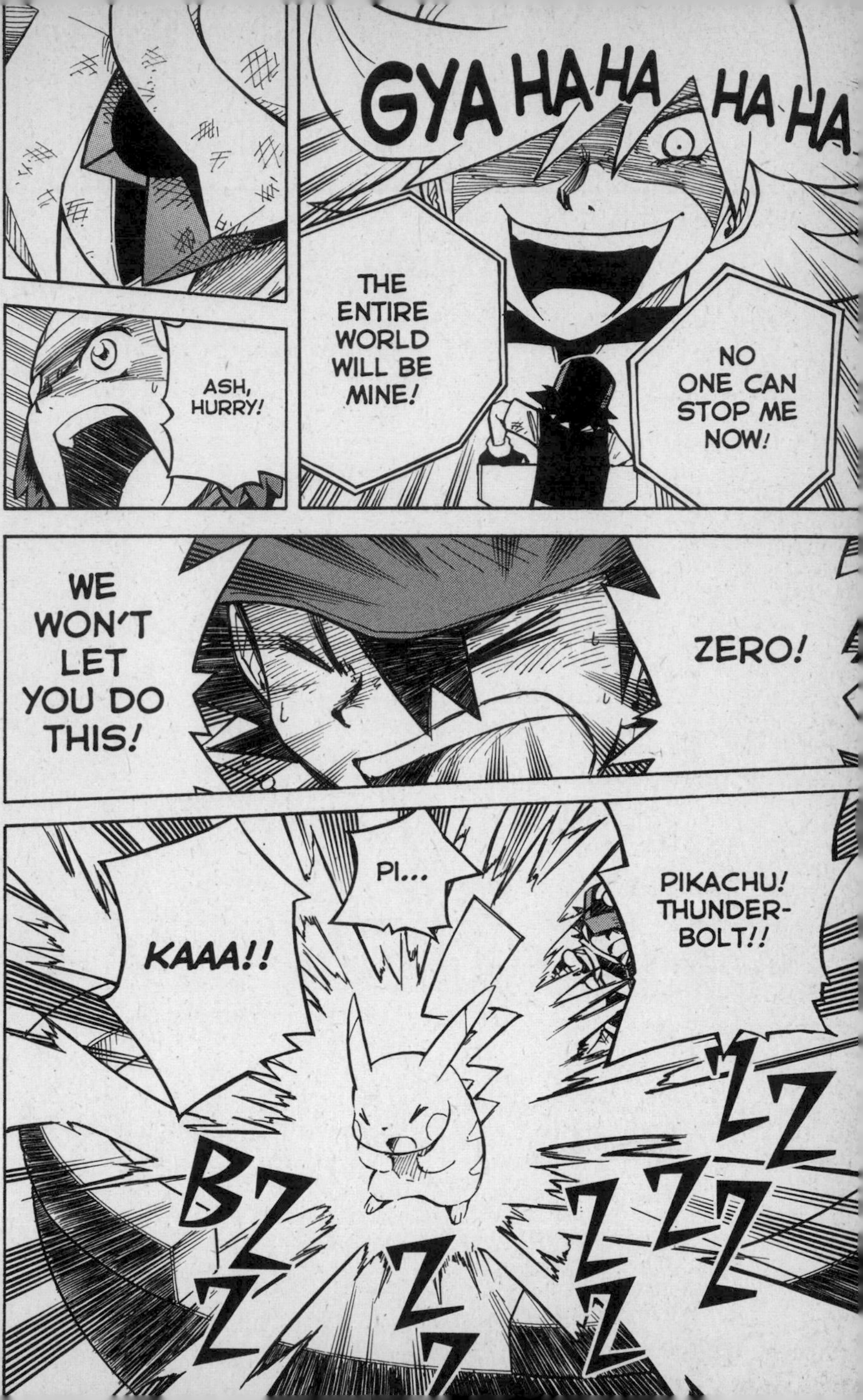
GYA HAHAHA HAHA
THE ENTIRE WORLD WILL BE MINE!
NO ONE CAN STOP ME NOW!
ASH, HURRY!
ZERO!
WE WON'T LET YOU DO THIS!
PIKACHU! THUNDERBOLT!!
PI...
KAAA!!
BZZZZZ
ZZZZZ

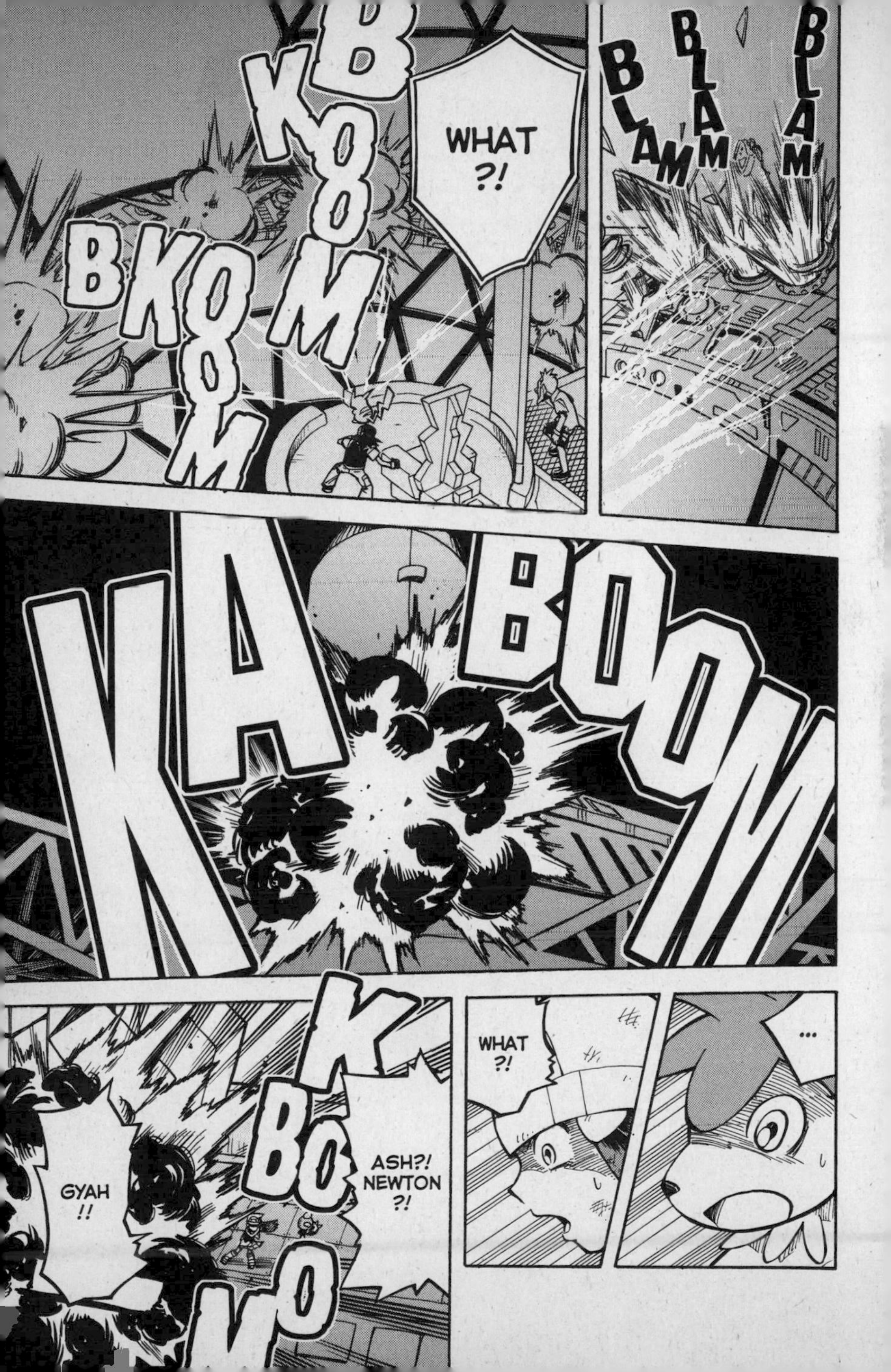
BLAMM
BLAMM
BLAMM
WHAT ?!
BKOOM
BKOOM
KABOOM
...
WHAT ?!
ASH?! NEWTON ?!
K BO O
GYAH !!

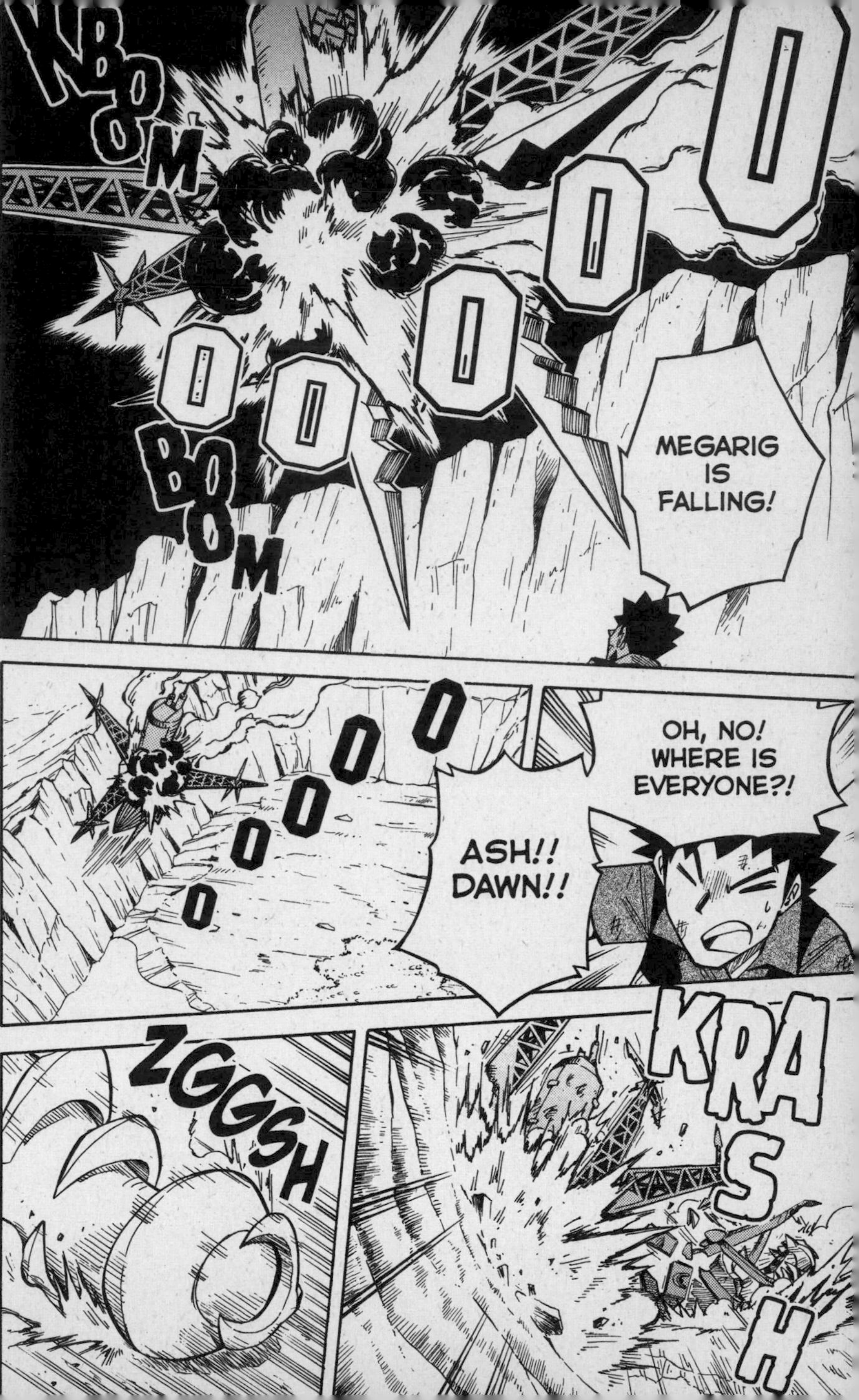
KBOOM
OOOOO
BOOM
MEGARIG IS FALLING!
OH, NO! WHERE IS EVERYONE?!
ASH!! DAWN!!
OOOOOO
KRASH
ZGGSH

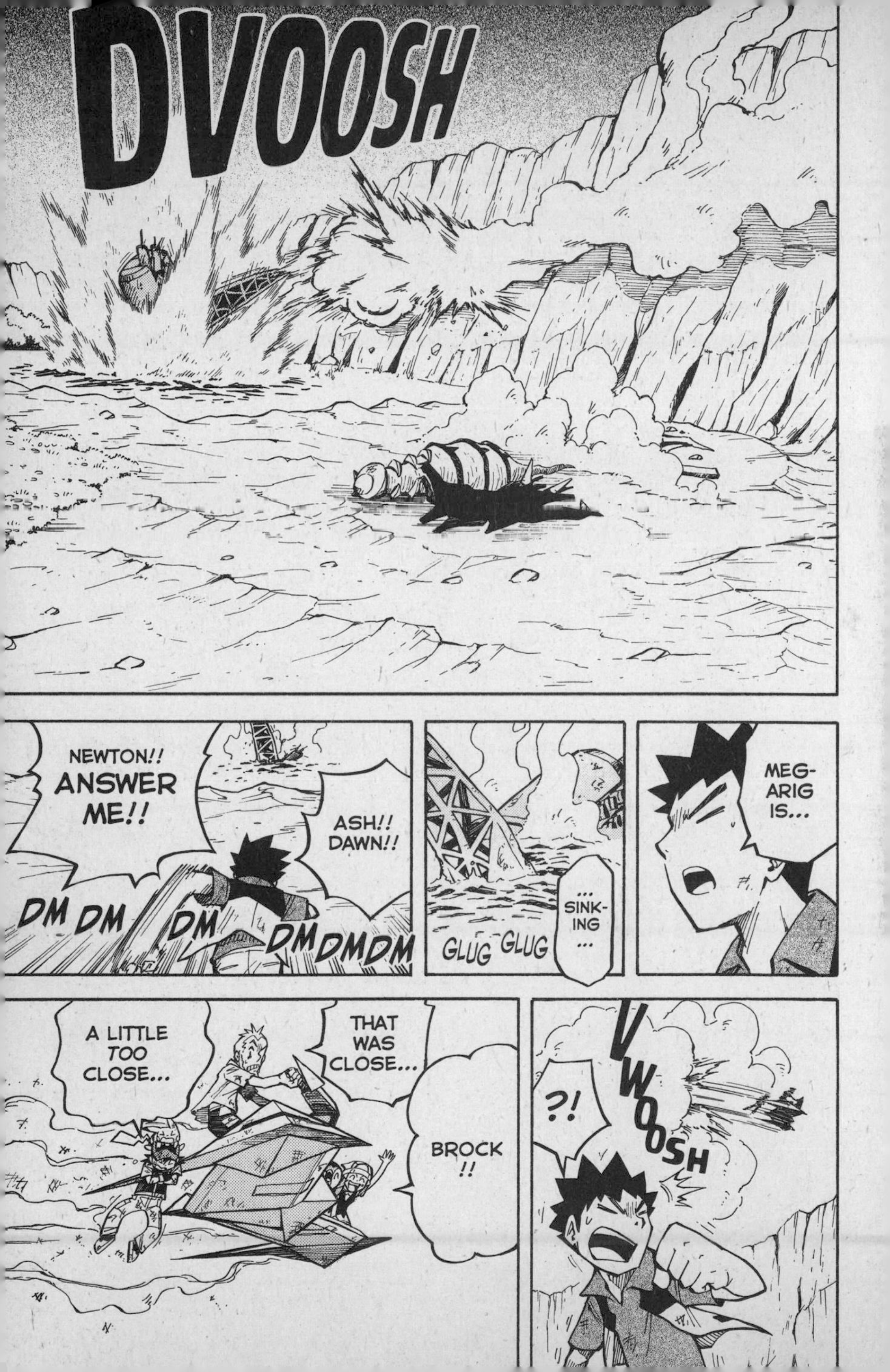
DVOOSH
MEG-ARIG IS...
... SINKING ...
GLUG GLUG
ASH!! DAWN!!
NEWTON!! ANSWER ME!!
DM DM DM DM DMDM
VWOOSH
?!
BROCK !!
THAT WAS CLOSE...
A LITTLE TOO CLOSE...

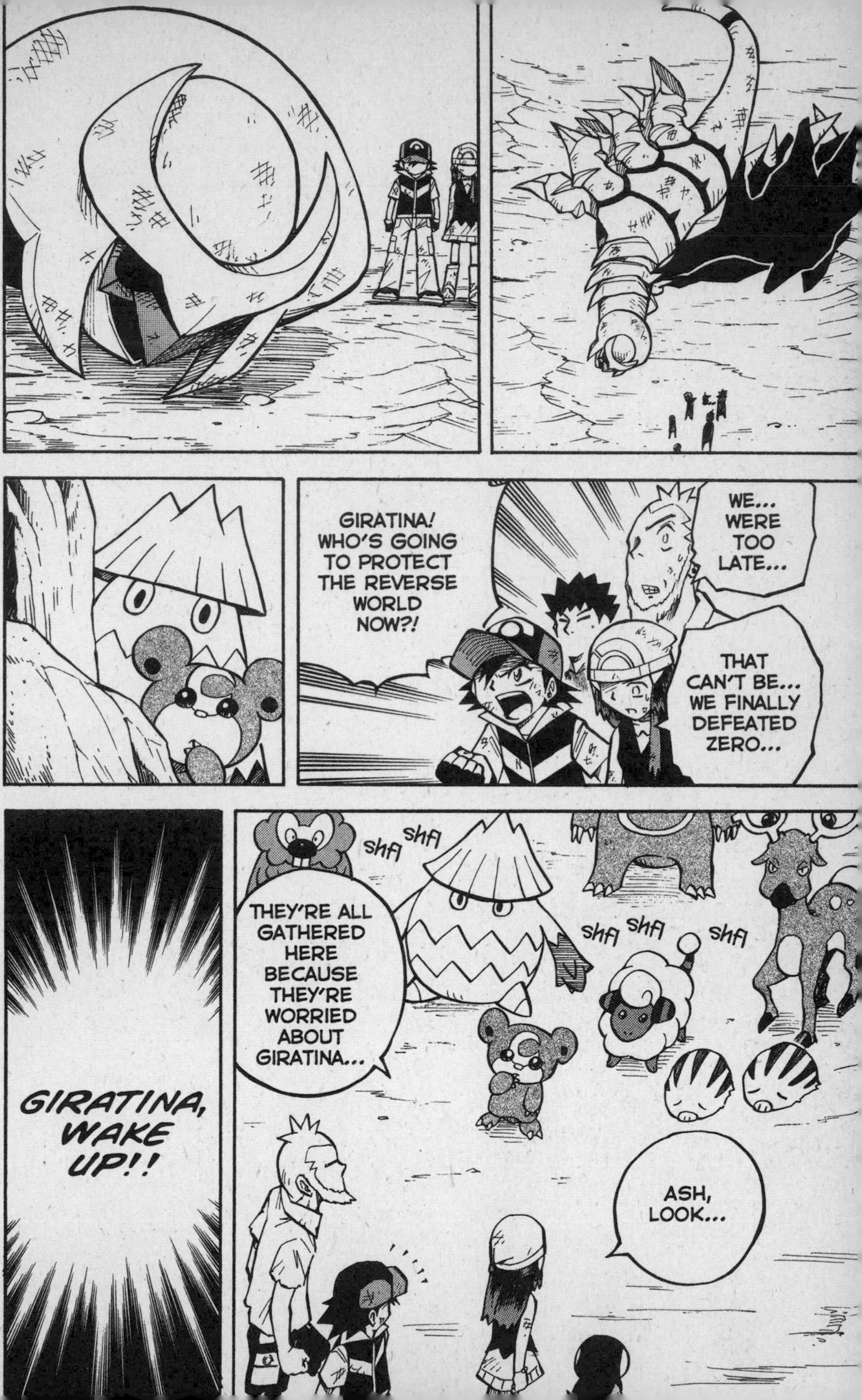
WE... WERE TOO LATE...
GIRATINA! WHO'S GOING TO PROTECT THE REVERSE WORLD NOW?!
THAT CAN'T BE... WE FINALLY DEFEATED ZERO...
shfl shfl shfl
shfl shfl
THEY'RE ALL GATHERED HERE BECAUSE THEY'RE WORRIED ABOUT GIRATINA...
ASH, LOOK...
GIRATINA, WAKE UP!!

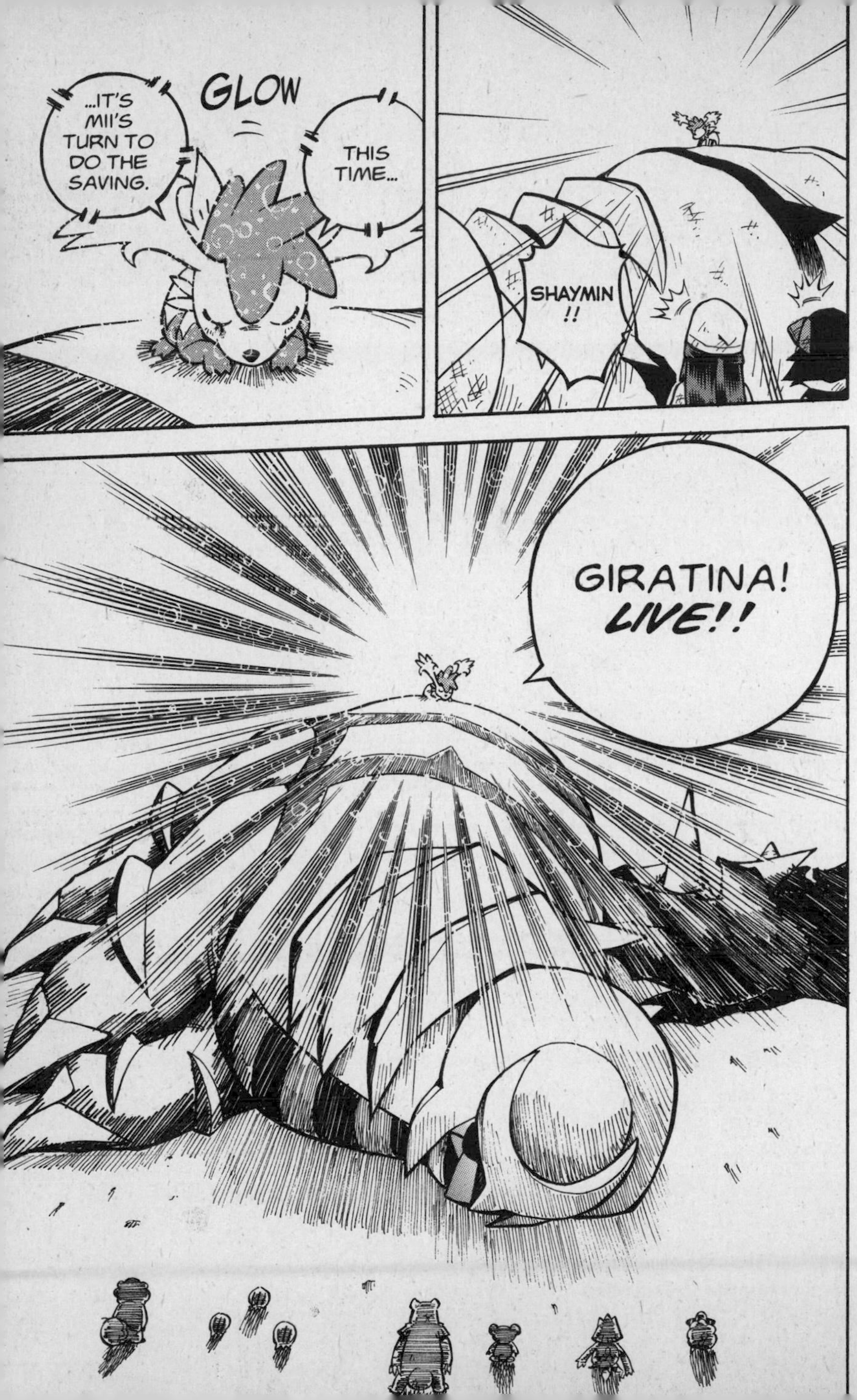
SHAYMIN !!
THIS TIME...
GLOW
...IT'S MII'S TURN TO DO THE SAVING.
GIRATINA! LIVE!!

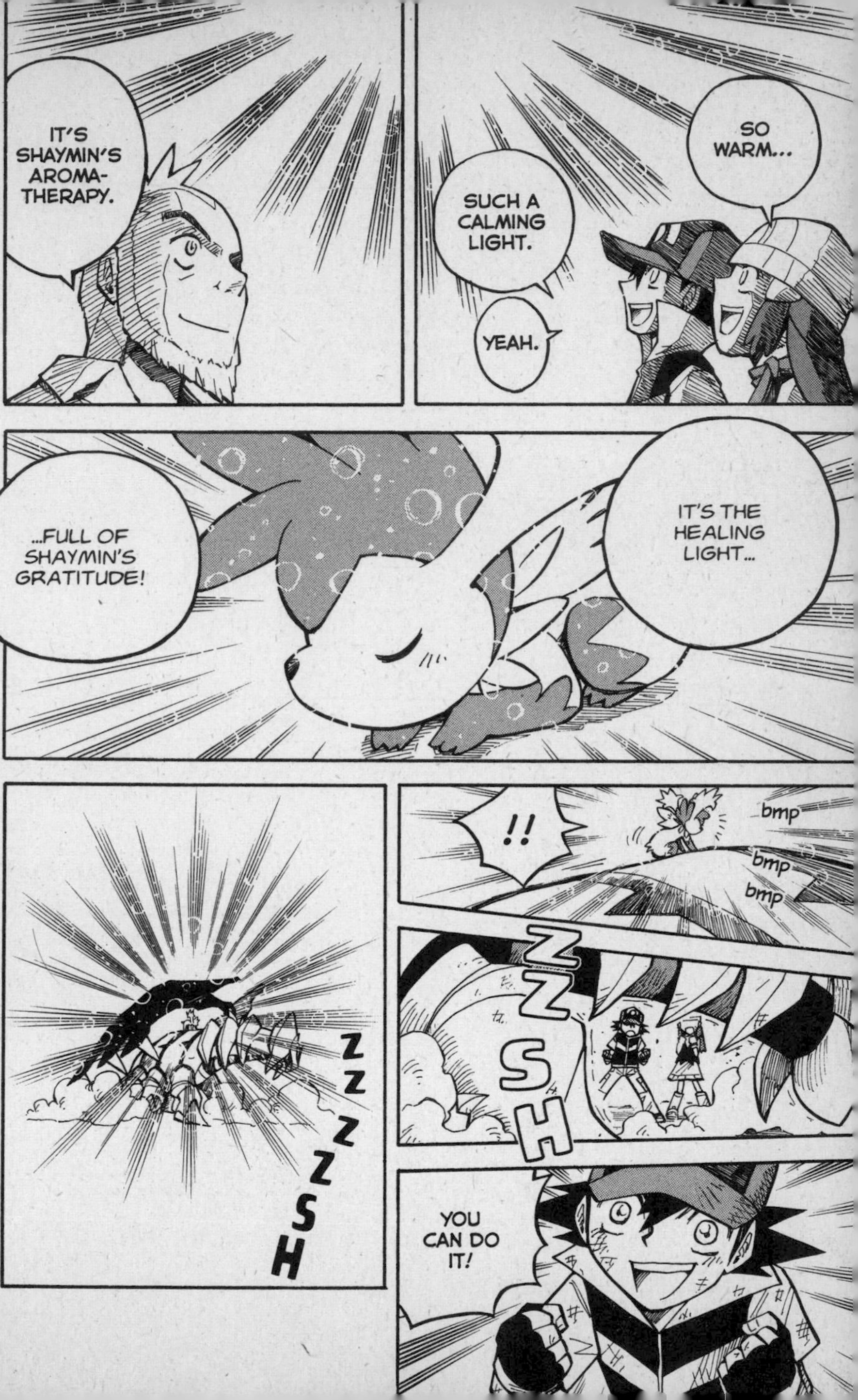
SO WARM...
SUCH A CALMING LIGHT.
YEAH.
IT'S SHAYMIN'S AROMA-THERAPY.
IT'S THE HEALING LIGHT...
...FULL OF SHAYMIN'S GRATITUDE!
!!
bmp
bmp
bmp
ZZSH
YOU CAN DO IT!
ZZZZSH

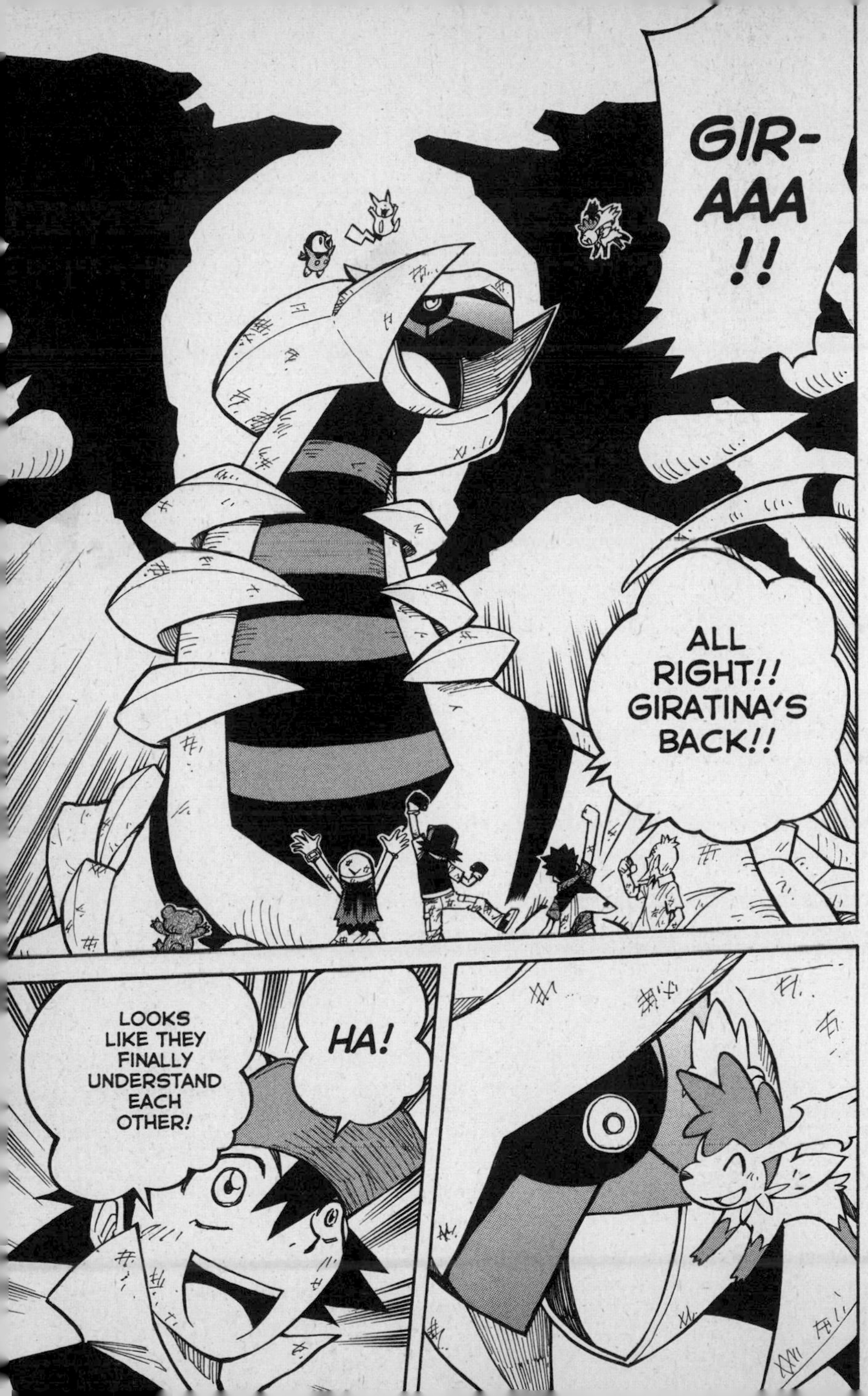
GIR-AAA!!
ALL RIGHT!! GIRATINA'S BACK!!
HA!
LOOKS LIKE THEY FINALLY UNDERSTAND EACH OTHER!

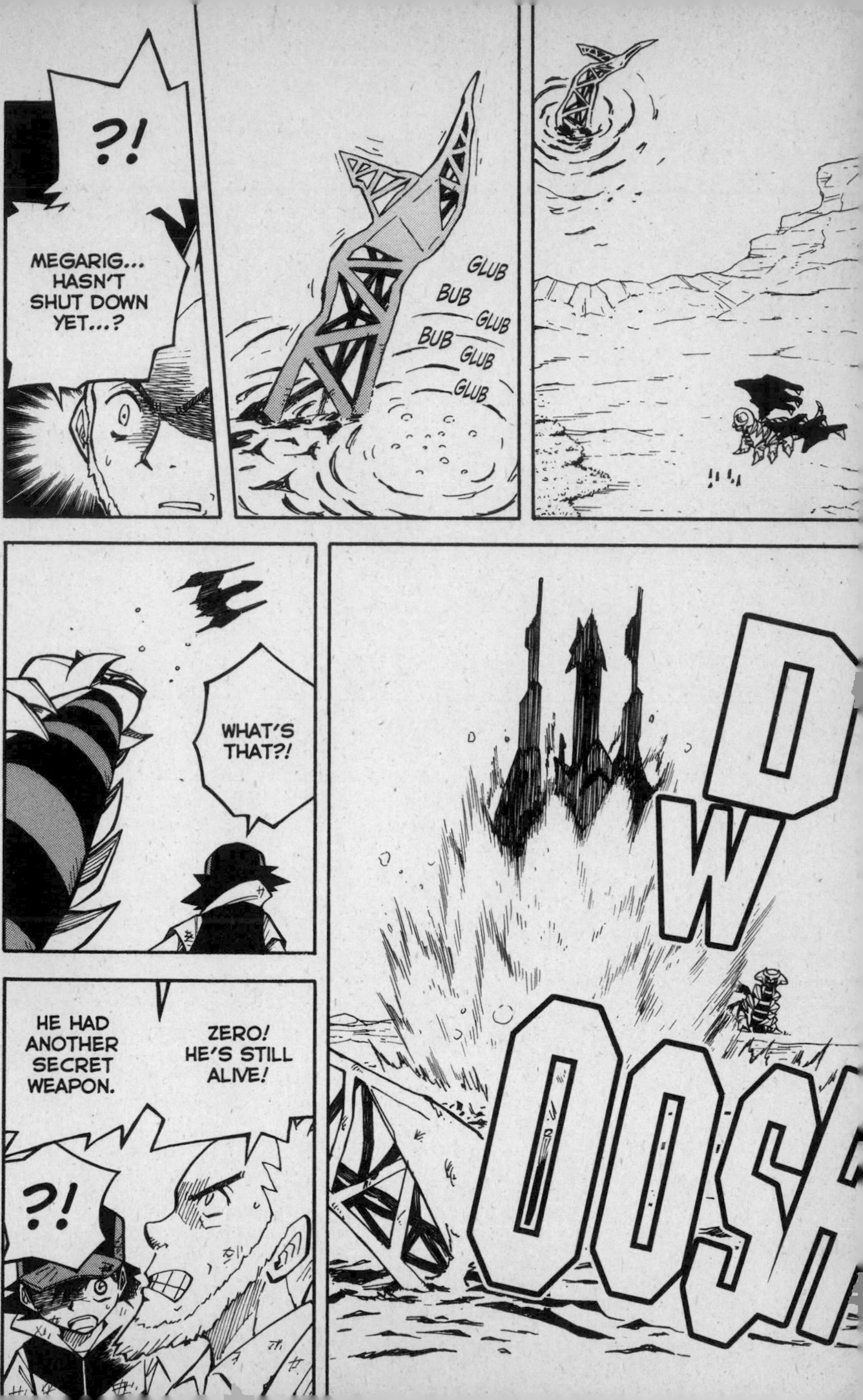
GLUB
BUB
GLUB
BUB
GLUB
GLUB
?!
MEGARIG... HASN'T SHUT DOWN YET...?
DWOOS
WHAT'S THAT?!
ZERO! HE'S STILL ALIVE!
HE HAD ANOTHER SECRET WEAPON.
?!

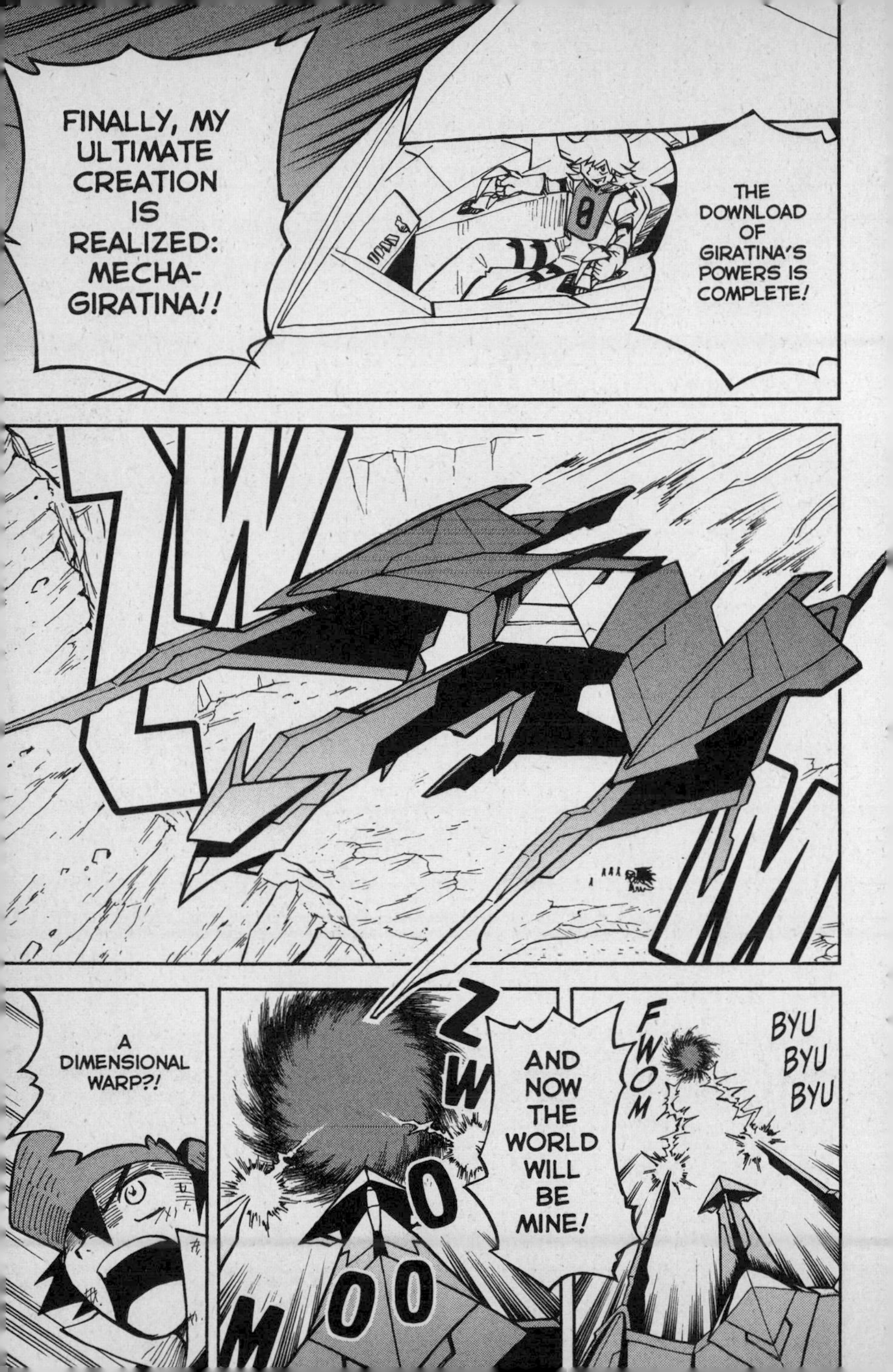
THE DOWNLOAD OF GIRATINA'S POWERS IS COMPLETE!
FINALLY, MY ULTIMATE CREATION IS REALIZED: MECHA-GIRATINA!!
ZWM
BYU BYU BYU
FWOM
AND NOW THE WORLD WILL BE MINE!
ZWOOOM
A DIMENSIONAL WARP?!

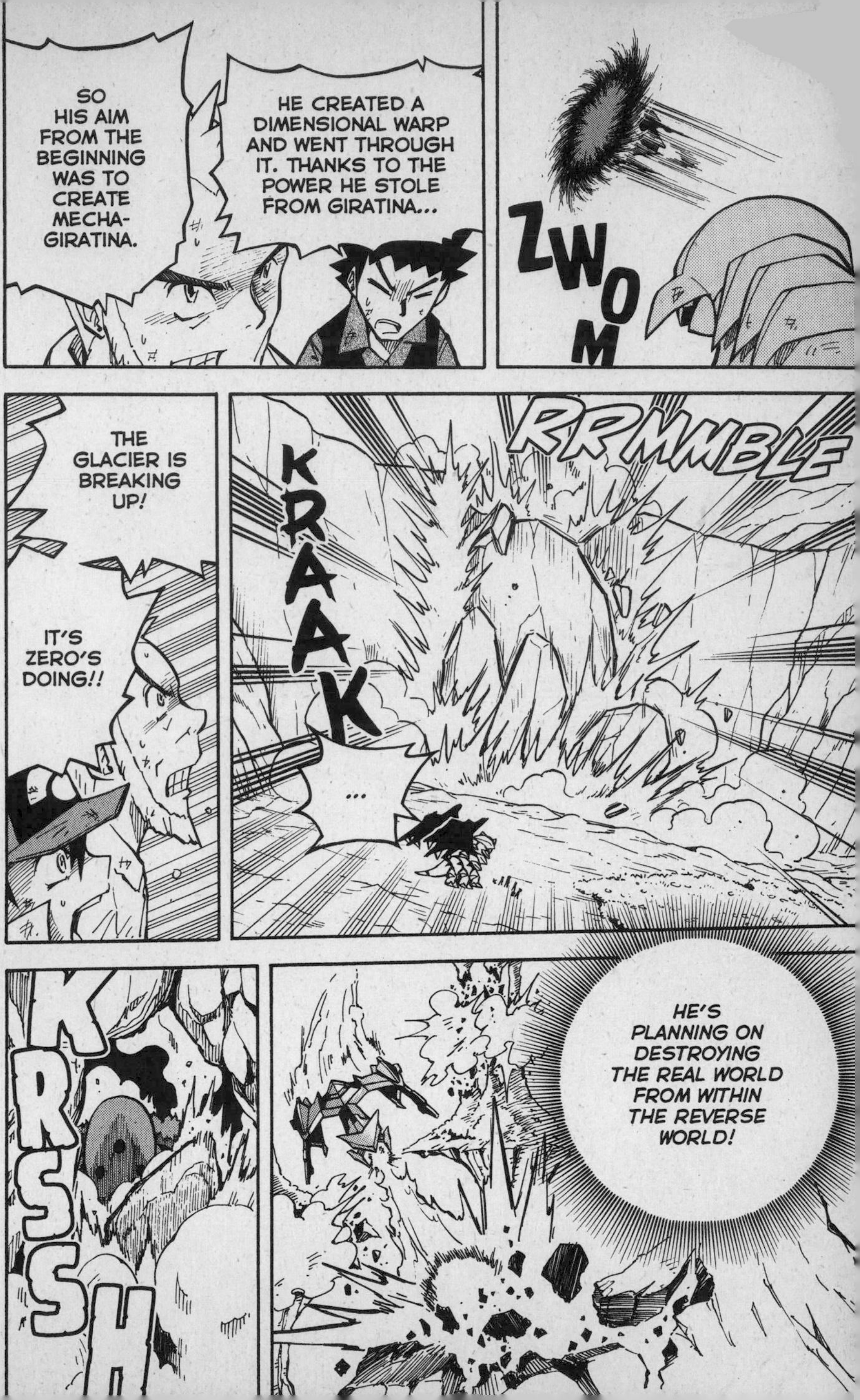
ZWOM
SO HIS AIM FROM THE BEGINNING WAS TO CREATE MECHA-GIRATINA.
HE CREATED A DIMENSIONAL WARP AND WENT THROUGH IT. THANKS TO THE POWER HE STOLE FROM GIRATINA...
RRMMBLE
KRAAK
...
THE GLACIER IS BREAKING UP!
IT'S ZERO'S DOING!!
HE'S PLANNING ON DESTROYING THE REAL WORLD FROM WITHIN THE REVERSE WORLD!
KRSSH

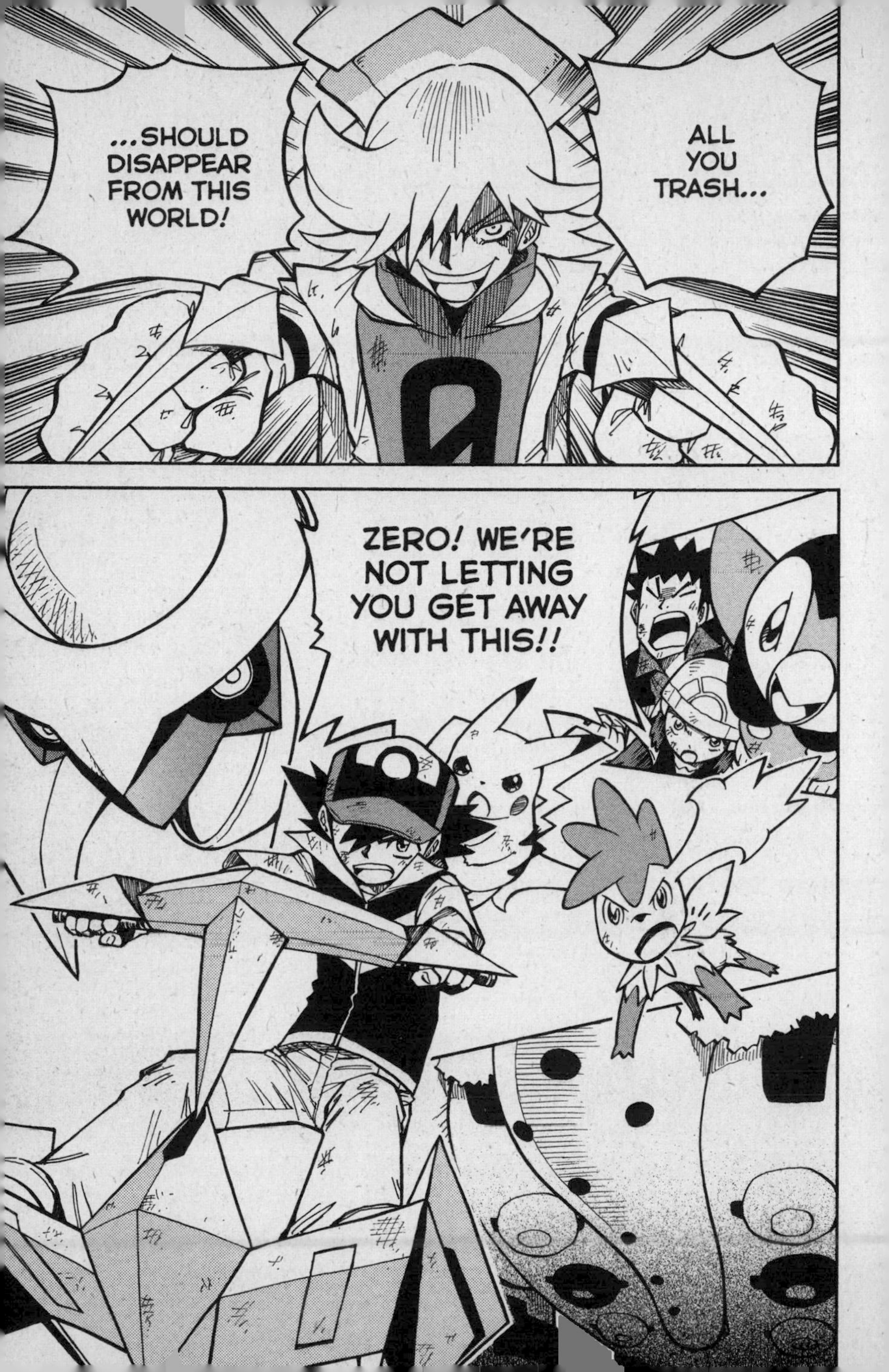
ALL YOU TRASH...
...SHOULD DISAPPEAR FROM THIS WORLD!
ZERO! WE'RE NOT LETTING YOU GET AWAY WITH THIS!!

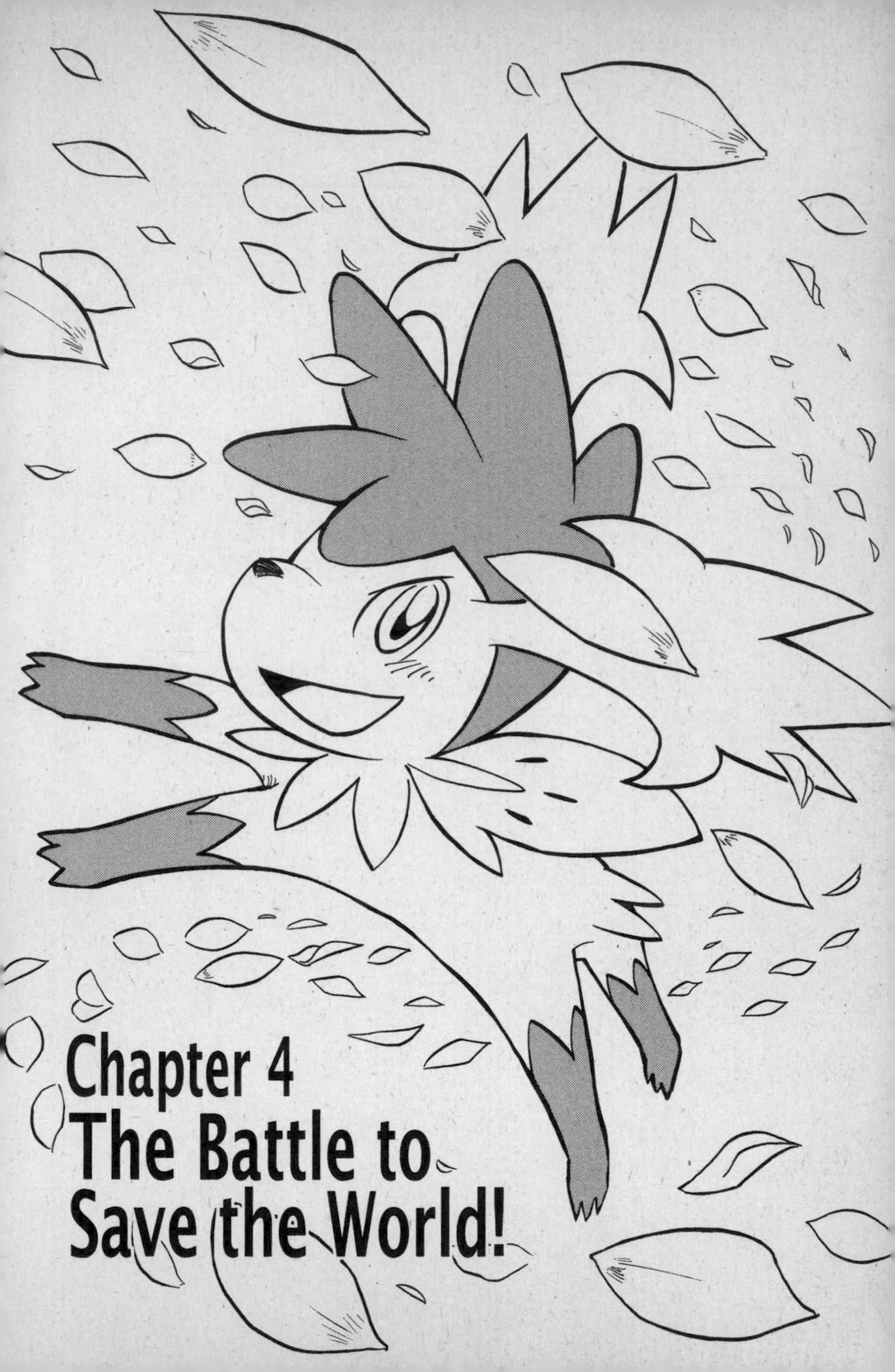

Chapter 4
The Battle to Save the World!

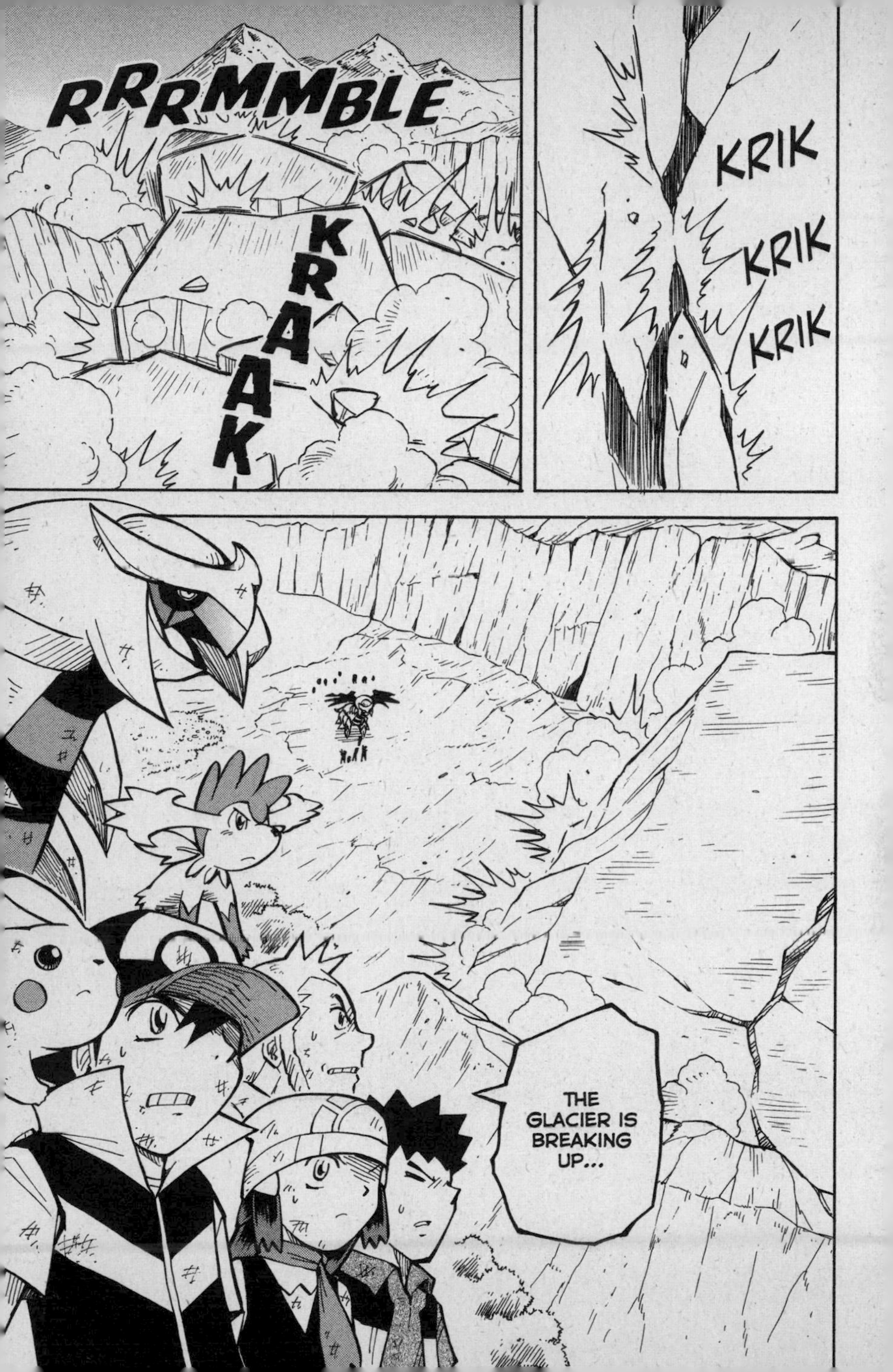
KRIK
KRIK
KRIK
RRRMMBLE
KRAAK
THE GLACIER IS BREAKING UP...

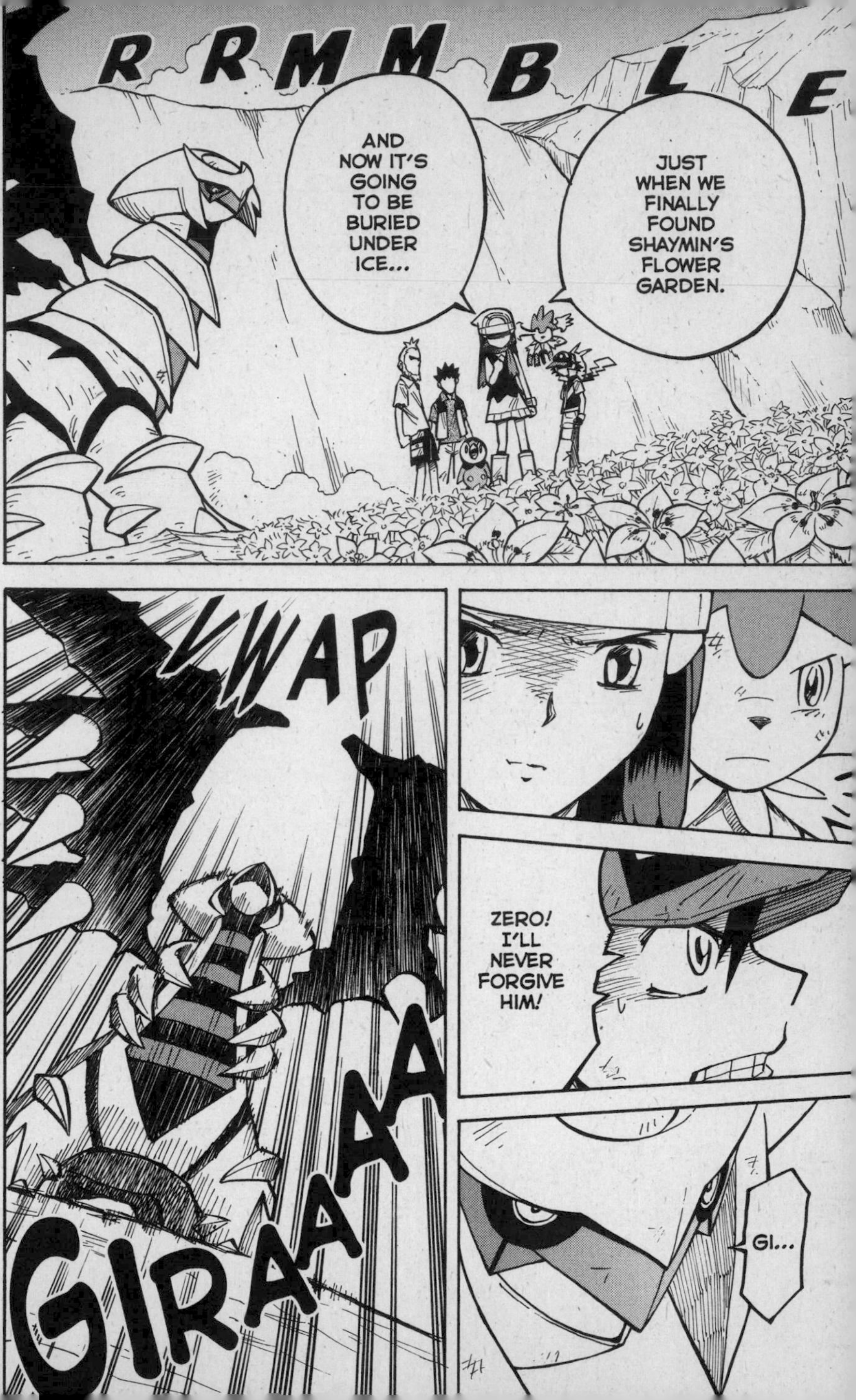
RRMMBLE
JUST WHEN WE FINALLY FOUND SHAYMIN'S FLOWER GARDEN.
AND NOW IT'S GOING TO BE BURIED UNDER ICE...
ZERO! I'LL NEVER FORGIVE HIM!
GI...
VWAP
GIRAAAAA

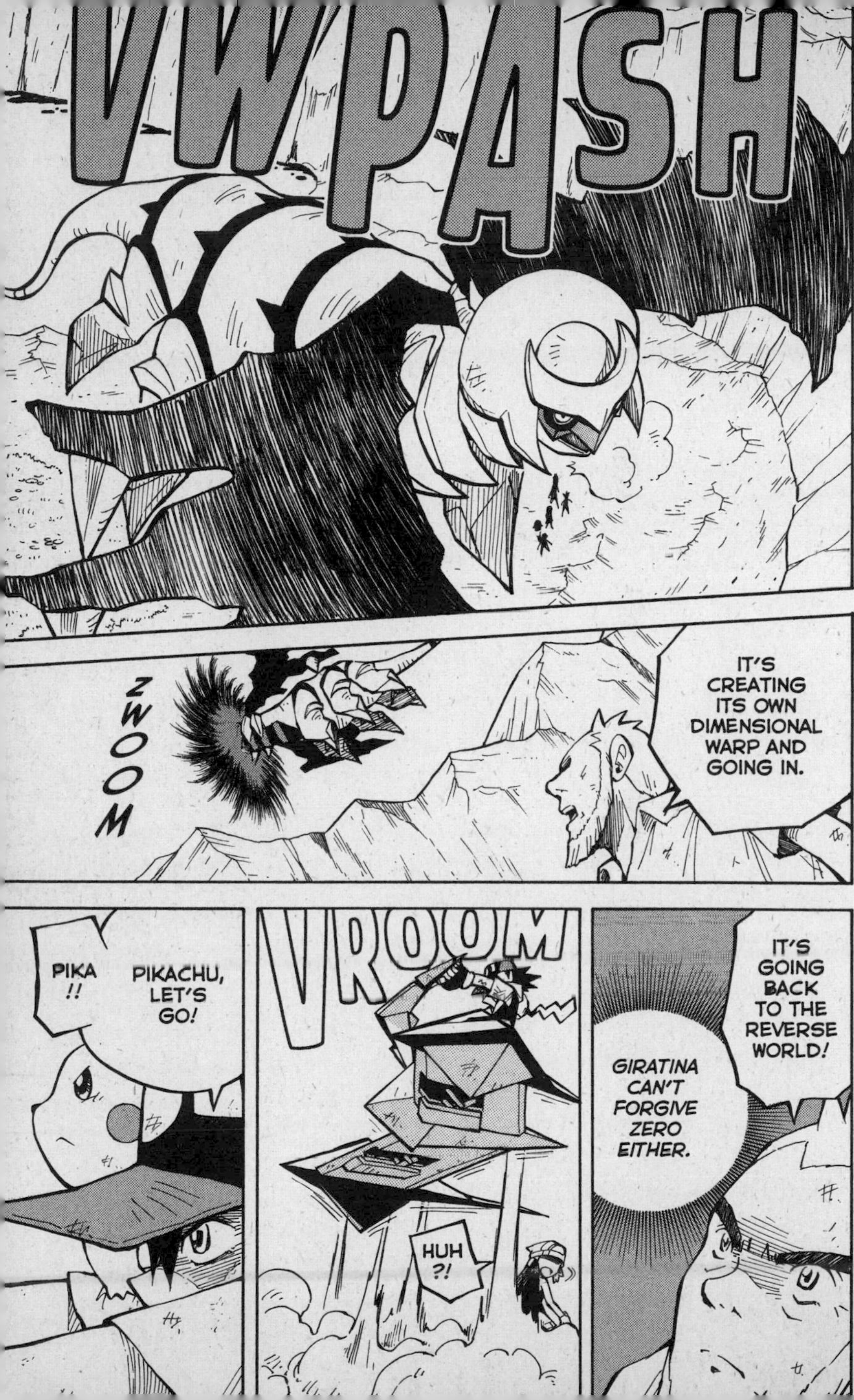
VWPASH
IT'S CREATING ITS OWN DIMENSIONAL WARP AND GOING IN.
ZWOOM
IT'S GOING BACK TO THE REVERSE WORLD!
GIRATINA CAN'T FORGIVE ZERO EITHER.
VROOM
HUH?!
PIKACHU, LET'S GO!
PIKA!!

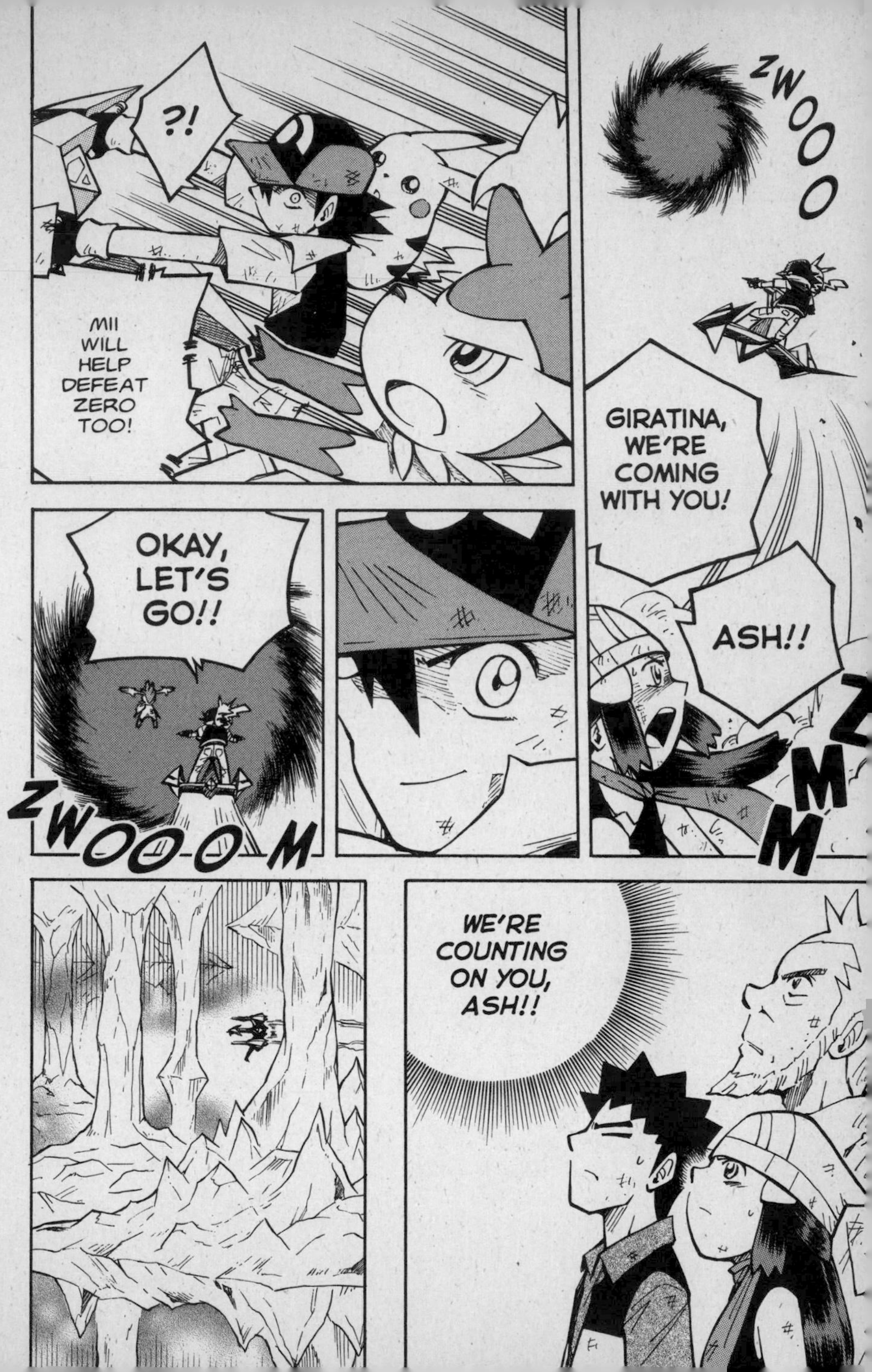
ZWOOOO
GIRATINA, WE'RE COMING WITH YOU!
?!
MII WILL HELP DEFEAT ZERO TOO!
ASH!!
ZMMM
OKAY, LET'S GO!!
ZWOOOOM
WE'RE COUNTING ON YOU, ASH!!

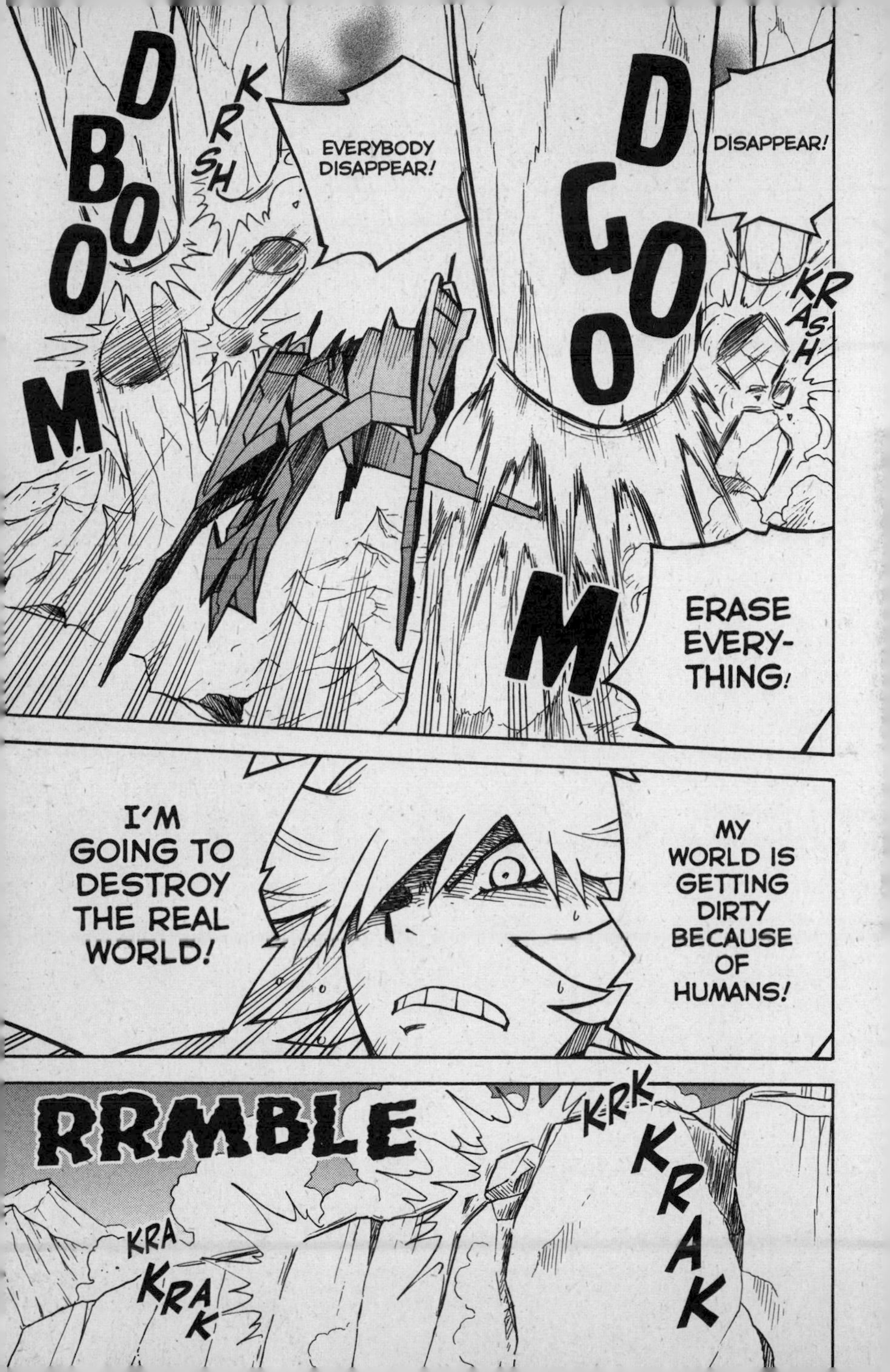
DISAPPEAR!
DGOOM
KRASH
ERASE EVERYTHING!
EVERYBODY DISAPPEAR!
KRSH
DBOOM
MY WORLD IS GETTING DIRTY BECAUSE OF HUMANS!
I'M GOING TO DESTROY THE REAL WORLD!
KRK
KRAK
RRMBLE
KRA KRAK

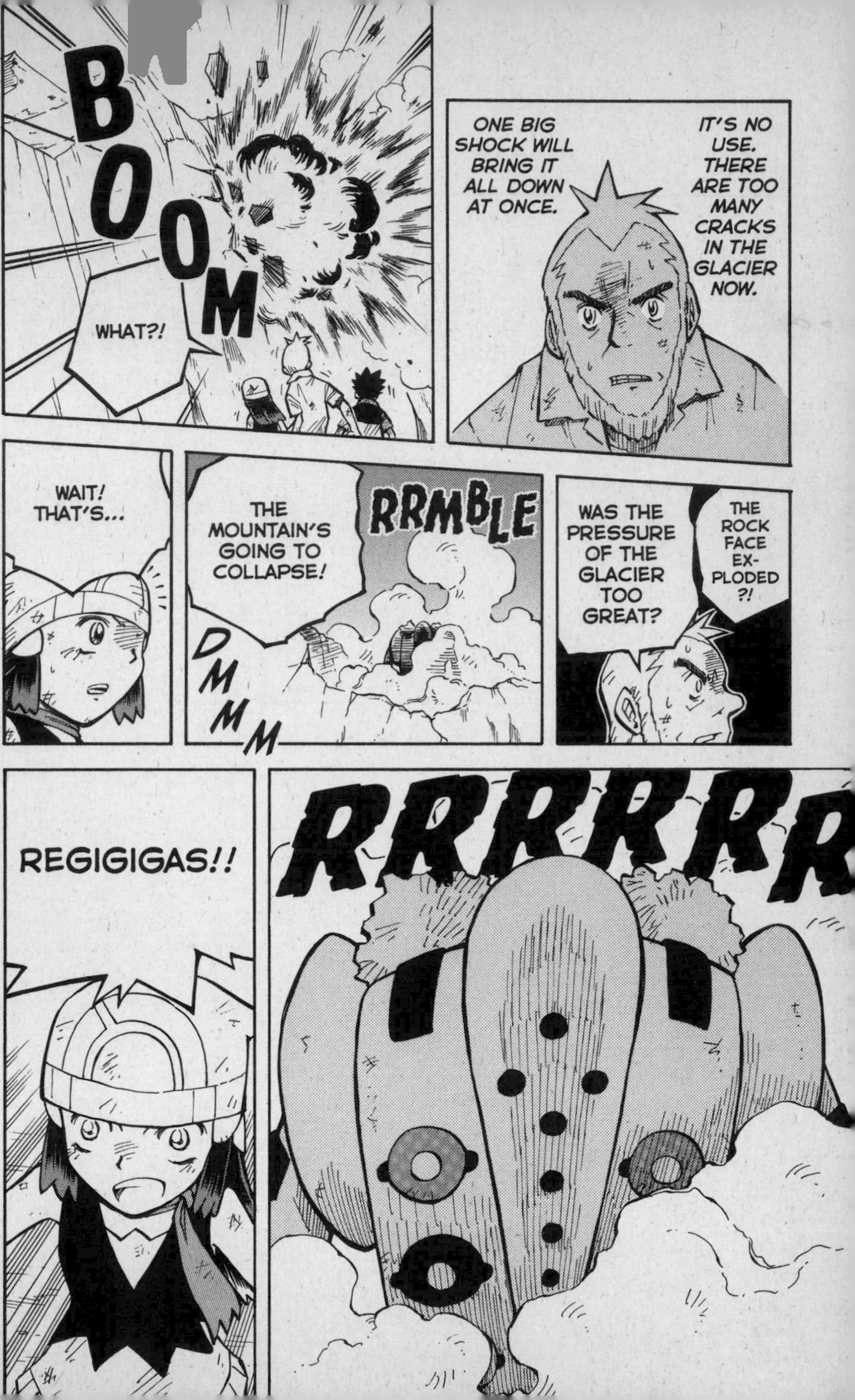
IT'S NO USE. THERE ARE TOO MANY CRACKS IN THE GLACIER NOW.
ONE BIG SHOCK WILL BRING IT ALL DOWN AT ONCE.
BOOM
WHAT?!
THE ROCK FACE EX-PLODED?!
WAS THE PRESSURE OF THE GLACIER TOO GREAT?
RRMBLE
THE MOUNTAIN'S GOING TO COLLAPSE!
DMMM
WAIT! THAT'S...
RRRRRR
REGIGIGAS!!

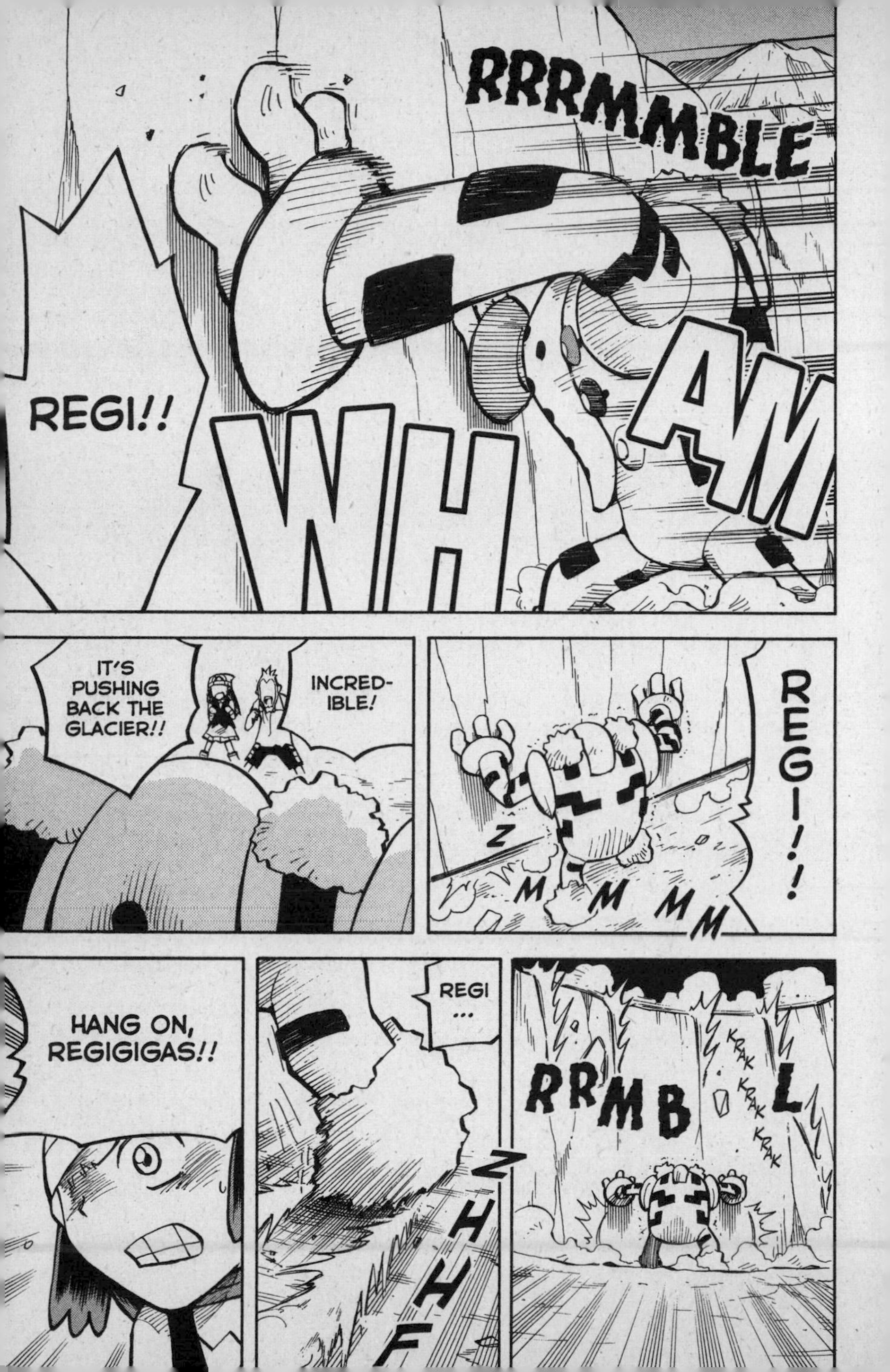
RRRMMBLE
WHAM
REGI!!
REGI!!
ZMMMMM
INCRED-IBLE!
IT'S PUSHING BACK THE GLACIER!!
RRMBL
KRAK KRAK KRAK
REGI...
ZHHHF
HANG ON, REGIGIGAS!!

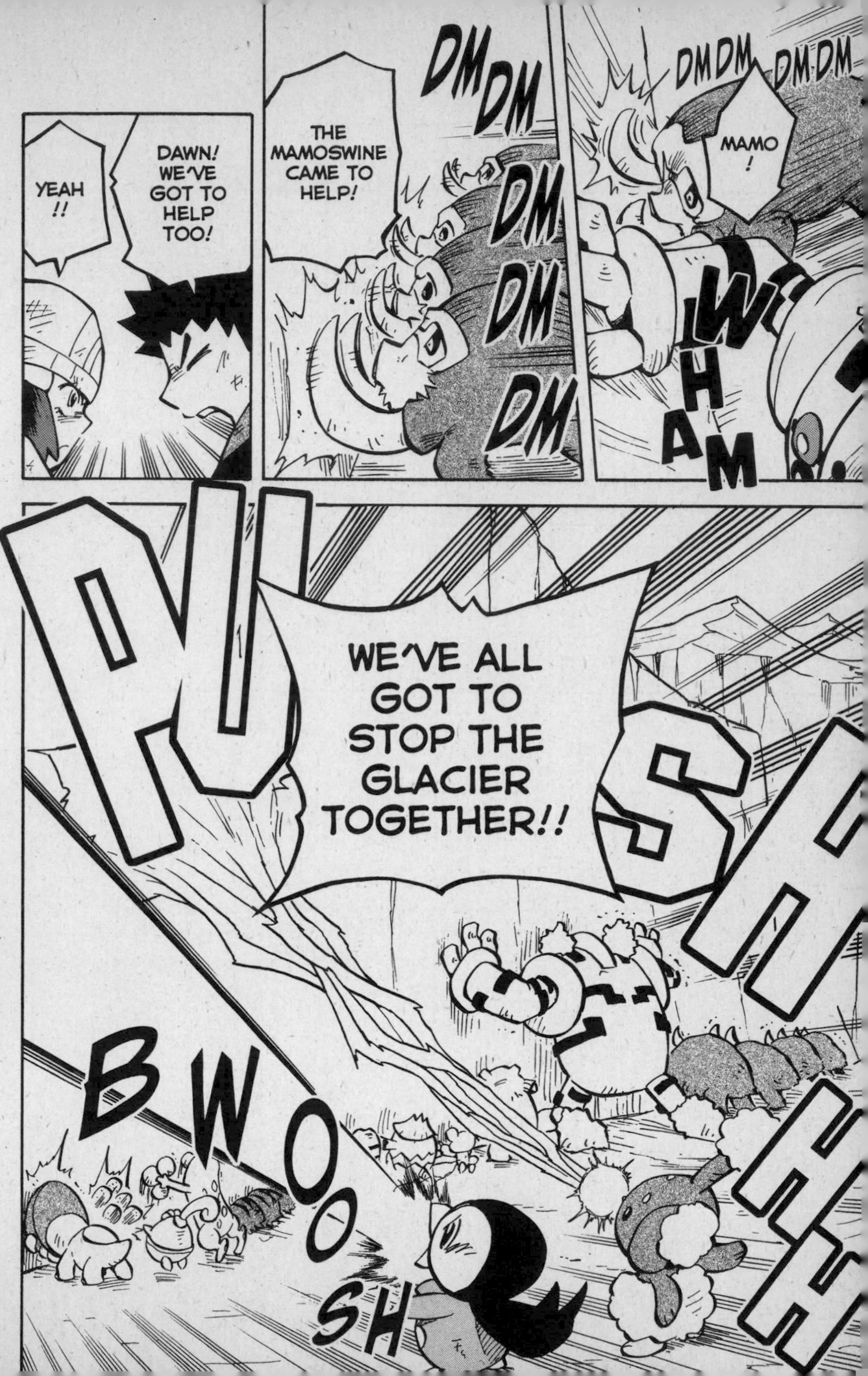
DMDM DMDM
MAMO!
WHAM
THE MAMOSWINE CAME TO HELP!
DMDM DM DM DM DM
DAWN! WE'VE GOT TO HELP TOO!
YEAH!!
PUSH
WE'VE ALL GOT TO STOP THE GLACIER TOGETHER!!
BWOOSH

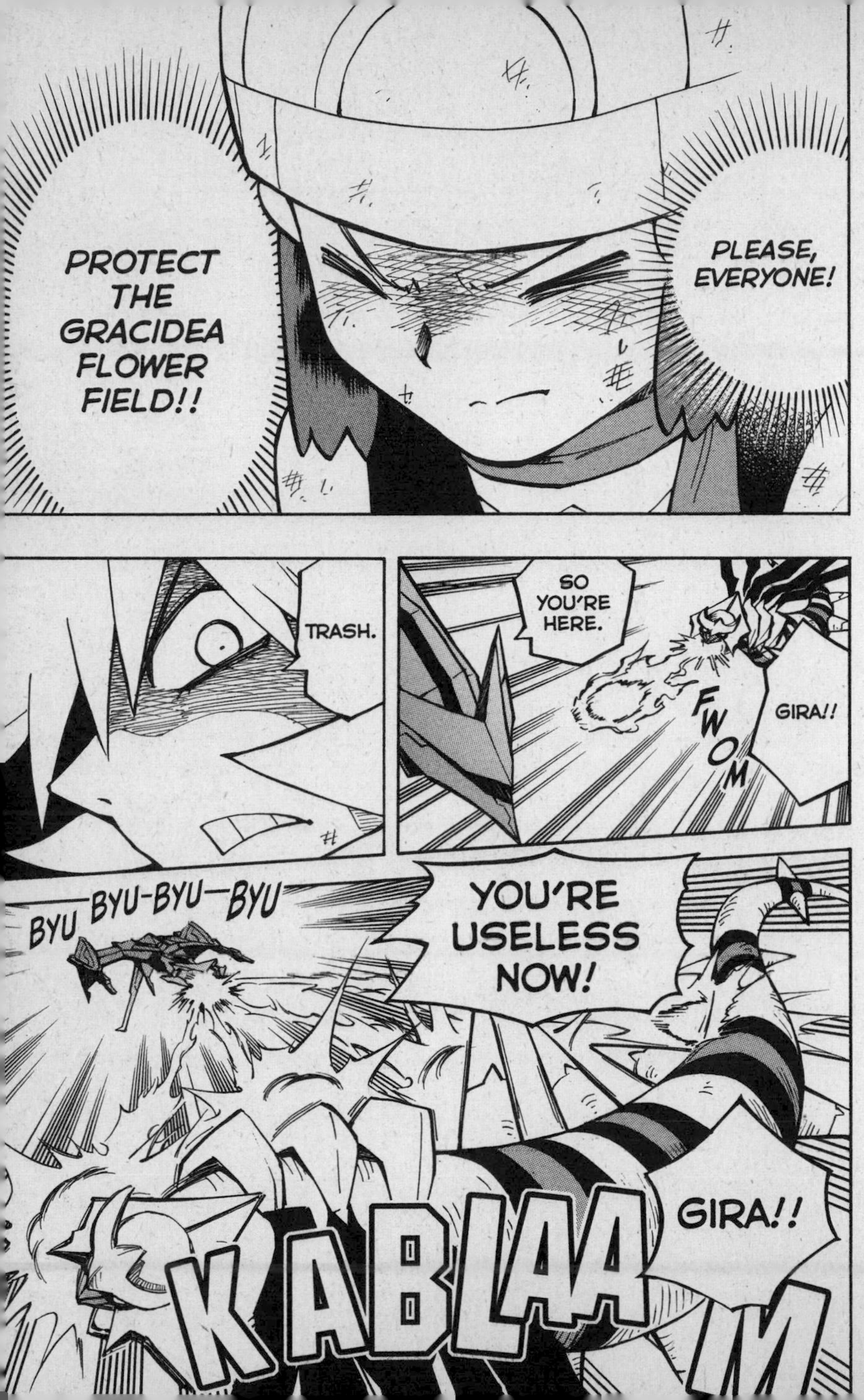
PLEASE, EVERYONE!
PROTECT THE GRACIDEA FLOWER FIELD!!
SO YOU'RE HERE.
GIRA!!
FWOM
TRASH.
YOU'RE USELESS NOW!
BYU BYU-BYU-BYU
GIRA!!
KABLAAM

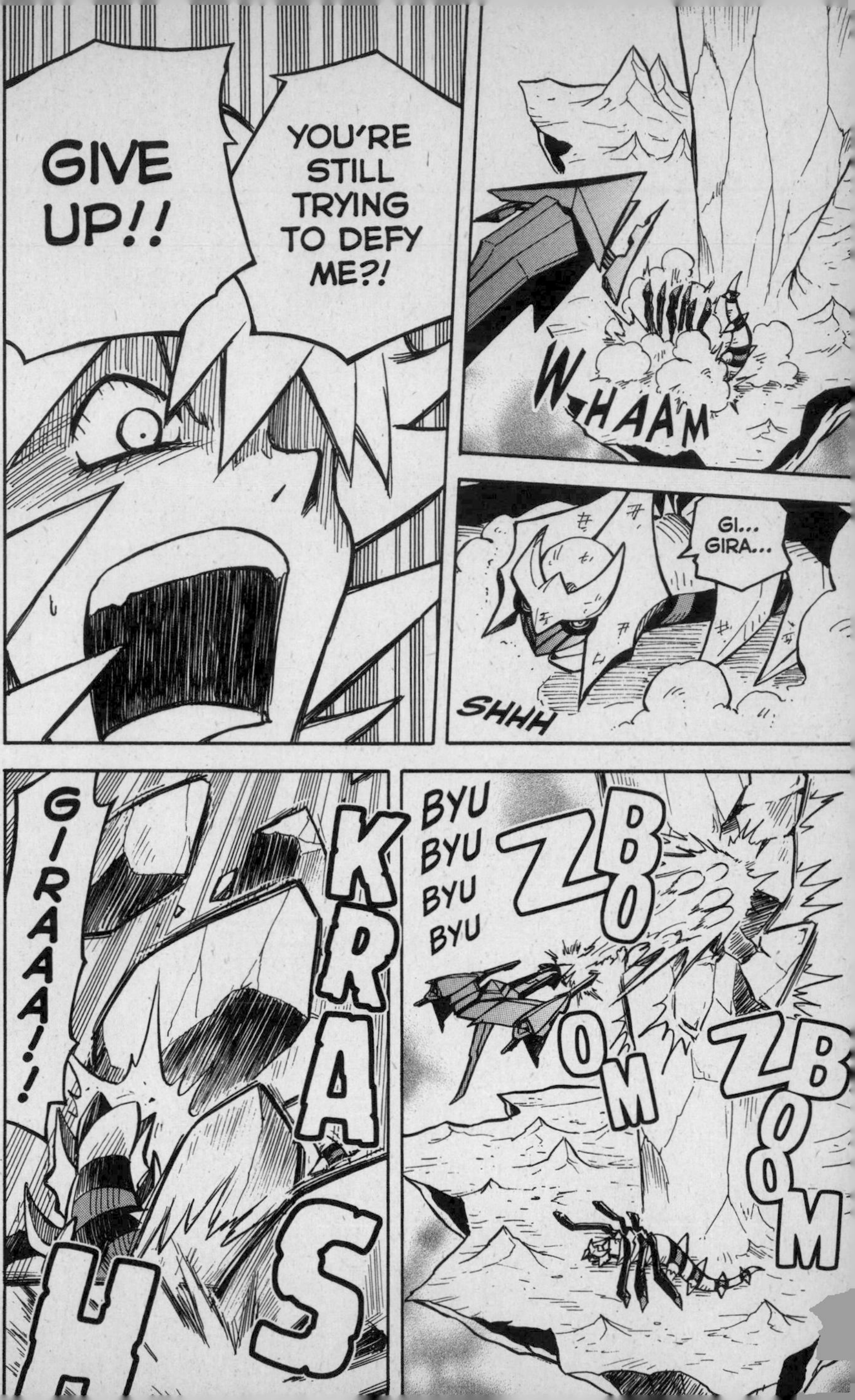
W-HAAM
GI... GIRA...
SHHH
YOU'RE STILL TRYING TO DEFY ME?!
GIVE UP!!
ZBOOM
BYU BYU BYU BYU
ZBOOM
KRASH
GIRAAAA!!

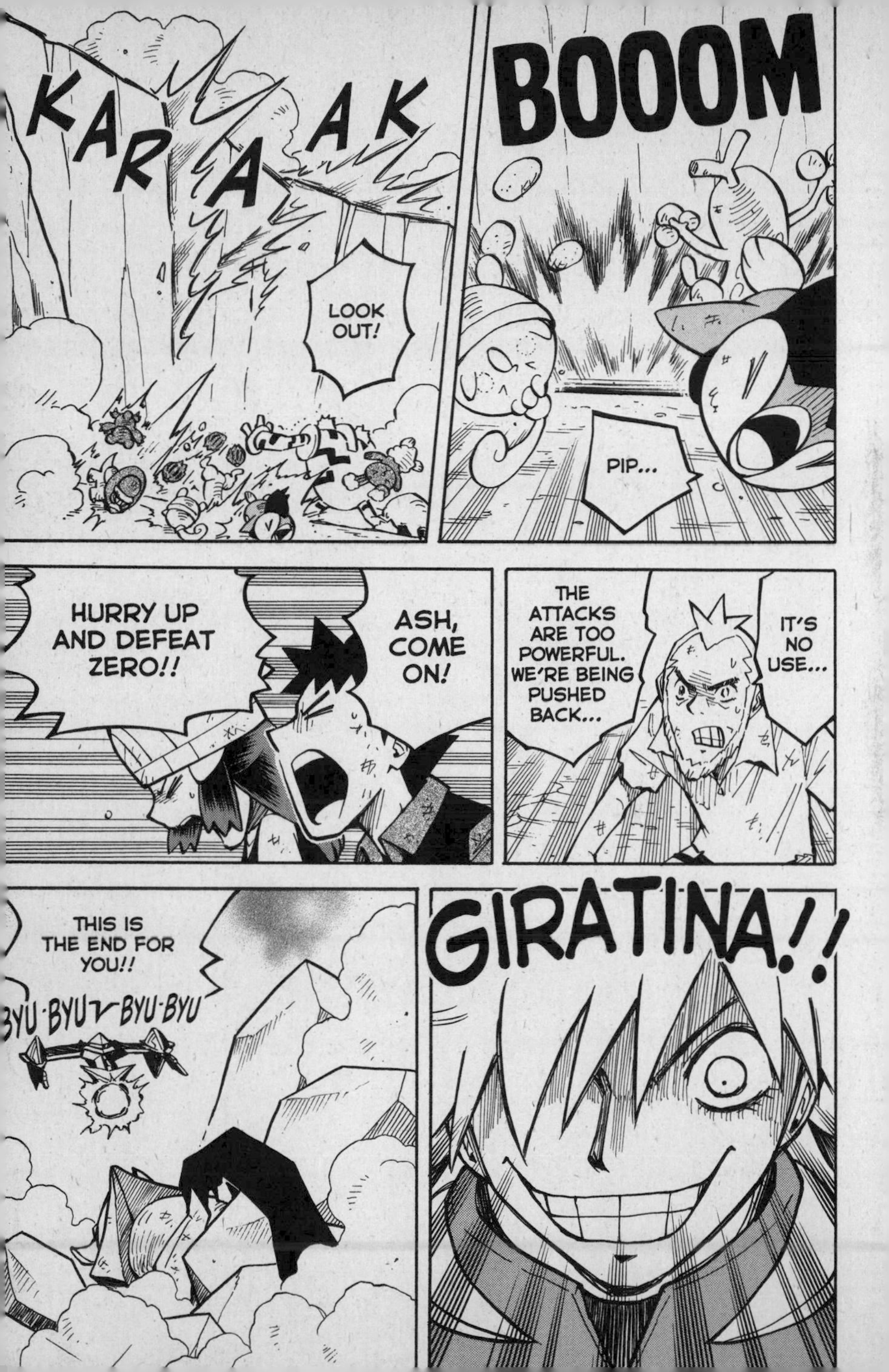
BOOOM
PIP...
KARAAK
LOOK OUT!
IT'S NO USE...
THE ATTACKS ARE TOO POWERFUL. WE'RE BEING PUSHED BACK...
ASH, COME ON!
HURRY UP AND DEFEAT ZERO!!
GIRATINA!!
THIS IS THE END FOR YOU!!
BYU-BYU~BYU-BYU

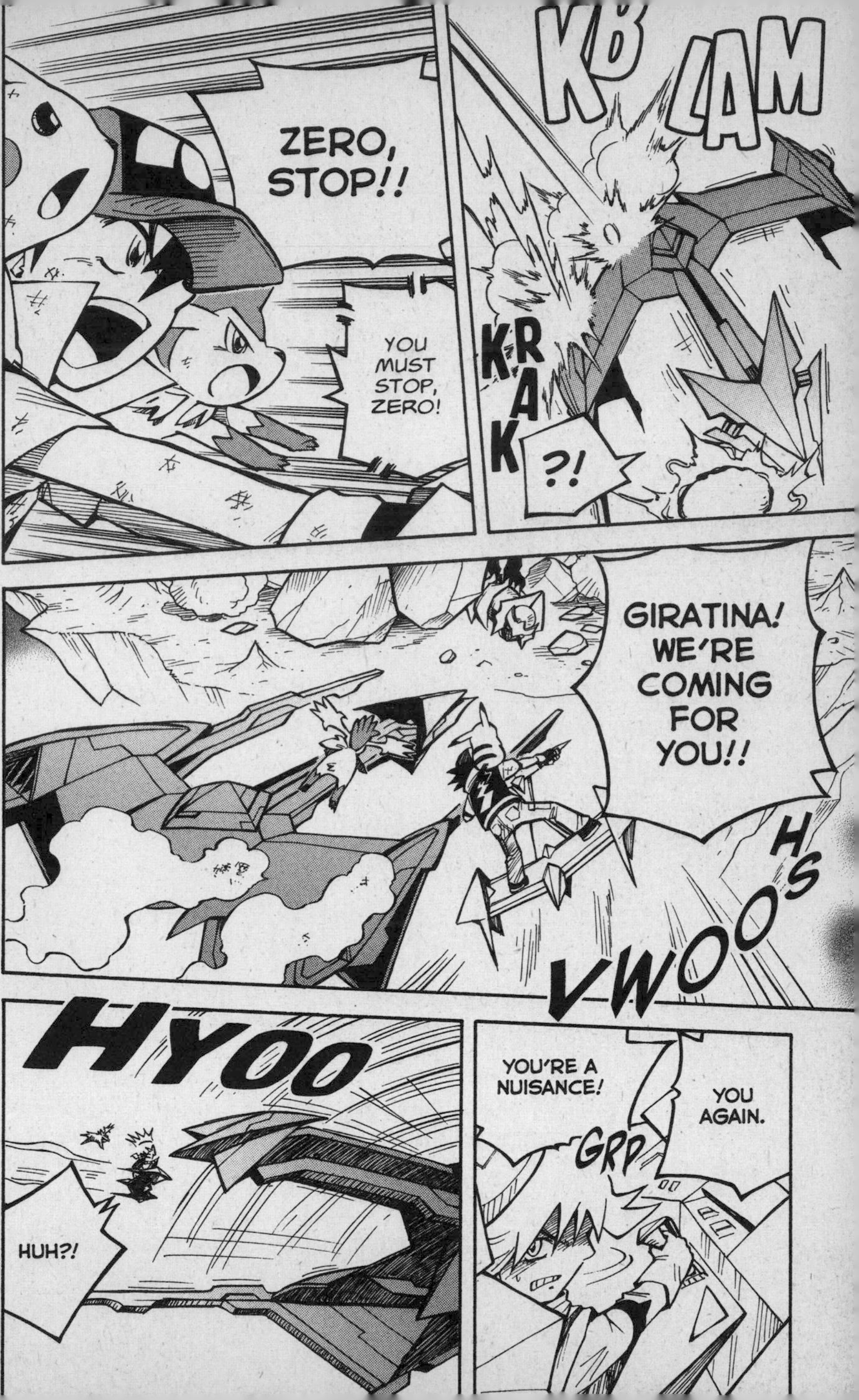
KBLAM
KRAK
?!
ZERO, STOP!!
YOU MUST STOP, ZERO!
GIRATINA! WE'RE COMING FOR YOU!!
VWOOSH
YOU AGAIN.
YOU'RE A NUISANCE!
GRP
HYOO
HUH?!

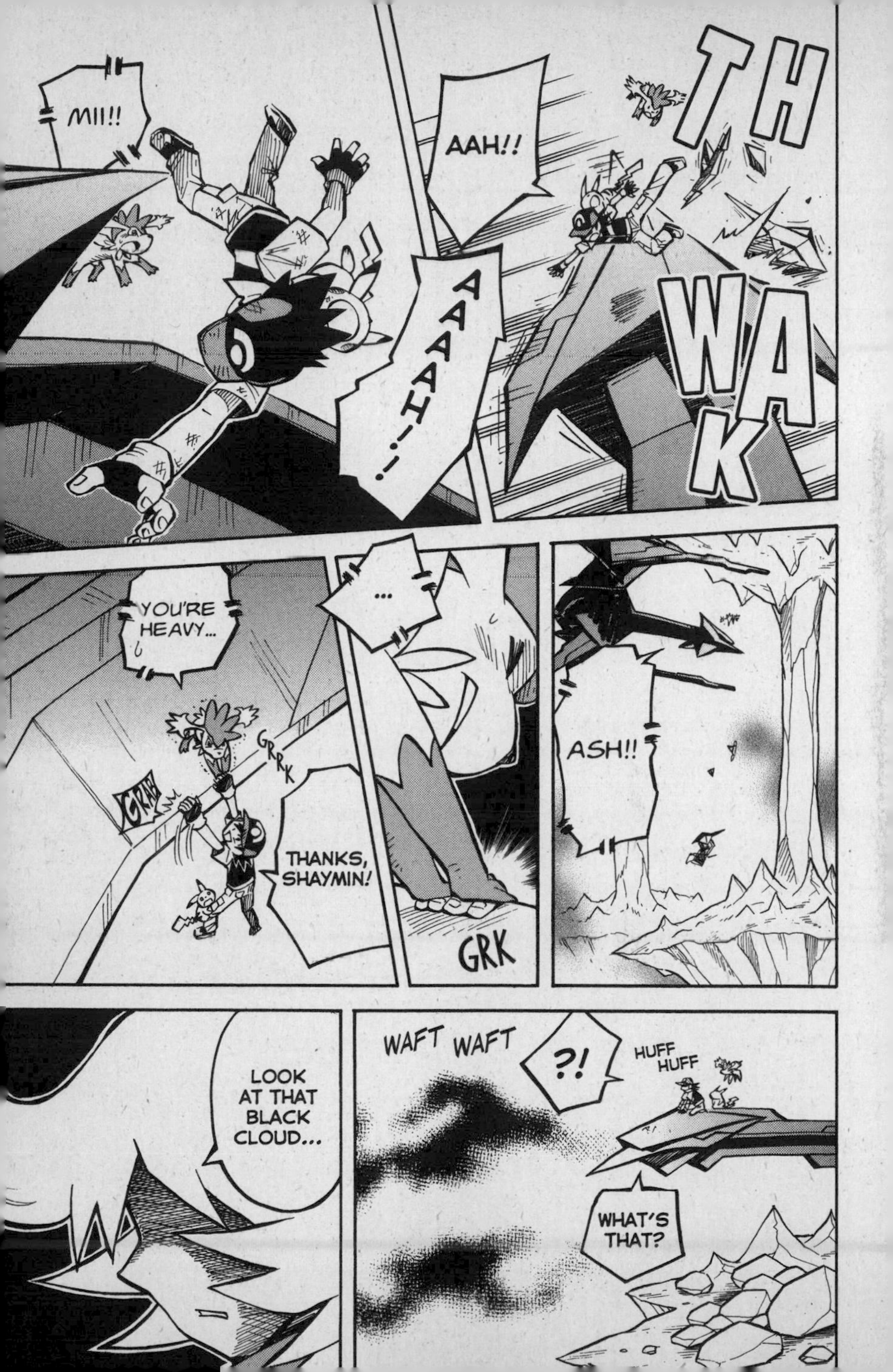
THWAK
AAH!!
AAAAH!!!
MII!!
ASH!!
...
GRK
YOU'RE HEAVY...
GRRK
GRAB
THANKS, SHAYMIN!
HUFF HUFF
?!
WAFT WAFT
WHAT'S THAT?
LOOK AT THAT BLACK CLOUD...

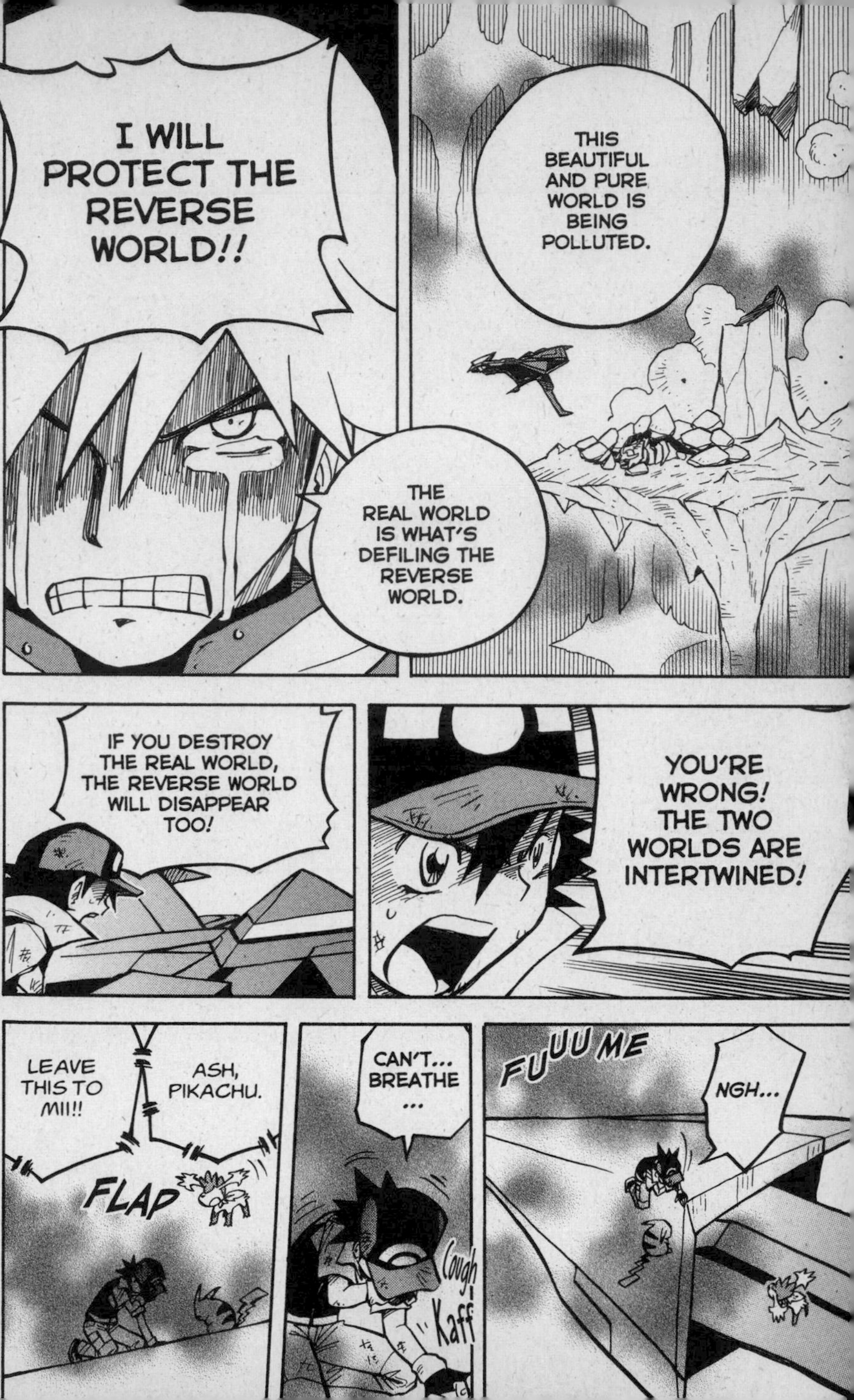
THIS BEAUTIFUL AND PURE WORLD IS BEING POLLUTED.
THE REAL WORLD IS WHAT'S DEFILING THE REVERSE WORLD.
I WILL PROTECT THE REVERSE WORLD!!
YOU'RE WRONG! THE TWO WORLDS ARE INTERTWINED!
IF YOU DESTROY THE REAL WORLD, THE REVERSE WORLD WILL DISAPPEAR TOO!
FUUUME
NGH...
CAN'T... BREATHE ...
Cough
Kaff
ASH, PIKACHU.
LEAVE THIS TO MII!!
FLAP

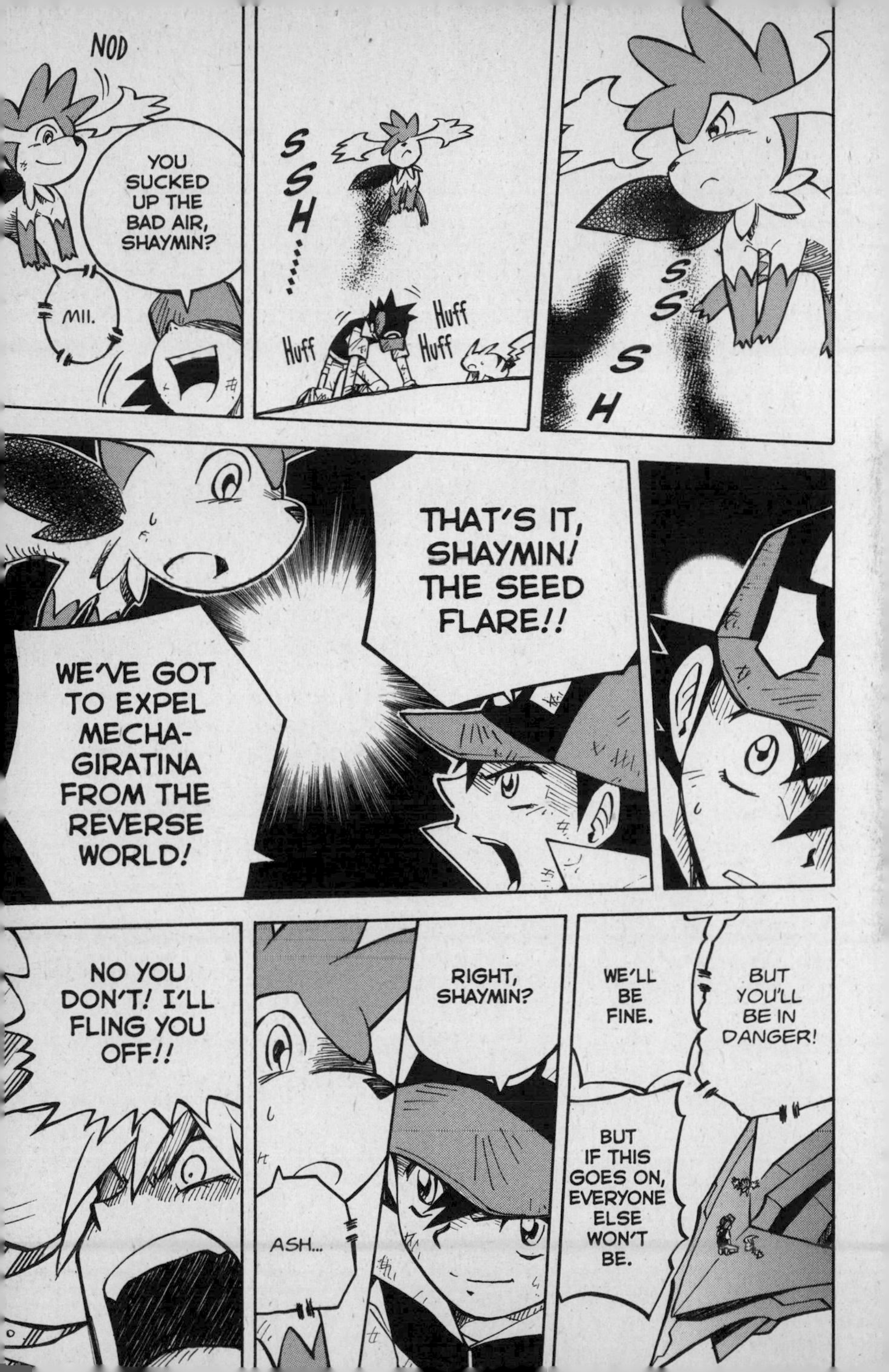
S
S
S
H
SSH...
Huff
Huff
Huff
NOD
YOU SUCKED UP THE BAD AIR, SHAYMIN?
MII.
THAT'S IT, SHAYMIN! THE SEED FLARE!!
WE'VE GOT TO EXPEL MECHA-GIRATINA FROM THE REVERSE WORLD!
BUT YOU'LL BE IN DANGER!
WE'LL BE FINE.
BUT IF THIS GOES ON, EVERYONE ELSE WON'T BE.
RIGHT, SHAYMIN?
ASH...
NO YOU DON'T! I'LL FLING YOU OFF!!

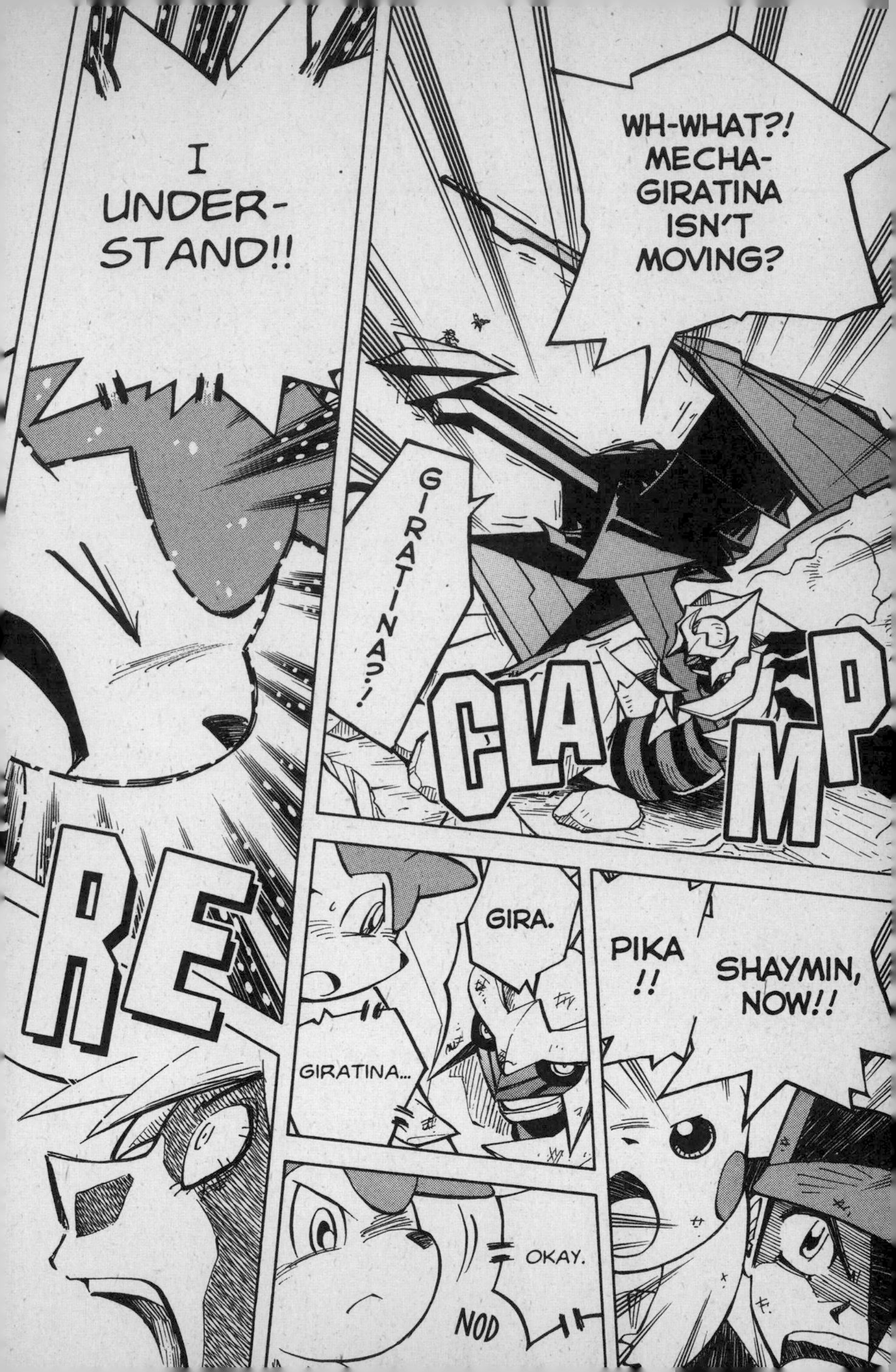
WH-WHAT?! MECHA-GIRATINA ISN'T MOVING?
GIRATINA?!
CLAMP
SHAYMIN, NOW!!
PIKA !!
GIRA.
GIRATINA...
OKAY.
NOD
I UNDER-STAND!!
RE

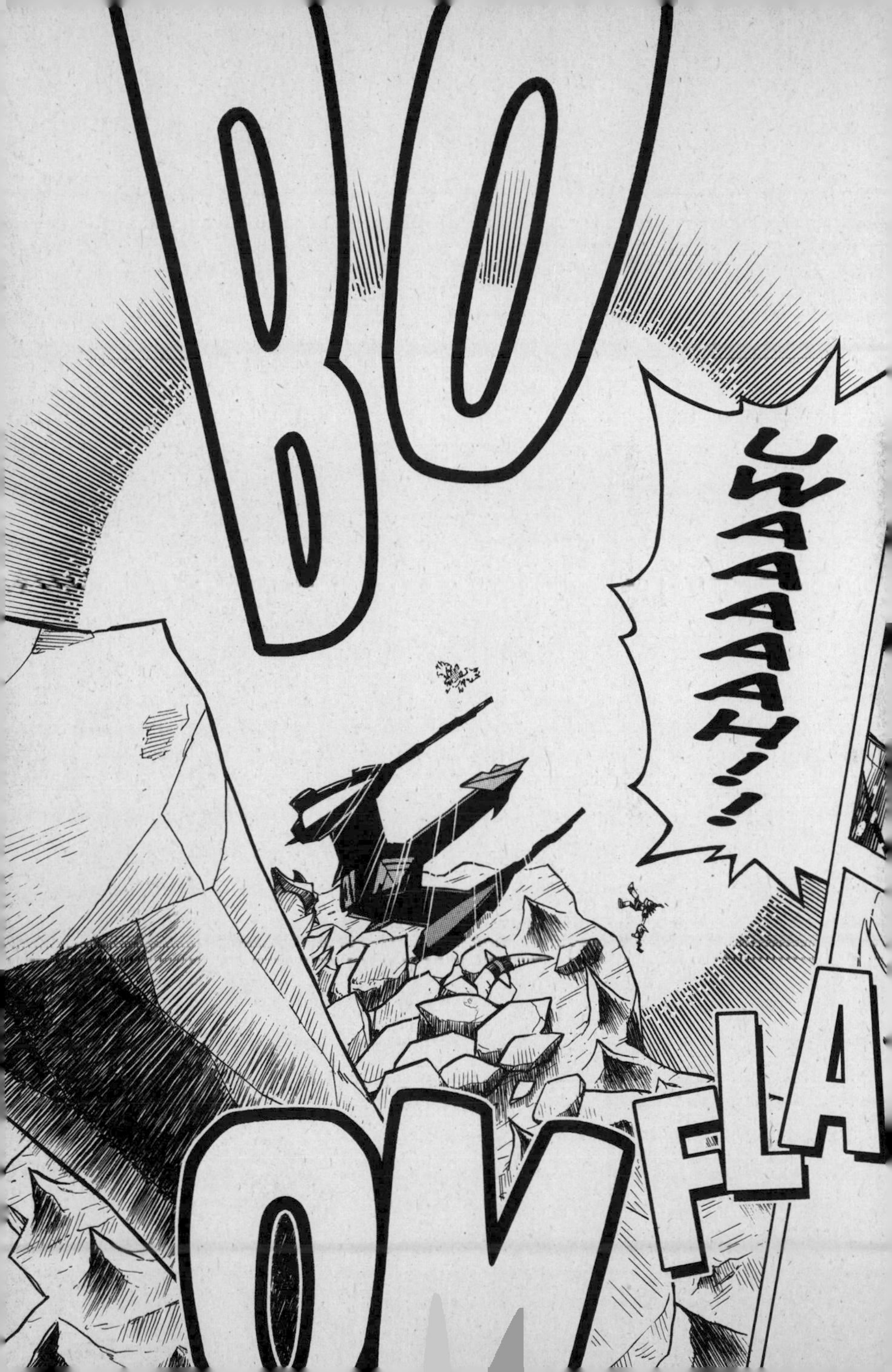
BOOM
UWAAAAAH!!!
FLA

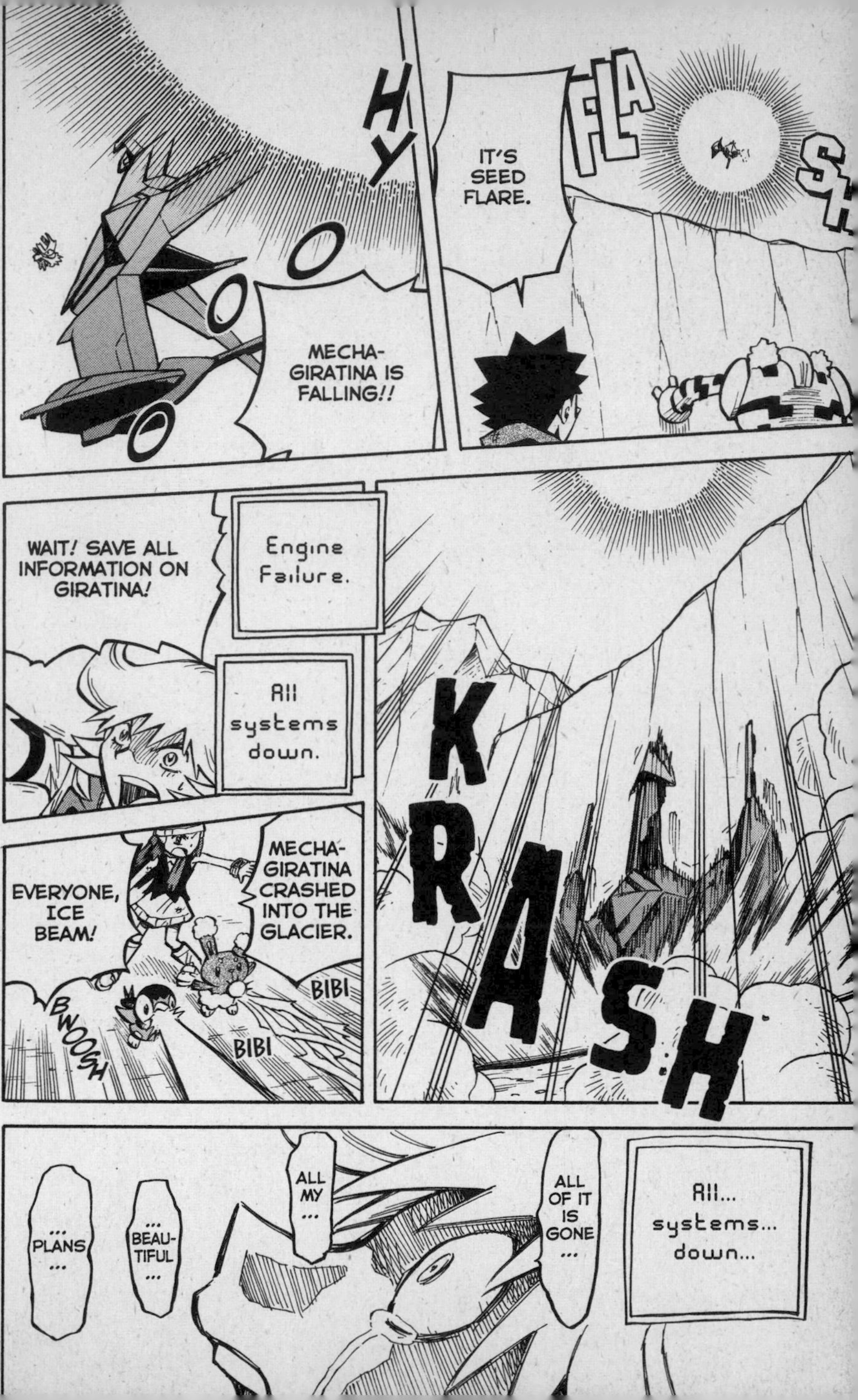
FLASH
IT'S SEED FLARE.
HYOOO
MECHA-GIRATINA IS FALLING!!
KRASH
Engine Failure.
All systems down.
WAIT! SAVE ALL INFORMATION ON GIRATINA!
MECHA-GIRATINA CRASHED INTO THE GLACIER.
EVERYONE, ICE BEAM!
BIBI
BIBI
BWOOSH
All... systems... down...
ALL OF IT IS GONE...
ALL MY...
...BEAUTIFUL...
...PLANS...

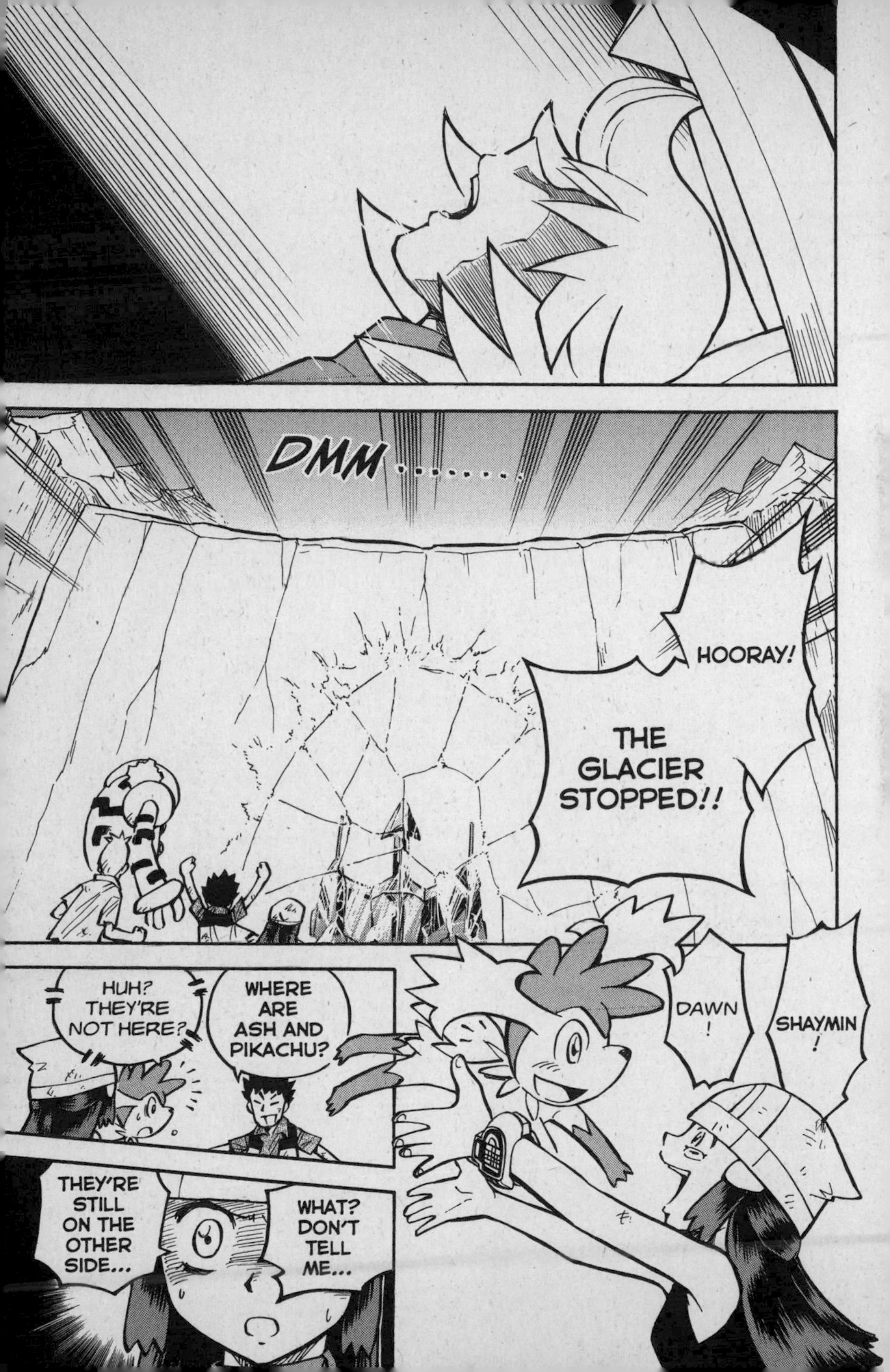
DMM ....
HOORAY!
THE GLACIER STOPPED!!
SHAYMIN!
DAWN!
WHERE ARE ASH AND PIKACHU?
HUH? THEY'RE NOT HERE?
WHAT? DON'T TELL ME...
THEY'RE STILL ON THE OTHER SIDE...

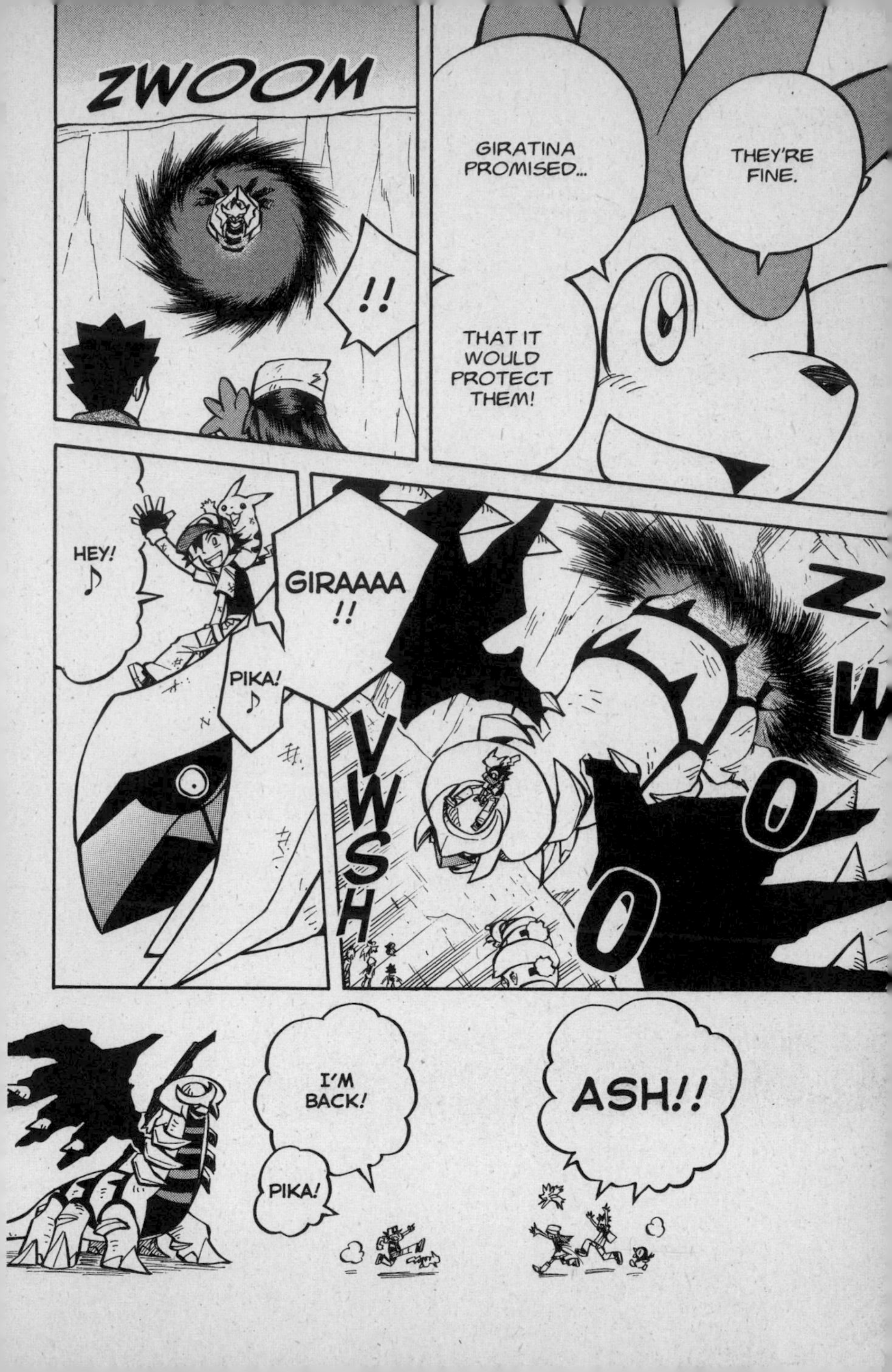
THEY'RE FINE.
GIRATINA PROMISED...
THAT IT WOULD PROTECT THEM!
ZWOOM
!!
ZWOOO
GIRAAAA!!
VWSH
HEY! ♪
PIKA! ♪
ASH!!
I'M BACK!
PIKA!

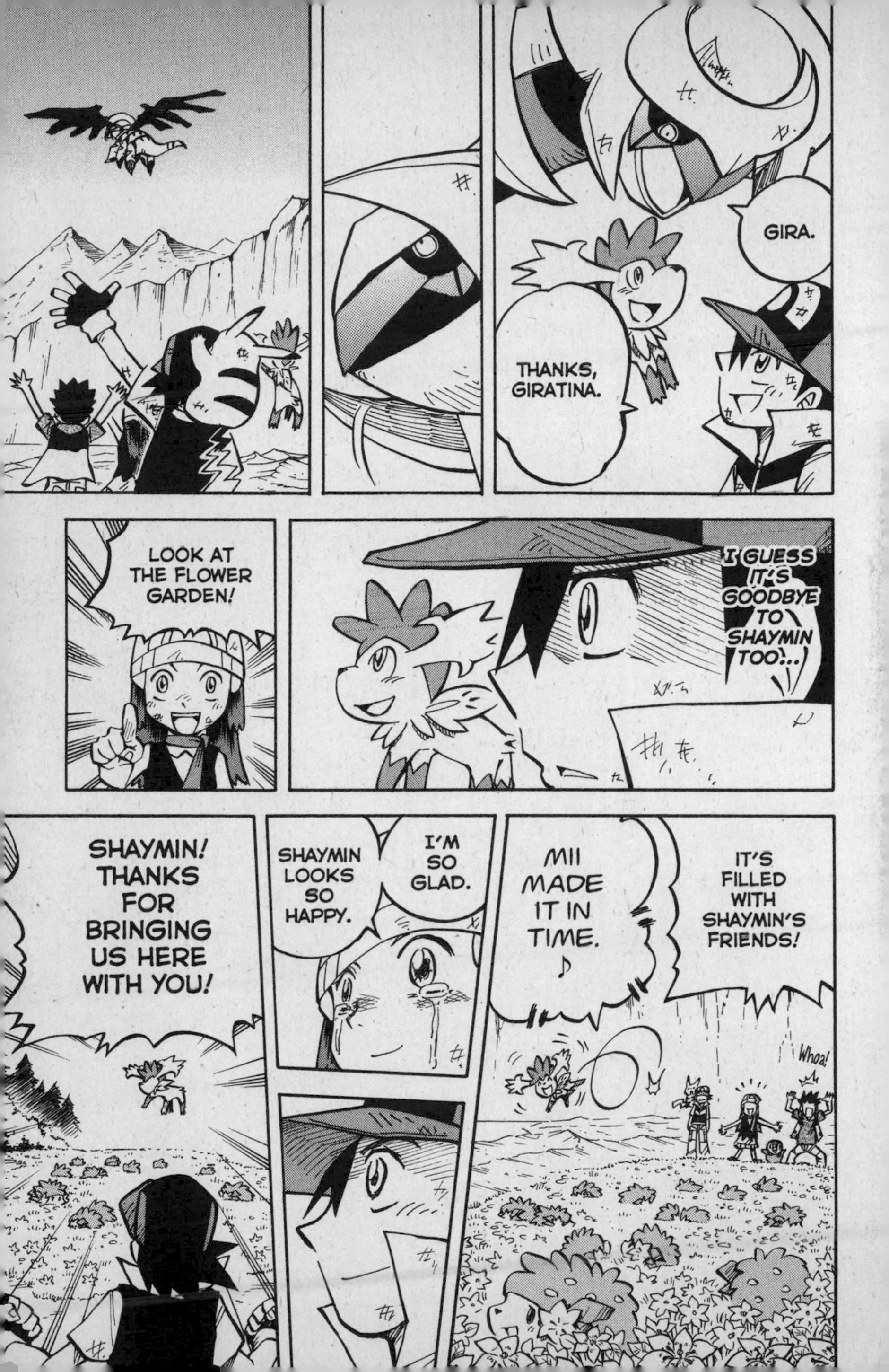

GIRA.
THANKS, GIRATINA.
I GUESS IT'S GOODBYE TO SHAYMIN TOO...
LOOK AT THE FLOWER GARDEN!
IT'S FILLED WITH SHAYMIN'S FRIENDS!
MII MADE IT IN TIME. ♪
Whoa!
I'M SO GLAD.
SHAYMIN LOOKS SO HAPPY.
SHAYMIN! THANKS FOR BRINGING US HERE WITH YOU!

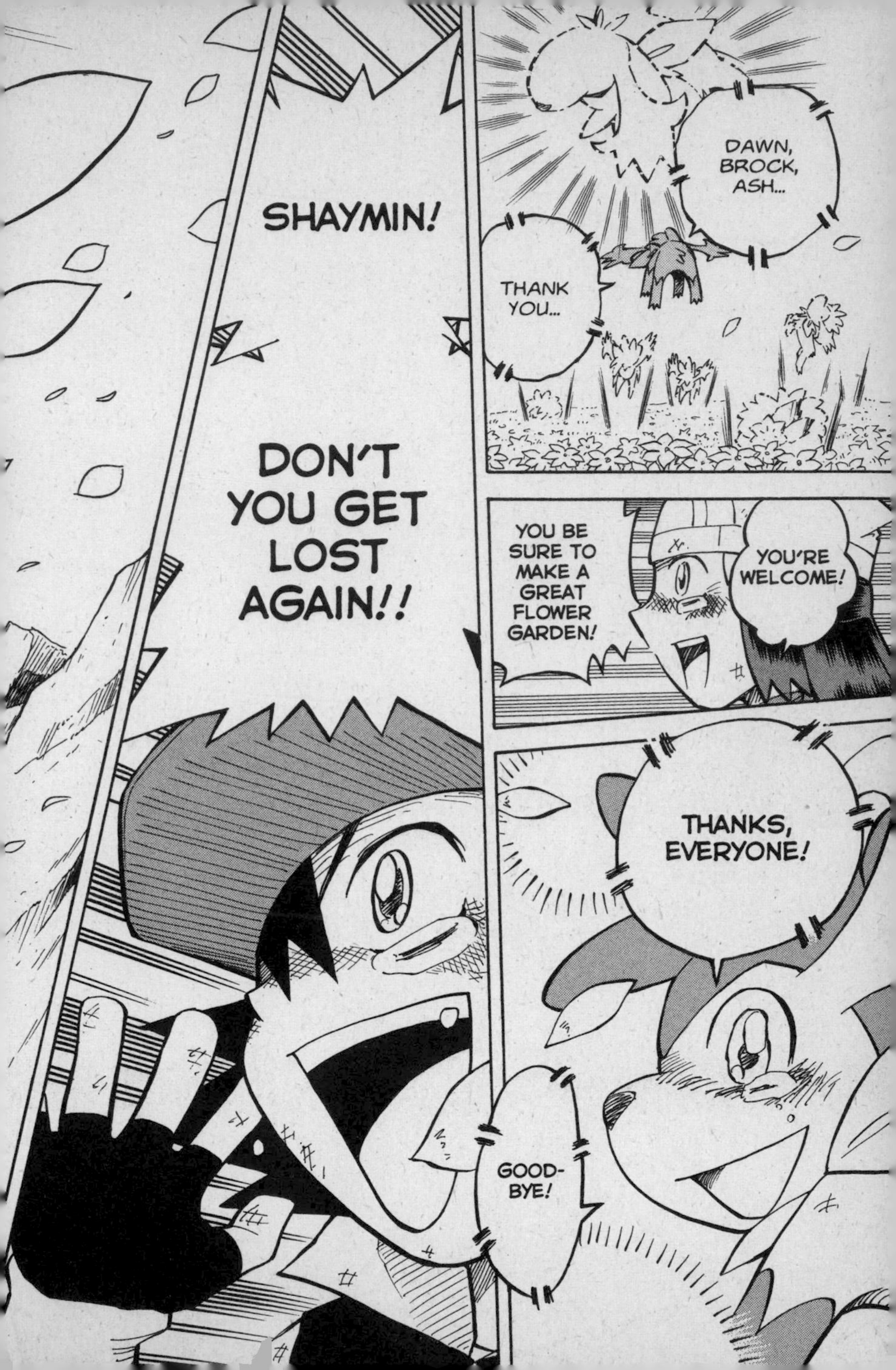
DAWN, BROCK, ASH...
THANK YOU...
YOU'RE WELCOME!
YOU BE SURE TO MAKE A GREAT FLOWER GARDEN!
THANKS, EVERYONE!
GOOD-BYE!
SHAYMIN!
DON'T YOU GET LOST AGAIN!!

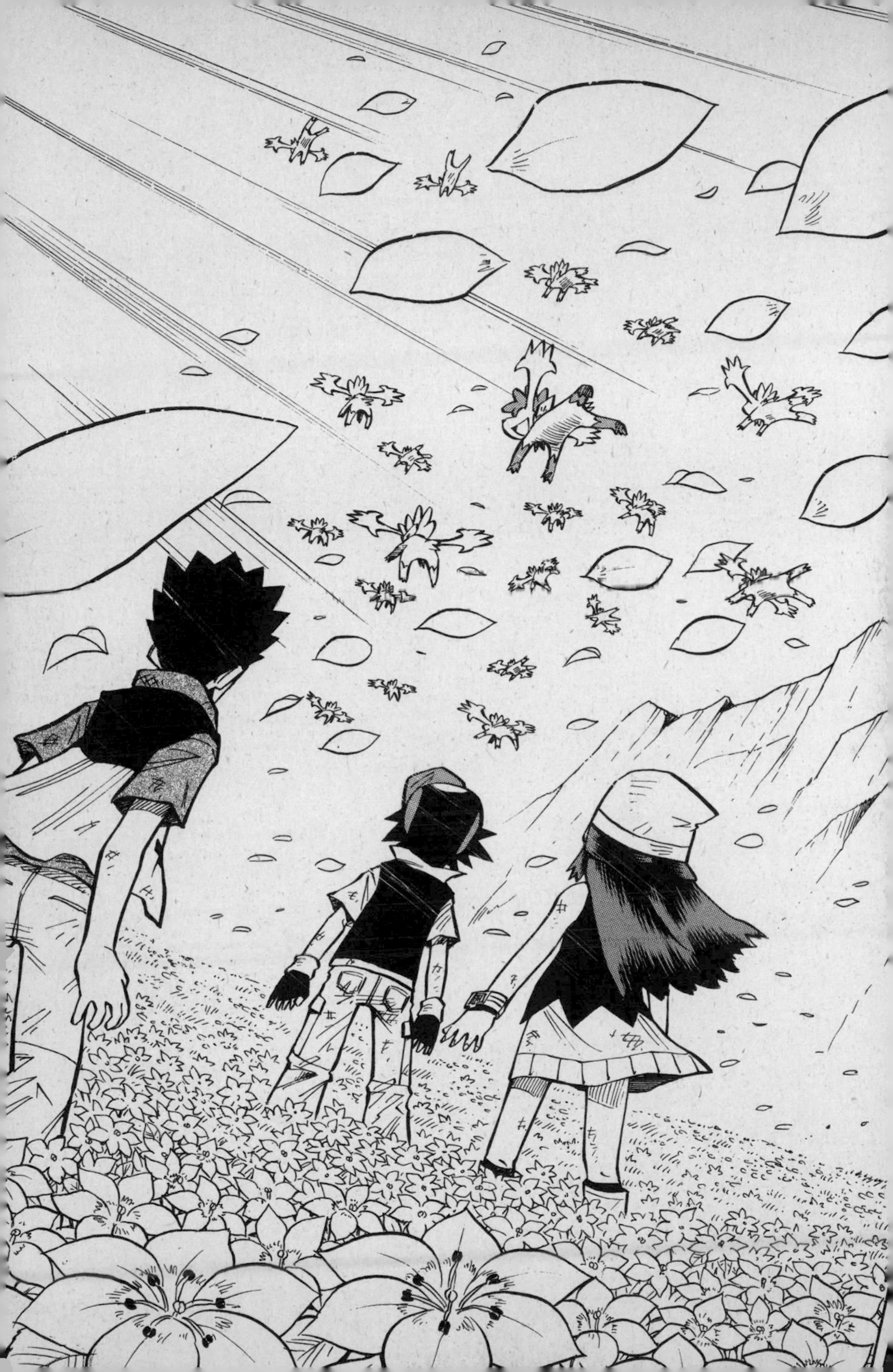

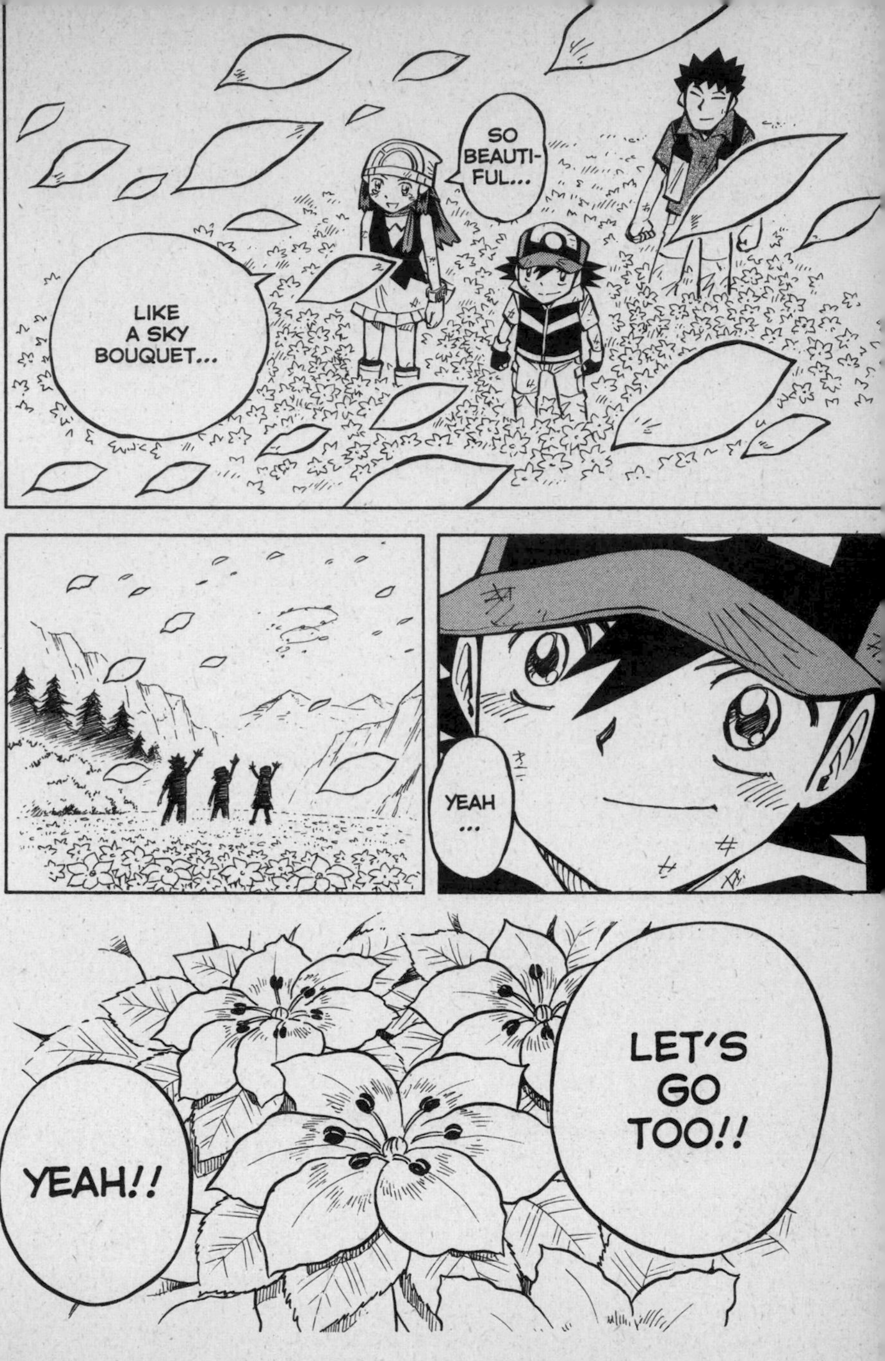
SO BEAUTIFUL...
LIKE A SKY BOUQUET...
YEAH ...
LET'S GO TOO!!
YEAH!!

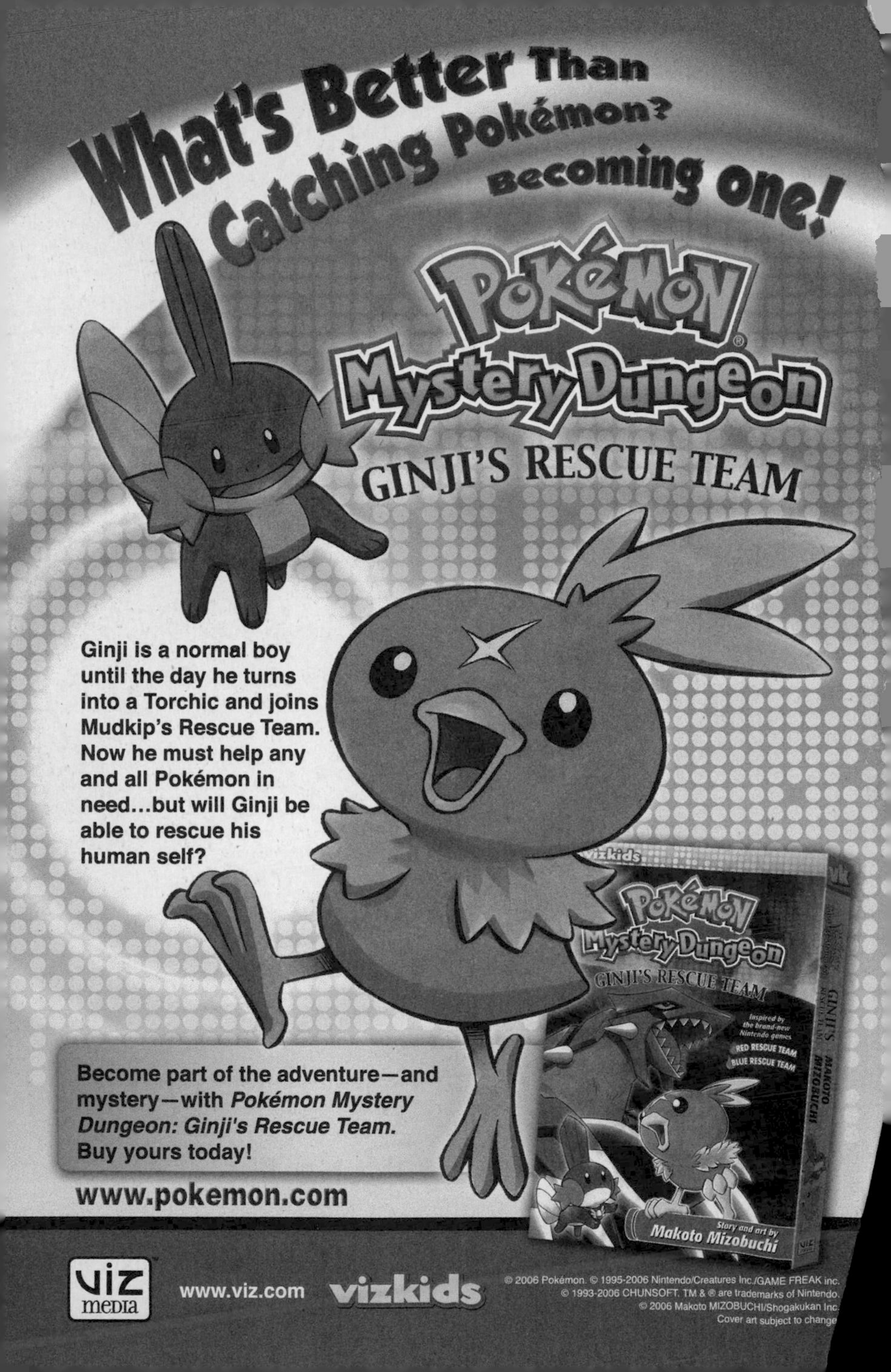
What's Better Than Catching Pokémon?
Becoming one!
Pokémon Mystery Dungeon
GINJI'S RESCUE TEAM
Ginji is a normal boy until the day he turns into a Torchic and joins Mudkip's Rescue Team. Now he must help any and all Pokémon in need...but will Ginji be able to rescue his human self?
Become part of the adventure—and mystery—with Pokémon Mystery Dungeon: Ginji's Rescue Team. Buy yours today!
www.pokemon.com
vizkids
Pokémon Mystery Dungeon
GINJI'S RESCUE TEAM
Inspired by the brand-new Nintendo games
RED RESCUE TEAM
BLUE RESCUE TEAM
Story and art by
Makoto Mizobuchi
VIZ media
www.viz.com
vizkids
© 2006 Pokémon. © 1995-2006 Nintendo/Creatures Inc./GAME FREAK inc.
© 1993-2006 CHUNSOFT. TM & ® are trademarks of Nintendo.
© 2006 Makoto MIZOBUCHI/Shogakukan Inc.
Cover art subject to change

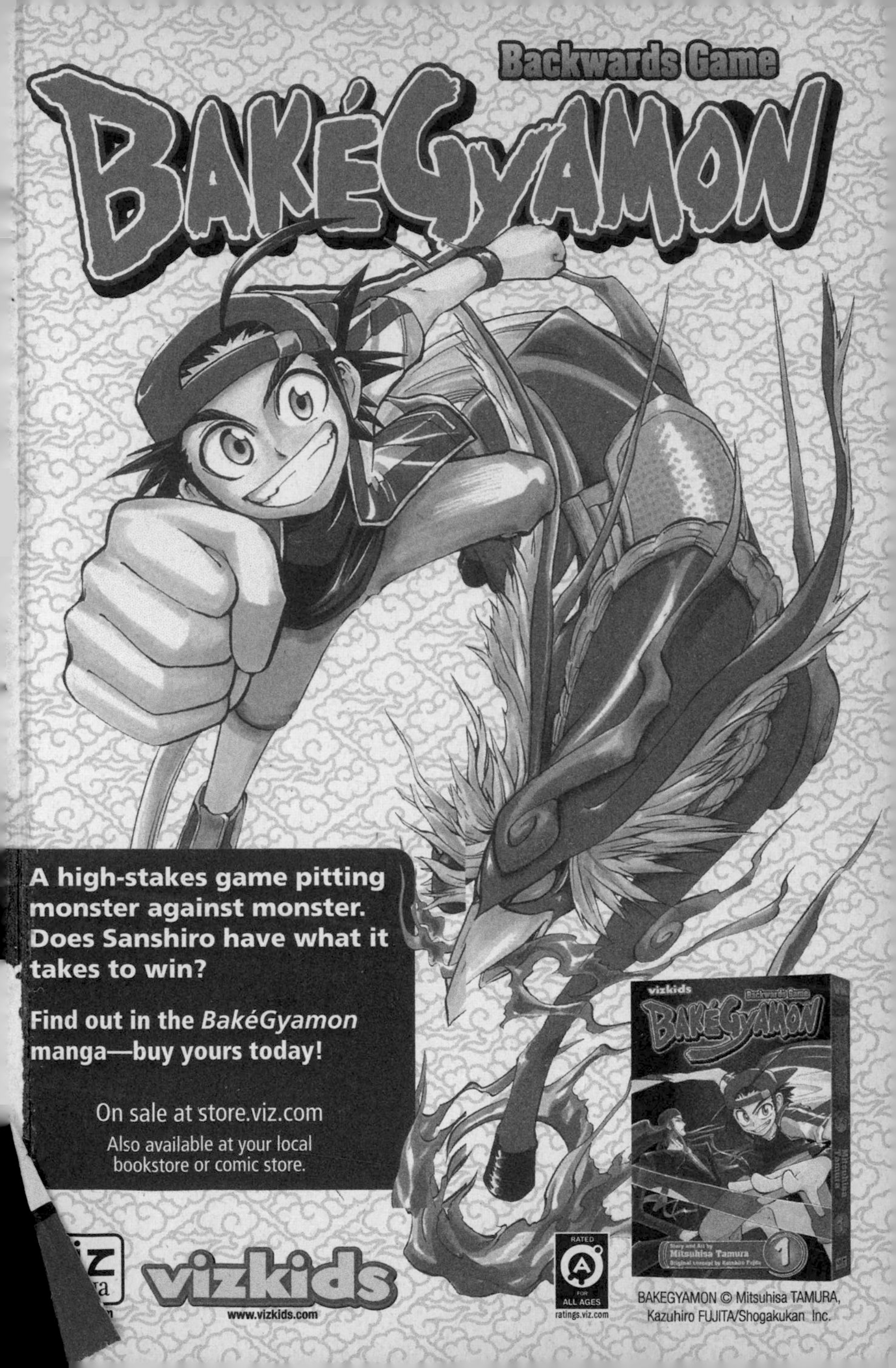
Backwards Game
BAKÉGYAMON
A high-stakes game pitting monster against monster. Does Sanshiro have what it takes to win?
Find out in the *BakéGyamon* manga—buy yours today!
On sale at store.viz.com
Also available at your local bookstore or comic store.
vizkids
Backwards Game
BAKÉGYAMON
Mitsuhisa Tamura
1
vizkids
www.vizkids.com
RATED
A
FOR ALL AGES
ratings.viz.com
BAKEGYAMON © Mitsuhisa TAMURA, Kazuhiro FUJITA/Shogakukan Inc.